The yellowbacks... classics of popular fiction

The yellowjackets or yellowbacks were a great series of bestselling adventure and crime thrillers that had its origins in the mid to late 19th century following on from the 'penny dreadfuls'. They virtually began the mass market revolution of the early 20th century with a clear standard format and imprint/series livery (what would today be called branding). Hodder & Stoughton published the yellowjackets in two main series with series run dates of: 1923-1939 and later 1949-1957.

As the tagline ('where thrillers really began') on the back cover implies, the imprint and series focused on thrillers that were the bestsellers of their time. This current reissue or retro revival if you will, brings back many of these masterpieces, now classics in their own way and extends it further by including key titles from that period that were either great crime or thriller or even general commercial fiction (including sub-genres of noir, horror, gothic, romance, westerns, etc.) influences of their time. There are some perennial favourites and many rarities either lost or not easily available being revived in the current series. Writers and characters ranged from adventure heroes like Bulldog Drummond, Allan Quatermain, Richard Hannay or the Saint through thriller grandmasters Edgar Wallace and E. Phillips Oppenheim, crime and mystery maestros like Patricia Wentworth, G.K. Chesterton, Agatha Christie and the Detection club, to western and swashbucklers like Zane Grey, Max Brand, Captain Blood and even romance or general fiction classics like Hermina Black, Denise Robins, Marie Corelli or Stella Morton. These were books that had storytelling at their heart and always entertained.

The yellowbacks had both hardback (with varying design elements) and paperback (which built the series look) versions with the latter still carrying the imprint 'yellowjacket'. The current reissues pay tribute to both and use an amalgam of elements from both editions while retaining the complete yellow (or 'mustard-plaster') livery with the author's name in blue beveled type with a 'simulated emboss' effect and a white outer 'outline', and the book title in black. These reissues retain the distinctive size of the original mass market paperback and follow the three main category variations—the thrillers (crime, westerns, mystery, adventure) had blue lettering for the author's name, while romance and softer general fiction had red; and other categories like humour had green.

For more detail and a full list of titles visit https://www.hachetteindia.com/home/yellowbacks

THE SEAMARK OMNIBUS OF THRILLS

VOLUME 1

THE SEAMARK OMNIBUS OF THRILLS

Seamark was the pen name of Austin James Small (25 July 1894–15 January 1929) – an English writer of thriller, detective, science fiction, adventure, romance, and western novels and short stories. Most of Small's titles appeared in Britain under the pen name Seamark, while his American publisher preferred using the name Austin J. Small. Several film plots were based on his stories. Small was born Austin Major Small in Luton, Bedfordshire, on 25 July 1894. He later changed his name to Arthur James Small. He ran away to sea as a boy and travelled the world, serving in the Royal Navy during the First World War, where he was a champion heavyweight boxer. He met and was inspired to write by Jack London and adopted the pen name "Seamark" to comply with Admiralty regulations. He began his literary career in the early 1920s publishing new westerns and detective stories in British pulp magazines.

In 1924 he produced a western novel, *The Frozen Trail*, and three romantic novels in 1925, before publishing *Master Vorst* a.k.a. *The Death Maker* (1926), a science fiction novel in which a secret society based in London develops a means of destroying the human species with the help of a bacteriological weapon. He went on to write half a dozen detective novels, another science fiction novel, and many short stories.

He was found dead in Kensington, London, on 15 January 1929, from suicide by gas inhalation.

THE SEAMARK OMNIBUS OF THRILLS

Austin J. Small

VOLUME 1

consisting of these famous mysteries

DOWN RIVER
—a story of cocaine smuggling in the Port of London

THE MYSTERY MAKER
—an adventure, in which the title role is played by Colonel Stayne, late of the anti-espionage corps

HODDER AND STOUGHTON YELLOW JACKET

hachette

The Seamark Omnibus of Thrills
First published by Hodder & Stoughton, UK in 1937

This Hodder Yellowback edition © Hachette India 2025
(Registered Name: Hachette Book Publishing India Pvt. Ltd.)
An Hachette UK Company www.hachetteindia.com

1

The texts in these editions in most cases have been reprinted as is, with minimal editorial changes and by and large no bowdlerizing for political correctness; though in some editions, a few words and phrases considered archaic, or those considered offensive now, along with archaic punctuation may have been modified in places to make the text more accessible to today's readers. The narratives, language, beliefs, social mores and/or cultural depictions, in these volumes are a reflection of their times and must be viewed as such. They may also contain certain cultural, racial and gender prejudices and stereotypes that may be outdated or clearly wrong then and wrong today; but their removal would be tantamount to claiming these prejudices never existed. The Publisher does not endorse or support those depictions or stereotypes; and these books have been made available for a discerning audience that will read it for entertainment value and a chronicle/record of popular fiction of past times.

Cover design by Priya Singh adapted from the original classic yellowjacket by Hodder & Stoughton.

Cover illustration by Ishan Trivedi.

Series note: Some of the books in the series (unless otherwise credited) may have cover or inside illustrations from the original yellowbacks or early editions, and while full restoration has been attempted, some images may be grainy or faded due to the condition of the original material. The end notes or bonus material or blurb details may have been sourced from the public domain or free use publications such as Wikipedia and attribution is hereby made also allowing similar free use reproduction from here. Sources requiring further specific attribution may write in and further detailing and/or corrections shall be made in subsequent printings/editions.

Reprint specifications may be subject to change including but not limited to finishes, paper, colour sections.

ISBN: 978-93-5731-804-4

Hachette Book Publishing India Pvt. Ltd.
4th & 5th Floors, Corporate Centre,
Plot No. 94, Sector 44, Gurugram - 122 003, India

Typeset in Electra LT STD 10/12.5 pt by Manipal Technologies Limited, Manipal

Printed and bound in India by Manipal Technologies Limited, Manipal

FSC www.fsc.org MIX Paper | Supporting responsible forestry FSC™ C043100

CONTENTS

DOWN RIVER

A story of cocaine smuggling in the Port of London, praised by the *Morning Post* as "A really good thriller, excellently written."

I

Grey dawn was breaking gently over the long reaches below the Pool of London. Dank river smells, cold and clammy, and as transient as the dawn itself, hung faintly on the air and fused into the sharp tang of the mist wraiths that swirled about like wisps of torn gossamer above the fast-running tide. Ahead of the chugging police motorboat the Tower Bridge reared up out of the mist; and beyond it, massive in its noble setting on the hill, the mighty bulk of St. Paul's arose in majesty.

All night long that police boat had been panting steadily up and down the tideway, and a discerning eye would have seen that the draglines were out. Murky and muddy, but as old as history itself, the water sucked softly by her bows as she headed for a lower reach.

Half a mile below them, heading upstream to her moorings by the Houses of Parliament, the *Spindrift* came, with her slim nose shearing through the water like a knife. She was a beauty, that long splinter of a boat, the fastest thing that marine ingenuity had yet devised. Thirty feet of her, thirty feet of aluminium and oak that could snore through the water at a shade over sixty miles an hour when her engines were screaming at their peak—and twenty feet of her lifting sheer out of the water once the fifty-mile mark was quivering on the gauges.

But just then she was throttled down to a bare crawl. Toby Essex, her owner, was one of those unusual characters, a man who had some consideration for the small craft cluttering the banks—the *Spindrift*, travelling at speed, sent up a young hill of water that would have made even a fully laden barge cock up on her heels and sock her old nose down till half her rudder showed clear.

Standing behind Essex at the wheel, clad in a soaking wet beret and glistening black oilskins, was as trim a looking little piece of femininity as the boat herself. Hillary Kittredge had wearied of horses for a season and had fallen under the lure of speedboat racing. The bewildering rush of it, the exhilarating smash of salt air across her face, the sting of the spume, whizzing at her from the streaming forefoot, the breathtaking, sprawling skids round the cornering buoys, and the general mad excitement of a trophy race vibrated to a similar singing note in her body. For two hours she and Essex had been putting their speed queen through her paces out on the flat level deeps beyond the Nore. Wet, weary, and as hungry as lumberjacks, they nosed along past Limehouse Pier and the Shadwell Basin and on through Wapping Station into the Pool.

Essex noted the stolid little ten knotter ahead.

"Care for horrors?" he asked, nodding towards the river police. "The J drags are out. Suicide, I suppose."

"I have a firmer leaning towards eggs and bacon," decided the girl. "If you could find it in your heart to let this decrepit tub of yours spraddle her old legs a little faster we might be able to get in before the breakfast menus are snatched off the restaurant tables. If you ask me—"

The rest of her sentence was cut off short, for the police sergeant at the tiller had suddenly reversed his engines and the other two officers with him were clambering hurriedly aft.

Essex brought his boat round to a rolling halt less than a hundred yards from them. They saw the draglines tauten and watched them hauled in. They saw the officers lean over the stem to get a grip on something that rose with a slow heave to the surface.

At that distance it was an indistinct, an inanimate, waterlogged something breaking the ripples there, and they could only just distinguish the helpless roll of lifeless limbs as four strong arms hauled it aboard.

Essex slid a silent eye round at the girl. She was white faced, and her gaze was fixed rigidly on the scene of tragedy, her mouth half open and her fingers drumming unconsciously on the narrow beading of the gunwale.

"Good heavens—look—Toby—a body!" she gasped.

Essex let the clutch in and the boat moved forward slowly. "Shouldn't let it upset you," he said. "Happens quite a lot up and down this old river. They scarcely even report that sort of thing in the papers nowadays."

The *Spindrift* was crawling along under the counter of a great ugly old hulk of a tramp steamer berthed up by Wapping Old Stairs. Simply to take his eyes off the unpleasant scene ahead, Essex glanced up at her rusted bridge, smoke grimed and salt crusted from voyages in far seas. And his right foot stole out and pressed the girl's toe.

She looked round hurriedly, caught his eye, and then she, too, followed his gaze up to the loom of the bridge. In that same split second she realised there was more than a mere suicide in the recovery of the last remains of yet another of the tragedies of old London River.

Leaning over the side of the bridge was one of the most evil faces she had ever seen in her life. It was Oriental, in a fat, obese way. There was a thickness and a slant-eyed placidity about it that bespoke its eastern progenitors, but the inhuman malignity that glared from every line of it was positively frightening. It seemed utterly incongruous that such a fat, reposeful-looking face could suddenly distil such a torrent of devilish hatred. The eyes seemed to glitter like white-hot coals, and the features were contorted with a spasm of demoniac rage.

He seemed to be oblivious of the long, shining speed monster right underneath him—his eyes were glued on the police boat, and he was glaring at the officers with all the burning virulence of a stream of boiling acid. If ever murder shone, stark and red, out of human eyes, it was literally blazing out of his. Then, slowly and with terrible deliberation, he raised his fist and shook it at the three men labouring in the boat.

The girl caught her breath and gazed up at him, fascinated. The savagery of it, the malevolence of it, appalled her.

"What—what on earth did he do that for?" she asked at last.

Essex made a little gesture of ignorance. "These young bucks of the river police are not what you might call popular—that is, not with gentry of his calibre. All sorts and conditions of humans make their home on this tideway in the course of a year—and some of them are not too savoury. He's probably got a grudge against the police—possibly scotched him on some lively little game or other and he's sending them a valentine about it."

"But—but, Toby, he's Chinese, surely. I thought his race was notorious for not showing emotion."

"'M—well—might be a half-caste. He certainly knows how to register disapproval, anyway."

Hillary Kittredge stepped across and took the wheel out of his hands. There was a determined look in her eye, not untinctured with a dash off defiance and her underlip was thrust up into a red bow of a pout.

"What's wrong?" asked Essex.

"I'm going over to tell those policemen what I saw," she said with the utmost decision. Essex had heard that tone before, and he surrendered the wheel without a murmur. He rather liked it. There was something delightful in being bossed about by a woman with a mouth like that—one, moreover, who could handle the throbbing beauty under him like a goddess.

As they went creaming along to the police boat he glanced at the tramp steamer's name. It was bold on both her bows, in letters that had been battered out of alignment by swinging seas—YANGTSE.

With a neat turn and a sudden rush of reversing water she brought the *Spindrift* alongside. The sergeant leaned over and tried to prevent her from seeing the dripping huddle in the well of the boat, but the girl waved an unconcerned hand.

"Please don't worry about us, sergeant," she said; "we saw what was happening down river and are not out hunting for sensations over some unfortunate's death. What I want to ask you is, 'Do you happen to know the man who was on the bridge of that big cargo steamer we just passed?' No, don't look round or he will know we have come over to talk to you about him."

The sergeant stared grimly into the little glass panel of the engine housing and tried to get the man's reflection, but the range was too great.

"The ship is the *Yangtse*," said the girl, "and I'm sure he is Chinese—or a mixture of Chinese."

"You can bet your life he's Chinese, miss, if he's on the *Yangtse*. They're all Chinese on that hooker. She's a Chinese boat, registered at Hankow, and I never have liked the slab-sided old scow since she first came to the river. Gets in here about twice a year—general cargo out of Hankow, takes back cotton and machinery. That's all I know about her, miss. Why—is there anything wrong?"

"I'm certain there is. As we were passing under her side just now a man with a fat Chinese face was leaning over the side of the bridge, shaking his fist at you and glaring as though he would have liked to see you as dead as that body there. His face and his gestures were positively awful."

"Fat feller? Rather on the short side? Pasty cheeks, and wears a little black skull cap with a red button on the top?" The sergeant did not seem to be particularly interested.

"Yes—that's him," said Hillary.

"Grosman. Half-Chunk, half-Dutches, Hell of a combination. Shouldn't worry about him. He's captain of the ship. And we are—how shall we say—a little strict with him when he comes in to be searched. He's always trying on some little dodge to slip something past the Customs. Get what I mean, miss? There's an eternal call for opium down past Limehouse way, and prices run high for those who can get it through. None of 'em like us. Call us Water Rats; and they'd do a two-step all over the river if we were to be done away with tomorrow."

The girl drew away from the rail. "Well, you can make light of it if you like," she said flatly. "But if I were you I would keep my eye on that gentleman. He wasn't merely venting a general spleen against the river police—he was doing his best to wish *you* off the earth. Not the river police—but *you*. He has a grudge against you for something you were doing right here and now; not for having given him a stiff time some time last week. He saw you haul that body out of the water. And that was when it happened. You watch him, sergeant. May be—Oh, never mind. I know what a man means when he smiles at me from behind his eyes."

The sergeant winked at Essex, who wasn't even smiling from behind his eyes. "Thank you, miss," he said cheerfully. "My name's Manning, and I'm very much obliged for your warning. But I think we know how to look after ourselves in the water force."

Essex winked back at him as he resumed the wheel, and Manning stood watching the glistening hull slide away through the seethe of yellow water.

"Nice kid, that," he remarked to his second in command. He was rubbing the tips of his fingers together, an odd trick he had subconsciously acquired in moments of hard concentration. "Grosman," he muttered. "Grosman. H'm. Now what the devil's *his* game?"

"Well—that's your second warning," said a quiet voice at his elbow. Procter, his second, was eyeing him curiously.

"I know it's the second," said Manning viciously." But I'm not telling everyone who comes up in a swell speedster. We shall have half the toffs of London messing about round here if we once let 'em get their noses in. Head her back for the station. Take the tiller and run her under the *Yangtse*. I'll have a look at the brute myself. There's something on the move again on this dam river—and Grosman isn't far off the centre of it."

The slow-going boat chugged its way back to the river station, Procter bringing her to within a few feet of the gaunt old cargo steamer. Grosman was still up on the bridge, but he scarcely seemed to notice the plugging little boat below him. He was looking out serenely across the smooth water, now lit by the purest vestal light of the morning, and his face was as peaceful as the image of a Buddha cast in bronze. Something of an almost babylike benignity had masked across it. It was not that it had suddenly become kindly or even friendly—it was just that a complete absence of expression had set in upon it. It was a vacuum so far as emotion was concerned.

"The old rat!" muttered Manning under his breath. He watched him out of the corner of his eyes and then waved an airy hand in greeting as befits a salute to the captain of a ship.

Grosman waved in return, and Manning watched him draw back from the bridge rail and go down the companion-way to the upper deck. His right foot dragged badly with an obvious limp. On that right foot he wore a thick surgical boot in an effort to correct his natural disability. As he made his way aft to the stateroom he passed a huge pile of old junk—rope, cable, cordage, canvas, worn-out scrubbers, tins of old ship's biscuit battered and water-soaked from the stores, coils of rusted wire, tins of caked paint, and all the general paraphernalia of old lumber that is thrown out from various parts of the ship after a long voyage.

He ordered the bos'n to get the stuff cleared off the deck and sold ashore. And the last Manning saw of him was his limping back view as he went through the bulkhead for his breakfast.

"I'd give a year's pension to know what graft he's trying this time," growled the sergeant as Procter brought the boat in to the landing stage. He climbed out of the boat and indicated the huddled mass under the tarpaulin.

"Get that round to the mortuary," he said. "And phone the surgeon."

He went through to his little office. On his desk was a neat pile of the morning's mail. Over by the wall another officer was correcting the pointer hand of the high-tide indicator in accordance with the printed tide-table.

Manning reached out for a portfolio and took a blue document from it. It concerned the case on which he had been engaged that morning. Against the only blank line left he made the simple entry—"Body recovered 7.50 a.m."

The other officer looked at him with a mute inquiry and Manning shrugged. And the tips of his fingers began rubbing softly together again.

For a solid half-hour he sat and stared at the wall, and printed up under his eyelids was the picture of the fat, ponderous face of the captain of the *Yangtse.* He hunted through the files and rang up Headquarters, but there was nothing known against him, not a thing that could possibly he construed as an attempt at an evasion of the laws of the country. His record was as clean as any other captain's along the waterway.

He gave it up as a bad job and turned his attention to his morning's mail. The second one made him knit his brows—and it also gave him an uncomfortable sensation of heat under the collar.

It was a note from Headquarters, short, but as pointed as the ends of forked lightning. Cocaine smuggling was again on the increase. Increasing quantities were coming into the market and the menace had assumed grave proportions. All the known sources had been investigated, and it was now known that the river was the point of arrival. Headquarters stated very definitely that the menace would be stamped out, and speedily or there would be an unpleasant tightening up of things in general down the river.

Manning sat back and the fingertips were jamming so hard against each other that the tips of them were white.

And then Procter came in, Procter with a look on his face that told of yet more trouble. Manning stowed the letter in his pocket.

"Get that?" he said sourly. "Headquarters are raising another howl. And it's at our end of the river."

Procter deliberately stuck out his tongue. "What is it this time?" he asked; "slovenly bearing in the boats?"

Manning shook his head. "Dope," he growled.

"Opium?"

"No. Snow. The real and only genuine cocaine. They've got it hot up topsides that we're letting it through."

"Well—you can't patrol seventy odd miles of river banks and wharves with a force of two hundred—including reliefs," snapped Procter.

"Headquarters says we can," said Manning bluntly. "And if Headquarters says we can—then we can, and to spare."

"But we couldn't search all the barges, let alone all the big 'uns."; Procter raised his voice to impolite heights.

"Nevertheless and notwithstanding. The blokes sitting at mahogany desks say 'Yes.' They say the dealers are flooded with stuff and that it's coming in in barrels, hogsheads, and tuns. And, what's more, it's coming in along our section. The Man Up Top informs us that we shall forthwith eradicate every tabloid from the metropolis. Failing which—and the rest is the mixture as before."

"Pity the Man Up Top can't have a night out in the boats with us now and then. Last night for preference."

"Why last night? It was warm, wasn't it? And calm?" Manning's voice was withering.

"Yes. But he might be able to get his teeth into something else. I've just got back from the mortuary."

"Well—is that a thrill to me?"

"Where did we get the first intimation of that suicide last night?"

"Deck hand on one of the boats bawled across to the station that he had seen a big splash from over on the other side."

"Where did the splash come from?"

"Dunno. He couldn't see. It was getting dark and he had only just got in, anyway—didn't know the shipping around there any too well."

"From somewhere by the Wapping entrance of the Western Dock?"

"Somewhere out that way. He was over on the other side by the East Lane Stairs."

"H'm. Well, we're going to hear a piece more about that suicide—a considerable piece." Procter took from his pocket a long piece of steel and put it on the table in front of Manning.

It was the blade of a dagger, about eight inches long, and it had been broken off short at the hilt. Manning picked it up and examined it. There was blood on it. And the breaking was curious, the break making an almost perfect V. Graven into the steel were some deeply etched marks which ran perpendicularly down the blade.

"That figuring—that's Chinese stuff," said Manning. "Was this—"

"You've got it, sergeant. That was no suicide we took from the river this morning. The surgeon has just taken *that* from his heart. Murder. That's what it is. Just plain murder."

Manning put the blade back on the table and eyed it dispassionately.

He was thoughtful for a moment and then said: "Procter, taking a line direct across-river from East Lane Stairs to the Wapping entrance to the Western Dock, what are the names of the ships berthed up there? I mean the ones you can remember off-hand."

"There's only room for three along that bit," replied Procter. "And I know 'em all. There's the *Stornoway*; she's been in there a fortnight, held up by a delayed cargo from the north; at the other end is the *Beau-delaire*, the French wine carrier in from Bordeaux last week; and in between the two is the *Yangtse*, mostly rice and cotton—the Chinese hooker that picked up her berth last Monday."

"And that's all, is it?"

"If you can find any more along that wharf you can have 'em."

Manning rubbed his chin and turned a gloomy eye on the tide indicator. "This deck hand," he said. "What time did you say he saw the splash?"

"Latish. Half-past nine, or thereabouts. It was getting dark, anyway."

"That would be when the tide was at full ebb, running its fastest. And that means that the man who murdered that poor devil thought that the body would be rolling about outside Sheemess by now. Well, a deep-sea man isn't to know that the bend of the river there sets up an eddy that would hold on to a body for days. The man who pushed that body over the side has as much knowledge of the river currents around here as a milk roundsman in Hackney."

"Now put the other two and two together and you've got your man," said Procter. Procter seemed slightly wearied at his senior's disinclination to jump at a transparent conclusion.

"Yes, I know. But the job is to prove it," growled Manning. "I've been sniffing at his heels every time he's berthed. And I've had the searchers over him with microscopes. But I've been bulldozing him for opium."

"And now it seems he has taken the jump into the big-league stuff," commented Procter.

"Yes. And we've got to get a line on his middlemen before we can nail him. Can't take him and leave the West End organisation to carry on under another head. We've got to get him for the whole boiling, West End dope running and all. Procter, we have got to make a complete clean up on this—then, maybe, we can pass our compliments back to the mahogany deskers."

"And please to remember little Procter when they hand out the stripes," said the second under his breath. "And if you want to know anything more about that knife, here's the surgeon himself. He said he wanted to see you."

The surgeon came in and tossed his hat on the table.

"Bad business this," he said shortly.

Manning nodded resentful acquiescence. "About as determined an effort as I've seen," he admitted. "Stabbing *and* drowning."

"Yes, and something more, too. I've just come in to give you a warning. You haven't been messing about with that dagger any more than you can help, have you?"

"Just picked it up and took a peek at it, that's all. The writing on it is Chinese."

"Yes—and so is the poison," said the surgeon grimly,

"The what?"

"That murder was a three-hander, Stabbing, drowning—and poisoning.

"I suspected it as soon as I raised the eyelids. The pupils were contracted almost to vanishing point. They were no bigger than little black pinheads. And yet the eyes themselves were dilated almost to double their size. Nothing but sheer inconceivable agony did that, the agony that comes from a toxin coursing through the bloodstream. It was obvious that the man was dead long before his body hit the river. There wasn't a drop of water in the lungs. I looked for the other cause—and found the knife blade in his heart. It had pierced both walls. A terrible blow."

"Sufficient to account for the breaking of the blade?"

"Yes. It was a downward blow and the steel had gone right through the breastbone. In a violent effort to withdraw it I should say the blade snapped off as you see it there. But even a wound like that did not account for the eye dilation. There was no other puncture on the skin; and yet it was all too plain that that poison had not been taken by the mouth. It was then that I examined the wound again. And there it was. The dagger had been impregnated with a deadly poison before it was thrust into that man's heart. It is being analysed now. And until I get the report through from the pathologist, I should advise you to handle that dagger blade as often and as carelessly as you'd touch a live rail."

Manning's reply was active. He picked the lethal thing up with his I handkerchief and dropped it in a drawer, which he locked.

"Has the body been identified yet?" he asked.

"His brother is round there now. You'd better see him."

"Does he know anything about it?"

"Yes and no. He says his brother was expecting bad trouble yesterday evening. I think there must be something fishy about the dead man's connections hereabouts, for the brother won't answer plain questions. However, that's your job, not mine. Perhaps you will be able to make him talk. He has definitely identified the body as that of his brother Gilan Maxick. Hungarian, I think. And that is about all I could get out of him."

"But he admitted there was trouble brewing for him?"

"Yes—in a sort of desultory way. You know the type. Can't open his mouth for fear of incriminating himself in an equally unsavoury connection elsewhere. Either that or he is frightened of the gang that has already put his brother out."

"Which is far more likely," said Manning slowly. "To me the whole thing reeks of gang-work—and a big, influential gang at that, with miles of real money behind them."

"Smuggling?" queried the surgeon.

"That's the line, sir. Had a scream from Headquarters about it only this morning. And we seem to have fallen right into the whole nest of it, without moving off the tideway. How the blazes he gets his stuff ashore I'm blest if I know. Our boys went over him with a small-tooth comb. And the man doesn't live who can run stuff through once the boys are on his scent. I've known those lads go through a ship with hammer tappers from forefoot to rudder-post and from keel to wireless gaff and come out of her at the end of the eighth day with thirty packets of saccharin, each one weighing an ounce. They collared each packet in a different part of the ship. One was buried in the flour tub in the cook's galley, three were behind panelling in the staterooms, one was sewn into the lining of an old dungaree coat hung up in the boiler-room, two were submerged in a tin of wet sand—the string was tied to the anchor cable eight feet below water: three were hidden away in a heap of ashes at the back of a cold furnace—they had to crawl in on their bellies to get *that* lot; one was stitched into the comer of the house-flag flying at the masthead. Another was tucked away behind an iron cleat. They had unscrewed the cleat, taken it out of the deck, chiselled the hole a bit bigger, put the packet in, and then rescrewed the cleat back in position. They actually got two from the top of the piston-head in the engine-room—stowed away there between the piston-head and the cylinder-top!

"But the point is that the boys got them—every packet. Every one that was aboard that boat came out. The mate, who was the culprit, confessed, with something like tears of incredulity in his eyes, that there wasn't a milligram of the stuff left fore or aft the ship. Our boys had found the lot. What with X-ray photographs and the new electrical devices for discovering the presence of other substances behind metal and wood, the plain, sneak-thief smuggler doesn't stand a chance."

"And yet this man is getting through?"

"Yes—and with bags of it, too, judging from the shriek we got from the Yard. And I'll say it isn't possible—knowing what

I know. Either he is getting rid of it before he makes the estuary or he has thought out a scheme so darned ingenious that nothing short of a miracle will expose it."

"Or luck," suggested the doctor.

"'M—yes. Maybe we might stumble on it by luck. But there's a notable shortage of that commodity down in this neck of the woods. You're reporting this to the coroner I suppose?"

"Of course. Ought to be an interesting inquest. When I get the statement through from the analyst I'll send you on a copy. Might help."

"You can bet your sweet life it will. What is the name of this brother, and where can I get at him?"

"His name is Ulrich and he left his address at the mortuary. He says he will keep any appointment you like to make—so long as you don't expect him to blab too much. Know what that means, don't you?"

"Yeh," grunted Manning. "Up to his eyes in graft himself. Still, I'll get something out of him if I have to put him on the grill all night. Many thanks, doctor—I'll be seeing you later."

The surgeon took his departure, humming a snatch of the latest musical comedy song-hit to himself. He was a prosaic individual. To him the life that surrounded him was just one seething fight for existence and, along the waterline, a pound earned by a trick was sweeter than two taken out of a hard trade. Over and above which that polyglot population had developed a queasy habit of hauling him out of bed at two in the morning to come round to the police station and perjure his soul by declaring it sober while it was apparent to even the most indulgent charge-sergeant that it experienced a mean difficulty in keeping its legs. One more or less was merely in the run of the common task.

II

The marine store-yard of Chinny the Junk stands just away back from the river. It clutters its startling wilderness of old ship's lumber in that murky section that lies between Wapping Wall and Silk Yard. A high board fence encloses it on two sides; on the other two the dismal backyards of rows of tenements come down to mask it in.

It is an oddity of riverside Chinese that they are either wholly crook or wholly straight. And when they are straight no old-established city merchant could rank higher in his principles. Chinny the Junk was one of the straight ones. He dealt fairly and legitimately, and the prices he paid and the charges he made were just. Manning had known him for many years. On occasion he acted as interpreter in the local courts and on innumerable cases his knowledge of ships and shipping had been of genuine worth to the police.

And yet, such is the perverse rigidity of the eastern code, had he known of the most villainous plot ever brewed along the waterway he would have breathed no word of it to a living soul. Not in a thousand years. That was the other fellow's business—no concern of his whatever. But if the police *asked* him—well, that put the case on a different footing altogether. His assistance had been requested. That, *ipso facto*, made it his business, and any information he might have was forthwith at the disposal of the authorities.

He was an odd little creature. An inch under five feet in height and as thin as a withy, he cut a queer figure surrounded by his enormous piles of rotted rope, cordage, and general old junk. His face was as wrinkled and brown as an old potato and, for some reason best known to themselves, his parents had heaped the final enormity of all insults upon him—they had bound his feet in infancy like those of a girl-child's.

His yard was an unbelievable riot of disorder. A stranger would have thought that ultimate chaos had descended upon the place. Enormous heaps of old iron and bent cans stood cheek by jowl with mounds of old brass and copper that had turned green in the acid rains of the years. Old car wheels and foothills of perished rubber slumped against them. There was a rough half-acre of rotted timber, and on beyond that a ship's anchor which, but for a damaged fluke, would have held the *Mauretania* in a typhoon. Two score other anchors were there and a litter of little ones, mudhooks. Steel cables and wire guys were massed there in tons. At one end a heap of old ship's biscuit boxes stood, some of them still full of biscuit, pulped and rotted where they had been burst and damaged in the perpetual jostle of long voyages. Miles of old rope and oakum reared up against a garden fence and scores of skiff and dinghy oars were piled against it.

Chinny the Junk—the derivation of his name is obvious—waddled out into the midst of his anarchy of odoriferous confusion. Somewhere in his tumble-down office a little bell had rung—a note that was barely audible three yards away. It told him, very distinctly, that someone had come in through his gate. The weight of a man had passed over a six-foot patch just inside his domain. Furthermore, that man had not presented himself at the office door to state the nature of his requirements. Although Chinny the Junk himself was as straight as a ramrod, he had personal evidence of the fact that others were not so particular.

Chinny left his dinner and toddled out into the sunshine to see Manning of the river police standing there casting a masterful eye over the gaudy litter.

"Can I do something, please?" he asked, and his face was as expressionless as it would have been if a lawyer had just informed him that he had inherited a million pounds, or if his doctor had just broken the news to him that all his six male children were unaccountably dead.

Manning eyed him steadily. "Yes," he said. "You can do a good deal for me—*but*—"

"I no speak—please." The reply was as placid as a woodland pool.

"Not even if someone comes up and offers you banky-note?"

"No—please."

"Swear on old Confucy?"

"I break a plate upon it—please. I blow out a candle if I may die."

Manning took him over to a secluded corner and sat down on an upended barrel. He took from his pocketbook a thin strip of paper. On it was painted a replica of the Chinese characters cut in the dagger blade.

"Know anything about that?" he demanded.

Chinny the Junk gazed at it; and the incredible happened, A further layer of wrinkles crimped into his withered face. He handed it back after a minute's hard concentration.

"It is not complete," he said in his queer, high-pitched sing-song. "It is not finish."

"Well, what does it say—what there is of it?"

"It is old proverb—old Chinese saying. It means—DEATH COMES WITH THE DAWN. Very true proverb out there. Plenty fever. Plenty malaria. When the dawn comes—then comes the cold winds. Plenty die when the dawn comes. They die—they go out like the thousand candles at the Feast of the Rains. Also—please—much too many girl babies born in China. When the dawn comes they float down the Yangtse Kiang—plenty—and down the Hwang-ho, too, and down the Hung Shui Kiang. Please."

"And how much of it is missing, Chinny."

"The las' word not there. The word Dawn, he not there."

Manning lit a cigarette. "Exactly what I thought myself," he said without a blush. It didn't do to show a complete hand of ignorance, even to Chinny the Junk. He blew a cloud of tobacco smoke at his fingernails and inspected his manicure minutely.

Chinny waited. He had the double advantage of a working knowledge of manners both East and West. He found they varied but little, fundamentally; mostly in the approach and the pauses.

Manning looked up through a smoke haze. "Do you happen to know a man named Grosman?" he asked. There was no need to disguise the curiosity out of his voice. Chinny the Junk's knowledge of the ways of the West would have corroded through any such veneer.

"Captain Grosman? Of the *Yangtse?*"

"Yes, that one. Ever sell him anything?"

Chinny pondered the idea. "No," he said. "I no sell him any. I buy from him sometime."

"Junk?"

"Shuar. All his ole rope. His bad biscuit. His ole paint. All the wire he no want. And sim'lar."

"Known him long?"

"Fi'—ten year."

"Tell me, Chinese. Which is he most of—Chinese or Dutch?"

"Chinese most, I think. He spik the best Chinese I hear for long time. Mandarin. Little red button on the cap—button of the mandarin."

At that moment another figure entered the yard, pushing a hand-truck. He came trundling up to where they sat and stood there, beaming.

Flat on the face of him he franked himself, a jolly old Hamburger. His face was a round, doughy blodge of fat, prosperous benignity, and he smiled on the entire universe through a pair of enormous and heavily pebbled glasses. The tortoiseshell rims were a quarter of an inch thick and the lenses seemed even thicker. They magnified his eyes to great blobs of pale blue blanc-mange, washed out and dim; but even that did not disguise the utter good nature that fairly oozed out of them. He radiated bulky benevolence. He silently informed all and sundry that, short of a direct attack on his pocket, you could have the earth and everything therein—and his unstinted benedicite went with it, yours for a makeweight.

"All right?" he asked in a rich, full-gutturalled bass.

"How many you want?" replied Chinny the Junk.

"Today thirty. Tomorrow some more."

He held out a soiled ten-shilling note. Chinny took it and waved him on. The Hamburger's face bunched itself into another beatific expanse of smiling geniality, and he waddled over to a mound of broken biscuit tins.

The old junk dealer watched him, with almost a hint of a smile in his own eyes. The Hamburger's cheerfulness was infectious.

Manning glanced round at him as he began piling the tins on his truck. He was too fat to bend with ease, so he contented himself with taking those about halfway up the mound. Chinny was carefully counting as the tins went bumping on to the truck.

"Who is the old boy?" said the sergeant.

"Him? Engelberg. Holland man. He buy all my ole biscuit. He keep plenty chicken. Ole biscuit very good for chicken. Big tin like that fourpence. Plenty cheap."

Manning waved the matter aside. "About this man Grosman," he said. "Do you know anything about him?"

Chinny lit up a foul little black pipe with studious care.

"Him no good," he said decidedly, between puffs.

"Know anything definite?"

The junk dealer shook his head. "No," he admitted. "I don't know. But he is the only one who come in here and don't try to swindle my prices."

"Is he liked around here?"

Chinny shrugged. "He no come ashore much," he said. "Stay aboard mos' the time. Nobody know him."

Manning played the approach direct.

"Do you know what his graft is?" he demanded.

"No—please. Me know nothing."

"Opium?"

"Maybe. Maybe not. All he do with me is sell me old junk."

Manning got up off the barrel. "Thank you, Chinese," he said. "That's all I want to know. There's no need to blab what I said all down the riverside. I'm just making a few inquiries, that's all. See you later."

He nodded affably and walked off. The store dealer, with a face as vacuous as a dinner plate, noted that the end of the cigarette between his lips was squashed flat and that the tips of his fingers were rubbing together in a queer little jerky rhythm.

In a minute or two Engelberg had finished loading his truck. The topmost of his tins wobbled precariously as he trundled them out of the yard. Chinny the Junk waved him a casual goodbye as he went.

Manning walked slowly back to the river station. His report on the case had gone through to headquarters, and he was expecting a visit from one of the heads—if not from the Chief himself. The Chief often took a personal hand in a case that presented unusual aspects; and this one certainly did. The deadly determination of the murderer was unique. The three different and distinct methods employed to ensure death were unprecedented.

He was not greatly perturbed at the prospect of having to meet the higher command. The Chief was amenable; and though he stinted his bouquets he was equally parsimonious with his censure. It was a comforting knowledge in the force that the Chief only condemned when the culprit was seriously deserving of blame—and then the culprit got it, hot and strong. A reprimand from the Chief was tantamount to a career cut short, but a pat on the back was as good as promotion. Manning had no qualms. He had done sound work in the few hours since the body was recovered, and he had definitely established his line of inquiry. But he wished he had had something concrete to show his overlord.

Procter met him as he turned the corner.

"Been looking for you," he said. "The Chief's down at the office. Going to put a C.I.D. man on the job, I think."

"Just my damn luck," growled Manning. "We only get a decent case down here about once in five years—and when it does come he shoves one of the nobs on it. They get bits of fat all the year round up at the Yard: why can't he let us have our whack when it comes our way? Is he still howling about the smuggling?"

"Never even mentioned it. I think he's too keen on this case. He hasn't issued it to the Press yet."

"H'm. That looks as though he regards it as serious. Who is he putting on it; did he say?"

"No. He wouldn't tell me, anyway. Minnows don't count among the mackerel. He's waiting for you. Better get along in."

Manning went straight through to the little office. The Chief was sitting there, a tall, well built, but rather slim man, with hair freely dusted with grey at the temples. He had the cold, aloof eyes of all of his craft, the eyes of a man who had dealt with crime and criminals so long that part of his nature was to suspect everyone until they proved their rectitude.

"Well?" he said, as soon as Manning pushed in through the door. And a whole ream could not have said more plainly: "Please proceed immediately with your report."

Manning coughed. The mere presence of that flint-eyed figure had an extraordinary capacity for unsettling a man.

"You know all the facts up to ten o'clock this morning, sir," he said. "If you will come to the window here I can give you the lie of the land."

He pointed out across the crinkled, dirty-brown water.

"The deck-hand who first notified us was on the upper deck of the *Windflower*—that red-and-black funneller over there. It was dark, and he did not know the names of the other shipping along here as his ship had only just come in to her moorings. But he states very definitely that the splash came from over there, in almost a direct line with him. He was so eager to see if the man broke surface again that he did not take his eyes off the water again—and so he could not sight the falling point properly. A very excusable thing to do, if I might say so, sir."

"From across there, eh?" said the Chief. "Well, that thins the field down to one of those three ships, does it not?"

"Yes, sir. The *Stornoway*, the *Yangtse*, and the *Beaudelaire*. There is nothing whatever against either the *Stornoway* or the *Beaudelaire*. They're dead straight—in the river here every other week or so and their crews have been aboard them for years. Most of them I know personally, and the officers tell me that no members of the crews are missing, and that to their very definite knowledge there is no feud or bad feeling among any of them. That thins the field down to the *Yangtse*."

"Well—and what have we about the *Yangtse*?" The Chief was shading his eyes with his hand against the sun-glare off the water.

"She's an all-Chinese hooker, sir, from the captain to the cook, and that's a bad combination. He is the only Chinese captain, to my knowledge, who has ever come into the river, and I've been treading on his heels for years. He's a half-caste. Speaks English well. And I've had him under my eye for opium-running. He is playing some game or other, anyway and playing it pretty big, too. The characters cut in the dagger are Chinese. I've had them deciphered."

"Yes?" The Chief wheeled.

"One of my friends down the river translated them for me. Apparently it's an old Chinese proverb and means 'Death comes with the dawn.' But the word 'dawn' is missing. The blade broke off short there. If we can get hold of that broken hilt with the rest of the writing on it we ought to have a real piece of evidence."

"His name?"

"Grosman."

"That is rather thick Chinese?"

"Takes his name from his hybrid half, I suppose, sir."

"And taking the line of the splash and the evidence of this dagger into account, you suspect him, do you?"

Manning looked uncertain. It seemed early to admit a definite suspicion with so little real evidence to back it up.

The Chief waited. "Don't worry about me," he said quietly. "If you think so, say so. You men down here live so continuously with the river population that you get intuitions and instincts that generally line up in the right direction. That's part of your job. And you know a good deal more than you care to put into words. Go on—tell me all you know."

"Well, sir, usually he isn't seen about on deck until the sun is high. He is not a cold-blooded mortal; what I mean is, he doesn't like the chilly winds of the morning, coming from where he does. But this morning find that he was up half the night, scrutinising us through night glasses while we were dragging for the body. I noticed him myself up on the bridge staring at us. And that was long before seven o'clock this morning. And then again, someone else came over and said they saw him shaking his fist at us. That was when we had got the body in the drags and trying to get it aboard."

"Must have been a fairly noticeable gesture if a third party came over and told you about it," commented the Chief.

"That's what I thought, sir. I didn't say so, but it was right then that I began connecting him with the circular letter you sent out this morning."

"About the cocaine? You can leave that for the time being. There are other stations that can take that matter in hand. For the present I want you to concentrate on this case. There are certain very serious features connected with it that make a conviction an urgent necessity. The history of Gilan Maxick has been traced. He is a drug middleman. And no one in his group can be persuaded to talk. They won't say a word against anybody. And that, to me, is iniquitous. It means that they are afraid. They all know who the murderer is, but they are scared out of their lives. They know that if they squeak the same death that happened to Gilan Maxick will overtake them. And such a state of affairs is intolerable. Gang-work—that's what it is. A gang has arisen that holds the fear of death over the river. Its shadow extends to the West End, where even the doperunners wince and shut up like steel traps when you mention the murder of Maxick. And they commit murder as calmly as they sell their drugs. And I'm not standing for it. I won't have it. I don't mind them working in their own little coteries and having their own little feuds and internal fights—it helps considerably. When a big job is pulled we know just where to go for our man, and if one faction doesn't squeak the other will. But when it comes to downright deliberate murder like this, murder committed with an insolently contemptuous disregard for law and order, then I say we've got to stamp out the whole gang as ruthlessly as they themselves work. This land is ruled by law; and so long as I hold office it is not going to be ruled by gangs of thugs.

An organisation of this magnitude, that holds the rest of the underworld in a reign of terror, is a direct challenge. It is the beginning of the Chicago gun-gangs here in London. And it has got to be stamped out—right here at its very inception. If this gang gets away with it, others will inevitably follow, and life will be rendered impossible for decent law-abiding citizens. If this one is broken up, stamped out, smashed, and abolished, then the others will have had their lesson rammed down their necks. But it *is* a menace—and a savage one. And it is going to be annihilated, once and for all. Have you seen the analyst's report of that dagger yet?"

"No, sir; it hadn't come through when I went out."

"Snake poison! That's what it was. The virus of the bushmaster, one of the most terrible vipers known. It contracts the muscles of the heart until the agony is horrible. Cases have been known where the eyeballs have burst. And they are bringing that sort of warfare to London. Well, Manning, we are going to kick it sky-high. You have as big a chance here as you have ever had in your life. See to it that you take it with both hands."

"I understood that you were sending down a chief inspector to take charge, sir?"

"So I am. But he will take one end and you the other. You will take the river. And if this case turns out as I see it shaping, you will be in for as tough a time as you have ever had in your life."

"That will suit me, Chief. Who are you sending down?"

"Sterling. He's the man for this job. And you two won't clash. There's enough for the pair of you to do. He won't interfere with you on the river. You know that end as well as any man breathing. Report to me each night at eight. By the way, you took the name of the informant who came over and told you about Grosman? Who was it—a waterman?"

"No, sir. As a matter of fact, it was two of them. Man and a girl. I've seen them up and down here for some weeks. Every other day they come down from the moorings up at the House of Commons and go out to sea in their speedboat, the *Spindrift*. Maybe you've noticed her up there."

"The *Spindrift?* Why, that's young Toby Essex's boat, the long sixty knotter."

"That's the one, sir. And the girl who goes with him is Miss Kittredge. I should think they're engaged."

"Hardly that—yet. But no doubt they are headed that way. The rumour in the City is that her father, Sir John Kittredge, will be the new Police Commissioner." He smiled quizzically. "There's an entry for your notebook. Keep in the little lady's good graces and you will land one of the big jobs yet."

He reached for his hat and went to the door. As he turned the handle he looked back at Manning and said: "If you want an illustration of how tough your job is going to be, I can tell you that Sterling raided Wallack's today. Biggest cocaine man in the West End. Collared him with over three hundred ounces of the stuff in his possession—and he wouldn't tell. That stuff was landed here within the last five days; snow has been at a premium until this cargo landed. He knows we know it. And still he won't tell. It was known at ten o'clock last night up in Soho that Maxick had gone west. Wallack can take three years or eight. Three years if he comes clean—eight if he keeps silent. Wallack is taking the eight. So now you know."

He nodded and went out.

Sterling arrived an hour later, a solid enough looking officer, but again dowered with that unmistakable eye.

"I'm Sterling," he said. "You're Manning? Got an edge of the table I can have, and a chair? That's all I'll want. You fire ahead on your own. I'll be seeing you every now and then and we can swap notes. No use fixing anything definite till we see how the case begins to form." In two minutes he was installed and at work, going closely over a mass of typewritten pages.

Once he looked up and remarked: "Maxick's brother is due here at any minute to see me. You can stay on and hear him if you wish. I want him first; you can tackle him after."

Without further word he was back at his notes, and he worked on steadily for three-quarters of an hour until a knock came at the door and a constable looked in to say that Ulrich Maxick was outside.

"Send him in," said Manning. Maxick slid in, looking back over his shoulder until the door closed behind him. He was spinning a big-peaked cap nervously in his fingers, and his furtive eyes never rested on one spot for more than a few seconds—and never on the eyes of the man he was talking to.

"Mornin', gents" he said hurriedly. "Wisht to Gawd you hadn't ast me to come 'ere. Makes it bad for me. The boys know already that you've been at me about Gilan. If they finds out I've been down here—and you nabs the murderer—they'll make 'oly 'ell for me. I'll get done in, sure as breathin'."

Sterling swung round casually in his chair.

"And who is going to do you in?" he inquired.

"Who? Who do you think?" snarled the wharf-rat, wheeling on him. "The Lord Mayor? What is it you want to know? Come on. Out with it. I want to get out of 'ere."

Sterling eyed him. Already he knew he was on bad hunting. The man was an unlovely specimen, little more than a youth; a slink-eyed, collarless, thin-wristed throw-out from the factory of life. He had an exasperating habit of talking out of the acute corner of his mouth, apparently under the impression that this subterfuge effectively disguised the fact, from anyone but the person spoken to, that he was speaking at all.

He carried on his emaciated figure all the symptoms of the cocaine addict. But the real sign manual was in his eyes. They seemed to swim in a bath of atrophied mercury. The fishy glitter that came from them was the spurious flash of a recent "shot" of his enslaving narcotic. That alone had braced him to face the Yard man. He stood there a symbol of the strata he occupied in life, one of a murderous gang, more afraid of his gang than of the police.

"You knew Gilan was coming down here last night?" Sterling's tone was friendly and conversational.

"Yes. He had a job to do down here."

"With whom?"

"I don't know. He never told me."

"But you must have had some idea? You are all in the same game. There are not so many people down here mixed up in your business that you wouldn't have some shrewd idea of who he was setting out to see."

"I tell you I don't know," declared Ulrich in his plaintive whine. "He don't tell me what he's doin' every damn minute of the day."

"But he left you to come down here?"

"Yes—and what of it?"

"Do you mean to tell me he didn't say to you, when he left you, 'Well, so long, I'm just off to see So-and-so'—or whoever it might happen to be?"

"Yeah! That's what I mean to say. And what about it?"

"What's wrong, Ulrich? Do you think we can't handle this job? What are you frightened of?"

"I'm frightened of getting what Gilan got! And he *did get* it, didn't he? You can't laugh that one off the minutes. And I got no private desire to go underground. An inquest may be all in the day's work to you. But to me, up on the slab, it's a great big pain in the stuinmick."

"Don't get rattled, son. We're out to help you as much as anyone else."

"Yes. And a few dead bodies scattered about the river don't matter a tinker's cuss to you so long as you get the main job cleaned up."

"Was it a steamer captain he came down here to see?"

The wreck flared up. "I don't know. And what's more, I ain't *going* to know. And that's all there is to it."

"Why won't you tell?"

"You know as well as I do. You are hintin' that you can stop the gang from gettin' me. Well, why didn't you stop 'em gettin' Gilan? Eh? Because you couldn't. Any more than you could stop 'em gettin' me. But you want me to squeal just the same, don't you? Well, I ain't going to. And you can't make me. And you ain't going to get *me* picked up somewhere out by Shoeburyness this time tomorrow."

"But you have already told the surgeon that your brother was coming down here on risky business."

"You're a liar!"

"You said he was expecting trouble?"

"That's different. You can't put something into my mouth I never said. You always *can* expect a bit of trouble down at this end of the river, can't you?"

"Maxick, you can find trouble anywhere—if you are out looking for it."

"I dunno nothing about it. Gilan wasn't out looking for trouble. He wasn't that sort. He was no fool. He knew the strength of what he was up against. Trouble just came to him. See?"

"You mean that you won't help us—not even to get the man who murdered your brother?"

"That's it, mate. Better to have one dead 'un in the family than two. He knew he was runnin' into trouble. But he wouldn't stay out of it. Tried to square it up—and got it in the neck. And now you want me to follow suit."

Sterling sat back and twiddled a pencil in his mouth. It was uphill work, trying to glean something definite from a man in the grip of such mental terror as was Maxick. But there are other methods than the approach direct—and patience brings its own rewards in the Force.

"Tell me one thing," he said at last. "How do you know Gilan was running into trouble?"

"How do you think I know?" The wharf-rat was almost snarling with hatred of the men in front of him. "I know because he told me."

"When was this?"

"Las' Monday."

"Morning or evening?"

"Night time. What the hell does it matter?"

"Thank you, Ulrich. That will be all today. It was on Monday the *Yangtse* came in. I just wanted the definite point of contact, that's all. Mark you—you told me nothing. I shall tell the boys so. I kicked you out of here because you wouldn't squeal. You can go now."

The degenerate did not even stop to nod his thanks to the detective. His cap was upon his head, the peak pulled far down over his eyes, and his feet were slithering towards the door. He did not walk, his leg action was more like that of a snake, except that it was perpendicular. He seemed to move without actually moving any particular part of his body, and he was as silent as a painted shadow. He opened the door just wide enough to slip through, and when the door closed there was not even a click.

Sterling grunted to himself. "There seems to be a grand wind-up around here," he said. "I think we can leave Maxick alone after this. They will be slugging him next. Still, we've got the line. If it was anyone else, that rat would have shot all our suspicion on to Grosman. That's why I gave him the chance. But no. He fought off like a wasp the moment I mentioned a steamer captain. That, and the incidence of the times, is enough for me, coming from a piece of ullage like Ulrich Maxick. You didn't want him, did you?"

"Not for a minute. He's no use to me. Pity I can't go and have a mop-up over on the *Yangtse*, though."

"I know. But you can't do it. Might get a little piece here and there. But you would wreck the big scheme. We have got to get those brutes cold. We should never get another chance, once we started nosing round there. Well—I'm going up West. Got two more raids ready to explode on dope handlers."

"Going to get them?"

"Sure to. But they're only small compared with this new one that has just arisen. Can't get on the track of him yet. Someone is covering up a trail mighty well. But there isn't a doubt they are all getting their supplies from him. And he is getting his from the *Yangtse* Chinese. London last week was a desert so far as cocaine was concerned. Dope loonies were paying up to five pounds a packet for it. And it was as scarce as Great Auk's eggs even at that. Now the channels are flooded with it. Last week they were selling twelve packets to the ounce—and over fifty per cent, of it was alum adulteration. Today it is eight packets to the ounce and as pure as the stuff sold under Government licence."

"Wish you luck," returned Manning. "If you want me at any time tonight call in at the Outward Bound little tavern, round the corner from the Stairs. Those Chinese use it a good deal at night. Got an idea something may turn up there in the way of a lead."

Sterling nodded and pushed out through the door.

III

Hiixary Kittredge yawned inelegantly and relaxed against an uncomfortable piece of canvas that was painted to resemble granite. Except for its gross roughness on the skin the camouflage failed notably.

At the far end of the dance floor an orchestra of seven, decked out as buccaneers of the Spanish Main, succeeded in creating enough blaring discord for twice their number, and the floor itself was far too crowded for anything more than a halting one-step. What had once been a chain of dilapidated old mews at the smelliest end of Soho had burst forth, under the name of La Caverne Diamentde, as the very latest thing in fashionable nightclubs.

The whole place represented a long, dank cavern, with lesser caves branching off at the sides, where little tables were set amid the glow of lamps that burned dimly from the depths of conch shells, and where, in place of chairs, one sat on grog barrels. Here and there fountains of real seawater played. This, in the opinion of the management, gave the place the authentic tang of the sea, and the bunches of kelp weed that clung in festoons from the walls and the cavern roof provided just that subtle atmosphere that was supposed to be redolent of caves long buried in the hidden deeps of tidal oceans. The waiters wore thick gold rings in their ears, grisly looking cutlasses hung at their sides, their half bare chests were richly tanned with

Number Four grease-paint, and their striped shirts and loose sailcloth trunks were fiercely piratical.

The head waiter could be distinguished by his skull-and-crossbones jerkin and the livid slash that coursed down his face and distorted one eye—quite the best thing in the show. Instead of glasses he set hollowed bones before you, glared at you out of his one good eye, and growled to himself a gory string of blue water oaths. Then he poured out drinks from a grinning human skull, fervently hoped that your eyeballs would burst the next time you went over the Line, and added a depressing sum to your bill which he carried in a leather bottle at his belt.

"Feeling tired?" Hillary was out for the evening with her brother. And her brother seemed quite willing to go home to bed, with or without notice.

She shook her head. "I am and I'm not," she said. "At any other time I would get quite a kick out of a hole like this. But tonight all I can see is the canvas behind the paint, the silliness of that orchestra, who would probably go into screaming hysterics if someone down here pulled a real gun and started letting fly. I can see the wives of those brigand waiters waiting up for them to give them a good, sound nagging for not getting home earlier, and I positively can *not* see why one should have to get into evening dress to come down here."

"Neither can I. Blame yourself. It was your idea. Not mine. You didn't think *I* wanted to come out toe-tapping in a shanty like this, did you?"

She laughed. "No, I know. But I'm all loose-endy and you're a dear to have dragged yourself out with me."

Her brother snorted. "I didn't drag myself out," he protested. "I was coming out anyway. But not with you!

"I had a date myself. But it seems that every time Toby Essex is not available you hitch your wagon to my star. What's he doing tonight? Why can't he attend to his own women? Hey? Me gal, answer me that."

She laughed outright and called for a black coffee. "He couldn't," she said. "He and the mechanic are tinkering up the boat. He will be working pretty well all night on her."

"Well—who is he going to marry? You or Miss *Spindrift?*"

"Don't be an ass. We are going to lift the International Cup with *Spindrift.*"

"That will give me an enormous kick! Meanwhile, this evening has cost me the best end of three fivers. You'll have two more dances and then you will go home to bed."

She leaned back on her arm. "I couldn't sleep tonight for all the fivers in the world," she declared a little wearily. "It's past two now, and we go down river again at five. I shall stick it out here till then. I saw a dead body taken out of the water this morning and—and somehow I seem to have been living with it all day." She shivered and turned to the filibuster who appeared with her coffee.

Her brother glanced sideways at her. She was gazing at the waiter and her face was chalky white. The grinning pirate was pouring the coffee out of the eye socket of a skull.

"Oh! Johnny," she whispered. "I couldn't drink that—now!"

"What did you expect in a place like this?" retorted Johnny. "A bunch of counter-jumpers serving it out of monastic chalices? Get on with it. Drink it. Do you good."

He turned to the waiter. "The crowd seem a bit merry tonight?" he remarked. He had been down there before and had generally found it rather a gloomy affair. The dancers forced their laughter and their gaiety was painfully assumed. But that night there seemed to be a genuine sparkle about the place. The jollity was real and the greetings and cross banter had the ring of complete enjoyment.

The look he got from the cutthroat astonished him. The greasepaint faded and the theatrical habiliments misted out against the look of bitter contempt and disgust that glittered out of the dolled-up servitor's eyes. He was no longer a hireling, paid to make a fool of himself for the presumed merriment of others. He became the privileged critic, the watching eye that saw the same scenes night after night and attended the same painful rites through dawn after dawn: and had formed an opinion on them.

"This 'ere lot, sir?" he said in a deep rumble. "Bah! You ought to have seen 'em last night—and the night before! Eyes like dead cods. Skin like old paper. Snapped and snarled at each other all night. I got swore at, reg'ler, every three minutes. Couldn't do nothing right for 'em. And the young 'uns was worse than the old 'uns. That's the crowd I mean, over in the corner there. Can't mistake 'em, can you? There's some excuse for the old 'uns. I'm gettin' on a bit that way myself; and I can understand how they feel. Tryin' to get back to the old days, sir; and the poor old fools don't realise they ain't got the youth in their bones no more. Them little gels they hire—you ought to hear what they say about 'em—after. Pitiful, ain't it? Look at that old josser there. Rich as a Crusoe, waddlin' round with that Gaiety kid. Wonder if he knows what he looks like? Terrible, ain't it, to see sixty kissin' sixteen like that? Oh yes. They are merry enough tonight."

Johnny looked at him oddly.

"Well? Why the sudden change?" he demanded.

The swashbuckler seemed surprised at the question. He inspected the patron before him for a minute as though speculating on the genuineness of the inquiry. He appeared to come to the conclusion that he was dealing with real innocence, for he made the most cryptically illuminating reply Johnny Kittredge had ever heard. The freebooter slowly closed one eye tight, placed a long forefinger down his nose, and said: "It—has—snowed!" And that was Hillary's first conscious contact with the cocaine set.

A page-boy entered, dressed up as a ragged powder-monkey. Folded over his arm was a bundle of the first editions of the morning papers.

She nudged him. "Get me a couple of papers, Johnny. And then you can go home to bed. I'm so sorry I kept you away from her tonight. Why didn't you say? I didn't realise."

"Better come home, kid. You want a good night's rest. Let the boat go for a day. Toby can manage it all right without you."

"You've never been on her, Johnny, or you wouldn't say that. Like most young ladies, she needs two to handle her."

"All right—have it your way. Here's your papers. Johnny thinks too much of Johnny's health to mess about like this in the first bloom of his youth. Night, night. See you at breakfast—perhaps."

Later on in the day he thought considerably about that last remark of his to her. It was odd that he should have added that "perhaps" in just that doubtful nuance of tone.

She watched him disappear through the yawning portals of the Caverne Diamente, where diamonds and rubies and emeralds glittered in the surface of the granite. The manager declared, not without a hint of pride in his own restrained erudition, that he had got the notion from a poem—a *real* poem!

> "Full many a gem of purest ray serene,
> In deep unfathomed caves of ocean lie."

And if a real poet thought that way about it, then it must be a good taste to have them in his cavern. *And* appropriate.

She turned to her papers and listlessly turned the pages. There did not seem to be a great deal happening in the news just then. It was sum-merish. News always seemed to lack a thrill in the dog days. People all appeared to be as loose-endy as she was herself.

Then she leaned forward with something of real interest showing on her face. Here was something that gave her a little crawling thrill down the spine, a nasty little thrill. It was only a short piece, but it contained all the facts; and the powers that be, scenting greater interest to follow, had given it a precious top of a column.

"Mysterious Thames Murder," the heading took her eye in a flash. "Man poisoned, stabbed, and drowned. Dagger Clue."

Her eyes raced over the subject-matter:

"A mysterious murder was committed late last night apparently on one of the ships moored at Wapping. Dusk was falling when a deck hand on the opposite bank saw a great splash in the water, and hailed the river police. The river at that point creates a long, slow eddy, and Sergeant Manning, of the Wapping Station, determined to drag there instead of proceeding downriver with the fast ebbing tide. Dragging operations proceeded all night, and at dawn their patience was rewarded when the body of a man, since identified as that of Gilan Maxick, Dean Street, Soho, was recovered from the water.

"At the mortuary the police surgeon made the extraordinary discovery that though the body had been in the water all night, there was not a drop of water in the lungs. Further examination revealed the fact that the man had been stabbed through the heart before being thrust into the river. The dagger blade had broken off short, and was still embedded in the body. On analysis it was discovered that the dagger had been heavily impregnated with a virulent poison, the exact nature of which has not been disclosed. Further investigations are proceeding, and an early arrest is expected. It is stated that some Oriental writing, cut into the blade of the knife, is part of a Chinese inscription, the English translation of which is known.

"It is thought that the murder, one of the most brutally premeditated and pitilessly determined Scotland Yard has ever been called upon to handle, is the outcome of gang feudalism, for Gilan Maxick is known to have been a member of a group of individuals who levy toll on the underworld of London.

"He has a criminal record, and has served a term of penal servitude for illegally trafficking in drugs. Scotland Yard regards the case as serious, evincing as it does the first hint of what may happen to gang lawlessness unless the threat is nipped in the bud."

Hillary put the paper down, and all the lassitude had gone from her. She was tingling with a new and strange excitement, a stimulation of anticipation that even the prospect of a fifty-mile race in the *Spindrift* could not give. Here was something personal, something intimate to herself, something with which she herself had direct contact. And it had blossomed forth as an important item in the news of the day. She had actually seen the recovery of the body. She had seen that other far more portentous gesture high up on the bridge above the policemen—and she had had the blessed intuition to go over and warn the officers of possible impending danger.

And here, definitely stated in as many words, in an important daily paper was a complete justification of all her instinctive fears. The thing had happened. It was murder! And gang-work at that. What had happened once would happen again. That evil Chinese figure, lonely and grim on the bridge, *was* definitely concerned in the presence of that shapeless thing in the water.

Here was something with a real live thrill in it, a ready-made road leading down to the docks, away from three hours of utter boredom. Somewhere on that forbidding-looking boat there were surely clues in plenty, hard and fast evidence of the captain's complicity in that terrible crime. The waiter's last sentence buzzed in her brain like a prisoned bee. "It—has—snowed!" And the sergeant had bluntly said that he had long suspected Grosman of drug smuggling. What a grin she would have on Toby if she could get aboard that boat and find something solid for the police to work on—Toby with his smug tolerance and his air of superior intelligence in the speedster that morning.

The car would get her down to the wharves in less than half an hour. There wasn't a scrap of traffic on the streets at that hour in the morning. Gosh! What a thrill it would be to get aboard the *Yangtse* in that dead hour before the dawn, when even the river slept!

Hillary herself was only vaguely surprised when she found herself, a few minutes later, gliding out of the garage, heading for the river and adventure, heading for the first real thrill of her life, away from La Caveme Diamente with all its tinsel glitter, its silly make-believe, its old roués aping juvenility and its young men struggling manfully to appear blasé.

The car swung away through Dean Street and the cluttering side turnings, where, during the day, the kosher markets spread their garish turmoil of confusion. Then across Leicester Square and up the Strand, down through the City, bearing east through silent deserts of streets where tall warehouses loomed black into the night and the only humans abroad were the occasional beat constables trying the handles of the doors as they passed; on past the Mint and East Smithfield, skirting the landward edge of St. Katherine Docks and finally she was creeping down Nightingale Lane into Wapping High Street.

She left the car there in a tiny cul-de-sac, locked the gears, and switched off the lights. Then she stole away to the river front, her small, stubborn chin stuck out, the tips of her fingers clenched hard into the palms of her hands and a blissful unconsciousness of the fact that she was walking on tiptoe.

The days of teeming river activity, when loading and unloading went on all through the night, were gone. No gangs of stevedores worked under hissing, fizzling flares, while steam cranes whined and whinnied above them, and full throated foremen bawled for more and yet more labour to get boats warped out on the tides as they rose. The whole sweep of the waterfront was wrapped in a pall of gloomy blackness. Except for the intangible smell of ships and the occasional glint of starlight on the inky water she might have been far away from the river.

The loom of a ship reared up above her, gigantic and enormous, into the nave of the night. She stepped over huge grasslines that creaked round the bollards, skinned a sliver of skin off her shin against a taut wire guy that was startlingly invisible in the darkness and crawled along the edge of the wharf to the bows where, straining her eyes upwards into the blackness, she read out the name, faintly luminous in gilt lettering along her blunt nose, *Beaudelaire.*

Nose to nose with that great bulk was another; and her heart dropped a beat or two as she deciphered the name *Yangtse.* She drew back into the stark shadows of a great store-shed that flanked the wharf. For some minutes she did not dare to move. In one overwhelming moment she realised that she had made a grandiloquent fool of herself. The huge towering mass of that darkened ship looked portentous; it *looked* as though murder, cold, and calculated, lurked there. There was something sinister about the very atmosphere of her, black, immobile, a plague spot of the East come to anchor in the West. And for the first time she felt a horrible misgiving in the pit of her stomach. It was one thing, in the lights and glitter of the Caverne Diamentée to make up her mind to go adventuring among murderers in Dockland—she found it a totally different thing to see it through once Dockland closed about her in all its naked rawness, its grim silence and with the soft lap-lap of the dark water gurgling about under the piles and licking along the squatting keels. Upriver a streak of lights strung out athwart the river where Tower Bridge stood sentinel as the first bridge at the seaward end of the great waterway. Far downstream a lone kittiwake screamed, circling high up between the coppice of masts and the tiny pinpoints of the stars. The sound of it made her shiver. It was like the cry of a restless soul endlessly seeking a sanctuary that did not exist. It brought to her again a vision of that cold thing being dragged out of the water. Every atom of her was calling upon her to end the stupid escapade; to cut her own pride and dignity in halt; to scuttle back to the safety and seclusion of the big sedan; to creep away home, hide her blushes, and say nothing to anybody.

And she knew she couldn't do it. And what is more, she wasn't going to. The Kittredge spirit did not countenance a quitter. It had taken the bearers of the name through generations of storm and stress, through wars in far lands and through hairbreadth political crises at home—and it had taken her, with courage high, through daredevil risks on the flying *Spindrift*. She would have that laugh on Toby though the stars burst and the heavens fell, though all the wide waterfront vented its spleen on her and though the entire crew of the *Yangtse* ranged up with the odds against her. She was mortally afraid, but she went through with it.

A dim light shone from one of the small portholes at the stern of the ship. She didn't now whether it had just come on or whether her eyes, accommodating themselves to the intense darkness, had only just picked it out of the encompassing walls of the night. At a long guess it might have been in the ship's stateroom. She was moving forward to investigate when there came the barest suspicion of a sound from higher up the wharf. She strained her ears to hear it, a faint tap-tapping that might almost have been the mocking chuckle of the water alongside the *Yangtse*, except that it was harder, more definite and far more regular. It came nearer, tap-tapping along down the wharf, growing slowly and steadily in clarity, very subdued yet oddly distinct.

Then the long shadow of a man crept between her and the winking streamer of lights across the Tower, a tall man dressed in a long thin coat that came down well below his knees and accentuated his unusual height. A battered old felt hat was slung on his head as though its wearer did not care whether it stayed on or fell off.

He was carrying something in front of him. In the darkness she could not see what it was, and she could not account for the persistent tapping that preceded his deliberate, slow approach. He seemed to be advancing over dangerous ground, for he was feeling his way with extraordinary care, as though fearful of putting his foot on a live bomb. He came amidships and halted by an electric warping capstan. There he seemed to be back on ground he knew, for he sat down on the capstan and the tapping ceased.

Suddenly a low piping whistle sounded musically on the silence. After a second or two it was repeated, this time from the upper deck of the steamer. Soon a light appeared, a hurricane lamp, carried by a pigtailed seaman. By its light she saw he was dressed in blue jeans, the jacket very short and the trousers very tight at the ankles; and shoes of black felt with thick, white soles.

He balanced the lamp on the guardrail and peered over on to the wharf below. A sibilant whisper passed, and the seaman, satisfied, began to lower a gangway with a hand-winch.

Anyhow, she thought, she had discovered something. If the police ever wanted to get aboard her, all they had to do was to give a musical whistle, something like the fluting pipe of the nightjar. And she had discovered that the gangway was kept up at night. The tall man passed up the gangway, and again the odd tapping preceded him.

As he came into the aura of the lamp she saw what it was. The man was blind; he was feeling his way with the aid of a long ash stick, and the thing he carried ahead of him was a hawker's tray of wares—studs, matches, bootlaces, pipe-cleaners, and the general run of the street trader's merchandise.

As soon as the man was aboard the gangway went grinding back up against the ship's side. In a minute the deep silence had descended again and the stillness of the grave settled down over the ship.

Hillary felt her heart pounding. Something was going forward aboard that forbidding boat. The whole thing reeked of suspicion. If everything was honest and above-board, why should they haul the gangway up at night; why should they have secret whistle signs and have to identify themselves with a password before they were allowed to go aboard? And why should a blind hawker come crawling down to her at half-past two in the morning? Could anything be more obviously innocent than a blind beggar? The more she thought of it, the more suspicious it looked. And the more determined she was to get aboard and find out what it was all about.

In any case, she reflected with a feminine flash back to sanity, if the worst came to the worst and she was discovered, she could always fall back on the natural cupidity of the male where the female was concerned. She could giggle and be shockingly abashed and say she had got tired of the highlights up in Town and had come down there for a lark. One of the Bright Young People, possibly, out on a lone escapade; she just wanted to see what the inside of one of those great old cargo steamers was like. And then she would confess that she had been thrilled to the marrow and assure the captain that she had gone one better than any of her girlfriends had ever done yet. Looked at in that light, it all seemed simple enough. And yet somehow she could not quite shake off the memory of that foul face gazing down from the bridge, could not quite abolish from her mind the probability that that was the callous devil responsible for the death of the man being hauled into the boat.

The seaman had disappeared off the upper deck. She had watched him accompany the blind man aft through a steel bulkhead door, and she heard the soft thuds of the clamping dogs as they were thrust home.

Cautiously she crept across the wharf and hurried again into the shadow of the ship. Great mooring lines fell away from the bows to the fat bollards on the jetty top, and astern she could faintly make out more, coming off her rounded quarter.

She decided for the forward ones. The light in the port was aft, and the two men had gone aft too, so it was natural to suppose that such life as existed in the ship was all down there. Therefore it would be safer to climb aboard the fo'c'sle and then make her way astern.

She inspected the grasslines and found they were too big to get her hands round. They were over four inches in diameter. But fast round the same bollard was a one-inch wire hawser. She leaned out and gripped it, then gently lowered herself out over the chattering water.

It was a twenty-foot climb, hand over hand, out to the high-flung bows, and upward all the way. Before she was halfway she thanked her gods for the steel wrists that made it possible for her to hang on to the fiercely bucking wheel of the *Spindrift* when the boat was shrilling all out in a kicking sea.

Slowly and carefully she swung along. The tiny creak of the wire on the fo'c'sle head sounded in her ears like the clanging of a dozen empty biscuit tins, and it seemed impossible that the sleeping crew would not hear it in the pulsing soundlessness of the night. She imagined a circle of scowling cutthroats waiting for her with grisly scimitars a couple of yards beyond the fo'c'sle rails.

But when she reached there and hauled herself up there was not a soul to be seen and not a sound to be heard. She swung a knee over the hawser and rested for a minute and then gently reached up for the first rail. She grasped it, took her weight on it, and slowly climbed aboard.

Away down aft the bulkhead door opened again, emitting a faint haze of light. She saw the seaman mincing forward again with his hurricane lamp, and she heard him cross the length of the deck and disappear into the mysterious depths of the fo'c'sle. She could actually hear him moving about under the deck she was standing on.

That wouldn't help her much, she decided. She took off her satin slippers and stuffed them down the breast of her evening gown. They stuck out by the heels and they were horribly uncomfortable, but in her stockinged feet she could move about as soundlessly as a ghost.

She crept to the companion-way past the bridge and went down. In a few seconds she had hurried across the upper deck and was prospecting the possibilities of entering the stem housing.

There were two great doors of iron, one on either side of the ship. The seaman had come out of the one on the port side, the side that was outboard to the river. With her heart in her mouth she decided to use the same one. She did not know how long it took her to get the great steel clamps off and to push the door open, but she managed it at last, and, moreover, she did it without making a scratch of sound.

It was neck or nothing once that door was open. She slipped through and gently pressed the door shut behind her. And in her ears she could hear the dull pumping of her heart; it seemed to be forcing the blood in her head up to an unbearable pressure.

Still farther aft and below her she could distinguish the faint drone of a voice, but up there where she was the place was deserted. The light came from an electric bracket let into the side casing. Farther along was a polished wooden stairway leading down, and there were other lights on the baluster heads.

She went forward and turned down the stairs. A wide red carpet ran down the length of it, and the whole place was unexpectedly well appointed. Grosman, sailor though he was, appeared to have a full appreciation of Western comforts. At the bottom of the stairs was a deep divan, built up of many cushions, and a line of old Chinese marine prints hung down each side of the stairway. Down below, too, were censers full of a sweetly aromatic scent, and a dumb waiter, pushed outside a door and apparently left by the steward till the morning, contained the remains of a rich meal. There was cut glass and silver cutlery on the trays and finger bowls with rose-leaves afloat on the top. Two passages went round behind the stairs at the bottom, and it was from the left hand one to her that the soft hum of voices seemed to proceed. She cautiously glided forward.

At the end of the passage a cabin door barred the way, but to her right another door stood open. It was marked "Service," and she knew that the gods of luck were with her. Her own knowledge of ships told her that that was the steward's service-room and that inside it there was every possibility of a little service grill opening into the dining-room beyond. She listened intently. Not a sound came from the steward's room. And the odds were all in her favour that the steward was long since turned in. Grosman was not the type to risk being overheard even by one of his own race. His affairs were too obscurely his own for that.

She heard an unmistakably Oriental voice say, in its queer clipped staccato: "Please to wait a moment. Sit down here, please. I will fetch him."

The voice had undoubtedly come from the dining saloon beyond the closed door. She slipped into the service-room and waited.

Nobody came out, and she reasoned that the captain's quarters must lie in a part of the ship still farther astern than the saloon. Not daring to strike a match, she felt along the nearside wall, fumbling in the darkness until her fingers encountered the expected grill. It was only about eighteen inches square, secured at the bottom by a small brass bolt. But it was more than large enough for her purpose.

She slid the bolt back and cautiously raised the panel a quarter of an inch. Glueing her eye to the crevice, she could just see into the room beyond. The blind hawker was sitting in an armchair, his tray of wares supported on the table in front of him. He was half turned away from her, his sightless eyes raised to the ceiling in an attitude of listening and waiting.

The saloon itself was ornate. It was panelled round completely with an exquisitely aromatic sandalwood. The dining-table was large and of solid mahogany, and across its length was a silk runner of deep Chinese blue, hand-embroidered with truly wonderful workmanship. A humidor of ebony and cut crystal stood beside a great silver bowl of cut flowers, and one side was a silver opium tray containing the little black pellets, the tiny burner, and the thin, slender pipe with a golden bowl no bigger than the cup of an acorn. The chairs, too, were massive, built to stand voyaging in wild seas, and they were secured to the deck. Perched on a wall bracket was a gold image of the obesely contemplative Buddha, its hands gently linked across its round belly, gazing down on the scene below with placid satisfaction. The lamps were glowing pomegranate fruits, with the dark leaves clustering up the supporting stems. There were many of them scattered about through the room, along the cornices, round the great mahogany sideboard; a tall bunch of them stood at the end of the table itself. The only other lighting was on the yellow idol, and that, she noticed, was flood-lit from below.

A door which she could not see opened and Grosman came into her line of vision. He was dressed in the gorgeous silk robes of a mandarin, the black skull-cap with its little red button drawn closely over his head. He walked soundlessly to the middle of the room and sat in a chair opposite the blind man. The blind eyes followed his every movement as though he derived some visual satisfaction from knowing exactly where the man was.

"That you, captain?" asked the beggar in that monotonous, querulous voice peculiar to the blind.

"I am here, Rudley. You have been long gone," the Chinese replied, and Hillary was surprised at the smoothness of his English.

"I've had trouble in getting through." There was anxiety in the voice, anxiety and not a little misgiving. "Lingard would not see me until I had sent him the final sign."

"Lingard is developing nerves. Something has gone wrong. What is it? Lingard must know."

"Warnings have gone down river. The police know that snow is flooding the markets. An official statement was issued this morning. Lingard has a copy of it. Things will not be easy after tonight, captain."

"Things can be made easy, Rudley. They have been made easy before."

The blind man shifted uneasily on his seat. "There's ways—and there's ways," he intoned stolidly. "What passes for normal in the treaty ports doesn't get by on the Thames. Lingard is worried. He wants to close down until you have cleared your papers and gone. The Water Rats suspect the *Yangtse*."

"The Water Rats always have suspected the *Yangtse*. It is Lingard's fault if he floods the markets while I am still in port. Rest assured I shall always get the stuff through to him though the river police *live* aboard this ship as long as I am in dock."

"He says he would feel safer if he knew how you did it. He would know how to fence back against the police when they get on his heels."

"Does he expect the police to get on his heels? That again is his own fault if they do. None stands more readily convicted than he who convicts himself. You will be seeing him tomorrow?"

"He says he won't see me again till you have spoken Aden."

"Till I am through the Suez, eh? You will see him tomorrow, Rudley. And you will tell him that no one on earth knows how I get my stuff ashore. And that he would be the last to whom

I would impart that secret. He lacks the final ten per cent, of courage."

"He says there must be someone else in your secret; the man who gets it to the warehouse after you have got it ashore."

"Rudley, there *is* no one else. I do it all. Which is why I shall continue to beat the police for as long as I care to deal in cocaine. There is no one to fool my plans. I alone get it ashore. I alone get it to the warehouse."

"He says he won't take any more from you this trip."

"He says that, does he?" Grosman's voice had sunk away to a soft purr. It sounded as gentle as the note of a cooing dove. But it turned Hillary's blood cold. For behind it was not the contented purr of the house tabby, but the first warning mutter of the king of cats—the snarl of the tiger.

"He says he is not satisfied with the arrangements. He is taking all the risks and only getting a fifth of the profits."

"He wants more money?"

"No. He says he wants less risk."

"The arrangements cannot be altered this trip. And he will take all the cocaine I give him."

"He says he won't take another gram."

"Lingard grows obstinate. Does Lingard, too, need a lesson?"

"I can only carry his message, captain."

"I appreciate that. He knows that I have come to England this time with the greatest cargo ever landed. And I am cutting out the opposition. You best know how! In a year the monopoly will be established. Then shall these fools pay for their pleasure. Thirty-eight pounds have already been landed. Before I sail for Hankow another hundred thousand pounds' worth will be safely in his warehouse."

"He told me to tell you he will have nothing to do with it."

"As coolly as that? Lingard needs reminding. But what has happened, Rudley? Am I so simple that I cannot see there is something more behind Lingard's attitude than this? Am I so much a stranger that you refrain from telling me?"

"He doesn't like the way things have been happening here, captain."

"Maxick?"

The blind hawker nodded deliberately with shut lips. There was a silence. The mandarin poured himself out a thimbleful of emerald-green creme-de-menthe and took a tiny sip.

"So!" he said. "I am to be chided by my servants? He knew that Maxick was being shadowed by the police and was likely to turn informer?"

"Lingard's argument is that that was very doubtful. Maxick was never given a chance. Lingard knew the police had been after him for weeks. Maxick hadn't squealed up to then. And he says there was no reason to suppose he would squeal when you came up river. He takes the opposite view; he thinks your presence here would have been a firmer muzzle than ever, were one needed at all."

"In this business one takes no risks. Whenever a danger arises, that danger is automatically eliminated. That way alone lies immunity. It has been a proven axiom in China for more centuries than this country has known."

"Lingard says that is all very well in China. Shanghai allows a lot that London won't tolerate for an hour. Maxick is dead and the police have the body. The London police will not stand for murder. You have seen the papers?"

"They amused me."

"Lingard says that all the avenues of investigation must eventually lead to him."

"In short, Lingard is frightened?"

"He protests that too much force is used in the wrong direction and at the wrong time. The result of the Maxick murder is to put the police hot on the scent. By tomorrow we will be fighting a running battle to keep clear."

Grosman took another sip from the minute silver cup. "There are other ways and means," he murmured. "In China we do not fight rearguard actions with the police. Lingard will discover that in time. Tomorrow you will see him—"

"He says he will not see me till the *Yangtse* has cleared for the East."

"Unless Lingard is very careful Lingard will find himself—supplanted," purred the quiet voice, and there was a shiver in the way he said 'supplanted'. "You will see him tomorrow—"

The hawker cut in with a gesture of exasperation. "What is the use of giving me orders I cannot obey?" he said plaintively. "Without eye I cannot find him. Without eyes I cannot find the traces to follow up."

"Nevertheless," the cold voice went on, "Lingard will see *you*. A blank post card sent to his address will suffice. Do you understand?"

"No, captain, I don't," replied the hawker bluntly.

"It is a secret signal we use between ourselves. Just a plain post card with nothing on it except the address." There was almost a chuckle from the depths of the bulky chest. "Some of those post cards have arrived two days late. The police must have had many thankless nights submitting those cards to acids and irons and alkalies in an effort to decode the secret message written there. There is no message at all, Rudley. Just a verbal understanding, that is all. When one of those cards arrives it orders him to appear at the warehouse within twelve hours of the hour of its receipt. Simplicity is always more efficacious than intricacy. I will send the card myself. Lingard will be there."

"Then you have no further need of me?"

"On the contrary." The silky voice went down a note. "I want to know on whose side you stand!"

The forehead above the sightless eyes wrinkled and the head turned sideways as though to catch a hidden meaning.

"It is obvious that a faction exists," went on Grosman. "Lingard is feeling his feet just a little too well. Just a little too well. He forgets that the source of supply is the fountainhead of strength. If there is to be internecine strife, Rudley, I need to know my forces."

The blind man stirred in his chair. "Why ask me?" he said simply. "For five years I have known comfort—when for fifteen I had known nothing but misery, I who have travelled the East and held the whip to a thousand slaves. Five years of comfort I owe you. My affliction is your safeguard. For twenty years now the police have known me, living on a pittance. They would laugh if anyone told them I was an emissary of yours. They have known me too long. I can go where I will, hear what I will. None bars my way; none denies me. I am Blind Rudley. I cannot hurt a fly. Neither, captain, can I live unless the stream of snow comes in with your ship. What can Lingard offer me? What can Lingard offer himself—without you? Why ask me on whose side I stand?"

"Tell me the truth, Rudley. Lingard *is* definitely antagonistic?"

"As regards the Maxick business—yes. He says it was a fatal thing to do and it is not counterbalanced by a possible benefit."

"Lingard does not even appreciate the intelligence of the West. What, do you think, is the effect of Maxick's death on the rest of them? Will anyone dare to turn his coat? A little judicious murder has a tonic effect where a dissatisfied mob is concerned. You will be seeing the others in the morning?"

"At ten o'clock in the coffee-house."

"I shall be in the Outward Bound at nine in the evening. Report to me there. You will get a message. Pass it to me in the usual way. It is possible that a Water Rat may be present. Do not hesitate. Just carry on in your usual way. I can attend to the rest."

There was a silence for some seconds. The mandarin rose, intimating that the session was at an end. Still Blind Rudley sat on, looking straight up at the captain out of the depths of his blindness.

At last Grosman jerked out: "Well?"

"What's wrong, captain?" asked the blind man quietly. "You have never done this before."

"Never done what before? I don't understand you," said Grosman with a puzzled frown.

"You've never had a third party listening in on me. Don't you trust me?"

"Trust you? Third party? I don't know what you are talking about. There is no third party here. There never has been. I am capable of handling all emergencies—myself."

Rudley laughed; and the laugh was not nice to hear. "You don't bluff me like that, captain," he said bitterly. "You might be able to bluff my eyes—but you can't play tricks with my ears. Twenty years of this blackness has taught me to recognise the voice of a friend in a chorus of a hundred enemies, to distinguish the step of a man I know from among a dozen of those who are strangers to me."

Grosman was eyeing his henchman intently.

"Would you mind explaining what you mean?" he said, and his voice was like a saw cutting into steel.

"Captain, there are three people breathing in this room!"

"*What?*"

"There have been, ever since you began to talk."

"You are mad. There is not a soul here except ourselves. There is nowhere a cat could hide, except in the sideboard."

"The third party is not there. The sideboard is behind me on my left. This person is behind me on my right. The breathing began one minute before you came in. That is, two minutes after the mate left to fetch you."

Grosman had not heard the last sentences. As soon as Rudley had indicated the direction of the breathing his super-sensitive ears had detected, Grosman's eyes had flashed across to the service grill from his still-room. He saw the panel raised a fraction of an inch. And he himself had closed it and bolted it a minute after his steward had turned in.

In spite of his bulk, he was out through the saloon door with the slippery agility of a cat. Blind Rudley sensed the position. He called to Grosman. "Steady, captain—it was a woman."

Grosman wheeled in his stride. "So!" he said. His great bulk was planted outside the service door. His clawlike hand went out behind him and found the handle. The door was shut to with a slam and the lock clicked home.

He stepped away from the door and crossed over to Rudley. "Come this way," he said. "I shall not need to see you again till tomorrow night." He piloted him out to the stairs and clapped his hands for the seaman.

Caught in a trap, Hillary, white-faced and frightened, hunted round in the darkness for the electric light switch. She had a horror of being caught in that narrow place with such a ferocious brute, in the dark. She couldn't find it. In a panic she fumbled in her bag. She found there a little book of cardboard matches, a souvenir from the Caverne Diamenée—and never did she wish so soulfully that she was back in its futile gaudiness.

A tiny wisp of flame seared into the blackness, and she saw the switch tucked away behind the door. She pushed it down and gazed around in the flood of light that blazed out. To a woman's eye there were weapons of defence all about her. Pewter mugs, teapots, vegetable dishes, entrde covers, soup tureens—every single one of them a possible missile, but not a thing that could hold Grosman off for more than a few moments.

She heard a faint chuckle from beyond the door. Grosman had seen the lights appear through the transom overhead. A few seconds later the lights went out with a startling blackout; Grosman had pulled out the master switch in the passageway. Hillary Kittredge began to realise something of the animal nature of the man into whose power she had thrust herself.

"Ying, take Mr. Rudley on deck. When he has gone see that the gangway is raised again. Lower it for no one. And you yourself—keep for'ard. Don't come abaft the funnel. If I want you I will ring."

She heard Grosman's calm voice giving his orders and, straining her ears into the silence, she heard the soft padding of the seaman's shoes as he took Rudley tap-tapping up the companion-way.

Then for a few moments she waited, tense as an overstrung violin string. For her, crouched in the corner, it was like that horrific interval that comes between the flash and the crash in a thunderstorm, except that the interval was drawn out till it became unbearable. She knew that her knees had gone as weak as unset jelly with sheer livid fright, and the back of her throat was as dry and rough as though it was coated with coarse sand. The docks were deserted. A few out-of-works might be lounging about the all-night coffeestall in Wapping High Street, but Wapping High Street was a long, long way away—and between her and it stretched acres of gloomily deserted store sheds and silent wharves. All the hysterical screaming on earth would not help her at that time of night.

Slowly the door began to open. A hard lump shot into her throat when she heard the ominous click of the latch. It opened a foot, and a faint blur of light crept in from outside. She saw the bulk of the Chinese, grown suddenly bigger in her frantic imagination by the black cast of his shadow against the wall, loom silently into the room. He paused inside the door, and a long pencil of light stabbed out from his hand full into her face.

For long seconds he kept it there. She was too sick with fright even to shut her eyes against the piercing glare. He looked her over as calmly and critically as a prospective buyer inspects an animal in the market-place, appraising the offering point by point, saying nothing, but retaining his own opinion.

"So!" he said at last, and in the utter silence the single syllable came like an explosion on her ear-drums. It seemed to put the onus of speaking on her. And for the life of her she couldn't open her mouth. That grim beast was capable of infecting steel with poison and thrusting it into the heart of an enemy—and she was as much at his mercy as though they were out on the broad, tenantless wilderness of the Pacific.

And yet in spite of it, at the back of her brain there functioned a little burning spark of the Kittredge spirit. She was aware of a wild surge of recklessness in the knowledge that her feminine intuitions had been right. If only she had had the sense to have come down there with Toby, or have bribed one of the river police officers to sneak aboard with her, she would have been at the pinnacle of her own self-esteem. And she would have wiped that tolerant smile off Toby's face for as long as he lived. No matter what happened, she had won her point—and proved it. It was not her fault that there was no one else there to see.

"So!" said the mandarin again, and he limped a few steps nearer, like an excessively fat perpendicular frog. "What are you doing aboard this ship?" he asked politely. In that horrible minute of scrutiny she felt as though he had dug into her mind and turned her every thought over, examining each one and tossing it back after picking out its secret.

"I—I—I'm sorry. I think I have got aboard the wrong ship." The words bubbled out of her mouth almost incoherently.

"What ship do you want, little lady?"

"The—the *Beaudelaire.*" She thanked her gods for the chance they gave her of reading that name out there on the jetty.

The thin eyebrows went up. "The French boat lying ahead of me?"

"Y-yes. That one."

"And who did you wish to see aboard the *Beaudelaire?*"

"The captain."

"The captain's name is—?"

"I—I don't know," she stammered. "It's a French name and I—I forget it."

"You have met him?"

She nodded, feeling more and more desperate. "I saw him one night this week—in a restaurant—and he asked me to come down and see him."

"Do you often do that sort of thing?"

The slimy inference was obvious. There was something of a clammy caress in the very tone of it. Hillary, with her cheeks flaming scarlet, threw her character to the winds that floated down the broad bosom of the Thames. She nodded again and tried to look away. But the slant eyes held her as though on the end of a lance. She wanted to get rid of the sight of them but she couldn't—for she knew she was far more eager to pierce their unemotional depths and prise a hint of his intentions from them. But to her they were like little ovals of agate coloured ice, without a shade of feeling in them.

"The captain of the *Beaudelaire* is Kidson," he said in a level sing-song. "John William Kidson. He is English. As are the three other officers aboard her. His wife travels with him. She has her stateroom next to his. He does not make chance acquaintances with little ladies of the restaurant lounges. Kidson is deeply religious. He is known along the river as Holy Bill. Rivermen take humour from the fact that he is rabidly teetotal, yet gets a comfortable living by bringing over most of the wine that comes to this country from France. Yes? You are going to tell me something?"

"It—it was someone who said he was the captain of the *Beaudelaire*." She was horribly conscious of the lameness of the get-out.

"Are you sure it was not a stoker, a fireman—or maybe a common deck hand?" That was a fierce one. Little ladies of the persuasion to which she had allied herself begin in a blaze of glamour up among the bright lights of the West End, but they finish up across the bridges. There are grades, even in the oldest of the professions, and once they get down among the common lodging-houses on the Surrey side they reckon to have got down to bedrock.

"What do you mean?" she gasped.

"If the officers are all English—you must be looking for someone with a French name. Therefore he is not an officer. The captain does not allow what you English call 'That sort of thing' on board his ship. You are looking for one of the crew. You need to do it surreptitiously. Therefore you take off your pretty shoes and tuck them down your equally pretty bosom. So. You can get aboard and into the fo'c'sle without being heard."

He crossed his hands over his middle and regarded her.

"That is not true. It's a disgusting lie!" she burst out.

"What is chaste in the officers' room is crime in the fo'c'sle head," he said gently. "You English have such quaint distinctions. Tell me, little lady, if you wanted to see this officer with the French name aboard the *Beauddaire*, why did you come aboard the *Yangtse*, creep down into this room without arousing the suspicion of my very light-eared Ying on the upper deck and—having discovered your mistake several times over—elect to remain here?"

"I—I was too frightened to move until you had all gone to bed."

"And is that why you so silently raised the grill of the service hatch?"

"I just—just tried to peep in. I wanted to see who was there."

"So?" He regarded her again with amused interest.

"You were the girl who was out in the reach here this morning," he said suddenly. "The girl in the long motorboat, the *Spindrift?*"

Hillary's quick look of startled surprise would have given her away anywhere. The sharpness of Grosman's eyes was as unexpected as Rudley's abnormally perceptive ears.

"Why, yes," he went on, as though temporising with himself. "But you were wearing a helmet then. And leather breeches. You look very well in breeches. Perhaps your friend on the *Beaudelaire* has already told you so? There was a man in the boat with you?"

She took a grip on herself and tried to bluff it out on the oldest bluff of all, that of sheer frankness.

"Yes," she admitted. "I was out on the river this morning. I'm often out. We go out through the Swins to the Black Deeps—we are tuning the boat up for the International."

"And do you know the river police so well that you slow down and go over to talk to them—when they are recovering dead bodies from the water?"

"We—we just wanted to see if there was anything we could do," she lied valiantly.

"Who is the other half of the 'we'?"

"Mr. Essex. With me, he is the owner of the boat."

"So? And do little ladies who are rich enough to own boats like the *Spindrift* and go to expensive nightclubs pay visits at this hour of the morning to unknown sailors on ships like the *Beaudelaire?*"

"It—it was just a silly adventure," she managed to get out at last. Grosman was slowly but surely driving her into a corner, and he was doing it with all the wicked delight of a cat playing with a lamed mouse. Under the beady glitter of his mesmeric eyes she felt more and more like a trapped animal every minute. There were centuries of cruelty and callousness in those soulless eyes. They held in them countless generations of the brutality that has, in the Oriental mind, regarded woman as nothing more than a vehicle for the appeasement of desire and a genitive machine for the production of heirs male.

"A very silly adventure," he concurred. "So silly that, even yet, you do not realise the full silliness of it. Or, perhaps one ought to say, the full gravity of it. A great deal has happened since you came up with the dawn this morning. Things have become rather more involved. The dawn winds blew. And, as you probably know, little lady, death comes with the dawn. Intricacies have arisen. Manning has called in Scotland Yard. Sterling is in charge of the case. My ship, to my great surprise and sad regret, is under suspicion. Tomorrow it will be under surveillance. But tomorrow will find little to survey. For the intricacies will be removed. The police will have been just those few hours too late. In five hours' time the dawn winds will blow again."

He spoke with the smoothest gentleness, as though trying to placate a somewhat restive customer, assuring him of his own personal attention in all future dealings with him; but behind his purring suavity she read the deeper menace, the horrifying threat that underlined every word.

"There are places on this ship," he went on, "that even the Water Rats cannot find. They take the ship's plans with them when they search for contraband; but the plans they carry are not the plans from which this ship was built. There are places here, little lady, where even Sterling and his men cannot find you. For the *Yangtse* was built on the Yangtse Kiang, where ship inspectors weary not and Boards of Trade do not operate. You will find that it is unwise to meddle with things that do not concern you."

She cowered back against the wall. Grosman did not attempt to molest her. Instead, his eyebrows puckered at her fright.

"Why so frightened?" he murmured. "I shall not harm you. To be sure, it would be a simple matter to be rid of you, for you are a danger, and it is unwise to harbour dangers. It is like suckling a viper to the breast. But there are other ways. The ocean is wide and the soundings are deep. Many have gone out in the holds of ships, stowed deep among the cargo. Two thousand miles out a body is thrown overboard, in the warm seas, where the horse-mackerel shoal. Have you seen the horse-mackerel? Their action is swift and eminently sure. They do their work well. I have seen a body picked clean in less than five minutes—just a perfect human skeleton, white as new ivory, left turning over and over on the surface of the water where the thousands of little mouths still champ hungrily at the bones and the density of the seething fish beneath still keeps it afloat."

He chuckled again, silently, inhumanly. "But such ways are for those with a purse to fill," he said. "You are just a dilettante—a little fool seeking a thrill. You shall have it. There would be awkward inquiries made were you to vanish. The police would be informed. Possibly some of your friends know where you have come tonight. It would not be pleasant. So you shall go back to your people, little lady. But not quite as you are now. There will be a little subtle difference in you when next you sit with your people. Do not shiver so. No one will notice it. Only you yourself will know what has happened. And you will not tell; for secrecy is only one of the virtues of the pleasant spell that I shall cast upon you. You shall not be disfigured; and, after a little while, you will feel no revulsion. Only a great kindliness towards me. You will look forward to my visits with a great yearning, as a maiden in love longs for her swain. You will study the shipping for news of the *Yangtse* and you will pray for the safe coming of my ship to the river. *Increasingly*, little lady, you will sigh for my return from far Hankow."

He broke off and the pencil of light suddenly snapped into darkness. She screamed, loudly, piercingly; a shrill peal of horror that pulsed out into the night. The sudden darkness again had overwhelmed her. Her nerves, taut as overstressed metal, broke; she literally *felt* him drawing nearer.

"Don't squeal," she heard him softly chiding her. "There is nothing to fear. Just a little unpleasantness, that is all, until you get used to it. You see I must safeguard myself. You have been listening. And you know what happened to Gilan Maxick. Your tongue must be sealed. Maxick could die and not much would be said. He was of the gutter. You are different. But—"

She felt herself taken in a pair of enormous arms, arms that in spite of their seeming flabbiness were hard as teak wood and as fiercely strong as an athlete's. She struggled like a maniac, kicking, biting, scratching, and screaming like a virago. His grip seemed to encompass her. He had taken her round the arms and was squeezing her till the breath was being crushed from her lungs. His great muscles flexed to steel, and he had locked his hands. Slowly the pressure increased. A numbness was creeping over her, and her head began to sing madly with the violent pressure of blood to the brain. A distant drum was throbbing in her ears. It shifted and began to beat behind her eyes. She knew that her screaming was no longer audible—it had sunk away down the scale to a hoarse croaking.

The crushweight of his bear-hug was all on the muscles of her arms and shoulders. He did not increase it. She could feel his breath on her face, breathing smoothly and evenly. Her feet were clear of the deck, but she no longer had strength to kick. It was as though lead weights bound her limbs and held them stretched. Then the palms of hands went cold and the wrists hung useless, numb. They were insensible, except to the pain of millions of pins and needles that were shooting through them. It was as though a savage tourniquet had been applied to both her arms. She gave a little gasp and relaxed in his embrace.

He bent his head nearer, listening for the sound of her breathing. Then with a heave of his body he swung her on to the broad top of the surface dresser, limped down to the door, and switched on the lights. She lay there inert. She was perfectly conscious and fully aware of all that was going on around her, but to save her soul she could not have moved a finger. The life seemed to have gone out of her muscles, her limbs were inanimate, and a dull lethargy was on her body, a listlessness that was heavy as the aftermath of alcohol.

Grosman came back to her. "Just one little puncture," he said, with an oily smile, "and you will feel better."

Her eyes followed him, half hysterical with dread. There was something in his hand, something that glittered and was bright with glass and nickel under the strong lights. It was a gleaming hypodermic syringe, its attenuated needle as fine drawn as a piece of wire. From his robes he produced a slim phial of colourless liquid and placed it on the dresser beside her.

The stopper was a tightly stretched piece of elastic. He took the syringe, pierced the elastic, and carefully filled the cylinder with liquid.

"Just one little puncture," he reflected malignantly, "one little puncture repeated at intervals. Gradually you will come to like it. You will look forward to it. And in the end you will need it with every fibre of that trim body of yours. It will be some days before the *Yangtse* weighs out for the East. And in that time you shall be my own charming guest aboard here. You shall live in the Temple with the God of All Knowledge and All Wisdom. With Buddha himself you shall live, in the House of the Hundred Prayer Wheels, where none but a mandarin has trod before you. Just a little at a time you shall have, gradually increasing the strength until, like the other little fools who have tampered with foolishness too often, you burn with the secret fires that cannot be quenched except by more of the fires that consume them, until you only find ease in the sharp kiss of the needle.

"You will go back to your people outwardly as sound and as well as when you embarked on a misguided urge for a night's adventuring down river. But inwardly you will be one of the rest of them, a confirmed addict, hiding your desires with all the cunning that comes to the votary of the cocaleaf, yet satisfying your craving as often as the old fires begin to smoulder.

"And you will not dare to tell. Your only horror will be that you should be discovered and that your supplies will be cut off, that the avenues of supply shall be barred to you. You will fight and pay stupidly to get what you need. Your daily problem will be to get more of the narcotic that has poisoned you, for cocaine alone is its own anodyne. Aha! You will long for the return of the *Yangtse* and you will pray for her safe passage."

He picked up her unresisting arm, slid the evening cloak away, revealing the clear whiteness of the perfect skin, white and smooth as porcelain save where a sullen band of red showed where his powerful arms had been. Deftly as a surgeon he stretched the skin, searched for, and found the vein and pressed the needle in.

Coldly, analytically, like a chemist measuring out a prescription, he injected the dose, a thin squirt of the exhilarating drug that coursed into her veins like liquid fire and yet, in some queer way, as cool as a press of menthol on the skin.

Hillary's eyes were opened wide with horror. A floodlight of understanding was drenching through her. By continual doses of the vile drug, added to day by day and strengthened dose by dose, he intended creating in her a cocaine fiend, a dope addict, with all power of mind and body sapped away and corroded until nothing but a drug-ridden husk of a body was left, a body that hungered and burned for more of the drug that destroyed it, a dull, torpid thing that was gradually voided of every scrap of willpower, with only one aim left in life—the acquisition of more of the deadly opiate.

The very beastliness, the inhumanity of it, swept her into a fierce rebellion. Life came back in a flood to her benumbed limbs, and she tried to fight back at him. But her muscles were lethargic; it was as though a long sleepiness had come over them. They did not move quickly; her nerves were seconds late in obeying the urgent dictates of her brain.

The devilishness of it appalled her. Such a monstrous malevolence could only have germinated in the brain of a ghoul. She saw her perfect young body cankered and rotted, lost to all sense of decency, a pod of loathsome desires and dehumanised appetites. And fighting availed her nothing.

He leered above her, all the hate of the East for the West alight in his bitter eyes. He was holding her hands with ease, smiling humourlessly at her maddened efforts to shake him off. In a few seconds he knew the drug would begin to take effect.

"Little interfering lady," he said silkily, "you have a proverb—that a burnt child dreads the fire. So shall you dread ever again to interfere in those things that do not concern you."

She tried to tear her thoughts from him, tried to concentrate on hope of later escape; surely, on a river teeming with life during the daytime, it was not possible to hold a woman against her will. If she could only keep calm, keep her senses, and watch for the opportunity, that opportunity was bound to come.

The captain might be master of life and death aboard the *Yangtse*, but his power did not extend up and down the length of the great waterway. There were the river police, constantly patrolling the water; there were lighters, slowly passing up and down day and night, strings of barges, dinghys, skiffs, grimy little tugs fussing and snorting about all day long, all the whole ruck and gamut of riverwise shipping passing up and down in continual pageant. Opportunities for escape must surely present themselves every hour. He could not keep her cooped up and hidden away there through the long days of lading and weighing out without *someone* noticing her presence there.

And then again, perhaps Grosman was only frightening her; perhaps he was only putting the fear of death into her, so that when he let her go she would have had such a fright that never again would she open her mouth as to what had happened to her aboard his ship in the silent hours before the dawn.

Yes, that was it. He was bluffing her. Really, at heart he was not such a bad old sort. No one with such a fat, placid old face as that could possibly be such a human devil as he was trying to make her believe. And, after all, she deserved to be frightened. She had broken into his own domain and had played eavesdropper, had dared to listen to his private conversations. Some sort of a punishment was only right. She had asked for it. And in giving her a scare like this he was surely letting her off with as light, but as horrifying, an experience as his Oriental brain could conceive.

At that point she surprised her own thoughts. Another self, another, more intimate, self inside her seemed to draw apart and point out to her the extraordinary course her thoughts were taking. She drew back with a start of horror. These stupid, easy, happy ideas, these fulsome, reassuring prospects for the future—they were all the brain-children of the drug, the first soothing effects of the filthy stuff he had pumped into her. Already it was working. She was aware of a feeling of languorous somnolence; a carefree outlook was sliding into her brain, and even the sinister presence of Grosman, leering down above her, did not seem so noxious to her.

It was his ship, anyway. He had more right there than she had. She had no right there at all, come to think of it. And in any case, what did it matter? What did anything matter? Everything would be all right tomorrow. And maybe it was only a dream after all. A foolish dream born of old inhibitions and long-repressed desires. Silly how these dreams came about. But that was the way they happened. If you wanted a thing, like riches, or lovers, or fame, or, say, adventures, and you repressed the thoughts about them with sufficient firmness, they stayed deep down in the half-dead chambers of the brain and then threw up again in dreams when the brain was no longer fully master of itself. Or something like that. She had read it somewhere. Freud? Was it Freud? The German chap. Someone, anyway. A foreigner. Certainly not Chinese. That was Grosman. Fat old Grosman. Trying like the very devil to frighten her.

But he didn't know her secret. She *knew!* It was bluff. In the morning he would let her go. He might probably make a few dark hints as to what would happen to her if ever she came near his ship again. And she could go back, have a good long sleep—and that would be the end of it. That is, if it wasn't all a dream. Which, of course, it was. Such things as this never happened to people in their wakeful hours.

Her inner self was slowly fading. Her present self seemed to be drawing it back again. Its panic-stricken warnings were muting. She heard them only faintly. And she disbelieved them. Her faculties were functioning as she wanted them to, along the easy, pleasant lines that were strewn by the coca-leaf. The inner self, the very mainspring of her willpower, grew vaguer, more misty with each passing moment. She scarce heard it at all. The solace of its going filled her.

It was gone. The last jarring note had dimmed and died away to nothing. Her arms hung limp in the mandarin's grasp. He leaned over and spoke to her softly. She turned her head with the slow, soft languor of utter contentment, and looked up at him. She smiled and her hand squeezed his, ever so gently. In any other circumstance it would have been the soft caress of invitation...

But the smile was at an odd hallucination which she had been harbouring but a few short minutes before. How on earth had she ever conceived the notion that Grosman was fat—or ugly? Queer how the brain warps conceptions at times. Grosman? He was positively a decent-looking old chap. Wouldn't hurt a fly. And certainly not fat. There was nothing obese about him. How she had first got the notion she couldn't think. And, what was more, she didn't want to. So far as she was concerned, she had amended her ideas. Grosman was all right. Friendly old soul. Wonder what his Christian name was. Heigho! She'd be asleep in a minute if she didn't look out. Well, the bed was certainly very soft and nice. A big, double feather bed probably. Generally she didn't approve of feather beds. But tonight she did. She'd tell the world she did. Why she hadn't liked them before passed her comprehension. Quite a lot of her preconceived ideas were being knocked cock-eyed tonight. And a very good thing too—if they were all as nice as these. Ee-yah ! She stretched her arms in a bliss of comfort. Time must be getting on. No wonder she was tired.

But was she? The secondary symptoms were beginning to manifest themselves. Somehow she didn't particularly want to go to sleep. At least, she didn't think so. She wasn't quite sure. In a little while she would make up her mind. Meanwhile there was nothing whatever to worry about. Everything was slowly coming just right and splendid. The world was very rosy, very desirable, a wholly delightful place to be in.

And old Grosman, too. There he was, bless his old heart, as friendly and as affectionate as anyone could wish. Nice old chap. Faithful old chap. Trust old Grosman to stick around.

There was a brightness in her eyes, a glisten that seemed to be born of perfect health, spirits running up to the pinnacles of the heights. A feeling of warmth and bodily well-being was sweeping her, a gentle tingle of exhilaration, that most perfect of all emotional sensations, was spinning about in her. Grosman waited on with a high-souled patience. Soon she was smiling intermittently as though a free but disjointed stream of jokes was running through her mind.

The mandarin spoke to her then.

"How did you come down here?" he asked. "By car?"

The girl nodded, too serenely lazy to talk.

"Were you alone?"

Again she gave a tiny little nod of her head. Grosman stroked her arm. "And you left the car handy here somewhere?" he inquired gently.

"Yes," she whispered, and tucked her head down against her shoulder.

Grosman bared her arm again, picked up the syringe, and carefully sought a second vein. He chose one in the firm flesh of the forearm. The needle went in, and with studied calculation he administered a bolstering dose.

In five minutes the bright glisten of her eyes turned to a dull leaden glaze. The springy tingle slipped away from her veins; and slowly, with many flickerings, her eyelids closed.

He watched her critically for a moment to make sure she slept. And when her breathing began to come in short, steady exhalations he picked her up in his great arms and carried her out into the saloon.

He settled her on a deep mound of cushions and rang for the upper deck watch. In a little while Ying arrived on softly padding feet. Grosman was busy with Hillary's little gold-meshed handbag, ferreting about among its contents for one of her visiting cards. He found one and read thereon the bald announcement—Miss Hillary Kittredge, Cawdor House, Finchley.

Grosman turned to the seaman.

"Go out into the neighbouring streets," he said. "You will find a car, probably a saloon. It will not be in a garage, but most likely in a side street or small alleyway leading off one of the dock approaches. Very likely its lights will be out. Find it and take it to Cawdor House, Finchley. That is on the road out of London to the north, through Regent's Park and Barnet. The name of the road I do not know, but you will find it in the telephone directory under the name Kittredge. If there is a garage attached to the house—and most probably there will be—look carefully over the ground and run the car in as quietly as you can. You should not have much trouble, for it is obvious that the family there are quite used to the owner of the car arriving home at any hour of the morning. If there is no garage leave the car outside and return as quickly as possible. I will be waiting up for you. Leave entries in the log in your own writing covering the next two hours."

Ying bobbed his head without showing the least concern at the oddity of the order, and went padding away up the companion-way.

Grosman crossed over to the massive sideboard. A cluster of pomegranate fruits glowed at one end. He switched them out, felt in one of the side cupboards for a hidden knob, and turned it till there came a faint "click."

Then he turned the lights on again. And as the soft glow flooded out the high panel in the centre of the board swung open, revealing a narrow, pitch black opening beyond. Grosman turned off the flood of light on the Buddha, picked the girl up, and passed through the opening. As he disappeared with his burden the lamps went out and the panel closed silently behind him. The locks clicked tight as the panel closed in and the lights came on again from under the golden Buddha, who sat serenely on his bracket and gazed down in placid contemplation at the ominous silence and emptiness that descended upon the room.

From far away over the massed cluttering of store-sheds and dormant cranes Big Ben boomed out the hour; four brassy strokes, enormous and mighty, that quivered on the walls of the night long after the hammerhead was still. From on beyond Wapping Wall the protesting drone of the first of the early workmen's trams snored along, and a red light, bright in the black blocks of shadows along the Surrey side, crept gently along, where a police boat chugged slowly up river.

IV

Johnny Kittredge awoke next morning and bleated his regret to the ceiling that he had not kept earlier hours overnight. It was a hundred per cent penance, he declared, to be afflicted with a sister like Hillary. She had more personal will power than a yearling colt, and she took about as kindly to the bit. All told, he informed his razor as he viciously jammed the alum stick into the second snick on his chin, it would be thoroughly satisfactory to all concerned if she found herself one of these days in an undeniably sticky mess, a mess from which it would take more than the machinations of her more influential friends to extricate her. Meanwhile, he hoped she was having a completely filthy time with a busted rudder somewhere out past the Swin, in the back yard of the estuary, where she wouldn't be picked up for hours and hours and hours.

He was late for breakfast, and the coffee was nothing to raise a thrill about. Among his mail was a letter that cheerfully cancelled him out of a round of golf that afternoon; another, delivered by hand and written in a mixture of gall and prussic acid, thanked him with feminine fervour for having been kept waiting in a restaurant foyer till the whole evening was well and truly sunk.

His father, Sir John, knew the portents. He had a knack of smiling with a dead straight face and an eye that never even lit. Johnny described it as a very slight diaphragmatic tremor—just that and no more. He cocked a knowledgeable eye at his son. "Out late last night, old man?" he asked.

"Yes," grunted Johnny. "But it wasn't with malice afore thought. Like a dutiful ass I was hanging on to a completely casual and exasperating piece of skirt—an unnecessary and uninteresting piece of skirt, mark you—keeping her out of the hands of murderers, body snatchers, evangelists, white slavers, and God knows who-what—and in doing so I everlastingly annihilated my own date."

"You had a date?"

"I'll inform the slant-eyed universe I had a date! With one of the most—sorry, *the* most wonderful, most adorable, divine, goddessy, *délice*, soul burnishing, faith renewing, eye soothing, loveliest, darlingest, most highly inflammable piece of dame you could meet in a fortnight of Ash Wednesdays. Looks well, talks well, rides well, shoots well, got a peach of a drive off the tee, smacks a hell of a dirty backhand volley, and actually understands cricket! Yes, sir. Slit my throat if I tell a lie! A bit uncontrolled with the pen, though. And if you want to see a pair of legs do the 'Varsity Drag—"

A ringing squeal on the telephone bell cut him short.

Father and son eyed each other across the table. Johnny carefully put down his knife and fork. The elder never batted an eye, but the son had a fairly shrewd suspicion that the diaphragm was publishing a tremor.

"D'ye hear that?" Johnny demanded, jerking a belligerent thumb over his shoulder. "That's it! That's her! Stranded somewhere out on the Hevnelpus Shoal. And she's vamped the lighthouse keeper into a swoon—and he's let her use the Trinity House phone. 'Hello, Johnny, darling, is that you?' With her mouth all screwed up pretty like a piece of sugar-coated sugar. 'What *do* you think has happened? Here's your poor little sister all wrecked on the Whatsemames. All wet '—I'll tell the world she's wet—' and so cold and *so* hungry. And you will be a perfect angel and come out and rescue her, won't you? The best way is to take a taxi as far as Shoeburyness, tell him to wait so that we can all go back in it, and then hire a yawl. Any of the boatmen there will know where the Blastemall Shoals are—just sixty-six short little miles Nor'-nor'-east-two-east of the Gorblimies. And unless you get your poor little sister home and tucked into bed *touts suite* she's going to catch a lungful of that horrid pneumonia and won't be able to win that case of silver thimbles in the International.' Yeaaaaaaaaaah!"

The maid entered and said: "A telephone message for you, Mr. John. Mr. Essex is on the line, waiting."

"Is he!" said John with a glare that would have gone through Harvey-ised steel. "She's passed the buck on to Toby, has she, the hussy? Got her poor tame aunt to do the 'darling-Johnny' stuff, eh? Whoops, dearie, wait till I get at him."

He went out and stuck the receiver against his ear. "Well?" he barked.

"Is that you, Johnny?" asked an anxious voice.

"Oh yes, this is Johnny. Spill the bad news. You can leave me the preliminaries in your will. I'm busy and want to get it over. Where are you? And what's the alibi? Magneto? Spark plugs? Steering gear? General debility of the motor—or just dam lousy seamanship?"

"Easy, Johnny, easy. This isn't a call for the life-boat. Where's Hillary?" There was an undeniably worried note in the tone of Toby's voice.

"Where? How the fiery Hades do *I* know where she is? Where did you decant her last? Did you skid her over the tailboard, park her on the mark buoy, or just slide her over side on a twin? And while we're at it, why not look after your own *femmes* in the evening? Hey? Why dump 'em on me—and at the tail end of the month, too? D'ye think *I've* got diamond mines working overtime for me, or a row of chain stores hitting me with dividends every Friday? Or do you take me for the long, curly lizard that passes the cakes at *this dansant?* Hey? What's the natty notion?"

"Listen, Johnny. I want to know where she is. I couldn't be with her last night. There was a six-hour job to do on the *Spindrift* and I didn't want her here. She couldn't help—it was all heavy lifting and overhauling, no work for a girl at all. And I sent her home. I thought she was going to have a good, long night's rest—"

"Well, you can put your left hand right down your throat and say she didn't. She went out on a skite. And what's more, she planted me on the pillion. I was running around behind her half the night—clawing for my wallet every ten minutes or so. She said she was meeting you at five, and she kept me up singeing the hours with her till two o'clock this morning."

"Then why didn't she turn up at the moorings today?"

"Because Jupiter wasn't in conjunction with Jehovah or some such damn rot. How the bombinating blazes do I know why she didn't turn up? Why don't you look after her properly? Keep a firm hold on her. Boss her. Be master. Knock her about a bit. But don't use me for her private halter."

"Johnny, be serious Hillary has never failed to turn up before when we have an important test-run scheduled. If she can't get here she has always phoned the pier. That is a fixed understanding between us. I'm sorry to trouble you, but I asked to be put through to her and the maid informed me that Hillary had not been home all night."

"Eh?" said Johnny blankly.

"I wondered if you knew where she had gone?"

"Not been home all night? What new game's this? And not out with you this morning? Then where is she?"

"That's what I'm asking you. Where did you leave her last night?"

"At the Caveme Diamentée. She said she had gone beyond sleeping and was going to bum out the hours there till it was time to go down to the boat. I bunged oft home and left the car for her—Here, half a mo',

I'll go round to the back and see if the car's in. Hang on, will you?"

He hurried out through the back way to the garden. The garage, big enough for three cars, was closed, but not locked. Johnny flung the door open wide. All three cars stood there. Two had been washed and polished overnight: the third, the big blue saloon, stood just as it had come in.

He looked in at the window and stared around with a puzzled frown at its emptiness. He felt the water-jacket of the radiator and it was stone cold. That meant that the car had been standing there for some hours, for the car was fitted with the thermostat valve cooling system which kept the water warm long after the engine was shut off.

Then he glanced at the dash-board. "That's dam funny," he muttered. "She must have done twenty odd miles at the wheel after I left her last night. That speedometer was set back to zero when I took her out—and I'll swear I didn't do more than ten miles in her."

He went back into the house and called into the servants' quarters: "Did anybody hear the saloon come in last night?"

Hopkins, the butler, appeared. "Yes, sir," he said. "I heard it come in. At least, it must have been the saloon because the other cars were in before dinner. I saw the chauffeur washing them. I was only half awake. I think it was the gears squeaking that woke me, because I remember thinking that Miss Hillary must be having trouble with the car; I had never heard Miss Hillary grind the gears before."

"Did you hear her come into the house?"

"No, sir, but it isn't very likely that I would. My room is right over here at the back. I wouldn't hear her unless the door was slammed. But I heard her close the garage door and so I thought everything was all right. I just sort of turned over and went to sleep again, sir, as the saying is."

"And what time was this?"

"Couldn't say to a minute, sir, but it was pretty late. I knew I had been asleep a long time before she came in. I'd say it must have been about four in the morning, sir—or maybe even a bit later than that."

Johnny clicked his teeth. "See that that car is not touched till I get back," he said. He went back to the phone with a deep drawn frown on his forehead.

"That you, Toby?" he said. "I say, there's something fishy here. Hillary came home some time after four o'clock. The car is in the garage with about fifteen extra miles showing on the Speedo. That is, if she went to Westminster at all. Hopkins says he heard her come in. And she seems to have bunged off somewhere. What's up—had a love-spat or something?"

"Good Lord, no! Haven't had a cross word for two solid months. And she was keen as mustard to make the test this morning. Where did you say you left her last night?"

"At the Caverne Diamentée. About two o'clock. She was all half-and-halfy Didn't want to go home and didn't want to go off on a binge, I left her at a table reading the early morning papers."

"Dashed odd, isn't it?"

"Ring off, Toby. I'll get on to her clubs and see if she went back to Town after leaving here. Maybe she thought out a new one and tried it last night hot off the griddle."

For twenty minutes Johnny rang up various clubs, hoping to hear that she had come crawling in at some unearthly hour in the morning and had been too tired to keep her appointment with Toby. But at each one he drew a blank. Hillary had not been seen or heard of in her clubs for some days.

He went gloomily back into the breakfast-room. Sir John was deeply immersed in his morning paper, but he had heard every word of Johnny's conversation on the phone. He was as worried and as perturbed as the boy himself, though it was in neither of their natures to show it to each other.

Johnny slumped down in his chair. "Sis has gone daffy," he moodily informed his fingernails as he inspected them minutely. "Gone loco. Got skull bugs. The sap has riz in her veins and she's capering about like a spring lamb. Brought the bus back at fourish this morning and then went off on a purely personal whizz. No one's seen her; no one knows where she is. All we know that she isn't out on the Hevnelpus, Toby went out alone this morning."

Sir John glanced up over his paper. "She was telling me about an adventure she had on the river yesterday morning," he said.

"Yes, sir. She and Toby saw a body being dragged out of the water. Down by Wapping. And she got the idea she was playing heroine in a blood-curdler. The police gave her the 'ha, ha' and she went all chippy about it."

Sir John passed over his paper without comment. The front page contained a report of the case almost identical with the one Hillary had read earlier on that morning. Johnny read it through and got up without a word.

He went to the telephone and got through to the Caverne Diamentée.

"Hello!" he said. "I want to speak to the manager or the secretary or somebody in authority. Eh? All gone home? Well, is the doorkeeper there? Right—put him on the line, please. Hello—is that the doorkeeper? This is Kittredge speaking. Yes—I was in last night with Miss Hillary. Do you happen to know what time she left? What? No, I went soon after two. She did? A few minutes after me? Did she take the car? Oh. And do you happen to remember which way she went? *Down* Dean Street? Thank you. Much obliged."

He picked up his hat and jammed it on his head. "See you later, sir," he called to his father. In five minutes he was on his way in his car to the river station at Wapping.

Both Sterling and Manning were in when he got there and he introduced himself. "My name's Kittredge," he said. "I'm the brother of Miss Hillary Kittredge, who saw you take the body of Gilan Maxick from the water yesterday. I believe she came over and spoke to you about it?"

"Yes, that is so," said Manning. "Miss Kittredge came over and spoke to me. My name is Manning. This is Chief Inspector Sterling of Scotland Yard."

Johnny nodded to them. "Well, what has happened," he told them soberly, "is that Hillary has gone."

"I don't think I quite understand," said Sterling.

"We were out together late last night. At the Caverne Diamentée. I left her at two this morning. She was going to wait on till five, when she was going out again on the *Spindrift*. I bought her some papers to read while she was burning time. Whether she read the report or not I don't know, but it's in this morning's papers as you are aware. She can't have been reading long because the doorkeeper assures me she left a few minutes after me. It was a front-page story, and she would be bound to see it first thing. Her car came back to the garage at four this morning. The butler's room is at the back and he heard the car come in. He says he was awakened by the squeal of the gears changing down to low, getting into the garage. Now I've driven with Hillary some thousands of miles in that car and I've never heard her grind the gears yet. She knew when to slip those gears in better than the man who made them. I'll even say she could drive that car better than I can myself. Moreover, the butler didn't hear her come into the house. And when she comes in late she always gives my door a wallop to let me know she's O.K. I didn't hear her last night. Being dog-tired I may not have done, even if she had banged. But I feel pretty sure she didn't."

"Was she in the habit of bringing the car in and going off again on foot?"

"Never done it in her life before. Why should she? Why should she walk when she has got the bus under her already?"

"What are you hinting at, Mr. Kittredge?"

"I'm hinting that I don't believe it was Hillary who brought the car back last night. It was a stranger who whinnied those gears. Hillary has brought that car hundreds of times up that drive. The gears went in automatically—she knew to an inch when to change them down. And there's another thing. When she left the Caverne she went *down* Dean Street; which is not heading up towards Finchley, is it? And there is a story in the mileage on the speedometer this morning. There are fifteen odd miles that I can't account for. The chauffeur puts all the readings back to zero every morning. He keeps a log on each car. And when I went out to look at the bus there were fifteen miles on the mileometer that never ought to be there, that is, if she just went down to Westminster and back. That fifteen miles would just take her comfortably to Wapping—and back to Finchley."

"And you say she hasn't been home all night?"

"That's so, sir. And it's not like Hillary. At the very least she would have phoned. She wouldn't let dad worry. Today, for the first time for three years, he overshot his office time by half an hour—and didn't know it."

"Apart from the badly changed gears and her failure to telephone the house, have you any other cause for suspecting anything wrong?"

"No. But it's enough, isn't it?"

"In a great many cases, Mr. Kittredge, it wouldn't be. Just because a normal rule is broken there is no need to suspect foul play. Most people break old-established rules now and then. That comes in the law of averages. But in this case I will freely admit there is cause for investigation. Where is the car now?"

"At home in the garage. It is exactly as it was when it came back last night. I gave orders that it was not to be touched."

"That's fine. All right, Mr. Kittredge. I'll get a man up there immediately. It's a twisty road up from the docks, and there ought to be plenty of fingerprints on the wheel. But if Miss Hillary should turn up give us a ring, won't you? We've got quite enough on our hands in this case without side tracking on red herrings. Keep us posted with anything else that crops up. And don't worry. We have a fairly tight grip on the job already. We shall have an even better one tomorrow. If your sister *has* got herself all tangled up in this business no doubt we shall have her out of it in a brace of shakes."

Sterling shook his hand, nodded pleasantly, and watched him go out, more worried than he cared to admit, but relieved to the extent that the authorities were informed.

Manning looked over as the boy went out and their eyes met significantly. The tips of Manning's fingers were brushing together, half abstractedly, and there were deep lines of heavy concentration on his face. Sterling's eyebrows went up half an inch in an eloquent gesture of inquiry. Manning nodded, very definitely, and frowned.

"Just the type who would do it," he muttered. "Headstrong and as self-opinionated as a man. She gave me the wire all right. And there are plenty of men who wouldn't have had the nerve to do that. No shyness about her. She just sailed in and spilled the beans. Knowing Grosman, I wouldn't be surprised if he didn't notice her,"

"You think she went down there last night?"

"Sure of it. Her young gentleman friend was a bit indulgent towards her. You know the attitude? She bridled like the dickens. Yes, I'm pretty sure she took the bit between her teeth when she read that report in the paper."

Sterling looked serious. "Then in that case she is in the devil of a hole," he said, "And she has nicely queered our pitch, too. Why the blazes can't women keep their fingers out of hot pies!"

"Going to order a search of the *Yangtse*?"

"Not likely! Old Grosman would smell a whole sewer full of rats. We've got to play blind. If he really collared her last night it was he who sent the car back. He would know she had a car there because she would be in evening dress. The Caverne Diamentée is a full-dress affair. If we raided him now he would know we suspect him of the whole boiling. No. Better lay off and work up as usual. Lull him to sleep. I've got a plateful getting ready for him that will give him indigestion for the rest of his life. Did anything happen round at the Outward Bound last night?"

"Nothing to notice. But I've an idea there will be plenty tonight. Grosman himself was in. He seemed to be waiting for someone. You know how these Chinese can disguise their feelings? Well, he was. But every time the door opened his slink eyes went sliding round into that long mirror that runs round the back of the bar. You can see the door through it. And he had his eyes glued on it all night. I wore my old lighterman's rig and was round in the public bar. He didn't see me—and I doubt if he would have known me even if he had. But on towards closing time I saw one of his Chinese passing him a signal, intimating that it was a washout for that night. If you could have seen Grosman's face you would have had an eye-opener. It was positively murderous. I knew then that it was no use waiting any longer—but I reckon his third party will turn up tonight or there will be another murder to investigate down the river."

Sterling acquiesced. "But this Kittredge business has complicated things badly," he growled. "If we don't get her off that boat her dad will raise merry hell, and if we do we shall be laying our whole hand on the table for Grosman to see."

"I'm not so sure we shall find her on the *Yangtse*," replied Manning. "Grosman wouldn't be such a fool as to leave the girl where the searchers would find her inside an hour. I rather fancy he's got her stowed away ashore somewhere. He *must* have a place down there, some sort of a dive where he stores his dope once he's got it through the barriers. And she won't have a very enviable time with that animal either. Forty-eight hours with him should convince her that the handling of murder jobs is best left to a sex that is unattractive to the Chinese."

Manning looked over at Procter with a grin. "Now's your chance, laddie, if you want those stripes," he said. "'Rescue of beautiful girl by young river policeman! Daughter of the prospective High Commissioner of Police. Daring rescue from a gang of desperate river pirates.' Can't you see the headlines? Gosh—you'd be able to pick and choose."

"One good mark will suit me," said Procter slowly. "I've a wife and two kiddies at home that I wouldn't swap for all the Commissioners' daughters on earth. One good mark—and the chance of a wee bit more on my pension. That'll suit little Procter."

"You had a night run last night, didn't you?"

"Yes. And a nice quiet night it was, too."

"What time were you passing the *Yangtse?*"

"I got in soon after four. I'd be alongside her berth round about when the clocks were striking."

"Anything doing on board?"

"Not a thing. Wasn't a light burning anywhere. It was like a house where everyone had died."

Manning got up and went out. "See you at the rendezvous tonight perhaps?" he said as he closed the door behind him.

He mooched slowly round to Chinny the Junk's and spent an hour nosing round there. He had a rooted conviction in his own mind that a perfectly tangible link existed in that jungle of old junk. It was there, skulking about in the offing somewhere, but he was just failing to make contact with it.

While he was poking about among some old paint cans at the far end Engelberg came in wheeling his creaking old handcart. He waved a cheery greeting to Chinny and sat down on the end of his barrow, mopping his brow.

"It iss hot," he declared, and went off into a long wail about the damage done to his coops overnight by a rogue dog.

"You want some biscuit?" asked the wizened little dealer.

"Yes, I want some biscuit. Not mooch—a leetle. But most I want some wire. I want some wire for mine coops. The dog he break 'em all down. Two—t'ree—four—he break 'em all."

For once in a while Engelberg was missing on his usual smiling note. His kindly old face was seamed with wrinkles of worry. Cost of overhead was, to him, direct loss, and the bare idea of expenditure on renewals set up a ferment of horror in the financial compartment of his brain.

Manning edged over to him and watched him, laboriously and with many grunts, disentangling various lengths of wire from an enormous mound of it by an overturned raft. He cursed a little, too, in a rich, well-rounded tongue, as protruding strands of broken wire scratched his podgy hands.

The Chinese gave him a helping hand. "How many biscuit you want?" he asked. "I pack them for you."

"Ten—dozen," replied the Hamburger perspirefully. "Not so many today. The dog—he kill lot of my chicken. Yah. He brrreak me!"

"Chicken for dinner all the week, eh?" laughed Manning.

The Hamburger growled an unhappy affirmative. "Mister Polissman," he demanded, looking up in righteous wrath, "if I put some poison down and I kill that dog—do I get some prison?"

"Not so far as I'm concerned," returned the sergeant. "But you don't want to tell me about it, Dutch. You want to keep that sort of thing under your hat. Yours isn't the first complaint I've heard about that dog. But don't advertise! It's people like you that get fellers like us into trouble when we wink an eye. How many chickens did he kill?"

"Sem'teen. Blitzen! It iss the third time he brrreak me. T'ree time he eat my chicken. Tonight he eat my"—his brow grew dark—"somet'ing you know noddings about. Phew! I t'ink that enough wire for the coops. You put some biscuit on? Yaas? I t'ank you."

The little dealer threw him in three extra tins of biscuit as a sympathetic offering towards his losses. Manning, too, was constrained to give him a lift.

"Have you any more room for customers on your list?" he inquired, "Room for a fresh-eggs customer?"

"Yaas, sir—plenty, "said Engelberg.

"Well, you can send me a dozen every week. Six on Monday and six on Thursday."

"T'ank you—I t'ank you," said Engelberg gratefully. He raised his hat to the river policeman and began to beam again. He paid for his goods and departed, waving a paternal hand to a bunch of urchins playing in the road.

Manning stayed on and chatted to the junk dealer for an hour. He pumped him dry concerning the doings of the crew of the *Yangtse*, and when he had got through with it all he was not much wiser than when he began. Manning was trying to discover a possible address owned by Grosman along the waterfront, but nothing the dealer could say offered him any enlightenment.

Chinny's knowledge of the Chinese end of the river embraced the whole sweep of the northern waterfront from Wapping through Shadwell and Ratcliff to Limehouse and far back into the mazy warrens of Tower Hamlets. And Chinny made it his business to know most of the Chinese sailors and coolies who came up river. He knew their haunts, knew where they spent their off hours, and was a sort of mediator between them and the various welfare societies that catered for their needs in port.

But even he failed to establish a connection between the *Yangtse* sailors and any special resort ashore. He knew that some of them frequented the Outward Bound, and there his knowledge ended. Manning found himself up against a brick wall. Would Chinny give Manning any such information as happened to come his way in the next day or so?

Chinny would be pleased to give Manning all the information in his power at any time, provided Manning cared to invite it in the form of questions.

Would Chinny have a quiet little prowl round at night and see what he could pick up in the way of news?

Chinny would be pleased to have a little prowl round that very night, if Manning so ordered. But Chinny was apt to be afflicted with a temporary blindness once the sun was down. He could not guarantee to see anything that was in any way derogatory to one of his own race, and it might even be very difficult for him to remember anything that he did see.

Would Chinny put on his night glasses if a little present, say, of a five-pound note found its way unaccountably into his hand?

Chinny already had many five-pound notes. One more or less would not make any difference to his eyesight. Would it not be better to accept the dictum, once and for all, that while Chinny did not object to passing on such harmless small talk as came his way, that hardly entitled the police to regard him as an agent?

Was Chinny no longer loyal to the police?

Most decidedly he was. But how could Chinny be loyal to the police if he was not also loyal to his own people?

Manning presented him with a smouldery curse or two. In some things the Chinese $ould be dumber than a "voice off"on the movies. Sometimes it had its uses. But...

Manning went moodily off out of the junk yard. The river station had little attraction for him. He judged there would be an acid hint from Headquarters that the disappearance of Hillary Kittredge could have been prevented by the exercise of a little intelligence on the part of the river police.

He made his way home for lunch. On the way he called in at the little dairy shop to countermand his standing order for eggs. Not unnaturally the dairyman inquired the reason. Had he given any cause for complaint? Surely after ten years' steady service Manning might have voiced a complaint before cutting off an order like that.

Manning explained. The Dutchman had had a bad break. Lost a good many of his chickens and had his coops badly damaged. He was giving the old boy a leg over the stile for a week or two. In future Engelberg was sending him his dozen eggs per week. The dairyman scratched his head and looked at Manning in perplexity.

"Sure you haven't made a mistake?" he blurted suddenly.

"Why should I?" grunted Manning.

"Engelberg, the Dutcher? The fat old codger who comes around here with a handcart sometimes? Is that the Engelberg you mean?"

"Yes, That's the one. What about it?"

"Only that he was in here half an hour ago ordering eggs off me! A dozen each week, to be called for—Mondays and Thursdays."

Manning blinked and wiped a sting of cigarette smoke out of his eye.

"M'm," he muttered. "Maybe. Still—leave it as it is for a bit. I guess Engelberg knows his own business best. No need to tell him, though, what you just told me."

Manning was walking out again, stolid, a bit phlegmatic. But his thoughts were spinning round like a ball-race. That single, rather fatuous piece of information had hit him with the force of a battering ram. In a blinding flash it had presented a possibility that was so extraordinary, so ingeniously intricate, and yet so smoothly simple, that he was almost frightened to believe it feasible. It seemed too clever, too brilliantly precocious to have sprung from the brain of a river bandit.

And yet it all linked up. It explained the failure of the ship searchers to discover contraband on the *Yangtse*; it explained how the drugs were smuggled ashore under the very eyes of the Customs; and it accounted for Grosman's immunity from detection through the long years of his visits to the river. Continual practice had worn the scheme into a regularity that had come to be accepted by the police. The more he thought it out, the more plausible it seemed. And the more blatantly improbable it seemed, too. Things like that only happened in films that came out of the more sensational Hollywood studios. It did not smack of the hard, matter-of-fact atmosphere of Thames-side smuggling; there was a garishness about it, a touch of the macabre that did not sit well on the shoulders of a drug-smuggling proposition.

He turned the whole thing over in his mind, picking it up piece by piece and examining it as closely as he could considering he was dealing with nothing more concrete than a sheaf of fantastic suppositions.

And he came to one very definite conclusion. He would have to sound the possibilities of his startling theory down to the very depths before he could lay it before the Chief. If it proved all wrong, just a fanciful freak of a high-flying imagination, he would be the laughing-stock of the force. And a stream of the Chief's choicest acid would be hosepiped his way under pressure.

No, he decided that where careers and pensions are concerned the inviolable law is to walk the safety line until proofs are established. And as yet Manning hadn't a single proof to offer. Just a wild idea—and a laugh at the end of it if he was wrong. Still, he reflected, it would be jam for him if it came off, about as brilliant a feat as had ever been performed down river.

And there was no time like the present. Already there was a chance to establish his first proof, before Engelberg came back, before even Chinny suspected him of getting on to the back end of the trail. Thoughts of lunch squeezed out of his head, and the next moment found him heading rapidly back to the junk yard.

The little dealer was not tremendously surprised to see him back so soon. The police had a way of working in spasms at times.

"Something you want?" he asked hopefully.

"Yes," said Manning, and took him gently by the arm. "I want you to turn right round and go back the way you came. And there is no need to take an occasional glance out of that filthy little window. Anything I pinch I'll pay for. Just keep right on with your own little job, and I will get on with mine. I will not be more than ten minutes."

"You wait for somebody?"

"Yes," said Manning deliberately. "Let it go at that. I'm waiting for somebody." He steered the little man into his office and gently closed the door.

There was very little chance of being overlooked from that office. Chinny knew how to obey an order as well as how to deflect one. Manning went right on up the yard and sat down on the other side of the great mound of old tins, out of sight of any casual customer. Then he critically inspected all the visible tins of damaged ship's biscuit. There seemed to be dozens of them scattered about in a riotous jumble.

He was hunting for particular markings, for a slight difference in the size of the containers, or even the faintest scratch that would distinguish one brand from another. But they all seemed depressingly similar. For the most part they were all of a single make and were put up in plain tins. A few bore the sign of the broad arrow and had come from the Government victualling yards—cast-off stuff from the Navy. But among the others there was not a scrap of difference that could be detected. Some were burst and the contents had all gone to a mash, rotted with sea water.

He picked up a tin and put it firmly between his knees. With a jack-knife he cut away the top and pulled out a few of the biscuits. Some were broken, but the majority were undamaged. He cracked them all carefully into tiny fragments and critically examined each little piece. There was nothing suspicious about any of them. They were all they purported to be—just plain ship's biscuit and nothing more. He delved farther into the tin and went over them all with the utmost care. But again he met with no reward.

He took another tin and tried that. Before he was finished he had examined a round score, taking one from every part of the mound. And in the end he admitted himself beaten. The chance to establish his first piece of concrete evidence had fizzled out.

He laughed shortly, in a half-ashamed way. Well, he wasn't too disappointed. The thing had been too preposterously impossible from the first. "A golden dream busted," he muttered, and scattered the biscuit wide for the waiting sparrows to eat.

For a little while he stood there, watching the birds with half-amused eyes. He had been hoping to find little tabloids of cocaine mixed in with the body of the biscuit, neat little cubes of the deadly drug covered with the thin veneer of the hardened paste.

There was just a chance that Grosman had been even cleverer than he had given him credit for. If that was so the sparrows would provide the proof. If Grosman had found some method of mixing powdered cocaine with the biscuit meal and then extracting it later, it would not be long before the birds showed the effects of it.

Five minutes passed. The birds clustered thickly round the unexpected feast. Ten minutes ticked away and still they greedily pecked at the morsels. A little later he had definite proof that the stuff was harmless. One little fellow, a perky little chap with half his tail gone, came flying back for another meal. Manning had noticed him at the outset; he was one of the first to arrive when the biscuit was scattered. And he had wolfed as much as he could conveniently carry. And now, after nearly a quarter of an hour, he was back again. To Manning it seemed reasonable to suppose that any bird, having been drugged with anything so potent as neat cocaine, would betray unmistakable signs of distress long before that. But there was the little bobtail dashing about as busily as any of the later corners.

Manning buried the empty tins down in the heart of the pile; and he interred with them yet another experiment in applied deduction.

He studiously avoided the station for the rest of the day, and after nightfall there emerged from his neat little house a lighterman fresh from his barge. At least, that is what he looked like, even to the deeply ingrained dirt in the corns of his hands, where years of toiling labour on the great sweeps had left their callouses. He wore a blue jersey that came high up to the neck, and a purple silk handkerchief was tied loosely above it. His coat was of blue serge and the trousers were ever so slightly belled at the bottom. His hands were thrust into his trouser pockets, raising the hem of the jersey a little. Beneath that hem showed a curve of leather belt, marvellously adorned with brass insignia and regimental crests. A large-peaked cap that did not quite hide a wisp of the plastered quiff over his forehead, finished him off at the top end, while a pair of squeaky brown boots completed the picture below.

He strolled quietly into the public bar of the "Outward Bound" and ordered a glass of bitter. No one in there knew him. The proprietor nodded and carried on polishing glasses. He had seen him in there once or twice before, always a quiet, rather reserved sort of chap who never had much to say to the other river men who made his house their shore headquarters. He had long since put him down as a stranger from some other reach of the river, one who only came up that way occasionally and lodged in a room locally while waiting for a tide.

He took up his old position, right up in the corner angle where he could see the whole of his bar and look through the big wall mirrors at the back of the counter and keep an eye on the full sweep of the saloon bar. Behind him was a frosted glass partition that led from the street to the saloon.

He put his foot on the brass rail and propped an elbow on the bar, lost in profound meditation of the foam on his beer.

"Busy?" asked the boss, polishing away industriously.

"So-so. Nothing grand. Bit quiet on the river these days."

"So they say. Things won't be much better till the harvests are in. What's your line—grain?"

"Cement." Manning drained his glass and pushed it across the counter to be refilled. He had learned the safety of cement. All the big cement companies run their own barges and they carry nothing but cement from one year's end to another. Cement men know nothing else of river life except the steady transportation of cement from one point to another. Their job never varies. If they don't join in the more general conversations of diversified "shop" it is excusable, for they have little to offer to the common fund of small talk. And cement men are known to be just a little clannish.

The proprietor nodded. It was good enough for him. And it accounted for the man's sporadic visits: cement men man the big sea-going barges and are often away round coast for weeks at a time.

"Cigar lights—pipe lights—cigar lights," a thin voice came tentatively through the bar. Shuffling footsteps sounded and a monotonous tap-tapping crept up the partitioned passage from the street. Blind Rudley came, fumbling his way along with his sightless eyes upturned to the ceiling.

Manning watched him with the friendliness of old knowledge. The uncanny skill with which he avoided the chairs and tables was interesting, almost unbelievable, until one remembered that he had been coming into those bars at the same times for years and years past.

He knew the position of every obstruction in the place—and in dozens of others in the neighbourhood. Blind Rudley had a free permit and a roving commission. Nobody minded him; nobody objected to him. He had the entrée to every saloon and café for streets around. And he was the most popular man on the waterside when the black river fogs came crawling up, blotting out even the crackling loading-lights on the quays; he piloted the drunks home at threepence a time, for black fog and bright sunshine were all one to Blind Rudley.

He tapped his way along the floor to the corner seat in the saloon, and Manning saw the ash stick go prospecting along the horsehair-covered bench behind it, as though exploring for a possible customer. There was none there, and he tapped his way back into the public bar, carefully missing a new fem stand that had only been put in position a few hours before.

Manning tossed a coin on his tray as he passed through. A little while later Sterling and Procter entered. They had a glass of ale together, talked for a moment or two, and went out again. Manning was conscious of a grin of satisfaction in that Sterling had not recognised him, although for one full second he had stared straight at him.

Procter, of course, knew him. It was the only disguise he had ever known Manning adopt; for Manning was wily enough to know that one good disguise well carried off was better than a hundred that did not ring true. A second identity began to grow around the disguise if it was seen with some regularity, a second personality that had some real basis of old-standing existence and into which one could step almost at a moment's notice.

The evening drew on, and Manning began to think he had picked on an empty spell when the street door swung open again and Grosman walked in. The bar was hazy with tobacco smoke, and Manning's end was crowded. Two women, with their husband's hats pinned in their straggly hair, were having a heated altercation about the clothes-line rights over a party fence, and two men on the other side of him were becoming equally aggressive over an argument that had arisen over a football betting transaction. It was the usual down-cast public-house atmosphere that inexorably begins to blossom as closing time draws near.

Twice Manning managed to get his arm jogged while drinking, and twice he managed to get his beer spilled over his boots. Each accident was followed up by a surly "Sorry, mate," and a look that challenged any further remark on the subject. Manning took it all in apparent good part, but he eyed the proprietor severely, as though to ask if that was the usual treatment meted out to customers who did their best to keep themselves to themselves.

The boss took the hint and leaned over the counter to him. "Better get round to the saloon, old son," he said. "They ain't over friendly to strangers in their own bar. Kind of think they own the place, see? You get round to the saloon. I'll only charge you the public prices."

Manning went round. He wanted to get near Grosman, and it would have raised a querulous eyebrow on several faces if he had gone round without the invitation. There is an etiquette in riverside bars that is highly susceptible to slights, however much presumed.

Grosman sat over on the corner bench where Blind Rudley had gone questing an hour before. He was right in the corner and commanded the view of the entire bar, and nobody could approach him without coming directly in front of him. He ordered brandy and milk in a long glass and sat on, taking as little interest in the other habitues as the stuffed owl in the glass case over his head.

Manning called for another glass of bitter and pulled out the evening paper. He sat alone at a table and opened the paper wide in front of his face. But to his left he could see into the big bar mirror, and framed in the centre of his field of vision was the bulky, uncompromising figure of Grosman.

Procter mooned in again, saw Manning, and unconcernedly picked up a position away from him where he could follow his senior's signals. A quarter of an hour from closing time the tap-tapping of Blind Rudley's stick sounded along the passageway.

"Cigar lights—pipe lights—cigar lights—buy a box of matches, sir?" the plaintive voice preceded him. A coin or two tinkled into his tin. He intoned his thanks and steadily tapped his way over to the corner seat.

Grosman ignored him for some time, and Rudley stood there, patiently waiting for the glass of beer that always came over the bar for him every night from the proprietor. Grosman glanced at him and seemed aware for the first time of the nature of the man's affliction. It was an unobtrusively perfect little piece of acting.

"A box of matches, please" he said, and expansively threw a sixpence on his tray.

Rudley acknowledged it with a muttered "Thank you" and a nod. His long, thin fingers fumbled over his tray, feeling for the matchboxes. He picked one up and his fingers slid along it. He dropped it back and held out another so quickly that Manning scarcely saw the movement.

Grosman did not speak again. He thrust the matches into his coat pocket and gently sipped his brandy and milk. Rudley went tap-tapping out of the bar again, wearily piping "Cigar lights—pipe lights—cigar lights—box of matches, sir?" as he went.

Manning sat back behind his paper and tried to think it out. He glanced over at Procter, and a suspicion of a question was gleaming out of his second's eye. Procter, too, had noticed it.

The sergeant pulled at his lip. There was a significance about that innocent little episode somewhere. Grosman was waiting there for a signal. Rudley had called before with it and Grosman had not been in.

He was dumbfounded. He had known Blind Rudley for years up and down those reaches and had never had cause to suspect him of even buying an ounce of uncustomed tobacco. And here he was a private messenger to the biggest menace that had ever landed in the river. It was a nasty shock to his pride in the grip he thought he had on things down the waterway. He wondered how much farther the Chinese tentacles stretched. If Grosman had roped in Blind Rudley, it wasn't safe to take even his own landlord for granted.

He felt he was getting out of his depth. The more he dug into the case, the bigger Grosman loomed. He admitted, with professional appreciation, the astuteness of working through such an unsuspicious character as Blind Rudley, but even that did not soften the scorch of it.

Grosman took out a slim silver case and selected a long black cheroot. Manning watched him with proprietary interest in the mirror. He absentmindedly bit the end off and felt for the matches. He took one out and lit up, puffing out clouds of pungent smoke around him. His eye slid cautiously round the bar to see if he was being watched. With the clock hands pointing to only a few minutes off closing time, the crowd at the counter was too busily occupied in catching the barman's eye to get a final charge into their glasses.

The only other occupant of the place was the lighterman, who couldn't possibly see him. An evening paper was spread out between his face and the seat in the corner. Quickly the long-nailed fingers slipped into the box again and emerged with a small piece of paper screwed up into a wad. Grosman straightened it out and, under cover of the smoke clouds swirling round his head, read the message written there.

Manning saw his eyebrows draw down thunderously over his beady eyes, and the tip of his cheroot glowed to a fiery red. He read and re-read the scrap of paper; and when he looked up his lips were pressed up viciously. With a muttered oath he rammed the piece of paper back into his coat pocket.

Manning looked over again to his second in command, and Procter looked back at him without a blink.

The barman looked over the heads of a crowd of others and asked him if he wanted another before they shut up shop for the night.

"Yes—fill it up," he said cheerlessly, and folded up his paper. He leaned his chin on his hand and gazed moodily at the floor. The other hand, the one away from Grosman, was resting on the seat of his chair.

Slowly the thumb of that hand began to twitch, just a little tremor that was hardly noticeable, and even if it had been it would have occasioned no more comment than a slight nerve quiver would have done. But it was twitching in an odd way, and Procter's eyes were glued on it. It was an old method of communication between them, an almost invisible system of sending Morse messages to each other.

The thumb twitched on, erratically flicking out the dots and dashes, and Procter read it out of the corner of his eye.

"We must get that paper. Stub your toe on the mat as you go out. Cannon against him. He will ward you off. I will be behind him and get it from his pocket. Argue with him till I can read it and get it back again."

Procter turned and bawled over the bar for another glass of ale. He tapped his foot irritably at the delay. And the tappings spelled out "O.K." The manoeuvre went off smoothly and more rapidly than they had expected. Visibly disturbed by the contents of the note, Grosman got up to go. He passed down the bar, the big surgical boot clumping along as he passed Procter. The police officer, too angry that he could not attract the barman's attention, stepped back to go farther down the bar. And all his weight came down heavily on Grosman's deformed foot, and he stumbled against him, almost upsetting him.

Grosman swore and pushed him off. At the same second Manning was behind him and his hand had flashed into the open pocket. It was all over in the twinkling of an eye. The crumpled note was out and crushed into the palm of his hand.

And his hands continued on their way to grasp Grosman's arms, who looked like falling after the collision.

"Steady, mate—steady," he growled. "No sense in falling about all over the floor." He solicitously settled the captain on his feet and turned away. The affair was no longer any concern of his.

"Clumsy brute!" snarled Grosman, wheeling on the wholly surprised Procter.

"Sorry, matey—sorry," said the officer soothingly. "I slipped. Can't help a little accident."

"Accident! Accident!" the captain rasped. "You stamped on my foot!"

"Couldn't help it, matey. Didn't know you was there. Never done it on purpose." The reply could not have been more blandly disarming, and the Chinese was turning away as though satisfied with having voiced his protest. That did not suit Procter at all, for he suddenly turned on him and said, in a fighting growl: "And what if I did? Can't you take an apology? What the hell are you slant-eyes doing in a saloon bar I'd like to know? Your place is round in the 'bottle and jug.' In quick and out quick. That's your ticket. Why don't you stay in your own chop sueys? Hey?"Manning had gone over to the corner. He had turned his back and was trying to light a recalcitrant cigarette. Under cover of the action he read the note.

> Have told you before it is impossible to see you tonight. You are mad to make contact with me. If Rudley comes again I shall leave Town till you are gone. It is senseless to take such unnecessary risks. The police are apprised. The warning has gone down river. Every station is on the qui vive. The G. M. affair was unforgivable. You have tied our hands and brought the whole pack of the police down on us. Why? What good has it served? Except to make every single one of us suspect—and to encourage

one of the gang to squeal to the police to save his own skin. And now you have added the crowning imbecility of abducting H. K. Don't you know who her father is? In two or three days' time the papers may enlighten you. She must be released immediately. Please note I am no longer at the old address.

(Signed) L.

Manning crushed the note into a ball again. A miniature uproar had started in the bar. Some were taking Procter's part and some were siding with Grosman. Those who knew the police officer were passing the word round to their friends to clear out as trouble seemed imminent. The proprietor, openly surprised that Procter should raise such a storm on licensed premises, was hurrying round from behind the bar.

"*I* couldn't help it, could I?" demanded Procter of the crowd. "I'd been standing here for ten minutes yelpin' for a final and not a son of a gun behind the bar would take a mite of notice of me. If it was a Chinese or a lascar calling, the drink would have been under his nose inside ten seconds. All I did was to step away to get farther down the bar where they were serving, and this yellow streak of skimmings off the *Yangtse* sticks his boot under me and dam nearly brings me down. And then he bawls me out I—the slab-sided lump of ullage!"

"Easy, boy—easy!" It was Manning's voice that came pacifyingly over the hubbub. "You don't want to start a row just at chuckin'-out time. The Chinese apologised, ain't he? Heard him myself. Let it go at that. Come on, matey," he finished, taking the captain under the arm. "Come on outside and go home. It won't do to argue the point with *that* bloke—he's one of the Water Rats."

Almost before Grosman knew it he was heading for the door with the peacemaking lighterman stepping along in friendly fashion by his side. And as they passed out through the door the crumpled note slipped surreptitiously back into the unguarded pocket.

Outside Manning nodded to him with a cheerful grin and waved him on. Scowling, but acknowledging the service with a polite hand-wave, the captain went limping down the street.

Manning turned away in the opposite direction. He reached the corner and turned, waiting for Procter, who he knew would be along before many seconds had passed.

The minutes ticked slowly along and Procter did not appear. Manning waited on. A few stragglers came down the road, homing from the "Outward Bound," where the last drinks had been served. The last one to appear, slightly tipsy, almost cannoned against him as he came round the corner.

He grunted an alcoholic "G'night, mate," and went slouching off. Manning recognised him—one of the old soaks of the neighbourhood, one with something of a record in petty crime. He was certainly no friend of the police.

Manning hurried after him. It was obvious that Procter was not coming back that night, and he wanted to make an inquiry. He caught the man under the arm and affected a slight bibulousness himself.

"Seen anything of that Water Rat?" he asked thickly.

"Eh? Who?"

"That bloke Procter who was in the 'Outward Bound' with you. Leaning up against the bar on your side."

The drunk turned and leered at him. "Why? Is he after you?" The question was couched in all friendliness, the query of one who had come off second best in the eternal feud with the common enemy in blue and was cheerfully willing to help anyone else who was experiencing trouble along that line himself.

"Yes." Manning nudged his arm meaningly. "He's had his eye on me all the week. He spotted me tonight. And now I've lost him. I'm bringing a bit of baccy ashore tonight, and I want to know where the blighter is."

"You needn't worry about *him*," the drunk assured him. "You land your baccy, mate. He won't interfere. He's gone off after that Chinese. After you left another slant-eye came in in a hell of a hurry, lookin' for the captain. He went rushin' off when he heard he'd gone. And just after him went Procter—the swine. I hope he gets a knife in his blasted ribs. G'night."

Manning watched him go. As soon as he was out of sight he went hurrying back to the "Outward Bound." But there was no sign of Procter there. A little group of men and women still lingered outside the locked doors, beerily chewing over the arguments of the evening. Lights were being turned out in the bars and from the big saloon came the clink of coin where the day's takings were being counted.

They were all old regulars in that gossiping group, and Manning knew he would get no assistance there. They neither recognised him nor would have given him any help if they had. He went back to the river station and waited there an hour. Still there was no word from Procter.

Manning got more and more worried. It was not like Procter to leave him in the dark when anything was moving. He was positive that his second had stumbled on something important, and he was equally positive that Procter was not keeping him in the dark purposely. The station was silent and deserted. The boat was away up river and would not be passing again for half an hour. One o'clock sounded, and still there was no sign of his colleague. The telephone instrument stood silent and dead on the table.

By half-past one Manning decided to go exploring on his own. He gave a final touch to his make-up, and a few minutes later his rolling, semi-drunken figure was lurching away down towards the black line of wharves where the *Yangtse* swung nose to nose with the *Beaudelaire.*

V

Procter was on the point of going out to rejoin his senior when the Chinese seaman slipped in. He heard the hurried questions about his master and heard the barman tell him that the captain had gone. There was perturbation on the seaman's face, and it was apparent that he had news of the highest import for him. Procter detached himself from the end of the bar and crept out after him.

He crossed over to the other side of the road and shadowed him as he hurried along. Grosman was still in sight at the top end of the street. He could see his bulky figure limping along. He turned the corner and the seaman broke into a run. Procter was many yards behind when he got them in sight again. The seaman had overtaken the captain and the two were engaged in an urgent conversation, the seaman making emphatic gestures to the captain. Grosman himself was equally demonstrative. For several minutes they stood jabbering at each other in Chinese. Procter stood in the shadow of a doorway, unable to approach any closer without being seen.

Then the two of them hurried off together. They turned away left and entered a maze of narrow side streets, doubling and twisting until Procter himself had lost all idea of his own direction. He knew he was still somewhere near the river, for the dank river smells eddied up from blind side turnings and welled coldly in his face from black alleys that sloped away down into the silent darkness.

They were in a neighbourhood of gloomy looking warehouses that towered up above them and merged into the night overhead. Here and there lone gas jets flickered yellowly, casting dim pools of murky light for a few yards around and making the surrounding blackness seem even blacker. There was not a sound save the distant padding of the two Chinese as they cat-footed along the empty streets. A wall of hush had descended upon the place. Here the slums with their thickly infested life had given way to the commercial areas of dockland. There were other smells in the air beside those of the river. The piney scent of pitch gave a pungency to the general mealy reek of grain that hung heavily in the air; soon it was the fresh smell of bacon that came drifting out of a great darkened curing factory and a little lower down a dozen different grades of cheese fought each other on the palate. Then high-scented toilet preparations warred with the rich aromas of roast coffee, and through it all drifted the unmistakable, undefinable smell of ship's upper decks—rope and oakum, engine oil, and the thin tang of dead steam.

The two men ahead turned sharply to the right and entered a long alley that was shrouded in impenetrable gloom. It was narrow and cobbled and so cramped that the buildings on either side almost leaned against one another.

Procter slowed down and prospected. The others had vanished into the darkness. It was a locality where night prowlers turned the street lamps out almost as soon as the lamplighter lit them—and the river man was completely out of his bearings. He wanted to be able to recognise that spot again in daylight, for he already had a shrewd suspicion that he had run Grosman down to his secret haunt. A feather in his cap for him, he reflected, as he stared around. This was the clue Manning and Sterling wanted. If he could get in there and unearth the mysteries that lay behind those gaunt walls they had the whole organisation of the dope runners in their grasp. It was worth the risk of playing a lone hand. Perhaps Mrs. Procter would be stitching those three stripes on his arm before so very long after all.

A solitary gas lamp stood at the top end, dismal and unlit. There was just a hope that the name of the alley would be printed there. He silently climbed the standard and peered at the glass panels. His heart gave a jump. There were some letters on the pane. He puzzled them out with painstaking care in the darkness—Gunn Lane.

"Well," he muttered to himself as he slid back, "Grosman will have to step lively now if he is going to get away with it." He went cautiously down the alley, listening intently for any sounds that might tell him of traps ahead. But the pall of silence was unbroken. The alley was about fifty yards long, and the two Chinese had gone right along to the end of it.

He crept down and stared up at the bleak walls. Not a glimmer of light showed; and there was not a sound from within. He tried to look in at the windows, but lengths of sacking were hung against the sashes from behind. There was a door, but it looked as though it had not been used for years. The dust was grimed thickly into the crevices and the letter-box was boarded up.

At one side was a high gate, big enough to admit a railway lorry. Procter knew there must be some secret way into the place, but he judged that that was neither the hour nor the opportunity to ferret out such details. He took his chances in both hands and went over the top. It was a high gate, and there were spikes along the top of it. But in five minutes he was on the other side creeping across the stone yard. The whole place in the rear was in a ruinous state of dilapidation. Procter realised in five minutes that it was a derelict warehouse he was dealing with. Great doors hung on their hinges above tumbledown platforms that had once been used as loading quays for drays. The entrances had been barricaded up, but even the barricades were falling to pieces. Windows gaped open, and broken panes were stuffed with rags. It was a mournful picture of desolation.

He climbed in through a rotted door and listened. Rats, unseen in the Stygian blackness, went scurrying past him squeaking shrilly. A dusty smell of rot and decay filled the place. The whole budding seemed to be creaking with age. Procter took off his boots, tied them by the laces, and hung them round his neck.

He went forward farther into the recesses of the place, feeling his way along foot by foot. He stuck cigarette papers over the lens of his torch and used the light when he got into difficulties. The building was a veritable warren. Cross passages seemed to lead off at every other yard, and now and then he emerged on a vast room whose deserts of space echoed emptily back at him. He began to perspire. There was a feeling of foreboding about the place that was getting on his nerves. It was as though there was a sense of waiting in the air. There were eyes up there among the dust-laden rafters, eyes that followed him about from room to room and peered down at him silently from the yawning holes in the ceilings where the plaster had fallen.

He had lost himself in the labyrinthine ways of the rambling building. The maze of rooms and criss-crossing passages bewildered him. They led nowhere, and they were all as tenantless as the rest. And the position was too full of dynamite to permit too free a use of the torch. Heavily shaded and held in his cupped hands, it spread but a pitiful aura of light, but in that vast tomb of blackness it stabbed out like the glare of a searchlight.

Those brutes from the *Yangtse* might be within two yards of him for all he knew, malignantly watching his every step. They might be leading him on to a sudden swift stab in the dark, and a burial that would never be known.

He took out his handkerchief and mopped his face. He was admitting to a sneaking private regret that he had not phoned the river station or got into touch with Manning before setting out on the heels of the dope runners. Manning at least would have known where Grosman went to earth. He seemed to be heading into culs-de-sac and brick walls whichever way he went.

He waited in the darkness, trying to think out his next move. Things were not turning out quite as he had expected. There was a nebulousness about it all that was in no sense helpful. He couldn't get on to a line that promised results. Grosman and his man had vanished, and he was left floundering about in the depths of a building that seemed to have neither beginning nor end.

There was nothing else for it but to try and find some sort of a connection along at the back of the building, if he could find the back—and if it *had* a back. He stepped along with his nerves on edge. And then all in a second it happened. He put out his foot and stepped into space. Sheer and plumb he fell, with his body still upright and his right foot still out in the act of walking.

With the natural nerve reaction of a sudden crisis his muscles flexed. He tensed in every tissue and his hands gripped up at nothing. Nothing, that is, save the torch. His fingers gripped on it madly as he went hurtling down. His thumb touched the button and the soft glow of light flooded out. The next moment he had hit the bottom with a body-shaking smash.

For some seconds he lay where he fell, wondering what on earth had happened to him. So far as he could discern, there was no violent change taking place in him; if he was dead, then death was the quickest and most painless accident that had ever afflicted him. He opened his eyes and looked around. His leg was doubled up under him and half the wind was knocked out of him, but otherwise he felt pretty much the same as he had done before he stepped over the brink. In a semi-daze he rolled over on to his side and came to the conclusion that he was not dead—not yet, anyway.

No, he had just come a terrific flop down a disused well-shaft, and he had landed on a huge mound of cotton waste at the bottom. The soft glow showed the sides of the shaft going up into the blackness above. He shuddered. They seemed to streak up there into infinity. His leg felt cold and numb and he shifted about on the cotton waste, trying to ease it.

The daze began to clear. From somewhere close at hand he could hear voices, gabbling away in the sing-song monody of a Chinese dialect. He switched off the light as though it had suddenly stung him.

He lay flat on his back, scarce daring to breathe. Among the excited babble of voices he had recognised the fuller, deeper tones of Grosman. He realised then why he had been stumbling about so long up there on the upper floor without getting on to a clue. Their hideout was buried deep down in the basements under the road-level.

He had come a fearful cropper down that shaft, but he blessed it. But for it he might have gone bimbering about all night up there in the emptiness without getting back into touch with his quarry.

In front of him was the lift entrance, the woodwork all broken to pieces and the struts all fallen awry. It was through that opening that the voices were coming. He stood up and tried his weight on the crocked leg. Sharp, stabbing pains went searing through the back of his thigh, and he knew he had strained the great major thigh muscle. With an effort it stood the strain, but he knew that if it came to a race for it the Chinese had got things all their own way. Procter could not have run ten yards without cracking up.

He hobbled out of the shaft and took his bearings. A dim glow of light came from farther along. A door stood partly open. He waited till his wind came back and then carefully approached. There seemed to be a bad-tempered conference going on inside, though he couldn't understand a word of it. Then a bell tinkled softly inside the room and the voices suddenly stilled.

Proctor took a sudden premonition of warning. Without waiting a second, he crawled painfully into another room that opened at right-angles to the one that was lit. No sooner had he got inside than Ying, the Chinese quartermaster, came gliding out. He disappeared through a long corridor, leaving the door wide open. From the black darkness of his own retreat Procter could see into the opposite room, with not one chance in a hundred of being observed himself.

Grosman was in there, together with three other Chinese, and, sitting in a corner, white-faced and frightened, was Gilan Maxick's brother.

Procter crawled away out of the light. Grosman was looking at the door and the whole assembly seemed to be waiting. The river man hazarded a long guess that the meeting was not yet complete and that Ying had just gone up to admit the missing member. He explored around silently in the room. It was a big stock-room with wooden shelves running round all four sides. There were lanes of shelves, too, traversing the room, and they were stocked full with tins. Procter examined them, and his forehead puckered to a frown. They were tins of ship's biscuit. He fumbled around with them, trying to elucidate the puzzle. Then he found one that was broken. He took out a biscuit and twisted it about in his fingers. It seemed perfectly all right, just such a biscuit as are sold in thousands to ships that make long journeys and are ill-equipped with baking facilities.

He broke it. The outer crust of baked flour crumbled away in his hands, and he found himself holding a thin, oblong case of soft tin, as thin and narrow as a cigarette-case. He tried to open it, but the thing seemed solid. He could find neither catch nor lid. He thrust it into his pocket, together with a couple of the biscuits. They could be examined where he could get more light to bear on the subject. It was a mere waste of time fumbling about there in the darkness. But his heart was pumping. He knew that he was getting at the heart of the mystery. The whole place down there was nothing but a vast cocaine store. And he had got the address.

Footsteps were coming back along the long corridor. He drew back into the deeper shadows at the far end of the room. Ying was coming back, stepping silently along a yard or two ahead of a man dressed in a huge fur coat. The collar of it came up round his neck and almost hid his face. He was wearing a shiny silk hat, and his build, without the added bulkiness of the fur coat, was big and powerful.

Ying went on in through the door and announced: "Mr. Lingard is here."

Lingard stood in the doorway and surveyed the group inside. His face was like a thundercloud. The light was streaming full on it, showing up its deep, hard lines and accentuating the bull curve at the back of his neck. He stared hard at Grosman and nodded, once, in that short, abrupt way that just acknowledges a man's presence on earth and no more. There was the beginning of a war in that nod; it was the gesture of a man who has his sword out and is hinting to the other man that he had better get his own out too.

"Well?" he said, and it was the voice of a man who was neither asking nor giving quarter.

"I am glad you have come." The mandarin was gazing back eye to eye, and he was actually smiling. But Procter felt the hair at the nape of his neck crawl with horripilic anticipation. The sentence was as calm and as placid as a summer pool, but an undercurrent at the back of it was quivering with wicked threats. There was something sadistic about it, a gloat in it that regarded its victim with the satisfaction and erotic pleasure of watching it die slowly and horribly. It almost added as an afterthought: "Because if you hadn't I should have been under the painful necessity of fetching you."

Procter felt a prickling shiver running through him. There was murder, grim and vicious, crackling about in the air between those two. Each knew it in his own bitter way and each faced it without a quiver. Procter felt for the wall behind him and leaned against it. His knees had gone shaky. He realised that, unless a miracle happened, he was going to be an eyewitness of about as fierce a riot of sheer gang-murder as any police officer ever saw. It was pregnant in the air. The very tension was alive with it.

They were good rivals, those two. The one with all the craft and venomed subtleties of the Orient running liquid in his veins, with all the inborn cunning and ferocity of his race vitally alive in his brain. The other, the man who organised the minions of a vast system and kept them out of the clutches of the law, the man who knew he could depend on the backing of the thugs he ruled and fed; each deadly sure of his own power.

Lingard stood his ground. He had advanced as far as the door, and it seemed that he was anchored there for good. He unbuttoned his coat and let it fall back on his shoulders. His face was as full as Grosman's; it was overfed and flabby with years of indulgence, but there was a courage and determination printed there as firmly as on the face of a gladiator. And they had met in a fit setting, deep down in the bowels of their own headquarters, within sound of the lapping tides of the river.

Maxick looked up and breathed with quick relief when he saw the frame of Lingard loom into the doorway. Something of the hunted expression went out of his face, and a gleam, almost of hope, took its place.

Lingard tipped his hat back and regarded the group. He was in full evening dress, and, in spite of its utter incongruity in that scene of desolation, somehow it seemed entirely in keeping. It was East meeting West—and the West was clothed in the garb of the aristocrat, the right attire for one who came direct from the night life of the capital of all the West.

"I came," said Lingard in a voice that was corked up to the last ounce of doggedness, "because I think it is time one of us realised there cannot be two generals in command of this business. I came, not because of your order or because of the insulting messages you have sent me through Blind Rudley, but because my limit has been reached. Either you are to run this group or I am. If it is to be you, then you will have to spend all your time here in the city keeping the gates open to ourselves and closed to the police. You cannot make it a part-time job. You cannot do it on an occasional trip to the river. It will tax all your ingenuity, all your patience, for eighteen hours of every day.

"And you will be much more human in your methods with the lesser members. They take the majority of the risks and only a handful of the money we make. They are getting restive. They won't stand for being murdered in cold blood simply, as a critical French satirist put it, to encourage the others. And what is more, you will do it without the assistance of Graham Lingard." He took out a cigar and carefully lit it. Grosman looked at him in a calm, level scrutiny. All the venom, all the ultimatum of it was wrapped up in that last challenging sentence. He had never dreamed that Lingard would threaten to leave him flat.

"This is no time to make angry speeches," he said smoothly. "These matters can be adjusted. As assuredly they will be." And in his own last utterances there was a devilish whisper of evil.

"I am not making angry speeches," retorted Lingard. "This is a blunt speech, and I have no intention of decorating my words with a lot of polite flap-doodle and fal-de-lal. Let us make an issue. Let us take a point and fight it out. For instance, what are you doing with Maxick there?"

Grosman's thick hands made a smooth, deprecatory gesture. "What I am doing with Maxick is an affair entirely between myself and Maxick," he said. "He has come to discuss a little matter with me."

"He has come because he knew that if he didn't you would send one of your yellow-skinned scum along to squirt him full of bushmaster virus or some such horror. Take a look at him. He is a jelly. And can you wonder at it? You slugged his brother as mercilessly as one would step on a beetle. And now you have hauled him along to administer the same dose. And I want to know what it is for. I am a better judge of Western concepts of right and wrong than you—and *I* will arbitrate on this matter."

"*You* will!" The words were like chilled daggers.

"Yes, I will. What is the nature of the charge against him?"

"He has been to the Water Rats."

"It's a lie! It's a lie!" Maxick, little more than a rat himself, was squeaking with fright.

"Have you any proof of this?" asked Lingard coldly.

"He was seen to enter the river station at Wapping. And he was seen to leave. He was over twenty minutes inside with Manning. It is serious, for Sterling was in there too. Sterling, who has just been put in charge of the case."

"And why was Sterling put in charge of the case? There would never have been a case for him to have been put in charge of but for your damnable brutality." He turned to Maxick. "Did you go to the station?" he snapped.

"Yes, sir. That's right, sir. The sergeant, he sent for me. Couldn't help meself, sir. That was after Gilan got his. I told 'em I didn't know nothink about it and that I hadn't got nothink at all to say. But the sarge he says if I don't go down and identify the body he'd supeena me. So along I has to go. And then Sterling says if I don't go along to the station he would rope me in for half a dozen jobs he's got framed up against me. I never told 'em nothing. He just asked me the old rigmarole, and I answered him. Wanted to know if Gilan had any enemies and all that bunk. I could have shopped the captain then if I'd wanted to, couldn't I? And I told 'em I wasn't even in Gilan's gang. And that was the truth, wasn't it? I don't work his end of the city at all. What the hell was I to do? If I went down there the captain would stick a knife in me liver, and if I didn't then

I goes up to the beak for a stretch on the moors. I get it either way. And it ain't right to stick a knife in me liver for that."

"The idea in the captain's mind," said Lingard patiently, "is that you squealed. You understand that, don't you? If you did, then I would be the first to consent to your elimination. But if you didn't, then there is no need to get agitated. I will see that the captain does not stick a knife in your liver—or anyone else's. Not even mine; which will be rather an extraordinary accomplishment. *Did* you squeal?"

"No, sir. So help me God! I never said a word."

"You can't prove it, Maxick, that's your trouble. The two of you are on a par there. You neither have proof. Except that you, Maxick, have the finest proof of all. To any normally sensible human being the fact that the police are not here tonight is proof enough that you were loyal. Mill, without that, your word is good enough for me." He puffed at his cigar for a moment and let his fishy eye roam over the group.

Then Graham Lingard declared himself a man. "Ulrich Maxick," he said, "get up."

The shivering man reared slowly to his feet. He stood leaning against the table, looking fearfully from Grosman to Lingard. The storm had brewed around his helpless head and he was as innocent of its cause as of its effect. But it was on him, nevertheless, that it had centred. But Lingard was out for a fight right from the first word "Go."

"Maxick," he said quietly, "put on your hat and go. Go right up and out of it. Don't hurry. Just walk up and out into the street. And you, Ying, you stay where you are. If you move an inch to follow him I'll splash your brains all over that wall." Lingard suddenly declared himself as a man with a gun—a great shining automatic spinning about in his fingers.

Not a soul moved. It was as though the whole group were leg-ironed where they sat, unable or unwilling to stir a finger. The Chinese sat as unemotional as a set of carven images. Not a sign of their thoughts was reflected on their faces. Except Grosman's—and his eyes were glittering like red-hot agates. Right at the back of them were two central cores of gleaming fire.

Lingard nodded to Maxick. The wharf-rat, with livid fear crawling alive all over his twitching body, began edging round the table.

Procter waited with bated breath, knowing that at any moment the bomb would burst. Almost from the first he had known it was to be a duel to the death, a duel, not for the life of Ulrich Maxick, but for the leadership and mastery of the whole organisation.

If Grosman surrendered that first challenge without striking a blow, then he had surrendered all he had. His fall would be as full and complete as though he had resigned; for in gang leadership the master is either undisputed king or one of the rabble with the rest. And Grosman seemed to be going down to defeat without stirring a finger, placidly watching his crown topple with all the monumental calm of the East.

Lingard moved to let Maxick pass. And then Grosman raised his hand with the slightest wave of command. Maxick stopped as though he had collided with a wall. He looked as though he expected to be murdered out of hand, and his glance shot over to Lingard in fresh affright.

Grosman turned his attention complacently to Lingard.

"Could this domestic brawl not have happened privately?" he inquired.

"That was entirely up to you. I have received messages from you and I have replied with discretion and restraint. You have deliberately gone against my urgent appeals for greater care at your end of the line, and all I have had in reply are *actions* that flout all the laws of decency and common sense Then you invite me to come along here at this hour of the night—this, after my third point-blank refusal. And what do I find? You alone? You in any condition to be approached privately? Any of the privacy which, in your opinion, you say the situation required? No I fou—surrounded by a court, two of whom don't understand the English tongue. Five of them. And every single one of them a member of your own race. And, I doubt not, with a brace of poisoned knives hidden away somewhere where they can be flashed out before a snake could blink. Sitting in judgment on a shivering wretch who is not even articulate enough to plead his own defence. The crowd of you, setting out deliberately to murder a poor devil who hasn't a ghost of a chance of getting even common justice."

His voice changed. It took on a newer, more savage timbre. There was a note of bottled-up anger, of sullen passion beginning to quiver in it. Lingard was rapidly shedding even a pretence at restraint.

"And do you think I don't know the reason?" he demanded, turning on the whole crowd of them. "Do you think I don't understand the inner meaning of this meeting—or realise why this scene was staged for me? It was your first foul attempt to send me scuttling back with my tail between my legs. I am to be brought to heel, knowing there is war between us. I am to be shown murder—stark and naked. A man deliberately done to death—a death presumably with a lot of appalling agony attached to if. It is to be a lesson to me, the same as Gilan's death was to be a lesson to the others, a lesson—that I must not question the rectitude of the powers that be. Having seen what you proposed to do to Maxick, I should naturally crawl away with my belly turned to water. I should turn craven and never, from that moment, would your ascendancy be questioned. It was your way of winning your war as quickly and as expeditiously as possible. And with another terrible lesson to the others bound up in it. The London Boss would have had his claws cut and his sovereignty would have been broken forever. Men neither honour nor obey cowards. And your drama here was staged with no other reason than to blazon me up in the light of a coward for all the rest of the gang to see. I was to stand quietly by and see Maxick done to death under my own eyes. The fact that that entails the death of another poor brute, who is as innocent of traitorous intent as any one of us, does not even enter into your vile head. It will be good for the gang—that is your excuse. And when you say the gang, you mean that it will be good for *you*. Well, Graham Lingard was never a coward from the time he was pupped. If you want an example, take a good long look at this one."

He suddenly turned and sent his enormous fist crashing into the face of Ying. The whole force of it impacted squarely on the smug face with all the weight of sixteen stone behind it. Spang! The quartermaster went sideways across the room like a catapulted stone. For one miraculous moment his face showed a moiety of emotion. It was that of sheer astonishment that so much physical force could be generated in the human biceps. With his nose as flat as a piece of putty that has been stamped on, he fell sprawling over the stomach of his master, arms waving and legs kicking. The collision knocked the chair flying, and the pair of them went over backward together in a welter of tangled limbs and staccato expletives.

One of the Chinese seamen half made a move to rise, but his eyes encountered the centre of the bore of the glittering automatic, in a dead line on the spot where the nose joins the forehead. Straight into its uncompromising eye he looked, a tiny black circle of death surrounded by a thin rim of polished nickel. And he read death there, sharp and abrupt. Lingard's forefinger was crooked round the trigger—and his horrified eyes saw the top joint whiten as the blood was squeezed back to the pressure. The seaman relaxed in his chair, and he turned his eyes away from the sight of that bullet waiting there in the cold breech to leap at him.

Lingard knocked the ash off his cigar. "That is my message to you," he grated."You should be able to read it, captain. It's written in your language. If you can't—no doubt Ying will interpret."

Grosman was slowly climbing back to his feet. He was gasping. Ying's hurtling body had taken him flat in the stomach. He kicked the seaman's legs savagely away from him as he rose.

Procter saw his hand twitch a signal at one of the seamen on the opposite side of the table. Lingard was unsighted to it, but the river man saw it unmistakably, and he saw the answering signal, fleeting as it was. Maxick leaned against the table, his whole body shaking. His fingers were beating a nervous tattoo on the table top, and he was licking at his dry lips. That sudden flailing gesture had spelt his end. He knew that Grosman would never forgive that insult. Lingard had spelled out his own doom, and in doing so had made sure of the end of Maxick. Neither could expect a grain of mercy after that.

But Lingard did not look as though he was experiencing any qualms. He stood his ground and drew steadily at his cigar.

"If you have anything more to say on this matter you had better say it now," he said, "because I have a few things to say myself."

The mandarin brushed his fingertips gently and calmly resumed his seat. He pushed Ying away behind him as though the quartermaster was no longer a creature of any moment.

"I understand your message," he said with an ominous calm. "A reply will be sent in due course. Believe me it will not fail to reach you and you will not fail to receive it. In China we do not resort to violence. Quieter methods are more discreet and less exhausting. You wish for complete leadership in this matter. Exactly what does that entail on my part?"

"A very definite subservience to me in all matters of policy. That, first and foremost. I alone will say what will be done and what will not be done. In matters of life and death a meeting of the section leaders will decide. You will be ruled out of it. And in *no* consideration whatever will you act alone. Your job is to bring the stuff in from overseas and to see that it is landed. There your authority ends. What goes on here in the matter of sale and distribution is our affair entirely, and we shall brook no interference.

"We want no more stuff to be landed. That is very definite. We already have more than we can handle for the next six months. Any more will only congest the market and defeat its own ends. No matter how much more you have back there on the *Yangtse* it must stay there and go back with you. You have kept your method of landing such a profound secret that we are completely in the dark. In the event of a police raid we are powerless. A man of Sterling's craft could bowl us out in half an hour—simply on our own ignorance.

"The cellars here are full of the stuff. We stated our requirements weeks before you left the East, and you have grossly exceeded your orders. Lying here it is as dangerous as dynamite. For all your alleged cunningness you have bungled this affair from beginning to end. You thought it marvellously adroit to buy this ramshackle great barn and leave it to moulder in rot and decay. But do you realise that it is the only warehouse on the waterfront that is owned outright by a Chinese merchant and has been left derelict? In China it might pass—but not in London. The authorities here know the Chinese for business-like, painstaking men of commerce. They have no eccentricities. This place is suspect on that account alone. And now that you have been maniac enough to shanghai Hillary Kittredge you can look for a police raid here at any moment.

"Scotland Yard are not the fools that you care to think them. They have an astonishing knack of ferreting out details and of putting one and one together. Is it possible to get that girl back to her people without her knowing where she has been? Or did your idiocy extend to letting her know that she was aboard the *Yangtse*?"

"You mistake yourself. I did not shanghai the little lady. She came aboard the *Yangtse* of her own free will. I caught her myself, eavesdropping on a conversation that was going forward in my own stateroom between Blind Rudley and myself. She had broken into my ship. She got aboard without the knowledge of Ying—a very clever performance and one that goes to prove that she had come aboard with an ulterior motive so far as I was concerned. She crawled in across the hawser. She was in evening dress, and her car was parked round the corner in a cul-de-sac, unlit and unattended. Her shoes were stuffed down the breast of her frock. Under those suspicious circumstances you will perhaps agree that the little lady had seriously compromised herself. And as the nature of the conversation between Blind Rudley and myself was not unconnected with the secret matters that lie between ourselves—it was urgently necessary to proceed without delay. Fortunately Blind Rudley heard her breathing. And we found her there, crouching in the service pantry. Perhaps, in your monumental western wisdom you will inform me what I should have done? Kiss the little lady and send her home with my kindest regards to her parents? Supply her with a little more information than she already had? Perhaps you will enlighten me—bearing in mind that she was not entirely unaware of your own august connection with this organisation."

Grosman folded his arms and waited for a solution to his riddle.

Lingard stared at him. "She came there?" he gasped. "She knew about the *Yangtse before?* She came scouting there of her own accord, and she listened in to you two talking?" Lingard's voice was high with incredulity.

"Undoubtedly."

"Good heavens—do you know what this means?"

Grosman very casually informed him that he did not.

"It means that, thanks to your foul murder of Gilan Maxick, the police already know about us. Sir John Kittredge has been talking to his daughter—and she went down there on her own account for a little thrill." He thrust his hand into his coat pocket and shook out a copy of the *London Gazette*.

"Do you see this?" he demanded. "An early copy—fresh off the presses. Sir John Kittredge was appointed High Commissioner of Police this evening."

"Is that surprising to you?" Grosman's voice was aggressive with contempt. "It was known to me many days ago that the appointment would be made. For that reason alone it was necessary for me to act as I did. No other way was open to me. Had the same situation confronted you how would you have acted? It would be amusing to know."

Lingard was visibly perturbed. His brows were knit deep in thought. "Is she on board there now?" he asked suddenly.

Grosman inclined his head. "Yes," he said, "And she stays there. I am dealing with her myself. Do not be alarmed. There will be no murder committed. On occasion we have other methods; as you will discover for yourself. Let this suffice; when the little lady gets back to her home she will remain mute on the subject of her temporary absence. She will return to them perfectly safe and sound—but she will be unwilling to talk about it." He smiled. "More," he added, "she will be fiercely determined never to open her mouth on the matter. She will guard our secrets as jealously as we do ourselves. You will agree it was the only way."

Lingard was biting his lips. "We are in the devil of a hole," he growled. "What with the murder of Maxick, the raids on the dope houses, and now this, the *Yangtse* will be a marked boat."

"I would welcome a police search," said the mandarin affably. "I assure you they would find nothing more than they have found on previous occasions. She is there—but far beyond the noses of such inquisitive fools as they."

Lingard was muttering to himself. He seemed to be thinking aloud. Deep lines were creased down his forehead, and he glared evilly at the Chinese from under his bush of brows.

"Kittredge won't stand for it," he muttered. "Not for a minute. He knows what has happened. Right on the first day of his taking office. It will score his vanity to the quick. He will move heaven and earth to wipe us out."

"And also, for the sake of his vanity, he will remain silent," purred the captain.

"Of course he won't. He knows where the girl is as sure as we're here. He will be the laughing-stock of the kingdom—and do you think he will stand for it? Not in a million years. He will make a clean sweep of the whole waterfront. Grosman, you're a fool—a lunatic to have landed us into this mess."

There was a silence for many seconds, a silence that prickled. Procter knew that the moment for battle had drawn terribly near. He was writing hurriedly in the darkness, writing with a stub of pencil on the back of an old letter. He could not see the words he made. Lines ran into each other and wandered all over the paper, but he knew that such as it was Manning would be able to puzzle it out. He was aiming to get up and out of the place into the open air. Somewhere along those mazy streets he knew he could find someone who, for a consideration, would carry the message to the river station at Wapping. That would leave him free to carry on observations on the gang from the street and keep in touch with them.

"Am in disused warehouse at bottom end of Gunn Lane," he wrote. "Grosman is here, also man called Lingard, and five Chinese crew of *Yangtze*. Lingard is head of distribution end and they are having fierce quarrel. Think there will be murder done. Have established that the snow comes ashore in tins of ship's biscuit. Have specimens with me. The girl is hidden on the *Yangtze*, apparently in some secret compartment. Suggest rush reinforcements and can capture them all. Entrance is over big gate on right. Gang down in basement. All are armed. Quarrel is over Ulrich Maxick. Grosman aims to kill him for squealing. Lingard is challenging him. Situation critical."

He finished the note and crept towards the door. He peeped out. Lingard and Grosman were glaring at each other, and so far as the captain was concerned the mask was off. The atmosphere was electrical. The Chinese were only being kept off by the grim threat of the automatic. Lingard kept it waving about slowly from one to the other, and the promise of death was burning morosely in his eyes.

"Maxick," he repeated, "get out of here."

The wharf-rat edged nervously towards the door. He crept round by the wall as though expecting a knife in his ribs from every one of the cutthroats he passed. Procter saw him appear in the doorway, his feet shuffling and his cap tugged down over his eyes. He hurried through and almost ran away from the door. Lingard watched him go and he held his ground. He knew that Maxick would lose no time in getting into touch with the rest of the gang. There would be a hectic meeting. Maxick would tell his story and the gang's loyalty to Lingard would be assured. There could be no other outcome. Lingard had faced death to go down there and save Maxick's life. And he had proved himself a match for even the dreaded Grosman. With all his Chinese minions there, Grosman had not been able to shake his courage. The gang would know in Maxick's own highly coloured language that in Lingard they had a champion who would not countenance any repetition of the Gilan Maxick affair. And if it came to a down and out war between the two factions then Lingard held the whip hand of numbers.

Procter attained to a sudden brain wave. Why not rope in Maxick? The man was petrified with fear. He had just escaped from the very maw of a horrible death, and he knew that his immunity would not last. Grosman would wipe him out of existence with no more compunction than he had killed his brother. So far as the dope gang was concerned Maxick was already a doomed man. If he came in on the police side he would be under their protection until the whole gang was rounded up. And Lingard could not hold Grosman's devils off forever.

He cautiously left the harbour of the stock-room and crept after the hurrying figure. Maxick seemed to know the way blindfold. He doubled and twisted among packing-cases that had long since fallen to pieces, finding his way without making a sound. Procter followed him as well as he could, and finally traced him to the bottom of a long spiral staircase that went circling away up into the gloom overhead. He could hear Maxick's feet clamping up the iron treads, hurrying as though the imps of the pit were flying on his heels.

Procter went up after him silently in his stockinged feet. He took the stairs two at a time, and in a little while he could hear Maxick's laboured breathing. Drug excesses had weakened the man badly, and he was gasping when he reached the top.

There was a trapdoor of some sort at the head of the stairs, and Maxick was manipulating the locks when Procter came up behind him.

Procter, too, was thankful when the landing was reached. His leg was aching as though it had been wrenched in a vice, and there were streams of hot razor blades running through his thigh. He staggered up the last step and lurched forward. Without a sound he put his arm round Maxick's shoulder and clamped a great hand firmly over his mouth.

Maxick tried to squeal. A mouthing yammer rose in his throat. It was muffled and stifled back into his chest and Procter felt it rather than heard it. So great was the man's fright that he all but collapsed on the little platform.

"Quiet, you fool," Procter hissed in his ear. "I'm Procter—you know me, don't you?" He shook the man, trying to pull him to his senses and whispered "Procter—of the river police. If you open your mouth or make a sound I'll brain you. Understand?"

Maxick nodded and his teeth chattered. The knowledge that it was not one of Grosman's men who had cornered him up there ran through him in a welter of relief. Even the shock of knowing the police had got their hands on him did not outweigh the dread of the suddenly expected death thrust. Procter stuck his face close up against the gangster's ear.

"Listen to me," he rasped. "You're in a bad way, Maxick, and I reckon no one knows it better than you. We've got the whole crowd of you in a trap. And it's up to you whether you save yourself or not. I've been listening outside that door ever since Lingard came in, and I've got the drop on every mother's son of you. You get that, don't you?"

Maxick nodded again hopelessly. His spirit had been broken down there.

Procter released him and jammed him against the wall.

"What it amounts to," he went on, "is that you get it either way, don't you? Either you get ten years from us or you get a nice quick trip to Paradise from Grosman. That's about the strength of it. Because you know as well as I do that Grosman is going to get you after what happened in that room. You haven't one chance in a thousand, have you?"

Maxick tried to speak. But his tongue had gone as dry as an old pack saddle, and when he tried to get the words out the root of his tongue rose up against the back of his throat and stuck there.

Procter regarded him, and there was not a scrap of compassion in his attitude. He was fighting for his rights as he saw them, and his job was to carry the fight into the other man's camp. And his fight was not unconnected with the three silver stripes. He had got his man on the run, and he was not letting go. That message had got to get through. Manning had got to get it—or the chance of a lifetime would fritter away.

"Well," he said in a breathy whisper, "you can take that one chance and get away with it. I'm offering it to you. You can take it or leave it."

"Lemme get out of here," croaked the dope runner. "I'll talk to you outside. Lemme get out. One of them swine will be up here before you can say knife—and they'll get me. You don't know what they are—you don't know what they've got lined up for Lingard. Soon's they have got him fixed they will be racing up here for me. For God's sake lemme get out."

"Open that trapdoor," grunted Procter.

Maxick wheeled, and the river man watched the dim white of his hands operating the combination. As the door slid open Procter gripped his arm.

"What is that combination?" he demanded.

"G.E.L.," whined Maxick.

"Is there any special significance?"

"Yes, mate. It's the initials of the Big Three."

"Who?"

"Grosman, Engelberg, and Lingard."

"Well—that's information. So the Hollander is in it, too, is he? We live and learn. I'll say the gods have been good to little Procter tonight. And what part does he play?"

"What's the use of asking me? I ain't one of the Big Three. I only peddles the stuff. I'm only a bit of dirt in this crowd. I never knew he was in it till the other day."

He swung the panel wide and turned to crawl through. But Procter hauled him back with a jerk.

"Not so fast, my cocker," he growled. "I want to know where you stand first. I'm making you the offer and I want to know if you are taking it or not."

"Lemme get out," whinnied the gangster. "I want to get to hell out of here."

"So you shall, Maxick. But you have got to side in with us."

Maxick wheeled on him in startled fright. "I ain't squealin'," he protested. "You heard what they were goin' to do to me down there. And that was all because they thought I was going to squeal on 'em. They'd tear me throat out if they caught me. It ain't fair to ask me like this. For Gawd's sake let up on me."

"Listen," said Procter. "They are going to get you, anyway. Grosman has got it in for you, right up to the neck. If you get out you will be dead in a few hours—and not a nice death either. Why consider Grosman? He is going to do you in—whether you squeal or not. One chance you've got, and only one. If you shout and raise hell now they will only suspect you of having let me in. They know you were down at the station yesterday with Sterling. They would strangle you for it. You'd better think quickly, Maxick."

"What can I do?" protested the shivering man. "I get it in the neck either way."

"Not if you side in with us. We can keep you clear. We can hide you away where all the gang men in London won't find you. You have more chance with us than with a thousand Grosmans. It's up to you. I'm not going to stand here all night arguing with you. I'll give you a minute to think it over. After that, if you don't like the idea, I'll hand you over to one of the men we've got waiting down below—and you'll be inside a cell within twenty minutes."

"What do you want me to do?"asked Maxick in a frightened whisper.

"Spill the beans. Come clean on the whole game. Give us the names and addresses. Tell us how the job is worked. In short, squeal—and squeal like hell. You'd better. Squeal and live—close your mouth and die. That's how it works out, my cocker."

Maxick was staring, bright-eyed, at the river man. Here was hope, here was a straw of salvation. He clutched at it. He knew that the police had ways and means of their own of keeping their men out of harm's way. He licked his lips and his eyes flung round at the vague blue oblong beyond the trapdoor where the night hung peaceful and still over the dark river.

"I'll do anythink in reason," he stammered.

Procter grasped him tightly. "Do you mean that?" he snapped.

"Crorst me throat if I tell a lie, matey. But you gotter promise to see me through. I'll tell you all I know. It ain't much, because I ain't in the know like some of 'em. But I'll tell you all I've got. You can round up the West End gang on it, anyway. That'll pay 'em back for the way they have treated me. The sons!"

"That's the spirit," breathed Procter in his ear. "Why not fight back at them? They have got you marked down for a rotten end. Have a go at 'em. You can see the whole lot off if you side right in with us. I'll see that no harm comes to you. You will be kept in along with us in one of the stations till we have rounded the whole bunch up. After we have got 'em all slammed into jail you can do as you like. There is such a thing as an assisted passage for those who help the police and want to clear out of the country. You'll be all right—but, by crikey, you've got to play square."

Maxick capitulated without reservation. He was holding both hands out avidly for the lifebelt that Procter was offering.

"I'll go right round to Scotland Yard and give myself up," he declared.

"I'm fed up with it. I'll come clean. And glad to."

"Well—that will do for me," assented Procter. "Only there is no need to go to Scotland Yard. The river station at Wapping will do. Sergeant Manning will look after you and see that you come to no harm."

"Righto, mate. I won't let you down. I've had enough of it. I'll do anythink you say. I'll get right round there now."

"Just a moment, I'll scribble you a note to take round to the sergeant. That will make things easier for you."

He wrote on the back of the letter: "Ulrich Maxick brings this note. He is ready to squeal. Get all you can from him. Have promised him that he is kept clear. He can tell you all that is missing from the letter overleaf. Hurry assistance. Am going back down below to watch events."

He tipped some cigarettes out of a cardboard packet and slipped the note in. Then he stuck a postage stamp over each end of the packet.

"Here," he said. "Take this. That will see you through. But yon will hand it to Manning with those seals unbroken. If either of those postage stamps is torn you can look out for squalls."

Maxick grabbed the box and slid out through the trapdoor. He muttered a fervent whisper of thanks to the river man and was gone, climbing silently down the fire escape outside.

Procter watched him go. They had emerged on the rooftop and there was a long climb to the bottom. Procter lost sight of him among the shadows beneath. He never saw what happened below there in the darkness, and it was as well for his peace of mind that he did not. For neither that letter, nor the messenger who carried it, ever reached the river station. Grosman had laid his plans too well for any squeaker, any informer against the organisation he ruled, to have a chance of success,

Maxick slithered soundlessly up Gunn Lane. And as he went a black, silent shadow detached itself from the wall of shadows by the warehouse gate and crept along on his trail. Fifteen yards in the rear the trailer went; and twice, when Maxick turned to throw a frightened glance back, the lane was empty.

But Ulrich Maxick never made to the end of Gunn Lane. When there were still three houses between him and the crossroad a silent figure came up with the speed of an arrow. There was the blue glint of a knife in the night and a shrill scream, and the sinister figure passed on, rapid and as noiseless as the passage of an owl across a cloud—and was gone.

Maxick fell where he stood, and another awful scream shrilled out on the air. He was writhing in agony, turning over and over in the gutter like an animal that had been mortally wounded. The hilt of the dagger stuck out between his shoulder blades and the knife was right through his backbone.

A window shot up overhead and a woman looked out, her eyes dilated wide with fright. She saw the coiling thing below her, half on, half off the pavement, and her own shrieks went searing out on the silence. Screaming was a custom of the country in her part of the river. It drew attention to the fact that something was wrong and it kept the screamer out of any possible entanglement. The instinct of self-preservation was the root cause of it, for the denizens of that locality wanted the police round as urgently as possible when the killers were out. Other windows went up. Old caretakers who lived in the attics above the glooming warehouses added their babel, and soon their menfolk added their hoarse calls of "Police—police" to the din.

But no one went near the writhing man in the gutter. That was no concern of theirs. And if they were found near it, or trying to render first-aid, the police automatically required their names and addresses for such objectionable procedures as inquests and magisterial hearings. And anything to do with the law is anathema along that section of the river. It does not always end in the courts. Gangsters are apt to take revenge at a later date.

Thus, when running footsteps sounded along the road and two constables appeared, flashing their lamps ahead of them, the yelling died as if by magic and the windows silently closed. The faces disappeared and the silence of the night settled back over Gunn Lane.

Maxick had long since ceased to scream. His throat had closed up and a constriction had set in on his limbs. There was froth on his lips when the constables got to him. His back was bent nearly double, with his head thrown back in a ghastly rigor. One of the officers pulled out the knife with an effort. A fluttering tremor ran through the body, and Ulrich Maxick coughed and was dead. "That's the end of him, Martin" muttered the one with the knife. "Got him right through the back."

The other nodded grimly. "Dead as a doornail, Tom," he said. "Looks to me like Chinese work. I saw one killed like that down in Rotherhithe—that was a Chinese job, too."

Tom shone his flash-lamp on the knife, and he uttered a sharp ejaculation. "That's dam queer," he said. "Look—that figuring on the blade! It's the same as the one they took from the body in that Maxick murder the other day. Remember? There was some Chinese writing on that one, too."

"Knew it was Chinese," replied Martin. They stood up and looked up and down the street. There was not a sound from anywhere. The tragedy was done and finished with. In sixty seconds it was begun and ended. Tragedies like that, grim little highlights that flickered in and out of the dull picture of East End life, happened without witnesses. The dead body had been thrown up out of the night, without clue or pointer, and the night closed down dumbly upon it.

"What do we do about it?" grunted Tom.

"Better run through his pockets. Might be something there to identify him. Looks to me like a gang job."

Tom opened the coat and felt in the inside pocket. He pulled out a handful of paper oddments, bookmakers' circulars, newspaper cutting referring to arrests in connection with cocaine traffic, a list of probable runners in a classic race—and a post card addressed to Ulrich Maxick at an address in Newington Causeway.

The constable whistled. "Here's a go." he muttered. "His name's Maxick, too! This is a gang job all right. We had better get a report through in a hurry. Headquarters is working on this job."

The other pulled out a notebook and made a few ponderous entries. "I'll get round and find somewhere where I can telephone," he said. "You'd better stay around and look after the body. The Chief is handling this case—he will want to know about this."

He crossed over to a darkened warehouse and thundered on the door. The silence grew deeper and he pounded again. He knew there was a night watchman, and he hammered away until it was obvious even to the watchman's stolid brain that he intended staying there until he got an answer.

The man appeared, grudgingly. In answer to the constable's questions he swore he had not heard a sound in the lane for the last hour. The officer knew he was lying, but it was not possible to force witness against the gangs down there. He ordered him to open the office, and in a few minutes he was through to his station.

"Got a murder job here, sergeant," he said. "Looks serious to me. I think it connects up with that Maxick murder on the river the other day. A post card on the body is addressed to Ulrich Maxick—maybe a relative of the other chap. Found him dying in the gutter at the top of Gunn Lane. He died before we could do anything for him. There was a knife in his back—the blade had gone clean through the bone. I pulled it out, and there are some Chinese markings cut into the blade the same as in that other case."

"Right; I'll get through to Headquarters at once. Have you got help?"

"Yes—Three Eight One is with me. He's with the body now."

"Where are you phoning from?"

"A warehouse in Gunn Lane."

"Any witnesses?"

"Not a soul. The whole place here is as dead as a grave. Not a sound anywhere. The watchman here was awake, but he swears he never heard a sound. And we heard the screaming two streets away. But you know what it is. They'd cut out their tongues sooner than run foul of the gangs."

"Hang on there and I'll send an ambulance. Probably someone will be coming out from the Yard."

The ambulance came, and with it came Sterling. By that time the constables had gone right through the dead man's pockets. It was Martin who came across the cigarette box. He was about to toss it into the heap with the rest when the oddity of the sealed ends caught his eye. He held it closer to the light and saw that the seals were postage stamps.

The two policemen eyed each other dubiously. That was a new one on them. They didn't run up against sealed packets of cigarettes every day.

"Going to open it?" asked Tom.

"Not me," answered Martin shortly. "I once did a clever thing like that on a job three years ago. We were looking for stolen jewellery, and I opened a camera to see if there was anything hidden inside—and I fogged a set of plates that would have got us a conviction. Got bawled at for a fortnight and a year's seniority went west. Since then I've left off being a detective. I'm a plain, ordinary copper and know it. Leave it to the Yard man. That maybe the gang's secret way of passing snow. I'm steering clear."

And as simply as that the chance was lost. They waited and the precious minutes ticked away. And when, half an hour later, the ambulance arrived the opportunity had gone.

Sterling hurried out of the car and took immediate charge. He called to the senior constable, and in two minutes was in full possession of the facts.

He examined the knife, looking grave. "It's the same type of knife and the same inscription," he said. Then he dived on the cigarette packet. The message fell out, and he seized it. He bent over it, trying to puzzle out the almost illegible scrawl. It was nearly unreadable. Some of the lines were written over each other.

"Quick! Bring those lights here," he called. The constables switched on their lamps and they pored over the paper, trying to decipher the message.

VI

Procter crept back down the stairs and felt his way back through the darkness. Long before he reached them he knew that things were rapidly coming to a head in the lighted room. Voices were raised in high altercation, and the language was heated. The river man tried to get back to his old retreat, but his passage was barred. Lingard had flung the door wide and he was outside it. His position was such that he could have seen the officer as he came into the aura of light streaming from the room.

Grosman was reiterating his intention of landing every ounce of the stuff he had brought over.

"There is no sense in taking it back," he declared. "It is here and it is going to be landed. You can just as well be hanged for a sheep as a lamb. If you can give me one single reason why it should not be brought ashore it shall stay on the *Yangtse*. But there *is* no reason. It is no greater risk to store two hundred thousand pounds' worth of cocaine here than it is one."

"And I tell you it's not safe," stormed Lingard. "What we have here I can handle. In a few days I can spread it out over other storing points. But all that takes time, and other places will have to be found. Not one of the old dumps is safe. The middlemen won't take an ounce more than they can handle. They know the stuff is here, and they are diffident about buying. The price has already gone rocketing down. They know we've got to sell—and the onus is on us. With the police raiding them one after the other they will only take just enough for current consumption."

"Then it is up to you to find new dumps. That is your job."

"But you can't do things like that in ten minutes. This place will be discovered by the police before long. It's bound to be. We can't stave them off forever. And I'm working like a maniac to get it cleared. If the police raided us now we should be ruined. Don't you realise there is pretty well every cent of capital we possess locked up in those rooms over there? A raid would be calamity. It would take us years to get started on anything like a big scale again. And here are you insisting in forcing another fifty thousand pounds' worth on me. I can't take it. And I won't! Land it if you wish—it won't come into this warehouse."

"You think not?"

"I know it!"

The signal came again, the merest flick of the hand. Lingard half turned, but before he could get round with his gun the seaman on his left had made a lightning movement. For ten minutes he had been preparing for it. Slowly, unnoticeably, so gradual was the movement, his hand had gone round into his pocket and back again. Then, when the signal came, that hand had flashed backward and forward in a split second. Something impacted with a soft thud against Lingard's temple, and the dope runner was down.

It was a neat silken bag of small shot, little bigger than an egg. But the bag was loose and that looseness made it a deadly weapon, for it stunned instantly, without killing and without leaving a bruise. The bag was limp in the air and cushioned slightly on impact, the shot spreading out with the force of the throw. As the bag crashed into his temple Lingard half spun round. A fierce burst of white light flashed across his eyes, and then a great blackness overwhelmed him. He sagged slowly to his knees.

Grosman had laid his plans well. Intentionally he had got his man's temper frayed. And as Lingard became hotter and hotter in his arguments his attention began slowly to focus on the captain. Grosman knew that there would come a moment when Lingard would be so intent on his duel that it would be safe to risk a movement on the part of one of his men. Ten minutes before that ruse would never have worked. Lingard would have been round on him with the gun before the man could have even shifted the weight of his body in the chair.

As soon as the drug runner crumpled, all the apparent choler seeped out of him. He rose from his chair, quiet, calm, as coldly imperturbable as ever.

He indicated the prostrate form. "Tie him up," he said.

Then came interruption, abrupt and sudden. From outside in the great hall of the warehouse there came the sound of the creaking collapse of wood and then a muffled fall. Procter, in trying to get round to see what was happening, had stumbled in the darkness. His knee knocked against an unseen obstruction, and the injured leg gave out. There was the searing scorch of burning acid running up the very marrow of the bone as he toppled against an old rotted packing-case. The case broke with his weight, and he fell headlong.

For one jolting second there was a tense silence in the inner room. The Chinese stood staring at their master; Grosman, with a startled frown corrugating his brows, was peering out through the door as though he expected a spectre to appear. Then with a ponderous jab of his great arm he swept his hand down a row of electric light switches. He had a courage of his own. Whatever peril it was that threatened out there he was facing it foursquare. The warehouse leapt into a flood of light, and the burst of brilliance showed Procter, half buried in the debris of the smashed case, kicking about helplessly among the timbers trying to get up. But the leg would not help. It let him down badly. He struggled madly and reared up halfway while the Chinese raced at him, and sank back with a groan.

"Here goes Mrs. Procter on the pension list," he muttered as the ferocious figures closed on him. Grosman barked something at them in Chinese, and naked steel flashed under the blare of light.

Procter died fighting. As the leader came at him he rolled over and kicked out valiantly with his uninjured foot. The flat of his boot came into violent contact with the man's face. There was a sharp crack, and the man was staggering round, screaming, his hands clawing up at his powdered jaw.

Grosman hissed again, viciously, and another seaman, obeying the order without a glimmer of resentment, swung the butt of a pistol on his skull. The steel sank in an inch, and the screaming ceased with a high-pitched squeal. Grosman was muttering savagely under his breath. The din the seaman had made was piercing, and he was fearful that it might have been heard outside. His mind was in a daze. How the position stood he had not the faintest idea. Procter might be in there alone or he might be one of a platoon creating an ambush for them. There might be dozens of others guarding the exits outside. At the very least it seemed beyond hope to suppose that Procter was in there on a lone raid. Grosman purchased silence at the cost of a life.

Three others had flailed themselves on the helpless river man. He was pressed back by sheer weight of numbers. Two gripped his arms and hauled him over. He felt the sharp sting of steel piercing up behind his shoulder blade, and with a shock of horror he realised that his end had come. That quick stab had killed him as surely as though they had severed his head. A shuddering weakness ran over him. It was just beginning to dawn on him that he would never see the little wife at home stitching those three stripes on his sleeve. It was the end. Life had been lived, with all its hopes and efforts and high ideals, life with all its trials and troubles and little victories—and the end had come, as shockingly swift as that.

Dying like a rat, gasping out life under a heap of silent Chinese who clung to him, mute and determined, while the arterial blood ran out. His back was warmly wet, as though a slow, creeping humidity was spreading over it. The realisation of it horrified him. It was all damnably unfair. They hadn't given him a chance in a thousand of making a fight for it. Procter, with wide eyes and blanching face, was staring into infinity.

A hot rebellion whelmed him, a fierce resentment that Fate should cut him off in such inhuman fashion. He cursed the Chinese with all the virulence of his river vocabulary. His fury centred on Grosman. At that moment, if he could have got Grosman's throat between his hands, he would have gone to his Maker with murder on his soul; the two of them would have gone out together, with Procter's fingers fast locked on the captain's thorax.

And in the midst of his passion there burned a hot spark of joy in the knowledge that, even in death, he had bested his murderers. Ulrich Maxick was already on his way to the river station. Manning had been notified, and it would not be long before a swamping rush of uniformed men would knock them off their feet. He had won his fight even in death. He had made a turncoat of Maxick. The wharf-rat's evidence would send the crowd of them to the moors and Grosman to the gallows.

He fought savagely to get at the man. But his strength was fast running out. Grosman looked down at him with a bitter smile of hatred.

"You are making your last run down river, Procter," he said in a slow, almost caressing undertone. "All the mysteries of life and death and the Great Beyond, all the secrets that have tormented the sages since time began, will soon be yours for the solving. I hope the knowledge comforts you. Interfering pig! You would not take a warning."

He regarded the weakly struggling man from under half-closed eyes. "He who plays with fire needs asbestos hands," he said. "You were warned—you and Manning and the rest.

You were told to keep your fingers out of matters that did not concern you. Maxick was given you as a warning. But you would not take it. Perhaps your death will be a warning to the others. For as surely as they interfere in my business they will die."

Procter spat at him. His face was shaking with fury.

"Son of a sow," he yelled, "you haven't beaten me yet! I've got the drop on the crowd of you! I'll have you all in cells inside an hour." His voice rose to a scream. In the access of his blind rage caution went flying to the winds. The knowledge that he had beaten them and that they were in a trap overmastered him. It was the fighting instinct of a dying man. Outnumbered though he was, he knew that he had outgeneralled them, and the surging knowledge of it sent a vengeful paean of exultation through him. And in his wild frenzy he lost his fight—threw away his victory at the very moment of its success. He was not going out without letting the Chinese know that he had beaten them and that from that hour the greatest illicit drug organisation that had ever existed was toppling to its fall.

Grosman sensed the atmosphere and snapped on it like a dog on a rat.

"Oh yes," he murmured, "you will have to move very quickly, my friend, if you are going to oblige us with the inside of a cell. I fear you have not more than two minutes to live. Ying is very adept with the point of a knife. It is not often he fails to puncture the heart with the first prick."

"I don't need to move at all," barked the prostrate man. "I've got you pinned where you stand. I know where the stuff is and I know how to fret it through. And you bladder of sin, I've sent the message through. Wrote it all down—and it's on its way to the station now. You can't shift all that stuff before the boys get here. You'd want a lorry to cart all that biscuit away—and three journeys at that. The boys will get you—and they'll give you hell, too, when they find you have stuck me." Procter was dazed by the savagery of his death or he would never have given himself away like that. Grosman's crafty eyes were devouring him. The message was already on its way to the station. That meant that at least two of them had got into the warehouse. And it also meant that that was probably all there were, just the two of them. For surely, had there been others, they would have come to their colleague's assistance. They would not have stood by and seen him murdered in cold blood. Grosman goaded him along. Outside was one of his men, waiting and watching in case Maxick managed to make his escape. Grosman laid his plans far ahead, and Maxick was doomed. It might be that his watcher would see the police officer leaving the building. And in that case he had no further need for qualms. That message would never get to the station. And the messenger would never live to carry another Judas letter.

He signed to the coolies, and they released the fallen man. He was far gone, and there was no further need for restraint. The life was ebbing; nothing but the fine fighting spirit remained, and its flame burned bright and high.

"Your message could never leave this building," said Grosman gently. "Do you think we are such fools as to leave our entrances unguarded? He will never get to the river station. Even if he eludes my man a fast car will be at the station before him and silent knives will lie in wait. It is unseemly for you to die with false impressions, Procter. Your messenger will never get through."

It was then that the gloat in the river man's heart blinded him to what he was doing. The astuteness of his move in winning Maxick over was too good a farewell bullet not to fire at the smug face above him. By sheer blind chance he had stumbled on the only messenger likely to get through the cordon—one of the gang's own members.

"Won't he? Won't he get through?" he snarled. "That's just where you step on the soap, you fat lump! My messenger was Maxick, the poor devil you were going to murder. He's under police protection now. Safe as houses. By tonight he will be where none of you will ever get at him. And he's in with us! You can kick a man all you like, but there are limits. You found Maxick's when you went out to murder him for damn all. I was in the store there. I heard you. There's only one real man in the whole of your rotten crowd. And that's old Lingard. And he dam nearly queered the lot of you. He got Maxick away out of it. And I got him at the top of the stairs. Got him and talked to him. Poor brute! Livid with fear he was. And he fell for me, fell for my way out of your clutches."

"Maxick turned renegade, eh?" said Grosman. "That was why he was booked for death, Procter. He was a prospective squealer from the first. So was his brother. That was why they died. For, believe me, Maxick is already dead." Grosman's voice had sunk away to a soft purr and he seemed to be almost fondling the idea of Maxick's death. It gave him an infinite satisfaction. It was the greatest stroke of luck that could have happened. For Maxick, of all people, to have proved to be the police messenger was a veritable gift from the gods. Maxick was the one person who was doomed never to leave Gunn Lane alive. And it was all against Grosman's soulless nature to let the river man die with the taste of victory in his mouth. He had his last contemptuous kick at him as his life ebbed away.

Procter glared up at him. "You don't kid me," he croaked. "Maxick is alive. I saw him go. And he's got the message with him. Wrote it all down for Manning to see. He will get it. and you'll all be on the run you swabs. Maxick won't let me down. We are his only hope. And he knows it. You don't kid me. I saw him hoofing it down the fire escape."

"And at the foot of the fire escape a knife was waiting for him." Grosman smiled his villainous delight at the thought.

It soothed his brutal spirit to watch the dying man's triumph turn to gall in his mouth. Procter looked up at him and the old courageousness began to wilt. He read the truth on Grosman's flabby features. Death and defeat. Procter stared them both in the face as Death swung the scythe back for him. The bright flame dimmed. Flat on his back, he stared up at his tormentor.

"You're a—damned—liar!" he said, but the voice was daunted.

Grosman smiled and leaned forward as though listening. Shouts began to echo faintly through the gloomy building, the shouting of men that merged with the screams of women. From far up Gunn Lane they sounded, growing in volume and intensity. Across the way a dog howled. Long seconds fell slowly away into eternity. The two men stared at each other, eye to eye. Suddenly the tumult died, ceased as abruptly as though a gigantic sound-pro of curtain had descended on the whole of the world beyond the warehouse.

Procter looked away, scarce able to believe that Fate could be so savagely heartless with a man in his last few seconds of life. He knew what that din portended. And, more definitely than that, he knew the deeper meaning of that sudden silence. The police had arrived. The murder of Ulrich Maxick was a *fait accompli.*

His head sagged sideways. "Well, I'll say the gods—haven't—been any—too kind—to little—Procter—tonight," he mumbled.

He coughed. There was a fullness in his throat, a warm fullness that was sickly. He gasped. The blood was filling his lungs. He never knew what that fullness in the throat was. His eyelids slowly closed. He gave them a last feeble effort. Grosman had to bend low to hear it.

"Polecat—the boys—will—get you—yet!" he yammered, and rolled over.

There was a scratch of sound from the inner room. Grosman wheeled. Lingard was trying to sit up. Groggy as an owl, he looked about him and licked his lips. A mist was over his brain, and there seemed to be a wall between himself and his thoughts. His brain was not functioning and there was an enormity of ache going round and round in his head; and in the middle of his left temple seemed to be centred the fountainhead of all the pain that ever tore a nerve.

Grosman pointed to the dead body. "Weight that and drop it through the trap," he said. "Hurry. We must get that message back."

The seamen broke out the woodwork from half a dozen windows and returned with an armful of sash weights. They stuffed them into the dead officer's pockets and dragged him away. At the first sound of the shouting Grosman had plunged the whole building into darkness. The only light in the place came from the inner room, which was effectively screened from the outside.

They opened a trapdoor in the floor, and a cold press of air wafted up in their faces. It was thick and foetid with the smells of river mud and stagnant slime. Far down below black water gurgled by, the walled-up remnant of one of London's buried streams. Fifty yards away the river passed in its mightiness. But that body would never reach the river. The feeder stream was tidal, and, heavily weighted with cast iron, the body was doomed to drift up and down between the warehouse and the outfall.

They dropped him over. After a second or two there came a dull, heavy splash from down below that reverberated with all the ponderousness of a heavy weight falling into deep water. The cold air swirled up again as the body disappeared and they silently closed the trap.

Grosman went through to Lingard. The big man propped himself upon one elbow and looked up at him, blinking uncertainly. The sight of the Chinese pulled him together a little. He blinked again and tried to puzzle things out. But that mountainous ache in his head precluded all consecutive thought. All he knew was that somehow his power had crumpled. He could not remember how, but he knew it was true. He felt the ascendancy of the other man. Something inside him whispered a warning that Grosman had declared himself master and had demonstrated the fact in no uncertain way. The pain in his head told him that the method had not been without force.

Grosman picked up the gun and thrust it into his own pocket. The movement recalled things to Lingard. That gun was connected in some way with his present condition. Little bits of the mist began to clear away. Grosman shook him roughly.

"Well?" he growled. "Perhaps you believe me now!"

Lingard passed his hand shakily over his face. He was beginning to remember. "Better pull yourself together," said Grosman. "There is much to do. That damned rat Maxick has squealed on us. Turned right over to the police."

The mention of the name Maxick brought him back with a rush.

"Maxick? A turncoat?" he said weakly. "I don't believe it."

"It does not matter a button whether you do or not. The police have been here and—"

Lingard looked up with a start. The police! His thoughts went off into a maze again.

"Don't worry," said Grosman. "There are ways and means of dealing with the police. Maxick, too, has been dealt with."

"But—but what happened?" Lingard looked his incredulity.

"No more than was to have been expected when you take on the staff such runts as the Maxicks. Procter got at him. That was only to have been expected, too. That was why I wanted Maxick out of the way long ago. I had anticipated it. And I had a man posted outside to deal with any emergency that arose regarding him. His orders were to kill him no matter what happened. Maxick must have given us away to the police; must have told them of this rendezvous and how to get in. Anyhow, Procter came in here tonight. It was just after you had your—accident. Procter had stumbled against something in the dark. He gave himself away. Well, he has gone where he won't give anyone else away."

"Procter! You've murdered him?" Lingard's grey face had gone ashen, his jaw sagged away. The imbecility of it numbed him. He saw all his carefully built up schemes crumbling to the dust. That act would bring the whole pack of wolves snarling at their heels and there would be no let up until the whole organisation was smashed.

"Yes. We murdered him. Slipped a knife into him and he is down the the trap by now." Lingard was about to break into hot protests, but Grosman silenced him with a sudden outburst.

"What else could we do?" he demanded. "Procter was wise to all we had got down here. He must have been listening to all that was going on since before you came down. He was out in the snow store. He knew where the drugs were. He knew all about the girl because we were talking about her in here; knew that she was still on board and that there was a secret compartment on the *Yangtse*. And then, over and above all that, he wrote down the whole story and sent it through to the station."

"Good God!" gasped Lingard.

"Nice to know that even you realise the position was serious. Procter admitted it all while he was dying. He boasted about it. Fortunately for us we were prepared. Procter was using Maxick as his messenger. After your theatrical release of the man the way was left open for him. Actually you are more responsible for what happened than amy of us. Procter had to die because of the knowledge he had gained. We couldn't keep him a prisoner indefinitely. He just had to die. But the trouble was, and still is, with Maxick. Procter got hold of him and actually passed his message over. Maxick got outside. My man got him and you can see how the position stands. Maxick is lying out there, dead. And the message is still on him. The police are there. They are going to find that message!"

Lingard was staggered. In a flash he realised the hopelessness of the situation. Once the police knew, even if it was only the address, the game was up. Thoughts of immediate flight shot into his mind. He stumbled to his feet.

"Quick!" he gasped. "They will be here. We must get out. We will be taken like rats in a trap."

Grosman regarded him coldly. "Easy!" he said. "You have got us into this mess and you have got to help us get out. We have got to get at that message and destroy it. If the police read it we are doomed. We can't commit wholesale murder; can't very well kill off the whole staff at Scotland Yard. That letter will have to be destroyed before they get a chance to see it. Panic methods won't help. We shall have to work as silently as cats. Running away will do us no good. And do you think I am going to run—with a hundred and fifty thousand pounds of my own money lying there in the store? You are a little less sane than I thought you were."

"But—how—what can I do? I'll do anything that will keep us clear. Anything short of murder. Murder I flatly will not be linked up with. My sheet is black enough now." Lingard was as near panic as ever he was in his life. His eyes were darting about like a hunted animal's, and his ear was cocked towards the door as though he could detect sounds coming from somewhere out there in the darkness. He shivered and tried to moisten his dry lips. But his tongue was like sand. A slow despair was beginning to gnaw at him.

"Listen, Lingard—and try to act like a man. The beat policemen are out there now. They will telephone a report. And a Yard man will be sent out. They will have instructions not to touch the body till the Yard man gets out there. That is the usual custom here, which you should know as well as

I. That gives us about ten minutes in which to act. It's too late to go out right away. We should be interrupted by the Yard man; or the chances are a hundred to one that we should. There will be eyes up at the windows till the Yard wagon arrives. I will deal with the matter myself. But you need not shiver. There will be no more murder tonight. I have a little gun here that is quite as effective. In this case even more so. You had better keep out of it. You haven't a mask. And a mask is very necessary when that little gun goes off."

"Is it a poison gas? That won't help us. They will still know about this place and raid us." Lingard spoke in short, clipped-off sentences. He was rapidly becoming a mass of nerves.

"No. It is not poison gas. And it will not kill them. It will not even render them unconscious. But after it has gone off there will not be one of them able to take that message away. And if they don't read that letter, Lingard, how can they know about this place? But we are still in grave danger. It will be known that we carry on operations somewhere adjacent to Gunn Lane. This place will be suspect, and the whole lane will be under police surveillance. Every visitor to this lane will be watched. It means that we shall have to move from here. The front entrances will be barred us. To use them would be suicidal. That is where you come in. You will have to get this stuff away at lightning speed. If you lay claim to being something of an organiser, now is your opportunity to prove it. You'll never have another chance like it as long as you live. The old railway sidings are out there at the back. You'll have to use them. Bring the lorries up under cover of night. Rent another dump until we can find our new place. Any old store will do until we can get fixed up again. It's a hell of a risk, but we shall have to chance it. Hardtack biscuit is uninteresting enough not to excite anyone's curiosity. But it's neck or nothing from now on. The thing is that it will have to be done immediately. This place might be raided tomorrow night for all we know. If so, then it's up to you to get us clear.

The police will come and find the birds flown—and a hundred and fifty thousand pounds will have gone with them. That's all. It's your job and it's up to you. I will see to the rest."

The seamen returned and for some seconds Grosman talked to them in a quick undertone. They listened without a word as Grosman gave them their instructions. Grosman produced from a cupboard in the room a queer looking instrument that resembled a revolver in some ways and yet was unlike any gun that Lingard had ever seen. It was short and stubby. There was a butt for a grip and trigger to fire it, but there the resemblance ended. It had no barrel; but where the barrel should have been was what appeared to be a strong steel pan, two inches wide. Across the pan were three flat-looking cartridges, lying side by side, held in place by little clips at both ends.

The seamen pulled masks from their pockets and adjusted them over their faces, so that they hung down to their necks. Lingard saw that they had no eye-holes. They were just thick pads of exceptionally heavy felt. They pulled them down so that their eyes showed, and Grosman, fitting his own in position, gave the signal to move off. They switched out every light and crept through the darkened building. From the top of the fire escape they could see the torches of the two constables as they stood guard over the body.

Grosman whispered in Lingard's ear. "You had better stay back here and wait till you hear me whistle. When you get the signal, make a bolt for it. Don't get excited—just walk off as though nothing had happened. The coppers will still be up there, but they will not be able to hurt you. They won't even know you are there. And whatever you do, don't move from here till you get the signal—or you might get a dose of what those policemen are in for."

Lingard nodded and buttoned his coat closer about him. He was shaking badly. Grosman grunted a scornful epithet under his breath and the murderous-looking group moved off.

They progressed as silently as a cloud passes over the moon. Like black ghosts they went down the escape and out into the lane. At the bottom they separated into two parties, each creeping silently along in the deep shadows of the warehouses. They got to within twenty yards of the constables and waited there, silent and motionless. In a little while the ambulance drew up. Grosman's thick lips pressed up into a scowl of hatred when he saw who it was climbing out. He recognised Sterling in the light of the car's headlamps; Sterling, in charge of the case, and who had sworn to get him. He reflected that fortune could not have served him better. Here was a luck-sent opportunity of paying two debts with a single cheque. It gave him a sense of infinite satisfaction to know that it was Sterling who was to be the recipient of his little present.

They saw him hold his conclave with the constable, and saw him go down on his hands and knees to examine the dead man's belongings. Then Sterling found the cigarette packet. They saw him open it and take out the sheet of paper. Grosman knew from his sudden excitement that he had found the message. Without a sound he began to close in on the group.

Sterling called to the other constable for more light. The seamen crept up behind with drawn knives in case Grosman's attempt failed. Their masks were right up over their eyes now, and they were feeling their way along by the side of the walls. The driver had climbed down and had joined the group. He had put the stretcher down by the body. Sterling's sudden jump of activity excited his curiosity, and he bent over the group as the constables focused their torches on the paper. All four heads were poring over the message at once, and Grosman stepped forward without a sound.

What happened next was so unexpected and was done so quickly that they were powerless to prevent it. Grosman's hand slid in between them with the revolver gripped in his fat fingers. Just for one startling second they saw it, a weird apparition that had suddenly appeared in their line of vision out of nowhere. Their eyes fixed on it, half in puzzlement, half tn surprise. And then the finger flexed on the trigger.

Grosman's other hand was up against his face, plugging the mask hard against his eyes. A sudden scorching sea of light welled out of the steel pan, blinding, searing, ferocious in its enormous intensity. It was as though the livid cores of a thousand suns was suddenly centred on that single livid spot. All the glaring, eye-killing light of a universe incandesced into an incredible brilliance, a brilliance so intense that the fierce, blinding stream of a searchlight was as the pale gleam of a struck match beside it. For just that one blinding second it lit the skies, throwing the surrounding buildings into a wild futuristic silhouette of black and white, as though a ton of magnesium had been fused into luminance through monstrous lenses in that terrific fraction of a second. The piercing glare of it was so tremendous that it progressed on beyond the normal whites of light. It achieved a colouring of blue; burning, disintegrating, electric blue that penetrated on through the gelatines of the eyes to the very optic nerves behind the retinas.

The four men fell back, helplessly pawing at the air, their faces screwed up in an access of agony. Sterling rolled over, kicking spasmodically, his hands gripped up at his blinded eyes, whimpering with the exquisite agony that had brayed his sensory nerves. He had taken the full force of the ray; the instrument was less than six inches from his eyes when the discharge came. The jelly of his very eyeballs was roasted.

Jerky, frightened cries began to break out on the night, the panic-stricken cries of men in the first throes of blindness, groping sightlessly in the midst of a new and shattering darkness. The paper fluttered to the ground. Grosman, evading the clawing hands, leaned over and picked it up. One of the constables, unable to believe the enormity of the thing that had overtaken him, was staring into the eye of his torch, feverishly stabbing the beam on and off, with the bulb pressed hard into his eye. And as fast as he moved the button his bewilderment increased, for, although he could feel the heat of the bulb against his eye, his brain did not register the faintest reaction to the sharp streak of light. He was as blind as though red hot irons had been thrust far down through the iris of his eyes.

Grosman turned and whistled, a low soft note that floated down the lane to Lingard. The drug runner, even at a range of seventy yards, had been affected by the blinding ray. He had been following the movements of the Chinese with frightened intensity, and when the glare came he was staring hard at the centre of the group. The beam died, and the resultant darkness, doubly emphasised after the shattering precipitation of brilliance, found him almost helpless. A wall of blackness enshrouded him, and he fumbled to the wall for guidance. He heard Grosman's signal, but it was some seconds before he could re-orientate his sight to the pall of the night.

The seamen had taken off their protective masks. Grosman sent one of them back to pilot Lingard away. The big man was still dazed. Grosman told him to hurry. He was tearing the message into infinitesimal pieces, tearing and retearing each fragment until it was smaller than confetti.

Grosman's car came purring round the corner and paused there.

"Is your car handy?" he asked Lingard.

Lingard nodded dumbly. He wanted to get away from the sight of the stricken men groping blindly about down there on the ground. Sterling could hear them talking, and he was making a last effort to get at them. But with the sudden onrush of utter blindness his sense of balance had gone. He could not remain upright for more than a couple of steps. Lingard's last vision of him was of a man, valiant to the last, making a series of body-shaking falls and staggering up again in a wild attempt to get at the man who had thrust the blackout of ultimate night upon him.

Lingard shuddered and turned away. "I have a car two streets away," he said. "For God's sake let me get away out of this."

"I will see you at noon tomorrow," replied Grosman. "Come to me with your plans. Hurry; the whole neighbourhood will be awake in a minute."

They climbed into the car, and the wheels were in motion before the door was slammed. The driver stopped just long enough to drop Lingard at his own car and then sped back to the side streets by the wharf. There they all separated and approached the *Yangtse* by different routes. Crouched in the far recesses of the store-sheds opposite, Manning watched them come creeping back. The gangway was lowered and one by one they silently stole on board. The last to come was Grosman himself. Manning saw him limping along by the mooring bollards, stepping heavily over the network of mooring lines and wire guys. The gangway rose again as his bulky figure went on board, and a minute later the silence of the night closed down over the river.

VII

Hillary opened her eyes slowly. A racking misery was crawling to life in her nerves. Her head throbbed maddeningly, and every heartbeat seemed to be bumping its way through her temples against a vast compression. She was in a bath of perspiration, and there was a feverish heat in her flesh that seemed to be consuming her. She tried to sit up, but the effort was beyond her. There was a palsy in her muscles, a flabbiness that rendered them lifeless; they were a part of her in thought only. She knew she had them, but they did not belong to her. There was a dead insulation between herself and her senses.

She tried to think, but her mind refused to concentrate. It forswore and denied her. She could not even arrive at the faintest idea of time. It appeared to be still late at night. At least, the electric lights were still burning. Then she saw that she was in a room without a porthole. Sunlight never penetrated there, and it might be blazing midday for all she knew.

She closed her eyes and relaxed. The streaming light, poised there a few feet above her head, stabbed at her eyes and hurt. It cut into her head like knives and gave her a feeling of nausea. It was as though she was being rapidly revolved in a spinning drum, with no chance of either stopping the drum or of getting out.

For many minutes she lay back, slipping back again into a state of comatose lethargy. All the beastliness, the misery, and the deadening lifelessness of the slow return from drugging was loaded heavily upon her.

Full consciousness began to return to her in a series of growing waves, and each recurring wave seemed to leave in its wake a greater and more profound sea of depression.

It was an hour before she had strength to move her body, and the action brought with it violent physical pains. She did not want to move, did not want to think, did not even want to breathe. It would have been a blessed relief to have quietly sunk away into oblivion, to have closed her eyes and let Death have his way with her. She did not want to live. An ocean of melancholic depression encompassed her. Gradually she opened her eyes again. The blinding jabbing in her head redoubled. A revolting sickness seized her like the aftermath of a long anaesthetising by chloroform. She turned over and wept in the sheer hopelessness of despair.

Hillary Kittredge did not know, but she was experiencing the first nauseating symptoms and reactions of the drug addict when the potence of the narcotic begins to wear off; a depression, a misery, a state of absolute mental bankruptcy that can only be warded off and nullified by yet another administration of the drug that caused it. In a little while her very blood would be burning for the spurious relief of cocaine.

Vaguely she remembered fleeting fragments of the events of the night. She tried to disentangle them from the webs of vacancy that surrounded them. She snatched at them blindly, and it exasperated her to realise that she always missed them. She could get nothing connected from the jumbled mass. It was another hour before it dawned upon her to look at the time by her wristwatch. The hands pointed to half-past two. But the watch had stopped, and it did not even occur to her to listen and see if it was still going.

Her eyes wandered vaguely round the room. It was about ten feet square, and she was lying on a heap of silken cushions in a corner. The walls were covered with beautifully worked tapestries. At the far end the gross figure of an enormous Buddha, stolid and complacent, gazed inscrutably down upon her. It was a hugely magnified counterpart of the one in the saloon. The squat bulk of it sat ponderously on a black ebony pedestal, and his eyes were focused on a small jade altar at his feet. A rich, heavily piled crimson carpet covered the floor. The room would have been quiet and restful but for those maddening lights.

Slowly it began to drift back on her torpid senses that she had been drugged. She turned her head listlessly to see if the tiny puncture was still there. And then she wept again in a revulsion of horror. Grosman had already started on his beastly plan to enslave her. There were not two, but four, minute red dots on the smooth whiteness of her arm. Already she was beginning to wish that she could get back to that calm rapture of the previous night—the first deadly symptom of the drug calling for yet more of the drug. She would have done anything to have got some of that fearful lassitude out of her body, to have got back to some sort of a mental poise, to free her head from the ceaseless drumbeats of her pulse in her temples.

But all she could think of was the four wicked little needle-pricks. They floated through her head and drifted past her eyes in an ominous procession. Even when she clenched up her eyes and tried to blot them out they persisted, portentous purple specks dug into the marble fairness of her flesh.

With a violent effort of will she sat up. Her head swam dizzily. Every nerve-end seemed to be quivering in fierce protest. She put up her hand to her bosom. It was fully five minutes before she realised there was something under her fingers, her brain was functioning with such dulled slowness. She looked down and saw a note pinned there.

It was written in the curious spidery scrawl peculiar to the Oriental. She read it. It was terse and frighteningly indicative.

Little Lady, (it ran)

I am sure, by the time you read this, you will admit your unwisdom in meddling with affairs that are in no wise feminine. Your cure has already begun. The treatment will be continued at six-hour intervals, gradually diminishing to three. In all other respects, little lady, you are unharmed. I find that white women, when under the influence of narcotics, are very uninteresting. No doubt we shall know something more of each other in a day or two when you are feeling more kindly disposed towards the acceptance of the needle. Should you require anything, you will find a bell-push in the bulkhead to your right. It rings directly into my cabin.

The Master.

She crumpled the note into a ball and shuddered. A wild phantasmagoria of thoughts went rocketing through her brain. In a startled effort to find a way of escape she swayed up to her feet. For a moment she stood, reeling, and then fell headlong to the floor. Her knees had no more strength in them than soft India-rubber, and there was a rancid biliousness in her stomach that made her want to get out and drown herself.

Her thoughts ran on disjointedly. Was this horrible nausea the inevitable result of the aftermath of every injection of cocaine? Did these numbing hours of wrecked physical powers always follow the indulgence of the habit? If so, human beings must be maniacs ever to pander to the morbid desire. This misery was not worth one single second of the brief exhilaration that had come to her overnight. Not worth a whole continuous day of it. But stay. Wasn't it? Wasn't anything better than this mind-killing, body-wracking torment? Would it not be better to make an effort to get just one more quick little dose of the soothing drug? Just one and no more? Certainly no more than one. After that the return to consciousness would be easier. She would know what to expect, and its effects would not be so terrible. But all drug addicts said that. They all thought along those self-defrauding lines. Just one and no more. They all carried privily in their own minds the secret thought that this would be the end of their troubles, that the next dose would be the last, and that from then on they could make the one magnificent effort that would get them back to sanity and re-establish themselves in their own estimation and self-esteem. Just one more dose. And then they would be in a condition to make the great effort. Always that "just one more dose"... and the effort that never came... Always it was the next time... and the next... and the next... until even they came to realise that, for them, the great opportunity would never come. Always it would be one longing for another healing draught as soon as the effects of the last had worn off. She could not conceive anyone enduring such a welter of abjection as she was experiencing just then... it was beyond human credulity... with the release so simple... just one more quick little stab with the needle... and then rest, release, soothing surcease from the burning aches that wracked her... "If you want anything you will find a bell-push in the bulkhead to your right."

And then the four ominous red dots came swimming before her blurred eyes again. They seemed to be scorching into the very tissues of her eyes. They were red lamps, danger signals that screamed their warnings at her. No one but a fool could be blind to their messages. Already she was falling, she, Hillary Kittredge, who had prided herself on the strength of her will, on the proud health of her young body, on the forthright sense and common intelligence that was part and parcel of her.

She shook herself and sat up against the cushions. Even if this miasma of crawling agony was the price to be paid for the winning back of her fine young fighting spirit, then it was worth the purchase. The first overdose had been so severe that the resultant reactions were doubly serious. Knowing, to the very last degree, the varying actions of all his drugs, Grosman had deliberately aimed to achieve that state to which she awoke. The necessity for just a morsel of the opiate would be too ravenous for refusal. He pictured the girl holding out that fair white arm, shakingly, tremblingly beseeching the relief of just a tiny injection of the filth that had hurt her.

She shuddered again. Memories had just come back to her of her thoughts about Grosman overnight. While the drug was taking effect she had actually begun to make excuses for the beast; distinct recollections came back to her of having persuaded herself into believing that he was not half so black as he was painted. And she had even doubted him guilty of having murdered Gilan Maxick. Great heavens, she thought, if cocaine made her conceive thoughts like that about the repulsive beast, where on earth would it end? If her hand had ever been in any danger of going out to that fatal bell-push, it was drawn back then, finally and forever. Hillary sat back on the pile of cushions and fought out her battle alone.

The little screaming devils that ran alive in the drug whispered, urged, goaded, tormented, stabbed at her, jabbed at her, poured scorn on her, pricked the very centres of her nerves with their poisoned lances, coaxed her, upbraided her, kidded her softly along, and then incontinently fell upon her in full force with a long-drawn attack of retching. Then a shivering ague seized her. And she sat through it all, shaking like a jelly, with her head in her hands—and the four red dots holding her grimly to her ordeal.

After two hours she began to feel the first relief of having held on. The fierce desire began to give way to an even fiercer hatred of the ghoul who had caused her sufferings. She no longer experienced the least desire to ring that bell or prayerfully offer her vein to him. All that was thrust behind her. Her head was beginning to clear and some of the frantic pains were going out of her bones. All that remained was a fury against Grosman, burning in the inner chambers of her soul like a fiery, white-hot coal. Strength of mind had come back to her, she was beginning to see things along a more level perspective. She got up and walked weakly round the apartment. That battle was over. The ordeal had been fearful; it had shaken her badly and left her weak as a kitten, but she had come through with it with scarcely a whimper.

And deep down in her heart a golden-clear exultant note was sounding. That same battle could be won again and again. Grosman could come in there and drug her, subject her to the hypodermic as often as he thought fit. By sheer physical force he could add to the number of those angry red dots. But he could never break that will—not now that she had already experienced the worst of it and come through with flying colours. As often as he drugged her she would fight back at him.

For she had made the great discovery—drug taking is the outcome of a purely mental state, the addiction to it is the result of a neuroticism already existing. Unless she herself wanted it, needed it to bolster an enfeebled nerve process, it could never get her enslaved in its toils. And she did not want it, she hated it. Her whole nature revolted against its sensualising effects. Afterwards, when the reckoning came, she could despise herself for the weakness of her thoughts overnight.

Womanlike, she peered round the place for a mirror. She knew that she looked ghastly. Her hair, wet with the perspiration of long endured pain, was draggled and matted into rat-tails, and her face was wet and shiny. There was not a spot of powder left on her skin, and her cheeks were the colour of fresh putty. But Grosman's Temple of Buddha had not been arranged to accommodate the requirements of a lady. The walls, rich in the luxury of priceless tapestries, were destitute of mirrors. She inspected the great Buddha. He was carved of a curiously smooth, oily stone, like soapstone, but of a far finer texture and much more beautiful graining. He was huge, towering up to the ceiling, and as firmly planted as a statue.

The whole place was overpoweringly hot. Without a single porthole or visible ventilation, the room had acquired a stuffiness that made, and kept her, drowsy. She wandered away from the idol. There, at the end of the pile of cushions, she saw her shoes, crinkled and shapeless where she had thrust them into her bosom before coming on board. With them, too, was her handbag. She blessed the bag if not the shoes. In it was a sufficient supply of lipstick and powder to make herself presentable and, glory of glories, there was a tiny magnifying mirror let into the flap.

For the first time she became aware of a serviette lying on the floor near the cushions. Under it was a tray of eatables—quite a palatable meal. There were some slices of breast of chicken, some cucumber shredded as fine as paper, a plate of bread-fingers, a little silver bowl of glaced fruits, and a glass of burgundy, and some water. She let the napkin fall over it again. The last thing in the world she felt like doing was eating.

She rolled back on to the cushions again and tried to think things out. But so far as she could see there was no way out. She would just have to lie there and make the best of it with Grosman's attacks, keeping up her fight till the river police discovered her plight and came through to her rescue. She took comfort from the knowledge that she had left at least one clue behind her. The car was left back there in the little cul-de-sac, idle and unattended. The police would soon discover the identity of the owner, and a few inquiries from Johnny would establish the connection with the *Yangtse*. The mere fact of her absence would send Johnny hopping round to Scotland Yard. And Toby himself would not be far behind. Between them they were not entirely lacking in brains. Johnny would certainly make inquiries at the Caverne Diamentée—he would discover from there that she had left within a few minutes of him. It might almost lead to the paragraphs in the morning paper.

She buoyed herself up with similar hopes until she began thinking it all out sanely again, and then suddenly it all seemed terribly depressing and hopeless. She set her lips and stuck out her chin determinedly. Thoughts like that would never do. There was nothing like keeping the bright side outward. Apparently Grosman had expected her to sleep much longer than she had or he would have been in to drug her again long before that. He had not reckoned on her fine young recuperative powers. With half her life spent in the out of doors, she had acquired almost the resilience of a man. That was the most comforting thought that had occurred to her. She got up again and walked about. She found that she felt better walking about. It was only when she rested flat on her back and let her thoughts run riot that the awful phase of depression returned.

She began feeling her way around the walls, hoping to find some secret hidden door. She knew there must be one somewhere, or a trapdoor in the floor. She hunted around, searching every tiny crack and crevice. But she could find nothing that even looked like a secret opening. She rolled back the great carpet, and underneath was nothing but the deck planking, thick, heavy, and as solidly founded as the day the ship came off the slips.

She decided it was time she sat down, had a cigarette, and made her toilet. And in the same breath she blessed the recollection of those cigarettes. There were seven left in her case, and somewhere in her bag there ought to be an automatic lighter. They would help to soothe her jumping nerves anyway. And it would be a good test of her will to ration herself—just so many whiffs off each cigarette and then carefully conserve the remainder.

And then, for some reason which she could not define, her attention was attracted again to the great stone Buddha. She sat on the corner of the divan and stared at him. And ever after she blessed the fact that the image distracted her from lighting that cigarette. She slowly put the bag back, unopened.

The possibility had just occurred to her of a secret opening being controlled from some fitment attached to the great god. She got up again and crossed over to him. She could not get behind him. He was flat back against the far wall and much too bulky to have been shifted. She inspected him from every angle, and there did not seem to be anything suspicious anywhere on his massive frame. She pushed and picked and probed, but every inch of him was as solid as Gibraltar. Then she climbed up on the jade altar to see if she could find a clue somewhere up on his benign head. And no sooner was her weight firmly set on the altar than she felt the whole thing give underneath her. The whole altar depressed a couple of inches. There was a soft click and the carved robe of the great god opened out like a door. The inside of him was as hollow as a box.

She gaped into the cavity. The god was packed full of cocaine tins. And on a ledge just inside the robe she saw something that sent a wild flush of thankfulness surging through her, something on which she fastened with all the savage eagerness of a cornered animal seeing the way of escape opening to it at last. It was a small silver case, beautifully chased, lined with puffed silk. But it was the contents that gave her her swift thrill. It was like Grosman to house ugliness in loveliness. For that beautiful example of the jeweller's art contained Grosman's private drug set. There were three crystal bottles of pure cocaine and two silver hypodermic syringes. A little of the cocaine had gone from the first bottle.

The colour came welling back to her cheeks, and there was a quick sparkle in her eyes. That was the very case which Grosman had used when he last administered the drug to her. It needed no brilliant inspiration to realise his method. He came in through the secret door, made sure that she still slept, opened the idol, and injected the drug from the case inside. On that supposition, he would use that same case each time he drugged her. She breathed a little prayer of thankfulness and seized the opportunity eagerly. Pure cocaine is colourless. And in the knowledge of that thrice blessed fact she saw salvation opening to her. Grosman had made the unconscious mistake of sending in a carafe of water on her lunch tray.

She hurriedly took out the bottles and drained out their contents, knowing that every second was precious. At any moment the Chinese might return and crush her newfound hopes. She carefully tipped out the liquid from the first bottle, pouring it over one of the bottom cushions of the divan. She rinsed the bottle with a little water from the carafe, and then carefully filled it to its previous level. The second she treated in the same way, filling the bottle to the top with the harmless water. She was about to empty the third when a newer and even more thrilling promise offered.

Tacked against the interior of the idol was a green felt tool satchel. It was a medical contrivance, divided off into thin perpendicular compartments and used for carrying forceps, tweezers, thermometer cases and general surgical paraphernalia. But this one contained the captain's own reserve of syringes. There were fifteen of them, of varying sizes, and some of the compartments were vacant. It was highly improbable that even Grosman's quick eyes would notice the absence of one, especially as only the merest tips of them protruded. She hastily selected one that would hold double as much as the one Grosman had used on her. In a few seconds she had filled it to its capacity and buried it under a cushion against the bulkhead. In it was enough anaesthetic to send a dozen men into unconsciousness, and, when she was lying there on the divan, it would be handy to her right hand. She rinsed and filled the third bottle with water, wiping the shining case with the utmost care, and then silently closed the door.

She leaned back against the wall, panting softly with excitement. The golden opportunity was taken and the preparations complete. There was a little trembling in her limbs as she contemplated the possibilities. And she half wondered if she would have the nerve to carry it through when the chance offered. Even under those frightening conditions murder was not an easy thing to contemplate—and there was every possibility that Grosman would be murdered if that ferocious dose ever got into his bloodstream. But the memory of the foul things he had done to her and the certainty of the still fouler things he intended, banished every squeamish thought from her head. She clenched her fists and swore that she would go through with it if it meant treating the whole loathsome crew in the same way.

She covered the meal tray with the napkin and lay back on the divan again. So far as she could see there was only one little thing in that cabin that could raise Grosman's suspicions, and that was so minute that the odds were a thousand to one that he would never notice it. The one thing was the level of the water in the carafe. She had lowered it by nearly half a pint, but he would have to raise the napkin to see it. And even if he did it was extremely unlikely that he would remember so insignificant an item as that. For the rest, she felt there was not a single loophole for her scheme to miscarry.

All she had to do was to lie there feigning sleep, and the mandarin would never dream she had waked. She thanked her lucky stars she had refrained from smoking that cigarette. The fumes would have given her ruse away to that sharp nose. She had eaten nothing. Even the wine was untouched. And her face was unpowdered, her lips innocent of the touch of the lipstick. Her whole appearance and everything in the room was exactly the same as when Grosman had last left it. All she had to do was to lie and wait and hope he came while the drug pallor was still upon her. Then, if anything of courage and her own tigerish fighting spirit could avail, she would force the way of escape from that hell place alive—even though she left a dead body behind her.

Her heart was pumping as the minutes slowly passed. Another cracking headache assailed her, and it was followed by a return of the shivering ague. But the attack was in no way so severe as the first. Not a sound reached her. The place seemed to be insulated from the outside world. She was watching with the intensity of an expert watching for the solution of a conjuring trick. All her plans and hopes depended upon whether she discovered the secret of how Grosman got into the room. Without that she was penned in there for as long as the captain himself.

At last, after what seemed an eternity of hours, each one of which ticked ponderously and singly through her very brain, there came the faintest sound from the far wall. Instantly she relaxed on the cushions like a log and began to breathe in long, steady exhalations, her lips slightly parted, her breasts gently rising and falling. The sound had come from a tapestried panel immediately on the right of the giant image. It was vague, like the sound of a faint scratching behind the wall, and she could not locate its exact position. She watched tensely through eyes that were almost closed, her long lashes veiling the narrow glints that shone in them.

Slowly, the tall panel revolved on a central pivot until it was swung out squarely into the room. Immediately the panel began to move the glaring cluster of lights overhead went out, and small groups of lights, dim and diffused, lit up in the high corners of the ceiling.

She waited on with her blood beginning to chill. Grosman did not appear. The girl lay back doing her utmost to appear as though still in a stupor, to control her breathing to the normal easiness of sleep. Soon she heard the soft padding of footsteps coming up what was apparently a passage behind the panel.

The captain appeared in the entrance, staring silently at the piled up masses of cushions, his eyes boring greedily at the picture of slim, feminine daintiness reclining there. He came slowly into the room and gently closed the panel behind him. And as the wards of the lock slid home the lights came on again. Apparently the lighting arrangement was a signal to him when in the Temple that the outer door in the saloon had been opened.

He was dressed in his ceremonial robes of rich blue silk, embroidered with a riot of marvellous colourings. Around his middle was a girdle of silk worked in gold. He raised his arms and bowed to the Buddha, and the sleeves of his robes fell away a yard from his wrists.

The girl lay motionless as he came towards her. He stood by the side of the divan, his hands loosely folded, staring down at her. She could hear his breathing, laboured with desire. For a whole minute she bore his avid scrutiny as he bent over her, listening to her half inaudible respiration.

He peered round the room, seeming puzzled at her long sleep. He touched her softly, stroking her arm that was snuggled up beside her head. Then he brushed her eyelids, and the lids did not even flicker. He glanced down at the tray of victuals, opened her bag and counted the cigarettes. He appeared to be satisfied that she was really asleep, still drifting through the drugged torpor of lazy unconsciousness, for he tiptoed to the Buddha, made another profound obeisance, and leaned his weight heavily on the altar. The side of the robe opened and he took out the hypodermic case. With deft, practised fingers, he took one of the syringes, inserted it in the neck of the bottle, and extracted a measured dose. He held it up to the light and examined it. There appeared to be a little too much for his requirements, for he carefully squirted a few drops back into the bottle. There was humour in the idea of the man taking such meticulous pains over a drop or two of totally innocuous water, but the comedy of it was lost on Hillary. She was beginning to feel sickeningly nervous. The horrible thought had just occurred to her that there in front of her was a human being who, in a minute or two, would be slowly sinking into the lethargy of death. That great virile brute would soon be drifting helplessly to his doom. He was taking the last few footsteps of his earthly life. Those precise, measured actions of his, as he graduated the dose, were his last. And she was going to be the agent responsible for his end. Within the next minute or two she was going to be a murderess; all her life she would be self-stigmatised with the knowledge that she had murdered a human being. She felt like a spider crouched in its lair waiting the approach of its unwary victim.

He came back to the divan and put the loaded syringe carefully on the floor beside her. Then he shook her gently, taking her by both arms and half lifting her from the couch. Her head lolled back, and she hung limp in his arms. He shook her again and let her fall back on the cushions. She felt her hand taken and squeezed powerfully.

"Little lady," he breathed huskily, "wake up. Wake up. You have slept too long. You must wake and eat. And in a little while, when the pains course through your body, you will cry to me for another kiss of the needle."

He shook her roughly and seemed determined that she should wake. Her eyelids began to flutter. The idea was dawning on her that it would be better to wake and speak to him. Then, when the opportunity presented itself of thrusting the needle into him, she would be able to move with far more hope of success. If she suddenly leapt into activity from an apparently profound comatose condition he would be so startled that the common instincts of self-preservation would make him grapple with her and then the opportunity would be gone forever.

She feebly opened her eyes and as feebly closed them again. A long sigh escaped her. Dense lines of pain creased across her forehead, and she put up her hand as though to shield her eyes from the bright glare of the lights. She heard a satisfied grunt from above her, and Grosman went back to the Buddha and closed the robe into position.

She tried to sit up but relaxed again as though the effort was not worth the pain set up in her limbs. Grosman came back and sat on the cushions beside her. She heard his oily, suggestive voice.

"Little lady, wake. Your little friend is here, your little friend the syringe that will smooth out all troubles, soothe away all pains, and show you only the brightness of life again."

She opened her eyes again and stared round her with a puzzled expression. For a minute she did not speak. He was too well versed in the symptoms of the drug addict returning to consciousness not to know that it is impossible for them to talk. It is many minutes before the first glimmerings of mental contacts return. She licked her lips and tried to swallow. Unconsciously she was repeating the same actions as when first she began to come to her senses. And all the time his gross fingers were fondling her as an over-fond woman caresses her babe. Her brain revolted against it, his great body against her was overpoweringly repulsive. She wanted to rise up and lash him across the face, to feel the tough bones of her young knuckles pounding into the fat flab of his flesh, to take a toll of physical pain out of his sensuous body for all her outraged sensitiveness of womanhood.

But she endured it. And her anger, her temper, and her determination grew. He pushed some cushions behind her shoulders and forced her to sit up. He rubbed her hands and shook her again. She tried to push him off, and it was the first actively conscious gesture she had made.

"Leave me alone—please leave me alone," she whispered faintly. Then after a little while she muttered: "My head. Oh, my head."

"Your head aches, little lady? I'm afraid it will ache for some time—and the ache will increase." His voice was infinitely soothing, infinitely compassionate. "But I have something here that will ease it, my dear, Something that will soften the pains almost before you know they are upon you." He stroked her face again; and she did not try to repel him. "One tiny prick with the needle—and all your sorrows will begin to melt away. You can count the seconds as they pass. As the healing fluid finds the troubled nerves all the aches and pains will gently go to sleep again. The world will become rosy with delight. The future will hold nothing but the rapture of dreams again. But you must *ask* me for it first, little lady. Never again shall I press the needle unwillingly into that sweet arm. I want you to ask me for it. Won't you. Won't you offer me your arm and plead for the soothing balm?"

The ingratiating voice purred on in her ear. She listened to him as though through a daze. Her uncomprehending eyes focused on him in a deep frown of puzzlement. Then she looked uncertainly from him to the great stone Buddha, and her eyes wandered round the luxurious appointments of the Temple.

"Where am I?" she gasped. "What place is this?" Then as though the effort of speaking was too much for her she lolled back on the cushions.

Grosman leaned over, flicked the napkin off the tray and picked up the glass of burgundy. He held it to her lips and tipped it. She felt the cold press of the liquid against her mouth and drank. There was no need for acting there, for her mouth was as dry as a kiln. She drained the wine and thanked him weakly.

She was in a quandary. She knew which panel opened, and had a fair idea where the panel led to. But she had not the faintest notion of how it operated. Already the way was being paved for her to make her escape—and yet, right on the threshold of freedom, the door was barred to her. If she used the needle on him the man would be unconscious in a couple of minutes. It was doubtful if he would have time to get to the door. And she would be penned in there with a dying man. In half an hour the dying man would be a dead man—and she, imprisoned in a soundproof room with a body! The thought was scarifying. It was vitally necessary for her to discover the secret of opening that revolving panel.

"Don't you know me?" crooned the slimy voice in her ear; it seemed to come up from the nethermost walls of sensualness.

She made a real effort to clear away the haze from her brain. For long seconds she stared at him, trying to concentrate on her surroundings. Gradually a fuller understanding returned to her, and a look of horror passed over her face. She put out her hands to push him away, but he caught and held them with childish ease.

"Gently, little one, gently," he murmured. "In a little while, when you are fully awake, you will not think so unkindly of me. You will dread the thought of me going away without giving you what you need. You will beg and pray of me to stay. But first you must eat. You have been too long asleep. Far too long. And it is not good for you. When you have had a little meal you shall have another tiny vein-sip of the sweet water. Not so much this time, little one. For I do not want you to go to sleep. I want you to get back to that radiant rapture of the first few minutes... you remember? When all the world seemed sweet and the troubles and worries were lifted away from you like a curtain? You shall get back to that blissful state, but, little one, you shall stay awake to enjoy it. And never again will you think evilly of the master."

He picked her up and set her uncertainly on her feet. Holding her by the arm he walked her round the room. He was reeking with scent and the smell of it made her faint.

"Leave me alone!" she panted. "I don't want any more of your beastly drug."

"Ah, but you will, my dear," he assured her. "In a little while when your nerves are again able to register properly, you will be crying for it."

And then he declared himself in all his vileness. "Even if you don't fall so easily as the rest," he said, "even if you fight against it a little longer than the others, it will get you in the end. Every piece of food that comes in to you will be faintly powdered with the precious dust. Every drop of water sent in to you will be impregnated with the water of delight. Even the burgundy you have just drunk—"

She broke from his grasp and started back with a gasp of horror. But he took her again and chuckled.

"Do not be alarmed," he said softly. "It was drugged, little lady, but not with cocaine. Oh no. There was something much more subtle, something much more—shall we say, interesting?—in that little draught of wine. Really, it was not necessary for *you*. You are young and in full possession of all your virile youth. That drug is only taken by those whose years are on the wane, whose powers are no longer on the full flood of glorious youth. But you have heard of such things, I am sure. You appreciate its point." The tones of his voice seemed to be stroking her in the same way that his eyes were devouring her. "It was just a little boost," he said. "You might not be feeling yourself, might not be—as the saying is—up to the mark, after your little ordeal of the past few hours. But you will be feeling much better soon, much better, little lady."

"You beast!" Hillary turned and faced him with blazing eyes.

Grosman frowned. Such violent passion, such heaping scorn and fiery indignation was foreign to one who had only just returned from the depths of a serious injection of cocaine. He looked at her darkly, the first faint rustlings of suspicion beginning to whisper in his brain.

"So!" he growled, and seized her violently, staring straight into her eyes. He read there the truth. The girl was play-acting at him. Those eyes were not the eyes of a girl still struggling to clear away the fogs of anaesthesia. They were clear, alive, and the brain behind them was active. He could feel the strength in the pressure of her arms. Her weakness was all a pose.

He flung her fiercely back on the cushions and forced his knee against her chest. The man went into a sudden frenzy. She punched and pummelled and kicked at him and tried to free herself, but his weight held her down. He seized her arm and bared it to the elbow.

She struggled frantically, hammering at him like a virago. The robe slid away from his thigh, and with a sickly revulsion of disgust she saw that the brilliant royal blue robe was the only garment he was wearing.

And suddenly, like a sunburst, the realisation broke upon her that here was the opportunity for which she had prayed, the God-given chance of ridding herself forever of the grim menace of the Oriental. The Chinese, holding her down by his bared knee, her arm held straight out along the cushions, was leaning over away from her to get at his hypodermic. The force of his grip on her wrist was agonising. She scratched at his leg and tore at him with a flurry of nails. Wildly she groped among the cushions for the hidden syringe. Her questing fingers found it and fastened on it with the viciousness of frenzy.

After such a savaging as she had scored on his thick skin there was not the faintest possibility of his feeling the tiny prick of the needle making ingress. And even if he did he would neither know what it was nor have time to prevent the dose from being injected. She pinched him with all her might over the purple blue of a vein, and then, before the nerves could react, she forced the needle point in and began to squeeze down on the grip.

She felt the stuff going in. An odd thought fluttered through her head; she had never imagined it would require so much pressure. If she had thought of it at all she had expected the drug would flow in as easily as though she was squeezing it into thin air. But against the tough flesh she found she had to exert all the strength of her lithe young fingers.

The piston head was halfway down the cylinder. Grosman had already received enough of the deadening narcotic to render him senseless for some hours, and she was aware of a sweeping thrill at the thought of having beaten him with his own weapons. Then came a tiny prick in her own arm, just a suspicion of a stab, so minute that she scarcely noticed it against the pain of his grip on her arm. She knew that Grosman had retrieved his syringe and was pressing the dose into her. And all in that wild, incredible moment she wanted to laugh, to burst out into peals and peals of hysterical laughter. In a mad, rabid way she saw the grotesque, macabre farce of Grosman's efforts—he trying to drug her with harmless water, while she had already pumped enough of the real drug into him to knock him into a stupor for hours to come.

She never knew what happened in the next few seconds. A whole age seemed to spin through her head with each moment. All she remembered was that after what seemed interminable hours she found that the piston head of her hypodermic was rammed down hard against the neck of the glass cylinder and that she was staring at it. She had taken it out and it was there in her fingers, her fingertips still cupped round the grip and the palm of her hand still constricting madly on the handle.

She thrust her hand back against the bulkhead and rummaged down among the cushions, forcing the instrument far down. The awful crush weight of Grosman's thigh was lifting from her breast. She saw him fling the syringe against the wall and stand up. He released her arm and stood there, glowering down at her as though he would have liked to have taken her up and torn the limbs out of her. He was panting with fury, and the perspiration of desire was beading out upon his forehead. His brows were dark as a thundercloud, and he mouthed unutterable things at her. His vanity had been torn to shreds, kicked and trampled on. Grosman, who thought he knew every infinitesimal phrase and nuance of cocaine consumption and its after effects, had been fooled by a woman, bluffed by the very girl on whom he had centred his lustful intentions. He was ravaged between the mastering emotions of fury and desire.

"So! Little brat! You would make a fool of me," he rumbled, and his words seemed to come from deep down in his chest, from a very tempest of fury that lurked there. His fat fingers were working in queer, spasmodic jerks, itching to get at her smooth white throat: but in his eyes was the burning gloat of dominance. She was at his mercy, alone, helpless, and, though she screamed her lungs out, no whisper of it would pass beyond those dumb walls. And she was white, and beautiful—even in her rumpled disarray she was beautiful.... The dark eyes glowed hotly.

She stared back at him challengingly, crouched back against the bulkhead. She was all flexed for a spring. It only required a few seconds now, and the great brute would be sinking down to the floor, and she was ready to claw the eyes out of him rather than let him get those foul hands on her again.

But Grosman was not eager to rush. He knew the potence of the drugs he had administered and knew their effects could not be long delayed. He watched her as a cat watches a mouse, his eyes fixed on her face, watching for the first symptom to become manifest. He knew what it would be, a gradual diminution of that animal fighting glare, a softening of that passionate, warlike defence. The slow amalgamation of the two drugs would be irresistible. In a few minutes she would be relaxing on the cushions, unable—and unwilling—to defend herself. She would be limp and responsive, a softly caressive little child who would look on him with eyes of pleasure.

Meanwhile there was an odd coldness coming over him, a spreading numbness that was not altogether pleasant. It was some seconds before he realised its presence; it seemed at first like a quickly passing shiver. He was not worried, his attention was centred too hungrily on the lovely little thing crouching there on the divan.

He waited. Still she crouched there, tigerish, vixenish with aggression. Suddenly, just for a fleeting second, she blurred before his eyes. It was all over in a moment, like a picture gone momentarily out of focus, but it was startlingly real. And that odd chill was increasing. His left leg felt extraordinarily heavy, as though he had to exert double the power to lift it as he did the right. He brushed a hand fitfully over his eyes. It was all very unusual. His faculties did not usually play him tricks like that. He had half an impression that he was experiencing the first rush of a terrific overdose of cocaine. Only once had he done that, when the strength of his drug had been unexpectedly changed and he had given himself a normal shot of a mixture five times as strong. But he banished the thought almost before it was formed. It was impossible. He had not taken a spot of the stuff for weeks. He only resorted to it when going down through the Red Sea, where the murderous heat was too much even for him who had been nurtured on the sweltering banks of the Yangtse Kiang; and a man must do something to get the thoughts of the sun out of his head.

He took a step towards her, and a puzzled frown spread over his face. For though mentally he performed the action of taking that step forward, he was bewilderingly conscious of the knowledge that he had not moved an inch. His nerves had moved, but his muscles and his body had remained immobile. He tried to move his leg again, but it remained rigid. He grunted gutturally and tried to pull himself together. Something had gone radically wrong. The whole of his left leg had gone dead. He could feel it with his fingers, but he could not feel it with his leg! He pinched his thigh incredulously, and his amazement increased. He could not feel it even though he dug the exaggeratedly pointed thumbnail deep into the flesh. He lifted the right leg and almost fell over, for the right leg seemed to be functioning properly, but the left would not adjust itself to the shift of his weight. And—and—somehow it seemed all utterly absurd and impossible, but the lustful heats were dying out of his body. He no longer desired that lovely creature with every fibre that was in him, he no longer regarded her as the ultimate perfection of feminine seductiveness.

The sweat on his brow was turning clammily cold, and his loins felt leaden. The left leg was completely gone. There was less feeling in the sensory nerves than if he had slept on it all night with the leg doubled up beneath him. All the numbing ache that preceded a drastic attack of pins and needles was coursing through it. He tapped his right leg jerkily, feverishly. That, too, seemed to be losing its strength. He could not move; and a vast "still" was coming over him, a lack of warmth and an entire absence of feeling that was positively frightening. Thoughts were slipping out of his head—he was not even worrying whether there were any thoughts there or not. All he knew was that he wanted to get away out of the lungchoking stuffiness of that cabin, out into the fresh air, out anywhere so long as it was away from that glittering-eyed little harridan in front of him, that fierce-eyed little beast who, for the first time in his memory, had refused to succumb to the dictates of cocaine administered direct through a vein. It was totally incredible, unbelievable. But there she was, full of fighting spirit still, a direct proof of the staggering fact that a girl can take a drug one day and lie unconscious for hours and the next day fight back as though her constitution was impervious to any toxin in the pharmacopoeia. His thoughts swayed up into a bibulous perplexity; he was flatly beginning to disbelieve the evidence of his own senses.

The palms of his hands were like slabs of ice, wet ice, and there was a continuous tremor running through his biceps. He tried to force himself, but he could not keep the muscles still. He blinked and stared down at the girl. There was a slight bump in the cabin, and he found himself staring *up* at the girl—Captain Grosman had slumped down to his knees.

And then she laughed, a shrill, piercing cackle of high-pitched laughter that progressed up the scale through breathless relief to wild hysteria. It rang though the room like a thunderclap and ceased as abruptly. With her hands clutching up at her throat she gazed down at him, fascinated. A man was dying under her eyes—and she had done it, she had administered the poison that was slowly and surely sending him out to his Creator. And there was neither remorse nor pity in her.

He blinked again as he looked up at her; blinked slowly, for the drug was spreading up to his head. She had found the great thigh vein, and the thin stream of the fluid, mingling with the blood, had gone quickly back to the heart, to be pumped to every part of him. He made a violent effort to collect his fast-scattering faculties. That ringing laugh had something to do with it. It pierced right through to his brain. There was something in the fierce note of it, something of triumph and savage mockery that was directed straight at him.

It came upon him with the force of a mule kick: these horrible sensations, these deadening waves of inertia that were sweeping over him—they *were* the symptoms of a fearful over-administration of cocaine.

The shock of it sent mental activity flooding back through his brain. He knew that in some way totally beyond his comprehension he had absorbed a tremendous dose of the killing drug. From the frightening sensations that were coursing through him he knew that a fatal dose had somehow got into his system. In a little while he would be writhing with convulsions. The urgent demand for action was hammering at him, kicking him into motion. His arms were still able to move, though terribly slowly, but a deadly, overweighted dullness was inevitably mounting to his brain. He felt its relentless ascent and fought against it with a cold vengefulness. The girl's face, the glittering look of triumph there that lit it up as though with a flame, told him that it was no accident, no astonishing freak She was responsible. She had premeditated it, planned it, and somehow, by some utterly incredible means, she had put her scheme into execution.

Something had got to be done before that fearful coldness enveloped him. By sheer physical strength he began hauling himself across the floor. He progressed like a great lizard, his legs trailing out uselessly behind him. His weight was on his forearms, and his action was a slow, gross waddle. The altar was only a few feet from him, and he exerted his last ounce of effort to reach it. He needed to get that great idol open again. There were antidotes in there, precious mixtures that would nullify to some extent the awful virulence of the stuff that was running amuck in him. His rate of progress slowed visibly even before he reached the altar. But he kept on, with ice-cold beads of sweat beginning to drip from his chin.

Hillary watched him with wide, staring eyes. The grim fight the man was putting up frightened her. His jaws were clenched up until the fines of his lips were almost invisible. She found herself praying feverishly for the man's powers to wane away into oblivion.

He reached the altar at last and hung there panting. She wanted to jump off the divan and force him back, to hold him down until the long sleep overtook him. Sudden misgivings assailed her. His actions were so definite, so purposeful, that she began to be afraid. He had some new trick up his sleeve, some unexpected expedient that was surely going to wreck her hopes.

It took him long seconds to get one great arm up over the altar. She could see the muscles on his neck standing out in thick cords, and the big blue veins were pulsing with the effort he was putting out. Slowly the other arm came up and, with an unbelievable exertion of sheer willpower, he hauled himself up. His weight came on it, and the jade slab sank. The concealed door swung open. The promise of life blossomed again for him, the precious antidotes were lying there within a yard of him, a little nest of bottles that seemed to be grinning at his helplessness. He fell away from the altar with a thud, and his hand went out shakily for the bottle.

It was a matter of seconds for Grosman. He moved as one moves in a nightmare when some horrible apparition is following, with limbs that were weighted beyond the strength to lift them, as though powerful elastics at full tension were attached to every muscle. Hillary covered her face with her hands. She had suddenly become frightened of herself. The very thoughts of murder horrified her. Now that the thing was done it became an enormity in her eyes. A wild scurry of thoughts flashed through her head. Why had she given him so much? Why hadn't she been content merely to have given him sufficient to have sent him unconscious for a few hours? She knew the quantity of the dose near enough. She had seen Grosman himself measure it out the first time he drugged her. A little more than that would have sufficed, and her whole purpose would have been served.

Grosman would have been knocked out long enough for her to have ferreted out the secret of opening that revolving panel. And even if he regained consciousness before she was free she could always have given him another shot from the needle. The big man never quite reached the bottles. He collapsed within a foot of them. His great shoulders slumped down flat on the floor, and only his eyes remained alive, staring sombrely at the little vials of salvation, beyond his reach by a foot.

Hillary found herself getting off the divan without really knowing what she was doing. A stronger, more domineering self seemed to have entered her and taken charge of her actions. Shakily she crossed the floor and knelt by the stricken man. It was apparent to her that there was something in that receptacle of which the man stood in dire need. She was eager to give him that much assistance. So far as she knew, she was administering a crumb of comfort to a man already beyond help.

Hurriedly she took the bottles and held each one questioningly before his eyes. She had to do it in dumb-show, for Grosman's eardrums were no longer working. As she held up the third bottle he signalled with a scarcely noticeable twitch of his face muscles that that was the one he wanted. She wrenched the cork out and held the neck of the bottle to his lips. Slowly the liquid trickled down his throat. When he had had enough he let his head fall away. And still that compelling, insistent command shone in his eyes. She realised there was something more he wanted.

Again she took up the bottles and held them before him. And again he signalled his need of one of them, a bottle containing a pale brown liquid. But when she held it to his lips he resolutely shut his mouth. For a moment she was dumbfounded. It was obvious that the man needed the mixture with every scrap of yearning that was in him, and yet he refused it. She looked at him distractedly, and still he was beseeching her with his eyes to give him the antidote. It was a desperate quandary, and she could see no way out.

She tried him again with the bottle, and a leaden look of hopelessness came into his eyes. It was as though he knew he was passing out, with salvation holding out both hands to him and only ignorance holding it back. She looked down at him in helpless remorse. And then she noticed the faintest twitching of the muscles of his throat. He was doing his utmost to speak, but the vocal cords were no longer able to vibrate. She bent her head until her ear was close against his mouth. A hissy whisper, so faint that it seemed to be part of his exhaling breath, said: "Wrist—inject."

She scrambled to her feet, cursing her blindness. It ought to have been obvious even to a child that a poison injected into the blood would require the antidote to be administered in the same way. She snatched a syringe from the satchel and filled it with a quick snapping back of the plunger. With a woman's intuition she ignored the wrist, realising that Grosman did not know where the drug had been injected. To her it seemed fairly plain that the antidote would do most good if given in the same spot as the drug itself.

By that time Grosman was too far gone thoroughly to appreciate what she did. He could not help her gauge the dose, so she gave him the whole syringeful. Before she had finished, Grosman was lying like a dead man. She did her best to make him comfortable on the cushions, but in her weak state it was many minutes before she could get his ungainly bulk raised and settled. Afterwards she had to sit and rest to still her shaking limbs.

A deathly quiet hung over the place. The only sound that disturbed the silence was the cramped, laboured breathing of the man on the couch. His face had taken on a sickly yellow pallor. She turned away with a shiver.

Her immediate task was to discover the secret of the panel, and she set about it with a will. It had not occurred to her that, having got the panel opened, almost certain recapture awaited her on the other side. All she wanted to do was to get out of that horrible place. She had not the vaguest idea whether it was day or night outside. If it was broad daylight the whole crew would be up and about and her chances of getting clear were slight indeed.

The deathly silence of the place made her flesh creep. There was something machine-like in the soft hiss of escaping breath from the man on the couch. For the sake of getting her nerves under control she began thinking aloud, telling her own inmost thoughts to herself, trying to co-ordinate the loose ends of her tangled ideas.

"Hillary Kittredge," she said with tight-lipped gravity, "you are in the very devil of a mess. And what is more, you darned fool, you got into it yourself. Grosman was right; I've got nothing more than I deserved for interfering with what was essentially a job for men. Hillary Kittredge, you're frightened. You are. You're dead scared. Gosh—I wish that beast wouldn't wheeze like that. If Toby saw you now, my girl, he'd laugh your head off. Or would he? Blessed if I know. You never know what men will do. Probably go mad and sink the whole ship, hook, line, and sinker. That'd be fun. Provided I was having a comfortable snooze about ten miles inland. Oh, for a nice hot bath and my own bed—nice clean sheets and the window open. All the windows open—open wide. Phew—this place is stifling. Wonder what the folks are thinking at home? There's going to be holy murder for me when I get back. *If I get* back. Dad will go pots. Probably already gone pots by now. Wonder if he's got that Scotland Yard billet yet? Wouldn't it be a scream if his first job was to haul his dutiful daughter out of a Chinese hooker by the scruff of her neck. M'm, jam for everybody but me. I'll bet he docks my pocket money for a month. And I'll bet I deserve it. Of all the born fools, Hillary Kittredge, you're the one outstanding first-class example. Will you ever poke your long nose again into other people's affairs? Yes, my girl, *you will not*—and well you know it. Well, having had the courage of your own insanity and admitted it, what are we going to do about it?"

She sat, very quietly, with her hands in her lap, thinking out the position. It had just occurred to her that, having got the revolving panel open, her troubles were by no means over.

"What would Toby do?" she demanded of the atmosphere. "Certain sure he wouldn't go bullheaded at the job of opening that panel," she muttered. "For all I know there may be half a dozen Chinese in that saloon. And then I *would* be in for a gaudy time." She shivered again and looked helplessly at the insensible Chinese. His face had lost even the yellow pallor. It had taken on a ghastly hue like solid quicksilver that had lost its sheen and only retained its leadenness.

"Even if I get out," she argued, "it's a hundred to one I won't be able to get off the ship. If it's daylight I'll surely have to wait for nightfall. And where can I hide till then? And how can I get a message ashore?"

That was an inspiration that gave her an idea. She was in possession of certain knowledge that would be of inestimable value to the authorities that were tracking down the gang. It was knowledge of which only she was aware. Wouldn't it be the sensible thing to do to write it all down as clearly as possible, actually to put it into writing, so that if the opportunity occurred of getting into touch with a friendly spirit, her message would get into the hands of either Manning or Procter with the least possible delay? The wheels would then be immediately set in motion for her rescue—and what was honestly more to her even in that pressing emergency, the police would have all the information they needed to arrest the whole gang. She decided that it was the most sensible idea that had occurred to her since that idiotic night in the Caverne Diamentée when she had first decided on the fool venture.

She opened her bag and took out a little gold pencil and a tiny memorandum book. Also she remembered the cigarettes. With a sigh of thankfulness she lit one and blew long blue streamers at the ceiling. The nicotine soothed her tormented nerves, and she smoked the cigarette right down to a stub.

Then she turned resolutely to the task of writing her evidence.

> This is Hillary Kittredge (she wrote). I am imprisoned in a secret compartment on board the "Yangtse,"

the entrance to which I believe is through the after bulkhead in the saloon. Grosman, the captain, is in here with me, drugged. I drugged him myself after he had already forced four injections of cocaine on me. I have no idea of how long I have been here, but it was about three o'clock on Wednesday morning when I first came on board. Grosman is the big cocaine smuggler the police have been looking for for years. It, I mean the cocaine, is stored in this secret room. You will find it in the great stone Buddha, here in what he calls the Temple. You can open the robe of the Buddha by leaning all your weight on the green jade altar in front of the god. I don't know how the secret entrance works from the saloon, but ingress to here is effected through the tapestry panel immediately to the right of the god. When I have written this I am going to try to force it. Grosman is probably dying. I gave him a whole syringeful of pure cocaine. But just before he went unconscious he managed to swallow an antidote which you will also find in the body of the Buddha. When I came here I got into the steward's service-room and listened to a conversation between Grosman and a man called Blind Rudley. Rudley is the man who pretends to hawk studs and things round the riverside public-houses, but is in reality the chief messenger between Grosman and a man named Lingard. From what they said it appears that Lingard is the head of the distribution organisation of the gang. Lingard is getting restive and Grosman has threatened him. They have a code method of communicating between themselves whenever Grosman wants to get into touch with Lingard on important affairs. It is this. Grosman sends Lingard a plain post card, and from that alone Lingard knows that something urgent has happened and that

Grosman wants to see him at once. There is no writing on it whatever—just a plain card addressed to Lingard. So that if you can discover Lingard's address you have only to send him a plain card and then trail him when he sets out to obey the summons for that card calls him to their secret rendezvous. Where that rendezvous is I don't know, but I do know from their conversation that there is one and that that is where they meet when there is important business afoot. Grosman brings the drugs to England and lands them and Lingard does the rest. How Grosman lands the cocaine I don't know and neither does Lingard. I think that is what the friction is about. But there is an enormous quantity of the stuff here in the Buddha and from what they said there is another huge store of it somewhere on shore in their secret rendezvous. If you can trail Lingard to that place I think you will get the biggest haul of your lives. There is one other thing I want to say, and that is, that Grosman is the man who murdered Gilan Maxick. I was present on the river when the police were recovernig his body, and I warned Sergeant Manning of my suspicions. Incidentally, I was thoroughly well smiled at for my pains. Still, that is neither there nor here. But it was in consequence of that that I find myself in this particular predicament, and I would mention that no one will be more delighted and relieved than myself if you will rescue me without any further delay. I have a good deal of information to impart, but it is of minor importance and merely corroborates what I have already written here. All my evidence is at your disposal, and, if Grosman lives, I assure you I shall not have the slightest objection to being a witness when he comes up for trial. But at the present moment I must say that he does not show any particular signs of ever seeing the inside of

> the dock. That is all. I will do my best to get this ashore by someone I can trust. But if I should be unfortunate and get recaptured, I am going to slip these pages in the heel of my stocking and trust to them being discovered. That is, if they should kill me—which wouldn't surprise anyone if you knew them as well as I do. There should be enough evidence here for you to trace them down and act accordingly. That is about the best I can do. Anyhow I knew I was right about what I said to Sergeant Manning on the river. And you would be conferring a favour on me if you would kindly carry this message to Mr. Toby Essex, whose motor speed boat lies up at the moorings by the Houses of Parliament.
>
> Yours faithfully,
>
> HILLARY KITTREDGE.

Having finished it, she read it through from beginning to end. Her efforts at clearness and concision at first amazed her and then disgusted her. "Well, I'm blest," she muttered. "If Manning ever gets hold of this he'll think it's come from a maniac—or a practical joker. And I wouldn't blame him either. Of all the fool bits of writing, it's just about the dotty limit." It did not occur to her that, despite the shock of her savage treatment and of the mental uproar that was still seething in her head, she had somehow managed to get every fact in her possession down on paper. And, womanlike, she had also managed to get in her own self-righteous "I told you so," at the people most concerned.

The fact was that Hillary Kittredge, thanks to the clean living virility and resilience of her young body, was rapidly getting back to the full use of her faculties. The fact was evidenced by her subsequent actions, for the addressing of her missive presented only minor difficulties. She tore out the pages, rolled them tightly into the cylinder of her pencil, leaving the edges slightly protruding above the pencil-case. Then she rummaged an old dance programme from her handbag and wrote a hurried note upon it.

"The finder of this pencil will be rewarded with a ten-pound note from Sir John Kittredge if he will take it, intact, immediately to Sergeant Manning at the river police station, Wapping."

She tied the programme to the pencil with the cord, stuck the whole lot in an old envelope and hid it in her dress. Then she turned her attention to the panel. She went over it with the care of a searcher hunting for a gold lode; she pressed it from every angle, sideways, up and down, lengthwise, and across the middle. And the result was precisely nil. She charged her whole weight against it and the panel did not even budge. She drew back and regarded the thing spitefully. In her own mind she had hardly expected to stumble on the secret at the first attempt. Grosman was too ingenious to do the obvious, she had seen too much of his methods not to know that.

The thought brought a brighter idea. Admitting that Grosman had a positive genius for hiding his methods, was it likely that he would leave the system of opening that panel to the accidental experiments of a stranger? Wasn't it far more likely that the trick of opening that panel would only be discovered after a covering secret had been elucidated? It seemed highly probable to her. Almost intuitively her thoughts turned to the great Buddha. That would be just about on a level with Grosman's general craftiness, to hide the secret of the panel inside the secret of the Buddha—an investigator would first have to solve the problem of the god before he could get out.

Without another thought she forced her weight down on the altar and the long robe swung open. For some minutes she ferreted about inside, but there was nothing there that even looked like producing a clue.

Then came a sudden interruption. The lights suddenly went out and the dim corner lights came on. Her heart almost stopped beating. She froze like a rabbit scenting a stoat. There came again that soft click from behind the wall and the panel began to swing open. For a moment she thought the trick that had been evading her for so long had sprung of its own accord—that some accidental pressure of her own inside the god had actuated the hidden catches.

And then her heart began to pound in her bosom. Soft footsteps were coming up the connecting passage from the saloon. She almost sank to her knees with the sudden nausea of fright that seized her. From the soft padding of the feet she knew it was one of the crew, someone who walked shod in felt. That almost silent scuff-scuff was unmistakable. She could have wept in her sheer helplessness and self-pity. After all her efforts and plannings it was bitterly unfair to be caught like that—Fate was being inhumanly vindictive. If that coolie caught her there and raised the alarm her life would not be worth the toss of a coin. Grosman's unconscious body lying there on the verge of death would condemn her out of hand.

There was just one chance in a hundred that the visitor might be so nonplussed for a moment that she could effect her escape. With her feet shaking so badly that they scarcely supported her she crept into the aperture and pulled the great robe close behind her. She left an opening of about half an inch, just enough to enable her to see into part of the room.

In a few seconds the visitor appeared. It was the steward, carrying a tray of Chinese foods, all daintily set out in little silver bowls, and there were glasses of cordials and syrups and delicate finger-bowls and towels. He came into the room and looked down uncertainly at the couch, a comical frown of perplexity on his olive face, the tray held sideways in sheer astonishment.

She opened the door as silently as a cat and stepped out. Some odd telepathic influence on the Chinaman made him wheel. He was so startled that he dropped the tray with a crash and stood staring at her. Then he jerked his head sideways to see if the noise had wakened his master. But the captain still slept on, breathing in odd, jerky gasps that seemed to wrack him. The lungs were not more than a quarter filling at each inhalation.

His gaze returned to the girl, and it was wide open with astonishment. For once the monumental Oriental calm was shattered.

"Lady, what iss matter?" he asked at last. And the girl suddenly felt all fear drain away from her. To him she was just one of a string of feminine visitors invited occasionally to share the privacies of the Temple with Grosman, one of a line of interesting but completely immoral young ladies whose presence on board was always entirely voluntary. He was merely obeying a long standing order when he entered with the refreshments; it was part of his normal duties. And he was as frightened as he was perplexed. She could tell that from the scared way he kept looking down at the wreckage of the beautiful things on the floor. Apparently there would be a heavy reckoning to pay when his master came to be informed.

The words tumbled out of her mouth. "Matter?" she gasped. "Your master is ill, terribly ill. He must have help. A doctor must be brought immediately. Help me to get out—I will run and bring an English doctor for him."

The steward looked at her uncertainly. He was at his wits' end. He only understood a half of what the girl said; his English was poor and she spoke so emotionally that he could only pick out a word here and there. But what he did realise was that his master was really critically ill.

Unable to put his thought into any other series of words he again bleated: "Lady, what iss matter?"

Hillary explained, doing her best to speak slowly and with sufficient emphasis to convey her full meaning to the man.

"Your master, he came in here to me, smiling, laughing, all right, proper—you understand? He no ill when he came in here."

The steward nodded rapidly. Yes, yes, he had got that bit.

"He came in and we talk. You understand, he talk to me and laugh. And he give me glass-wine—big glass-wine. Look."

She whipped the napkin off the tray and the steward nodded again and grinned. He knew all about that glass of wine. He had seen many prepared for the same purpose. Yes, yes, he understood all about the glass-wine.

"He sit on the cushions down there with me," she went on. "And then he cough. Plenty cough. No can stop. Then he go very white. He stand up and try to open the door. But he no can get there. He fall back on the cushions. And he gasp, and gasp, and gasp. And then he lie very still like you see him now. He no move. I get frightened. I hammer on the walls, I shout, I scream. But no one hear me. I think he die. Why don't you come before?" She barked her last question at him and advanced threateningly. The steward cowered back and threw up his hand as though to ward off a blow.

"Lady," he protested. "I no can hear you in here. Shoot a gun I no can hear. Me no hear you shout. Come pronto if I hear you. Master he say, no come in for one hour. Not allowed to come in here at all unless he say. He say come in one hour—in one hour I come in. That iss right, lady."

"Well, you'd better show me the way out. You savvy? Take me to the jetty. I get doctor for him. Maybe he die without doctor. You get me there pronto, I tell master I break those things."

The steward brightened at once. Here was a blessed way out of what looked like being a highly unpleasant business for him. If the white lady was willing to take the blame for all the broken crystal on her own pretty shoulders that would suit him admirably. Grosman was notoriously as lenient with his own little charmers as he was harsh with his servants.

"You come back?" he stipulated, unwilling to see his scapegoat leave. White women had a habit, when trouble brewed, of slipping off quietly and leaving the sailormen to clear up the mess with the police as best they could.

"Yes—I come back," she assured him viciously. "He no pay me yet!" Again the steward grinned. That was assurance enough. If the white lady hadn't been paid then most decidedly she would return, and with a doctor. For how could the master pay her unless he woke from his extraordinary sleep?

"And you tell him it was you who break the tray?" he asked hopefully. "Yes, yes, I tell him. I tell him I knocked your elbow as you came in." He nodded, satisfied, and beckoned her towards the panel. She stepped in after him and he piloted her through. As she had surmised, she emerged into the captain's saloon. The place was empty then, and she turned curiously to see by what means entrance was obtained through to the Temple of Buddha. She saw the steward slam the side of the great sideboard into place, and the knowledge thrilled her, for she knew that a couple of constables with hatchets could smash the whole thing down in ten minutes.

They went through to the upper deck and she waited there with her heart in her mouth. It was broad daylight and she was terrified lest Ying should put in an appearance. And almost in the same moment she calmed her fears. There were more than a dozen white men busy about the deck. The *Yangtse* was loading for sea. The men were stevedores and ship labourers, tough, hard-muscled men who would not stand for any hanky-panky stuff from the Chinese where white women were concerned. The riverside folk boasted no high intellect or cultured refinement, the very nature of their livelihood precluded it, but there was one thing that ninety per cent of them definitely resented—at times actively resented—and that was the association of Chinese with white women. Hillary knew that she only had to open her mouth and start screaming at the top of her lungs to have the whole of that uncompromising looking crew tearing in to her rescue.

"Wait here, lady, I see first officer; tell him," said the steward.

She glanced round, looking hungrily for the gangway. But it was up. The ship was loading by electric crane from an enormous line of packing-cases piled on the wharf. A big, brawny craneman passed her, and smiled at her cheerfully. He knew all about it, did that craneman. Well, it was the kid's own business. Nothing to do with him. If she wanted to consort with a lot Chinese it was no affair of his. All that was implied in his grin and his nod.

And then he stopped and looked at her again. He was a man a cut above the average of his calling. There was something about his eyes, a twinkle in them, perhaps, a little finer shade of tolerance; it made her take a quick half-step towards him. He noticed the gesture, and eyed her shrewdly. She was no common riverside bought woman. The cut of that dress was not that of a common little Southside Magdalen. She was something out of the ordinary. Grosman certainly knew how to find them. There was a niceness about her, too, a grace that placed her above her mere presence on the *Yangtse*.

"What's up, miss?" he asked abruptly.

She stepped right up close to him and there was no mistaking the urgency in her voice. A rush of words whispered in his ear.

"You look a decent sort of boy; would you help me in trouble—serious trouble? I don't want money—it's not that—I'll give you some. Plenty. But I want someone I can trust, someone who will get off the boat right now and carry a message for me. Will you? Will you?"

"Nothing crook, is it, miss?" The answer was as solid as anyone could have asked. She could have gone down on her knees and kissed his fingers.

"No, no. That's the last thing I'd ask of anybody." He nodded. He had already formed that impression himself.

"What is it? I am going off with the next shift."

She snatched the pencil out of her dress and thrust it into his hands. "Quickly—take this," she whispered. "Take it to the Thames Police Division. Their head station at Wapping. Don't ask me any more. Just take it there and leave the rest to them. And above all, don't try to find out what it's all about. There is a message in the pencil, but it is for the police alone. You will be better off if you know nothing about it. If they ask you any questions tell them. Tell them the truth. Tell them where you saw me. And tell them I swear that what is in that message is true—every word of it. You will get ten pounds for your trouble. I'll promise that myself. And maybe a gold watch, too. Will you? Will you do that for me?"

The man nodded again, ponderously. "Yes, miss" he said good-naturedly. "There's no harm in that. I'll see it gets there."

"Quickly, then. Hide that pencil. Deliver it only to a police officer. Leave your name and address at the river station and the money will be forwarded to you. Hurry."

The wharf foreman was bawling raucously from an overhead crane, and the man moved off. She watched him grasp a chain and step on an empty hoist that went swinging up from the deck. In a few moments he was lost to sight.

She turned to see the steward heading back towards her. A tall, thin Oriental was at his side, a man dressed in an officer's uniform with two gold rings on his sleeve. The hoist came rattling down again with a fresh load, and, clinging to it was another man, hanging on to the chains with both hands. She did not see him, did not even notice that the hoist paused at the upper deck to enable him to step off before continuing down into the hold. Her attention was fixed on the two Orientals.

The officer bowed to her, but his cold, analytical eyes were boring into her. She sensed hostility in him from the first moment.

"When did you come on board?" he asked. It was the voice of a cross-examiner, chilly as a wind off the poles.

"Last night," replied Hillary, shrinking. "It—it was very late. He asked me to come down to see him—I think it must have been nearly three o'clock."

"I was on duty myself between two and three last night." There was no mistaking the frigid unbelief in the tone of that quiet voice. It implied that she was telling a calculated and very ill-formed falsehood.

"But it's true," she broke out. "It was all very dark and you may not have noticed me."

"It was not all very dark, madam. The arc lights were burning all night. I myself was on deck from midnight till four o'clock, when my watch terminated." His English was clipped, definite, and precise. The calmness of his statement staggered her.

"But—but I assure you you are mistaken," she said. "There were no lights at all. The whole place was deserted. There was not a soul about. That was why I came. Captain Grosman told me himself that no one would see me if I came at that hour." She spoke in a flurry. She realised that something had gone wrong. The man's attitude was aggressive. It was impossible to suppose that he was speaking anything but the truth. And yet so was she. She was perfectly willing to have told any lie to have got off that ship, and yet the very clash of their statements held her prisoner there.

"Madam," he said icily, "the fore and midship holds are fully loaded and the hatches battened down. If what you say is correct, and that no one was working on this ship all night, the stevedores must have broken all records for rapid loading by many hundreds of tons and by fourteen hours. We are now loading the last hold."

She gasped and looked wildly around. It was true. The tarpaulin covered hatches were battened on the fore and midship holds. It suddenly swept across her senses that she had spent not merely a night in that hidden room, but at least thirty-six hours. A whole night and a day and another night had passed since she first made that perilous boarding over the wire guy. The *Yangtse* was loading in haste. Day and night shifts were working on her.

"I—I'm sorry," she managed to get out, looking beseechingly at the officer. "I made a mistake—foolish of me—of course, you are right—it wasn't last night at all. But I've been down in the room with the captain. There are no ports there, and honestly I did not notice the passage of time. The captain—he was indiscreet—he gave me more snow than he intended. I'm not used to it and it made me sleep too long. I've only been awake a few hours since I came on board—the—the night before last."

Something of the hostility faded off the man's face. That was a likely story. It rang true. He took another good long look at the girl. Yes, it was more than probable that she was not a drug addict. And if the skipper had given her a normal dose for one who frequently indulged the craving, then it was highly possible that she would sleep the clock round.

"Ask yourself," she urged. "How else did I get on board unless the captain invited me? How else could I get into the Temple unless he took me? Why, I couldn't even get out. Mr. Grosman has been ill for over an hour, and I've been hammering on the walls till my hands are sore. And I've screamed myself hoarse. For God's sake let me get a doctor. He will die without medical attention. And then all the ghastly mess of it and the inquiries will fall on me. If only you would realise—he's terribly ill. *Please* let me get him a doctor."

"Hold that girl! Grab her—don't let her go!" A strange voice bit suddenly into the conversation. She spun round and gaped at the newcomer. It was Blind Rudley, his ear thrust out towards her to catch the inflection of her voice. And the expression on his sightless face was bitter with animosity.

"That's the bitch," he rasped. "She came aboard here the night before last. I heard her, listening in at the service hatch. The old man grabbed her and took her through for treatment. She's a police spy."

Before she could speak or utter a sound a tough, yellow hand clamped over her mouth from behind and she felt herself lifted off her feet and carried swiftly back through the bulkhead door.

One or two dockhead workers saw the little by-play, fleeting though it was. They turned and stared after her as she vanished into the black recess. It was all over in a couple of seconds. But they were not unduly concerned. They grinned and spat on their hands. That sort of thing was not unusual. Also, it was just as well not to interfere with officers' women. That was the way good jobs were lost. And no doubt the girl knew what she was about, or she wouldn't be on the boat. The bulkhead door slammed to with an iron clang, and the handles of the clamping dogs thudded home.

VIII

Manning sat moodily in his office. Things were going badly. The Chief was on his way to the river station, and he knew what that portended. He was in for the carpeting of his life.

The Chief came in, looking grim. He nodded to the sergeant.

"I think," he said, without preamble, "that this is where we proceed to make things happen. Have you anything further to report?"

"No, sir. Not a thing. Constant watch has been maintained on the *Yangtse* both from the river and the shore. She is loading, as you know, for a hurried departure. She is the first ship on the river for eight months to employ day and night shifts. Short of a sudden raid by about a dozen men, we seem to be up against a brick wall."

"A raid is out of the question," replied the Chief stiffly. "It can't be done. At least, not yet. We must get the whole crowd or none. If we raid now, all we get is the smugglers, and the big West End crowd goes free. And it's the West End organisation I want most. We can take the others any time they come in. The *Yangtse* won't get away with it again. She goes right through the sieve next time in—and every time in. But it's the controllers we want—the men who plant the drug all over the country. We have the chance and we've got to take it. We won't have another opportunity like it till the *Yangste* comes again. And that will be months too late."

"Is Miss Kittredge back yet, sir?" asked Manning hopefully.

"No—and is not likely to be. Sir John is raising the very devil. He knows as well as we do where she is. But thank Heaven he's sensible about it. He is as anxious to come in with a grand slam as we are ourselves, and he knows that if we raid the *Yangtse* we show our hand. The West End crowd will take fright and lay low. But he is like a cat on hot bricks. He knows what is likely to be happening to his daughter with that crew."

"Must be pretty tough for him, sir," said the river man slowly. "I reckon if I had a daughter in that position I'd raid twice an hour for a fortnight."

"And that is why you will never be Chief Commissioner. Every second of this waiting is going through him like a knife. But it's one of the things that have to be done when you hold the reins. Other people matter more than your own." He broke off and stared out through the office window.

"Sterling and the other men are in a bad way," he said quietly. "Harley Street has been in."

Manning leaned forward. "Is it likely to be permanent?" he asked.

"The specialists won't say. But they are hoping. The light was so strong that it paralysed the optic nerves. They are in hospital and, according to the doctors, they will be there for months. Three months is the very minimum before the bandages come off." He turned back to the river man. "Sergeant," he said, "we are going to take that crowd—and take them alive. We'll get them so suddenly that they won't get a chance to commit suicide. Grosman would be likely to take a quick dose, and so would the rest of his crew. But they aren't going to get the chance. If we have to knock every single one of them senseless we will take them alive. They are going to pay for what they did to Sterling and the others."

Manning was rubbing the tips of his fingers together. He appeared not to have heard the Chief's last utterance. But very quietly he muttered under his breath: "Just five minutes with

Grosman—just five sweet little minutes—and you can have the pieces, Chief. But I'd like that five minutes first."

"We begin a long comb out in the Gunn Lane neighbourhood today," went on the Chief. "But the trouble is the locals won't talk. They are scared out of their fives. Can't get a word out of them. Can't say I blame them. They have the lessons of Gilan and Ulrich Maxick staring them in the face. But it makes a devilish long job for the men working the case. Practically means a house-to-house search. The whole place is a rabbit warren, and all the back areas adjoin. We shall want an army of men there to hold them all up once we have located them. But that's where the rendezvous is—as certain as I'm alive. And Procter got on to it. Poor devil! I'll swear he got on the tail-end of it all and was coming through with the news. Those Chinese surprised him and stopped him before he could get through."

Manning looked up with a sudden start.

"You don't think Procter's dead, do you?" he asked, and there was a quick whitening of his weather-beaten face.

The Chief was silent. His hawky, wintry eyes focused on Manning's and held them. "Know the type of men you're dealing with, don't you?" he said in a curiously level voice. "And you know Procter's habits. Ever know him stay off on a job more than three horn's before without coming through on the phone? If he was sick he would send word. The only word we have had is from his wife—asking where he is. The last you heard of him was heading off on the trail of the Chinaman two nights ago. Think it out, Manning. The Chinese are adept at disposing of bodies." Then very slowly he added: "No, I'm terribly sorry to have to say it, but I don't think you will ever see Procter again, alive."

Manning looked away shakily. The dope gang was taking a savage toll.

"That is why I say," said the Chief, "it is time we *made* things happen." Another silence fell, a silence that seemed interminable. Manning was on touchy ground. Again that bitter reprimand had not matured. The Chief was becoming more and more of an animan to him humanned to be feeling the tragedy of events as deeply as did Manning himself. There was nothing of the autocratic bully about him, nothing of the inaccessibility of the man at the top of the tree who did nothing except demand results and hand out curses if those results were not immediately forthcoming. Instead of scolding he sympathised; he knew and appreciated the difficulties of the road they trod.

As though from the midst of a faraway reverie, he softly inquired: "I was waiting for a report from you last night, Manning. Where were you?"

Manning shuffled his feet uneasily. "I was out at the Wapping Wharf, Chief," he said. "When Procter didn't come back I got worried. You know how things are, sir. His missus and mine—well, you know, we are pretty well next door to each other and he—he was about the best man on the station. Booked for his stripes if ever a man was. We were friendly. Perhaps a bit too friendly. And it seemed to me he was going wrong. He was taking up the land end of it. And that's no part of our duty."

He lapsed into a moody silence and then added: "Our job is on the river. If Procter had stayed on his own job he would be here now talking to you. But it's hard to strike the dividing line on a job like this, if you know what I mean. You can't always run it according to the rules. If Procter was on the job then he had got on to a clue from the land end.

"I stuck around there for the best part of twenty-four hours. I knew there was something fishy going on on the *Yangtse*. And when no word came through from Procter I got out to the store-sheds there and waited in the shadows. That was long before they began loading for sea.

"And along towards about three in the morning, or it may have been nearer four, I saw around half-dozen of them come crawling back to the boat. If it had been just after the taverns closed, or if they had all come back together, it wouldn't have mattered so much. But they came off in dribs and drabs, one at a time, creeping through the docks as though they were scared of being seen. And the last of all to arrive was Grosman himself. As soon as he was on board they raised the gangway. That would have been a couple or three hours after Procter last went out on the trail of Grosman.

"It looks more and more as though you were right, Chief. Procter trailed them to their secret rendezvous—and they collared him there. That would be about the time the police were called to the second Maxick job in Gunn Lane. He would have had time to get out there—and to have got murdered, too."

The Chief pondered, with his eyes out over the distant river. "You told me you had nothing further to report—and yet you tell me this," he said, and he spoke as though he was going quietly over his own inmost thoughts. He pulled out a notebook and studied some entries there.

"Procter left you at eleven o'clock," he said in a barely audible undertone. "The first call came through to the Limehouse police just before one o'clock, roughly two hours later.

"Well, suppose we take things as they ran and leave a fair margin for supposition and error. And I freely admit that most of this is nothing more than mere supposition, with nothing whatever to substantiate it, except the deaths of Ulrich Maxick and Procter.

"Supposing Procter got on to the real live end of a clue; that is, supposing he actually trailed Grosman to that secret rendezvous. It is fair to presume that something like that happened. The gang were in a turmoil. Gilan Maxick had been slaughtered. The call had gone down river. Dope distributors were being raided every hour. Every single individual in the West End known to be associated with the dope traffic was being watched by hot men. Something had to be done about it.

"A hurried emergency meeting was called. It was called in so much of a hurry that the usual methods of communication could not be employed" Somebody in the Outward Bound' that night gave Grosman the wire that a meeting was called at the rendezvous to discuss the situation. Or it may have been the other way about—Grosman, getting nervy, called the meeting, and word came through that his aides-de-camp would be there to meet him.

"He set off to keep the appointment, and he was so deeply absorbed in his problems that he did not notice the dodging shadow of Procter creeping along behind him. The other supposition, and by far the more feasible one, is that he was protected, and that a third party, one of his Chinese crew probably, was trailing along in the wake of Procter.

"Now, I admit, we come to what is nothing more or less than a presumption. Grosman was frightened of a squealer. We know that from the fact that he murdered the first man he suspected of being one. Grosman murdered Gilan Maxick for no other reason than that he suspected him of being too friendly with the police. Maxick had a brother, and it is not stretching credulity too far to suppose that brother Ulrich would not be too favourably disposed towards his leader after such a wanton act as that. Working purely on a psychologic knowledge of the Oriental mind, who would Grosman be most likely to suspect of being the next to turn police informant?"

"Why, I should say Ulrich himself," said Manning. "Knowing the gang had turned a sore eye on him he would be more likely to try and get police protection than to assure the gang of his loyalty. Grosman acts first and thinks afterwards. Ulrich would be the most likely to squeal—provided he knew the police would look after him when the gang was busted."

"Exactly. And now supposing, merely for the sake of trying to fit the events together as they happened in chronological order, supposing Ulrich Maxick was called to attend that meeting of the heads of the gang, supposing he was there in person to answer their questions, on trial for his life if you like.

"We know that their headquarters are based somewhere in that network of intercommunicating buildings that litter the neighbourhood of Gunn Lane. And it seems to me that Procter traced them to their lair and somehow succeeded in getting into the building. It might be that he overheard much of what passed at their secret session. The Ulrich Maxick business would be only a small item on their agenda—maybe he was already marked down for death as a threat to the others."

"Well, they killed him, anyway," grunted Manning. "And out in the open street at that."

"Which is precisely what I mean. One of two things happened. Either Maxick got away on his own wit and was making his escape, or Procter was instrumental in getting him out of the clutches of the Chinese. But in any case he was booked for death. Someone else outside was detailed to follow him and murder him if he happened to be lucky enough or smart enough to get clear of the gang in the building.

"If Procter helped him to escape then it is more than excusable to suppose that Maxick had decided to throw in his lot with the police. Probably he had already turned informer to Procter, or, equally possible, Procter had promised him police protection provided he came straight through to you and told you all he knew. Personally, I incline towards the second theory, otherwise the blinding of Sterling and the other constables was senseless.

"Maxick was carrying a written message. We have that from the depositions of Sterling himself. He was trying to decipher a particularly atrociously written scrawl when the light smashed his eyes. And you know what that means, Manning? That message was written in the dark.

"There the line of deduction runs clear. Procter got the message away by a man who was doomed to be murdered as soon as he was reasonably free of the building. Then the gang surprised Procter. They may have seized him before, and Procter in a moment of triumph, may have boasted that a message was already on its way to the police. Or, as I say, the whole thing may have been preconceived in the brain of Grosman, and the shadower may have warned the gang that Procter was in the building.

"It is, I repeat, inference based on happenings. Maxick was murdered at a time that conforms entirely to that story. And having murdered him there would be nothing but madness in the idea of committing a further assault on the police at that hour of the night when the whole neighbourhood was aroused—unless it was to recover a damning document. The alarm was raised, and within a few minutes two constables were on the spot. They phoned the Yard; they knew it was a relative of Maxick lying there in the road. It was the same type of dagger. You see what I'm driving at, Manning?"

"Yes, sir, I'm afraid I do," said Manning, looking away from his Chief.

"Procter did his job, that's what I'm driving at. He got away with it. And both of them were murdered in cold blood. Murdered in the moment of victory. The whole thing knits up somewhere. Procter found the junction between this ship and the shore. And that's why we can't raid."

There was a tap on the door, and a duty officer pushed his head in.

"Sorry to trouble you, sir," he said, "but there's a man out here who says he must see Sergeant Manning. Says he's got something important for him. Something to do with the *Yangtse* job, from what I can make out."

"Who is he?" demanded the Chief, rising.

"Says his name's Tom Bristow, sir. He's loading on the *Yangtse*, and a woman gave him a message that must come through to the station here. Won't tell me what it is. Says he must see Sergeant Manning."

"A woman? That must be Miss Kittredge," said the Chief with a rush. "Show him through, officer—show him through."

Tom Bristow was ushered in, looking round nervously, not quite sure of himself. Bristow might have been as honest as the day, but men in his walk of life are apt to regard the police askance, for, in their eyes, the police are not so much the guardians of law and order as an inconvenient body of men who are liable to haul human beings off to jail at a moment's notice.

"Good morning, gents," he said from out of the depths of his broad chest. "I understand one of you is Sergeant Manning?"

The Chief pressed the sergeant's toe under the table and told him with a penetrating look to take charge of things. A man of Bristow's type might be free enough in his speech with a sergeant, but he would be likely to freeze like a puddle in winter if he knew he was talking in the presence of the reigning monarch of the whole force.

Manning pushed his chair back and rose. He held out his cigarette case. "My name's Manning," he said. "There's no need to be uncomfortable, old man, just sit down and tell us what's wrong. This is another police officer here, and you can talk as freely as you like in front of him. The duty sergeant tells me you are from the *Yangtse*. Is that right?"

"That's right, sir. Name of Bristow. Crane signalman with the Wharfingers' Alliance—loading on the *Yangtse* now, at Wapping."

"That's fine. We have been hoping for a message. What is it?"

"Well, it's a bit unusual, sir, if I might say so. I was just coming off my shift a little while ago—twelve o'clock to be exact—when I saw a female party coming through the bulkhead leading to the officers' quarters. The steward was with her, a Chinese, and she was looking all upset and worried—at least so I thought. The steward left her for a bit to call an officer, and she came straight up to me and asked me to give you this pencil."

He held it out, and the sergeant inspected it with beetling brows. The cap was screwed back in place and it looked as ordinary a gold pencil as one 'ould see in any decent jeweller's window any day of the week.

"She said there was a message in it, sir," went on Bristow, "and she told me I was to bring it here to the river station and nowhere else. She said I would be on ten pounds if it got there without anyone else seeing it—but I suppose that's all poppycock."

"Shouldn't be too pessimistic about that tenner if I were you," advised the sergeant. "What was she like, this woman?"

"Very good-looking piece, sir. All dolled up in evening clothes, but they was all so rumpled you wouldn't know they was made of good stuff. On the slim side, and fair. Somehow she didn't seem the sort to be down there playing the game that she was. You know what I mean, don't you? It ain't legal, and I know the gels can get into trouble if blokes like you get hold of them. But it was obvious enough what she was doing on that hooker—and—and, as I say, I was a bit surprised. Seemed a cut above that sort of thing. She was a West End tart, anyway—she wasn't one of the general Lizzies you can pick up in the pubs that side of the water."

Manning read the message on the dance programme and the next moment the cap was oil and the spill was in his hands. He unravelled the tiny pages and read them hurriedly. The Chief knew from the quick glitter that leapt into his eyes that he was on a discovery of the first importance. As he read each page he passed it silently across to his superior.

"Mr. Bristow," he said, "you have done us a very great service in bringing this message through to us, probably a greater service than you imagine. Have you read those pages?"

"No, sir, I brought it along just as the lady gave me it. She said if I read them I wouldn't be on the tenner. And I could do with a ten-pound note. Things haven't been too good on the river these last few months—and a tenner would take the missus and kids away for a bit."

"You will get your tenner all right. I'll see to it myself. Probably a good deal more will be coming your way. Now tell me, does anyone know you were bringing the message to us?"

"Not so far as I know, sir. Only the lady herself."

"I mean, was there anybody knocking around on the deck when she had the talk with you, anyone who would have guessed that something was wrong and that you were coming straight along here to us?"

"I can't say. The only people knocking about were the hands loading the ship, stevedores and such like. One or two of them may have noticed me talking to her. She seemed in such a hurry that as soon as I had got the message I just stepped on a hoist and left the ship. And I came straight round."

"Did any of the Chinese officers see you talking to her?"

"No, sir. There weren't any on deck. Not even the steward. He was gone through to the officers' quarters to call the officer."

"Better than ever. I'm only telling you this for your own guidance, Bristow. This case happens to be connected with the dope running job that has been in the papers the last couple of days. Grosman, the head of that gang, is captain of the *Yangtse*. Two of his men have been murdered for suspected squealing, and I think it is only fair you should know what you are up against. You hadn't better go back to the *Yangtse*. I'll get you a job farther down river. Know the Woolwich end at all?"

"Fairly well, sir."

"Right, I'll have a talk with one of the foremen down there and see that you are all fixed up. You'll have nothing to worry about; but until the whole thing is squared up it's just as well that you should not be seen. From what you say I don't think anyone there knows about you, but there are as many eyes on the *Yangtse* as there are rats in a run. Now, about this lady. You say she was looking worried?"

"I'd say a bit more than worried. She was looking real frightened to me Looked as though she wished she could get off. That was what drew my attention to her. But there was no gangways on that hooker. The tide was right down, and she couldn't have got off unless she had climbed the piles of the wharf."

"She actually looked as though she was being held a prisoner there?"

"Not right at that minute, because she was all alone on deck. But from her dress and the way she looked I'd say she had been held there against her will for some time. Looked downright ill to me. All white and kind of glittery about the eyes."

"Did she get oft the ship after you left?"

"Can't say, sir I got right away out of it as soon as I stepped ashore. When I looked back she was talking to the first officer."

Manning took him by the arm and piloted him to the door. "Thanks very much, Mr. Bristow," he said. "That will be all I shall want from you today. If I should want any more information from you again I will come over and see you. Meanwhile, if you call in here later on in the evening I'll leave you a note telling you where you can start in the morning."

Bristow, looking profoundly uncomfortable, thanked him and was gone. Manning went back to the Chief with the light of eagerness on his face. For the first time since the case broke he began to see success shining ahead.

"Looks as though we have got a line on it at last, Chief," he said.

"Twenty-four hours should see it all cleared up, Manning," replied the Chief quietly. "But every avenue will have to be tackled at the same moment. There will have to be a zero hour, and it will want organising down to the last second. What a brick that girl is! It's a hateful thing to say, but I don't think we need worry about her yet. She seems more than able to take care of herself. And, from what she says, she has given that captain enough cocaine to keep him quiet for some hours."

"Well, she certainly has given us something to get on with. And she is right about that secret rendezvous too. That's the place out at Gunn Lane, the place poor old Procter found."

The Chief was pulling at his lip. "Lingard. Lingard," he muttered. "That name is familiar. Now where does he link up?"

"Nowhere in connection with cocaine, Chief. I can tell you that definitely. I've gone over every drug dossier for the last ten years, and there is no such name on the records. I think I could recognise the name of every suspect off-hand. I've pored over those files till I'm sick of them."

"I didn't for a moment think he would be under the drug headings. The gang organises itself too well for that. As soon as a man becomes suspect on that count they would pass him out and bring in someone whose record is clean. Just a moment."

He reached out for the phone and called Headquarters. "Put this call through to 'Records,'" he said, "and tell them I want all the Lingards they can trace. Initials, addresses, records, and convictions, if any."

In ten minutes the call came back, and the officer at the other end reported that the archives contained the names of eight Lingards who had been prosecuted in various parts of the country since the end of the war.

Slowly the voice enumerated them, and as each one's record was called over the Chief slowly ruled them out. There was a coiner, a confidence trickster who sounded promising until the filing department told him that the man was still serving a long term in prison, an arson expert who specialised in insurance fires, two housebreakers, a long-firm swindler, and a diminutive little area sneak who only measured four feet two and had never been known to possess more than five pounds in his life. Regretfully the Chief drew his pencil through each.

"And now the suspects." And at the first one his heart gave a jump.

"There's a Graham Lingard down on the list, Chief," said the voice from the other end. "But we can't seem to get anything definite lined up against him. He's a proprietor of dud nightclubs, but he never runs them in his own name. Been a pest to us for years. He gets a cat's-paw to register them in his own name and pays him well to take the rough stuff when the clubs are raided. He has four running in London now and he mushrooms a few more round the coast for the summer seasons."

"Yes; anything more about him? From your end, I mean."

"Well, sir, we have had our eye on him for a long while as a possible distributor of cocaine. But there is nothing concrete. All we know is that lots of the stuff is collared in his clubs whenever we stick him up on a raid. But it may be that his places are just central meeting-grounds for runners and addicts. They all seem to gather round him, anyway. As soon as we close one club down he opens another, like as not next door. Cool as a snowball. He knows we suspect him, but he doesn't care a rap. Pays his men well, and they stand by him when trouble comes."

"Thank you, officer that will do splendidly. And the address is?"

"The Everglades, Loughton. Got a big country house there, with a full staff of servants and all the trimmings. When in Town he generally sleeps in a flat over one of his clubs. The latest one is that new flashy one in Soho, La Caverne Diamentée. 'Scuse my French, but that's the way they pronounce it. I'm told he has a very luxurious suite of rooms just over it. Do you want him watched, sir?"

"Yes. He's the man I want. Get after him. Put two good men on him. And have a messenger report his movements here every hour—here to the Wapping station. I'll have a man at this end to take all phone calls."

He put the telephone down and turned back to Manning.

"Well, what do you make of it now?" he asked.

The sergeant was busy writing down the addresses. "I think I've got my end of it, Chief," he declared. "There is only one link wanted now—and it looks to me as though we shall find it in Chinny the Junk's store-yard."

"Taking, at the same time," said the Chief, "particular note of the activities of Engelberg. There is a strong connection between him and the Chinese captain. The facts now are obvious. Grosman is the only one who sells biscuit to Chinny. And Engelberg is the only one who buys it from him."

"And he certainly doesn't buy it to feed to chickens," said the river man warmly. "I asked for a dozen eggs a week from him, and he had to order them from the local dairyman. That chicken business is only a blind. He's in this business somewhere—in it up to the neck. That is why I want to get another look in at the junk yard. If I can trace Engelberg's game down I think I shall have something worthwhile to report."

"You should have good hunting," said the Chief, smiling grimly. "Grosman swears he will land the rest of the stuff—whether Lingard can accept it or not. By tonight the pace should be red-hot. Lingard will keep out of the way. It is a thousand to one that he will stay at one of his clubs tonight and let Grosman stew in his own juice. At a long shot we shall locate him at the Caverne Diamentée. I'm going to try it, anyway."

"Are you going to send him that post card, sir?"

"I surely am. The postal authorities will have to help. But I've no doubt that will be the simplest difficulty. Get me our department at the General Post Office, will you? I'll speak to the Superintendent myself."

The call went through and the Chief took the telephone.

"Is that the Superintendent?" he called. "This is the Chief here. I want you to send a man to Wapping and to mail a plain post card there. The address is: Graham Lingard, La Caverne Diamentée, Soho. I want it to be imprinted with the Wapping stamp, and the time must be back-marked to ten o'clock this morning. Do you get all that?"

"Yes, Chief; I understand perfectly."

"And I want that card to be delivered to him at the Caverne Diamentée by the nine o'clock post. That is very definite. You will have to trace it right through and see that that card is included in the mail delivery there at nine. Nine is your last delivery in Soho, isn't it?"

"Yes, sir; nine o'clock is general for last mails right through London."

"So much the better; it will be all that much more natural. You will see that it is done?"

"Without fail, sir. I will see that it goes through privately. It shall be sent over by special messenger for delivery at nine. It has already missed the routine sorting schedule; but it will be there by the last post."

He hung up the receiver. "I'm going over to the 'Outward Bound,'" he said. "I want to take a particularly good long look at Blind Rudley. There appears to be a good way of approach through that gentleman. Maybe it can be done. Is Chinny the Junk on the phone?"

Manning wrote down the number on a card and passed it over.

"Good. I'll get through to the office here as often as possible. If you have anything to report, leave the messages here for me. You will have all your work cut out in the junk yard."

He put on his hat and went out. The "Outward Bound" was less than ten minutes' walk away, and he went in through the saloon door. The place was almost empty, and he attracted little notice sitting in a corner by a table.

He slid a pair of semi-dark glasses over his eyes; one of his discoveries was that if the eyes are masked half the face is masked. And in that company there was not much fear of being recognised.

It was fully an hour before Blind Rudley came tap-tapping into the bar. The Chief rose at the same moment and ordered another drink. And from then on his eyes never left the blind man. He watched him as though he was scoring a photographic likeness of the man on his brain. His scrutiny began at the crown of his head and continued right down to the toes of his boots. And then, having taken a carbon copy of every tiny detail of his dress, his gaze went back to the sightless face, recording on his memory every line of it. Every wrinkle was taken keen notice of; even the angle at which he held his stick came in for attention.

The blind man, hearing a strange voice calling for a drink in the saloon bar, came tapping round chanting his monotonous "Pipe lights—cigar lights?"

The Chief tossed him a coin and took the opportunity of examining him from the nearer advantage of a close-up.

Rudley did not appear to be waiting for anyone especially. He seemed to be paying one of his usual camouflage rounds. In a minute or two he started out again, heading for his next house of call.

The Chief followed out behind him, keeping far enough away not to be heard by those uncanny ears. For the greater part of an hour he trailed him and then abruptly turned and went back to the river station.

There he found a message from Manning to say that Engelberg had already taken away a load of biscuit and that the dealer expected him back again during the afternoon. Grosman was also likely to put in another appearance.

While he was reading the flimsy, Manning himself came through again.

"Is that you, Chief?" he said. "Just been trying to get you. There is certainly going to be a spot of liveliness here before nightfall. Both Engelberg and Grosman have called again. Neither of them know I am here—Chinny is on our side so long as he is not asked to take any active part in our operations. The *Yangtse* got her papers cleared and manifests through at noon today. So it looks as though Grosman is clearing for sea within forty-eight hours. I got that from the Port of London Authority. Do you want me to take any steps to hold her up if she tries to leave?"

"Not on your life. I knew she was doing everything to get out to sea, knew it as soon as they engaged double shifts to get the cargo stowed. Let her run. If you put obstacles in her way they will smell every rat in our bag. No; I'm aiming to have everything squared and ready before she slips her moorings."

"Right, Chief. I may not be coming through again for some time. Things seem to be working up nicely for a quick run for me. I have a chance of inspecting that new consignment of biscuit again, and if it turns out O.K. I am going to trail Engelberg. I'll come through again as soon as I have established the connection."

Manning turned away from the phone and beckoned to the little dealer. "If either Grosman or Engelberg comes in, keep him busy here for a minute and slip me the word," he said.

Chinny the Junk nodded affably and turned back to his accounts.

Manning went out into the yard to the pile of battered biscuit boxes. Another fifty cases had just come in and been flung on the heap. They were brought on a dock truck by one of the seamen from the *Yangtse*. Manning had watched him from the gloomy shadows of the tumbledown office.

And the gesture had been as innocent as one could imagine. Manning knew off-hand that the coolie had not the slightest knowledge of the contents of those tins. Grosman was too crafty to bring them himself. No captain in his senses would dream of doing such a thing as carting his own old junk about.

And Manning could not help feeling a glow of appreciation for the nerve of the man. He employed the most innocent and unsuspicious of his dupes to do the riskiest of the work. And it was done with such a *naivete* and openness that only by blind chance could his method become suspect.

He saw the whole scheme as soon as he approached the heap. On each of the freshly arrived tins a little group of scratches were scored. On such battered tinware they looked natural enough. But to a discerning eye they were too regular to be accidental. Moreover, they were etched on every side of the tin. Manning hunted for one that was more battered than the rest. He found one with a deep crack down the edge, and he smiled grimly when he noticed that the biscuit inside was as dry as stale bread.

He carefully prised the crack open and shook a biscuit out. Cupped in the palm of his hand, it looked as harmless and innocuous as any other ship's biscuit; but before he cracked it open he would have wagered his head that the outside paste was only a thin veneer covering the drug.

He crushed the biscuit in his hand. The outer covering fell away and there was the neat, thin case of cocaine wafers left in his fingers. He did not need to open the case to know that the drug was there.

He admitted to himself that it was the neatest thing that had ever been put over on the river police. The whole system was revealed in that moment. Grosman had been as thorough as only a really fine organiser could be.

He occupied the greater part of his journey from the East in putting up the cocaine into biscuit form, packing the disguised article in any old battered tin that came to his hand These he kept hidden in the secret Temple until the examination by the Customs officers was complete, And even if, by chance, the ship searchers stumbled on the secret of that Temple, it was unlikely that they would suspect the great Buddha to be hollow. A man of the captain's fanatical religion would be quite likely to carry a replica of his own deity on board. Much less likely things come out of the East.

For all anyone knew some of the prepared tins might even have been kicking about the upper deck when the Customs officers were examining the ship. No one but a madman, or a sheer genius, would have dreamed of suspecting broken old tins of biscuit thrown out on the open deck, awaiting a possible purchaser from the marine stores, bundled up with a lot of old rope and perished wire and rotted canvas, of containing enough drug to have poisoned half London.

And as soon as the examination was complete the ship became open to all the normal comings and goings of dockside work.

It again spoke a great deal for Grosman's craftiness that he was not in a violent hurry to get rid of the stuff the moment the Customs officers left the ship. He actually had the nerve to leave it knocking about the ship for several days before mentioning to Chinny that he had a littering of old junk that might as well be cleared off his upper deck.

And all unsuspectingly Chinny would call around and give him a price for it, small sums enough in all conscience, for the stuff was scarcely worth the labour of carting away. Grosman might have chosen any one of a dozen other mediums for the transport of his cocaine ashore, but in fixing on old ship's biscuits he had undoubtedly put an unerring finger on the one commodity that not another soul on earth would want to buy. Henkeepers in Wapping are scarcer than elephant tracks in the Strand.

What it amounted to was that with his colossal impudence he could leave thousands of pounds' worth of cocaine lying about in someone else's junk yard, open to the rains and the suns, knowing perfectly well that it was as safe there from molestation as though it was securely locked away in a safe deposit vault. The stuff was wheeled round to the yard by one of the seamen told off for the job in the normal course of the day's duties. He simply tossed the cans on the heap and went back to the ship.

The only weak link that Manning could see was that the method involved the employment of a second confederate ashore. But in Engelberg he had to admit the Chinese had found the perfect cover. The cheery old Hollander was the last man anyone would suspect of being concerned in anything so risky as cocaine running on the grand scale.

With his disarming, affable old face and his benign manner with the children around he was an ideal go-between. The thick pebble glasses added to the illusion of general harmlessness and good nature.

His end of the business was simple. As soon as the word came through from Grosman that a load was awaiting him in the junk yard, he ambled round to Chinny's, passed the pleasant time of day with him, and slung as many tins of biscuit on his truck as he cared to take away that day.

The tins he wanted were all plainly marked on every side, plainly, that is, to anyone who happened to be looking for that particular group of insignificant scratches. On the day that Manning had last inspected the biscuit, Engelberg had cleared the heap of every tin containing cocaine. And as often as a fresh supply came over from the *Yangtse* the Hollander came over and cleared it. There were days, of course, when there was no cocaine, but he came over and bought a few tins just to keep up the deception.

Whether Chinny knew the true nature of Engelberg's activities was a matter that did not enter. Chinny was above and beyond any possibility of entanglement. And any such knowledge as that was deeply buried in the inscrutable soul of the wizened little man himself.

All the Hollander had to do was to cart the stuff away to his master's secret rendezvous. And there his labours ended. It was, Manning decided, a thoroughly neat and ingenious scheme; one, moreover, that had proved effective through all the visits of the *Yangtse* to the river. By adhering strictly to the laws of the

Port Authorities and by utilising the tiny loopholes left between the rules, cocaine in enormous quantities had been smuggled ashore right under the very nose of the preventive squads.

And right there, Manning reflected, his own labours began. All he had to do was to get on to the rear end of the Hollander's shadow the next time he called at the yard and the trail would lead him straight to that hidden store.

He crawled under an upturned dinghy and awaited developments. They were not long in coming. A bare twenty minutes after he had installed himself he heard the creak of the Hollander's handcart coming into the yard. Manning could see under the rim of the gunwale, where the curve of the boat made a slight concavity against the ground, by pressing his face flat on the earth and looking out with one eye.

The junk dealer did not give away the position by so much as the blink of an eye. He glanced up from his preoccupations at his rickety desk and waved the Dutchman on with a nod.

Manning was less than ten feet from the pile of tins, and he saw Engelberg come to a halt beside them. And every tin he picked up was scored with the little groups of scratches. To a casual eye he seemed to be picking them up from anywhere, one after the other, just as they happened to come to his hand. But to Manning, watching underneath the boat, it was all one of the cleverest pieces of discrimination he had ever seen. Somehow it seemed to Manning that the cheery old soul was unwell, if not downright ill. He was dripping with sweat, as he bent down for more tins Manning heard him groan.

He actually picked up a couple of tins that bore no marks at all. And in flinging them on the barrow he made a bad shot. The tins rolled off again, and he kicked them carelessly aside.

When he had taken enough he went ambling back to the gate. Chinny the Junk and Engelberg had known each other too long for the little dealer to need to check the quantity. The Hollander was as honest as the day.

He padded out on his fat old feet, beaming and waving his hand to the urchins around. As soon as he was gone Manning hauled himself out from under the boat. A hurried inspection of the pile showed that not a single marked tin remained. He signalled his thanks to the little dealer as he crept out through the gate. Engelberg was just turning the corner at the bottom of the street. Manning hurried down after him and kept him in sight through more than a mile of squattering side streets and dank alleys. It was not a difficult task. Engelberg had made the journey so often that he had attained an exaggerated idea of his own immunity. It was a foolproof proposition. Nothing could go wrong with it. Dozens of times he had pushed that innocent old barrow through that maze of human burrows and nothing had ever happened.

Everyone along that route knew what it was he carried. Chicken food. And damaged chicken food at that. It was not worth anyone's while to knock him down and rob him. And, besides, the Dutcher was a decent old sort.

Manning knew in a hazy kind of way that they were drawing near Gunn Lane. At least, he knew they were in that locality, but somehow they seemed to be off the line.

The man ahead turned in at a high gate that abutted on a railway siding. And so sure of himself was he that he did not even pause to see if he was being followed. Years of immunity had brought a false sense of security.

Manning crept ahead and cautiously opened the gate an inch. Engelberg was away at the top end with his load, piling the tins on the siding platform. The river man surveyed the scene. At the far end was another gate, a high one with a frise of spikes along the top. He realised that that was the entrance from Gunn Lane. He had come in through the back entrance that led in from the railway. And that was the entrance probably used by the inner members of the gang. If that was so he required a redoubled caution. Unseen eyes were liable to be hawking at him even then.

Engelberg vanished into the gaunt wreck of the main building. The sergeant watched him approach a door and turn the handle. He seemed to turn it an unconscionable number of times, and then he gently pulled it towards him. The handle came away in his hand, and Manning saw that it was attached to a stout wire from the inside. As he pulled he pressed on the door itself. The wire raised a drawbar inside and the door swung open. It was just another adept contrivance planned in the brain of the drug-runner. It was self-locking on the inside, and, as a double merit for a safety device, it could be worked from either side by one man. And only a man who knew the secret of it could operate it from the outside.

From Engelberg's actions it seemed likely that he was alone in the place. He had given no sign of his presence to any hidden watcher and certainly no one had challenged him from the building. Manning was feeling more sure of himself. If he only had to deal with the fat old Dutcher then there was no excuse for that queer swimmy sensation that was drifting about under his belt. His own conviction was that if he couldn't double that old boy up and wrap him round a tentpole then he was willing to eat his own hat.

He slipped inside and softly closed the gate. There was a thrill of exultation running through him. If the Chief had only done half as well at his end the loose ends were rapidly being drawn together. But his chief thrill was more personal to himself, a more human one. It was the kick that he got from the knowledge that his first surmise was right. From the first moment he had seen Engelberg stacking tins of damaged biscuit on his handcart a secret little imp of knowledge had whispered feverishly in his ear that there was something suspicious about it. An inner chord in him had vibrated to the warning that the connection from the ship to the shore was there in that old junk yard and that Engelberg's actions were definitely linked up with it.

And here he had tracked it down. Here was his justification. Any man likes to know, by clearly proved demonstration, that he is still master of his own craft, and in tracing Engelberg down to that common meeting point he knew he had every excusable reason for satisfaction. He crawled round by the crumbling walls and explored the possibilities. He did not relish the idea of gaining admission by the same door as Engelberg. For all he knew there might be an automatic alarm attached to the drawbar inside. If he knew anything of Grosman's methods it was more than likely that there was. It would be all in accordance with his self-protective methods to cover one trick device with yet another. He was not the man to lay himself open to a surprise raid from the very entrance which he used himself.

Seen in daylight the place was more dilapidated and depressing than under the softening shadows of night. The roof sagged heavily in places, and it had been found necessary to prop great shoring timbers against one of the walls.

Entrances there were in plenty to anyone agile enough to haul himself off the ground. There was not a window anywhere in the building that was not smashed and gaping open. The ease of ingress made him all the more suspicious of that mechanically controlled door. The one thing that he did not know was that that trick door was the one direct entrance to the more habitable sections of the building. Procter had made that discovery for himself when he put out his foot and suddenly found himself hurtling down that broken lift shaft.

Manning gripped the edge of a windowsill and drew himself up. He listened closely. From far away down below him he could hear the soft shuffle of footsteps. He listened again—and the hair along the nape of his neck began to crawl. The footsteps limped!

He heard the dragging clip-clop of the heavy surgical boot. Grosman was down there. He took the bit between his teeth. Well, that made two to get on with. Provided he hadn't equipped himself with another charge of that damnable light or some other such lethal horror, Manning was ready and willing to tackle the pair of them. And if either of them saw fit to start what was colloquially known as the rough stuff so much the better. There would be a peculiar satisfaction about having five mad minutes in a wild free-for-all with the brute who had killed Procter and blinded four others of his working confrères.

He climbed inside and gently lowered himself to the floor. The boards creaked abominably. They were rotted almost to decay, and it was difficult to find a place anywhere to step that did not set up an immediate squeaking protest.

Manning did the same as Procter had done. He took off his boots, tied them together, and slung them round his neck. Thereafter progress was less noisy though more painful to the soles of his feet; splinters abounded, and he seemed to find them all. By tortuous paths he made his way down. He could hear the Chinese moving about down there, and now and then guttural mutterings floated up to him.

He, too, found the yawning lift shaft that had seen Procter go crashing down, but in the dim lights that filtered into the great barn of a place through the broken windows and breaks in the roof he saw it in time.

He knew there must be some other way down besides that lift. In so huge and rambling a place as that there would, of necessity, be several different stairways. But amid the lumber of old crates and packing cases all the doorways seemed to be impossible of access.

Grosman had planned it that way. In spite of the immensity of the place there were only two ways of getting through to the basement. One was down the lift shaft and the other was through the trick door from the back. To get down by the circular staircase one had to mount the fire escape outside and come down through the roof.

Every other communicating doorway and means of access was barred up with masses of packing-cases piled up in high profusion. To have tried to disturb them would have brought the top masses down with a crash. Manning decided to use the lift shaft, lowering himself down by his fingertips, hanging on like a limpet to every little projection that offered.

When he reached the bottom he crawled through to where he heard the sounds of Grosman's boots shuffling about. It was in the inner room and the lights were full on. He hugged the shadows of the far side wall, again precisely as Procter had done before him. It was a coign of vantage and by far the safest approach. He peeped in, and his brows came low over his eyes in sheer astonishment. It was not Grosman in there but Engelberg. At least, the body and the face were the body and the face of Engelberg, but the feet, with the deformed ankle, were the feet of Grosman.

And the man was apparently in terrible pain. Beads of perspiration were standing out on his brow. He was holding his head in his hands and rocking from side to side in an access of physical misery. Manning stared at him in amazement. After a while he saw him lay his watch on the table and sit staring at it. Minutes ticked by, and still the man sat and waited, his jaws clenched up till the muscles at his temples stood out in tight pads. He seemed to be concentrating all his will power into one dominant determination to watch the hands of that watch crawling round. The fat hands were clenched till they were bone white, and he cursed the slowness of the passing seconds in a language that was neither born of Dutch nor Saxon. The fascination of it held the river man spellbound.

The spasm seemed long in passing. The Hollander took out a gaudy bandanna and wiped the perspiration from his face. To do it he put up a palsied hand and removed the thick pebbled glasses. Then he thrust his finger and thumb into his mouth and pulled out two pads of cotton wool that had been stuffed up inside his cheeks, between the flesh and the top teeth. Shakily he wiped a piece of oiled lint across his eyes and a faint smear of pigment came away with it.

Manning almost gasped aloud. In ten seconds the benign visage of Engelberg had disappeared and he found himself staring at the hard, brutal features of Grosman, captain of the *Yangtse*.

And all in that moment the full realisation thundered across his brain. Grosman's method of running drugs ashore was complete and watertight to the last final shade. He did not even need another confederate ashore. He himself was his own confederate. Engelberg and Grosman were one and the same. He did not even need to send word through when a fresh load of tins was waiting on the dump. He had put them there himself. All he had to do was to go back, and in fifteen seconds he had changed himself completely.

True, now the river man came to think of it, the two men were remarkably similar—identical in build and of the same height to an inch. Engelberg was a bit fatter, perhaps, but that could easily have been accounted for by a subterfuge in dress. And anyhow, both men were naturally bulky.

But it was in the more subtle characteristics that they were so utterly different. And in that, again, Grosman had evidenced his remarkable genius. It was in the natural divergencies of nationality that the difference was so marked. The one was a scowling, bitter-looking brute who never spoke unless he was spoken to, and even then had no good thing to say of anyone or anything. A surly devil, a drug running suspect, a man who fiercely hated all thought of authority and resented the calm rulings of law and order with a fiery passion. Some of that was a pose, a magnificently carried pose, to throw into higher relief the sweet-mannered, affable-minded benevolence of the other identity.

It was a masterly disguise, and he owed it to his dual parentage that it was feasible at all. The merest touch of flesh-coloured pigment under the eyes and the slightest suspicion of brown above them and the eyes were altered out of all recognition. And then the master touch of filling out the cheeks with the dry wad of cotton-wool shifted the whole line of his features. The face did not merely look different, it *was* different. Then the thick glasses, with lenses so heavy that they completely obscured the eyes behind them, gave the final touch that knit the illusion.

Two entirely different identities could blossom and bloom in twenty seconds, and the difference from one to the other was astonishing. No one would dream that the grim, masterful owner of the *Yangtse*, tyrant over his men, contemptuous enemy of the Customs, could possibly be one and the same with the delightful, placid, rotund-faced old Hollander whose one harmless vice was that he kept hens and whose chief characteristic was that he was the most pacific old fellow in the whole locality. It was inconceivable that anyone should associate that sinister Oriental with the cheerful old Dutchman who delighted to give pennies to the gutter urchins when times were good, and who still had a smile for them when times were bad.

Manning leaned back against the wall and tried to convince himself he was not dreaming. Four hours ago he had read a message from Hillary Kittredge saying that the man was pumped full of cocaine. Something had gone wrong with the evidence; the two things did not link up.

And while he looked he saw the man breathe a sigh of relief and take a hypodermic syringe from his pocket. He filled it and waited till the hands pointed dead on the hour, and then injected the whole dose into a vein in his wrist. In a minute or two the twitching of his tortured nerves stilled, and a slow calm settled over him. The glassy, yearning look died out of his eyes, and he rested his head on his arms, outflung before him on the table.

Grosman had had a fearful time. In those last four hours he had gone naked through the fires. From that moment when the steward and the officer had gone through to him in the Temple nothing more than the exercise of a gigantic will had kept him up and going.

He had taken a terrible dose, but it was not the full strength that Hillary had thought it was. After the first injection Grosman realised that only a very weak solution would have the desired effect on the girl, and he had diluted it down accordingly.

And it was only the expert knowledge of his first officer that had pulled him round. He and the steward had marched him round and round the narrow confines of the Temple of Buddha until their own brains began to swim. They flogged him with rolled towels and rolled him on the floor till he was black and blue. They dosed him alternately with showers of icy cold water and then with water so hot that it turned his skin the colour of a boiled lobster. Anything to get those nerves alive and crawling again, anything to get some semblance of consciousness back again into his brain, no matter if it was only a glimmer. Every twenty minutes they injected a stiffening dose of the antidote and set about their efforts again, wind-milling his arms and legs until he gasped with unconscious exhaustion. It was artificial respiration on the grand, the merciless, scale.

And gradually it had its effect. The deadly pallor went out of the face, the awful leaden hue faded from the skin. A spot of feverish, hectic colour began to burn on each cheek. The hard labouring of the lungs, pumping in oxygen with the labours of his countrymen, began to revive him.

There came a faint twittering of an eyelid, and after that they never let up on him. If it were humanly possible, they redoubled the severity of the treatment they inflicted on him. And when full consciousness finally began to seep back into him it was from no other reason than that the nerve centres could assimilate no more induced pain and action and not react.

For the next hour Grosman had literally to *will* himself to remain awake. They ran him up and down the long alleyway of the ship and soused him again in the cold water. He knew what they were doing and he allowed them to do it without protest. For he knew it was the only thing that would stave off a return of that deadly lethargy that was clamouring to retake possession of his faculties.

The craneman had seen the girl talking to Bristow and he had seen her press something upon him. He could not see what it was, but he knew it was something tangible, for he saw him thrust it into his pocket. He would not have opened his mouth about it in the ordinary way, but the Chinese officers had gone round making inquiries. And as there was a five-pound bribe held out for information the craneman was not the one to quarrel with his bread and butter. He had told. And the first officer knew that a warning had gone through to the police. It was when that knowledge was finally hammered into Grosman's torpid brain that the man made his monumental fight for consciousness. And he almost fought his own powers to a standstill. There was just a chance that he could get through with it before the dogs of the law were snapping at his heels.

A big raid would take an hour or two to organise, and he had just that hour or two in which to get clear, for surely the river police would soon be upon him. And with such evidence as that girl could have given they would not rest until they had unearthed the secret of that hidden compartment. They would tear and batter at the bulkheads until every inch of the ship lay open and exposed. His only hope was to get the last of the drug out of the ship and away. The line of evidence of the biscuit tins would be followed through to the lumber yard. And that made it imperative that the double task of getting it out of the ship and out of the lumber yard again should be performed without the loss of a second.

He flung caution to the winds. The store dealer might become suspicious at so much biscuit being brought into his yard. He couldn't help it. It had to be done. He might become curious to know why Engelberg should always appear a couple of minutes later and cart the same identical cargo away. He couldn't help it. It had to be done. It was a crisis to be met with emergency measures. The next time the *Yangtse* came to the river he would have a new scheme worked out. Meanwhile it was a case of neck or nothing.

All the biscuit was now gone from the ship. He had cleared the last of it away on that final journey from the junk yard. Great heaps were stacked on the railway siding, waiting only for darkness and the arrival of Lingard's lorries.

Once that was done two of the three main ends would be clear of suspicion. Grosman could invite investigation. The police could raid there till all was blue, and they might as well raid Westminster Abbey. They would meet with nothing more than the galling knowledge that their information had broken down; the certainty that though they knew they were on the right hunting ground, the quarry had removed itself to pastures new. There would not be a jot or tittle of evidence to show.

All that remained was to clear the *Yangtse* itself of the drug. And now that the ship was free of the Customs and all examinations were over that would be a simple task. It was merely a matter of redisguising himself again on his own ship. Not a soul there knew him in his dual personality.

In his character of Grosman he could tell the deck watch that the Hollander would be coming along to the ship in person to clear some of the captain's own junk out of the cabins. The stuff could be stacked in readiness in one of the less frequented alleyways, and ten minutes later Engelberg himself would arrive with his truck to get rid of the last of the damning evidence.

But it was a fearful strain. His head was like a leaden ball poised on the top of his neck, and its weight seemed to increase with every breath he took. His whole body was crying aloud to be allowed to lie down and sleep off the deadly coma that was relentlessly gnawing at him. His limbs seemed to be things apart from the trunk of his body. They did not belong. His feet were like lumps of dough, without feeling, without shape; and there was a hard, cold lump in his thigh where the needle had gone in. If all that tremendous dose had found the bloodstream he would have been dead within an hour. But much of it had missed the vein and it hung there in the tissues, an enormous local anaesthetic that numbed his flesh and deadened his sensibilities. Every half-hour he had rationed himself a bolstering dose of the antidote. And the last ten minutes of each half-hour were a yelling misery to him. Every fibre of him was crying for the soothing relief of the antitoxin. But he knew that too much of it, or doses administered too frequently, would have the same killing effect as the drug itself. With an iron restraint and with the perspiration pouring down him, he waited till the safety margin of the clock was reached.

The adoption of the Engelberg disguise was a torment. Every scrap of the Chinese, the sullen, resentful, bitter shades of his nature, was surging up in him, hating the very shadows of the men he met; but through it all he had to preserve the calm, placid, wholly equable temperament of the Dutchman, beaming on all and sundry, remembering only the Dutch tongue, trying to forget the tearing ache that seared through his eyes from the magnified pebbles in his glasses. Every nerve was twitching, every muscle shaking, and his joints seemed to have removed themselves into all sorts of odd corners of his bones. Down there in the quiet seclusion of his rendezvous he permitted himself a let-up that he would never have shown to a soul above ground, though all the devils of hell were clawing at him.

Manning crept backwards into the store-room, holding his breath. In the brooding hush down there it seemed as though every scratch of sound was magnified a thousandfold. He scarcely dared to breathe.

The store-room was almost stripped of the huge quantities of the drug that had been stored there a few hours earlier. The greater part of it had been removed and was heaped up on the loading wharf of the railway siding, ready for Lingard's coming later on. There were still a few shelves packed tight with the stuff, but it was obvious at a glance that somebody had been frantically busy down there in the last few hours.

Grosman got up and helped himself shakily to a large glass of brandy. He drank it neat, and the glass slipped from his nerveless fingers with a crash that made Manning jump. The Chinaman stood against the wall, breathing deeply, slowly getting a grip on himself again.

Manning decided that he had got enough evidence there to make an arrest out of hand. The cleverest lawyer on earth could not have explained away the mass of material evidence that was piled up against him in that basement. There was the disguise and the knowledge that he had been working the same scheme for years. Chinny the Junk could be subpoenaed to prove all that. There was the fact that Grosman himself rented the derelict warehouse. And there was the great accumulation of the drug stored up there on the siding and the rest of it down there in the store-shed. There was the letter from the girl establishing the *Yangtse* connection with the whole affair. Though the arm of coincidence were made of elastic, it could never be stretched sufficiently to explain away all that with any attempt at verisimilitude.

Grosman had lifted his club foot on to the chair and was busy with a little instrument on the heel. In a few seconds the heel opened out on a hinge and a cascade of raw cocaine tablets poured out. Manning blinked and stared. From forty to fifty pounds' worth of the drug came tumbling out on to the chair. It was then that the reason for the odd use of the surgical boot became obvious. The Chinese captain had no more need of a specially adapted boot than had Manning himself. And Manning admitted to himself that, in confining the limp to the Chinese character, Grosman had illustrated his genius to the highest degree. It would have been so easy to have used the limp for the Hollander, on those intermittent occasions when he came to London river. That would have left him free to use his natural walk through all those months while he was away.

But the Chinese brain had worked on a higher plane. He wilfully thrust upon himself the penance of having to wear that clump boot in all his normal comings and goings. It made the disguise of the blind, easygoing Dutchman so much the more natural. One could watch that fat old figure for hours and never detect the trace of a limp or even a suspicion of a laboured walk, trying to eliminate a limp that really existed. It was not that Grosman limped even in his role of himself; it was the build and construction of the boot itself that *caused* the limp. As soon as the boot was off, Grosman could walk as naturally as any man.

Manning admitted that the man was a doughty opponent. Even though he was finally traced down as Grosman the drug runner and the warrant went out for his arrest, every officer in the force would be looking for a man with a pronounced limp. The very ingenuity of that trick alone would probably have kept him immune for years.

The boot, too, served the double purpose of inducing a limp and acting as the receptacle for small quantities of his drugs. If he could take away forty or fifty pounds' worth of narcotics every night sealed up in the hollows of that boot and distributed them among his clients down river, the net sum represented highly acceptable pickings.

That was the final touch that made Manning's case complete. Neither Grosman nor anyone else could explain away that boot and its contents to a jury of twelve.

Manning tiptoed to the door and entered. "Grosman," he said, "I arrest you on a charge of smuggling drugs through His Majesty's Customs."

Grosman whipped round as though he had been stung, and he stared at the river man as though he thought his brain was playing him tricks. But the sergeant's grim voice went on: "And I warn you that it would be unwise for you to say anything on your own behalf at this juncture; for it is my duty to tell you that anything you say may be used in evidence against you."

Grosman's soul seemed to wilt. Manning had caught him at a moment when his powers were at their lowest ebb. Neither mentally nor physically, at that moment, could he have been a match for the hard-bitten, tough-built river man. If it came to a fight Grosman did not stand one chance in a million. He could scarcely move his arms except at the expense of wracking pains, and his brain was as torpid and dull as a stagnant pool.

He swayed weakly against the wall and gently slid down to the floor. Reaction had come, abrupt and sudden. Nerves that had been holding out against overmastering lethargy for the last four hours cracked in when the vision of the uniform of the law presented itself.

Manning was halfway to him, but he stopped in sudden indecision. The breakdown was so unexpected, so unlike the relentless, fighting devil that was Grosman that it found him hesitant to proceed. It was difficult to believe that the man was really out. He was aware of an acute sense of distrust, a sea of suspicion that swept over him like a cataract.

He looked for the subterfuge and failed to find it. The man was so palpably in a state of collapse. His chin was sunk away on his chest and he was breathing as though each inhalation tore at his lungs with knives. His eyelids were lowered drunkenly, and about him were all the signs of a slow relapse into a dead inertia. The fight had been too terrific and the effort too prolonged. When the pendulum swung back it went back to the limit.

At least, that was how it appeared to Manning. A hazy idea began to float through his head that the man could not possibly be play-acting. Perhaps Hillary had been right in her message and she really had managed to drug him. And maybe his own doctors had performed the miracle on him and brought him round. The fact that he had injected something into his wrist bore out that possibility. Perhaps he was fighting a drug that was still potent in his body, unfit to fight, unable to put up any sort of a show against a man whose muscles were limber and whose faculties were still unimpaired.

He fumbled for a pair of handcuffs and moved round the table towards him. A man of Grosman's calibre was better manacled than left to make another fighting recovery. He had got the brute down and out and he did not intend to give him a chance of ever getting up again—not the flimsiest ghost of a chance.

Grosman sat like a dead thing. Manning could not see that the eyes beneath the drooping lids were burning bright as glowing lamps; he could not know that the thick muscles were flexing for one last valiant effort. Grosman could force a last trick out of his brain even when it was fast going back on him. His legs were drawn up under him and the broad of his back was pressed against the wall.

And just when Manning was coming round the comer of the table Grosman made his last effort. He suddenly sent the soles of his feet crashing against the leg of the table. With his back stanced against the wall and his forearms stiffened against the wainscoting, he was able to get every ounce of his weight to bear on the lunge. The corner of the table rammed into Manning's stomach with the force of a steam-driven battering-ram. There was a strangled gasp from the river man, a gasp that was cut short almost before it began. The lungs ceased to function in that same hundredth of a second. A great white mist launched itself over his brain.

The table had impacted on that same vital spot known to boxers; it was as though he had taken a tremendous punch in the solar plexus. There was an instantaneous suspension of the respiratory organs, every atom of breath was knocked out of him.

He went over with a sprawling thud, his arms out over his head, rolling over in an access of agonising pain. Grosman hauled himself up to his feet and stood swaying over him. His own head was swimming with the violence of his effort. There was a blur before his eyes, and his heart was pumping like an engine. But in the midst of it there was a fiery core of hatred, a white-hot centre that burned and blazed against the river man.

All his innate ferocity centred on that helpless figure. To him it epitomised the embodiment of all the forces that had so nearly brought all his years of labour and dogged endeavour to naught. Right on the very threshold of ultimate success the arch-enemy, uniformed officialdom, had butted in and all but wrecked him. He kicked him savagely as he writhed there.

His thoughts were going round in erratic circles. What did the presence of that man there portend? What was the mass of possibilities that lay behind his sudden appearance? Had the girl got her message through already, and were the police acting on it? Did any more of those damnable busybodies know the secrets of that derelict warehouse? Was Manning's advent only an advance-guard of a numerous raiding party already on its way out to Gunn Lane? Or was it just an accident of Fate—had Manning merely stumbled on that building in the course of the wide investigations that he knew were being intensively carried out all through the district?

And in either event, what was his own position? Was it safe to stay there and make the complete clean-up? Or did the whole thing call for instant flight? If he stayed and the police arrived in force, he might as well hold out his neck to the rope, for with all the accumulated evidence there he did not stand one chance in a million of ever getting himself clear. And as soon as the police got him into their clutches it would be all over with him; there would be dozens ready to turn informer on him. For the chance of a slight lessening of their own sentences half the gang would squeal on him, especially about the Maxick affairs.

He had no illusions about his reputation with the gang. He ruled them on fear alone—and both he and they knew it. Tyrants always ride for a fall. He had the example and precedent of all the East to draw on for that altruism, and the subsequent history of all the West to corroborate it. But he had chosen to rule on terror. And as soon as the tyrant falls the serfs rise up and rend him. The bully was torn between conflicting fears, fear of the vengeance of the gang and the sharper fear that his apprehension regarding the police might be groundless.

If he threw up everything now, right at that moment when final success was in sight, and fled, leaving the reams of evidence as it stood, then he would be a hunted man for life. True, he could kill Manning and drop him down through the trap. And Manning was the only soul on earth who knew about the double identity. While the police were feverishly hunting for a man with a disabling limp he could be organising a fresh business under yet a third identity. But always he would have the fear of the law hanging over him, dark and portentous as a cyclone about to burst. He would never know peace again for any single hour of his life. For he knew that the ramshackle old place was bound to come under the police microscope before many hours were passed. It was inevitable. The inexorable comb-out was getting nearer and nearer to that building every minute.

And yet there was the bare chance that Manning was an accident there, a visitor who had stumbled on the place by sheer fortuitous chance. And if he fled now he would be flinging his whole harvest to the winds, throwing it away without the slightest necessity. If the police stalled off for just a few more hours, if they could be kept away until nightfall when Lingard's lorries had cleared the place of the last trace of illicit drugs, then there was still a chance, still a fighting, worthwhile chance that the thing might be pulled off.

He slid heavily down to his knees beside the prostrate man. There was a wicked glint of determination glittering in his eyes. If a stake was worth playing for it was worth playing for right up to the last final fling. And he was not throwing away the labour of years so long as there was one chance in a hundred of bringing off the great haul. Let the police come. Half a million pounds was worth a last battle, a fight to the death if necessary. And if the worst came to the worst there was always that great cameo ring on the middle finger of his left hand. One fierce press on the cameo with that stiff thumbnail of his and the tiny hollow needle would sink into the flesh.

And while they questioned him, while those fools of the law hammered at him and fulminated their streams of questions at him, the poison would be gently and surely trickling through to his heart. A gentle death, a quiet death, a death shorn of pain and shame, a death relieved of the ignominy of being led up like a patient animal to the dim silhouette of a gallows in the pale grey of a dawning... of being legally killed by those loathsome hirelings of established law and order. Such a death as a mandarin of the East might desire to die, and not be ashamed of, when he was gathered up into the innumerable caravan of his fathers.

He took the handcuffs from the river man's nerveless fingers. In a few moments he had fastened them securely on the unresisting wrists. He tried to drag him along to the trapdoor, but his strength petered out. The river man was heavy and the captain's strength had been taxed to the uttermost. He leaned against the doorway and glared at him, all the concentrated ferocity of a wild animal gazing on its age-old enemy smouldering in his eyes. "So! Lie there—sow!" he said pantingly. "Lie there till I come back. In a little while other hands shall fling you down into the darkness. You shall drown like the rat you are. And I will listen above, at the open trap, and your cries shall be music to me."

Manning was beginning to come to. Something of the livid paralysis was going from his respiratory muscles, a tingle of returning life was suffusing the diaphragm. He opened his eyes and looked up. At first he comprehended nothing. Neither the glowering face of the mandarin nor the dilapidated appearance of his surroundings implied anything to him. He was like a man only half returned from a dream, a man still on the borderline between sleep and contact with his own brain. The solar plexus blow has that horrible stunning effect when the mind as well as the physical body seems to slide off on to another plane. Grosman kicked him again and cursed him gutturally under his breath.

When he finally began to drift back to his senses he could not move. He could see Grosman busily changing back into his Chinese clothes. Manning himself was bound hand and foot. Lengths of old canvas had been torn into strips and twisted to make ropes strong enough to have fettered an elephant. A Hercules could not have broken them.

He rolled over on to his side and looked in through the open door. He cursed himself for having let the drug runner catch him on so apparent a ruse. It was nothing less than blind folly. He might have suspected some sort of a trick from that cunning brain. But he had walked into the trap like the veriest novice. And his bitterness grew. Ten short minutes ago he had had that unutterable beast cornered and trapped; he had taken him single-handed, and nothing but a miracle could have prevented him from getting the manacles on him and marching him along to the lockup.

And in that short interval the tables were turned. Grosman had him at his mercy. He could have bitten his own tongue in sheer self-execration.

For some minutes he tried to think out a way of escape, fought his own brain for a trick equally as effective as the one Grosman had played on him. But Manning was cast in the stolid mould. He lacked that quick spark of electric ingenuitv that was ever gleaming in the mind of the Oriental. He struggled with his bonds, and his only reward was to feel the warm trickle of blood over his wrists where the harsh canvas rawed through the flesh.

And then he heard a sound that made him stiffen with expectancy. It was slight, ever so far away, seeming to come from right away in the back end of the building. For some seconds he harboured a wild, sweeping hope that the Chief had altered his plans and was raiding without waiting to connect up with the West End gang. And then the sound clarified itself, identified itself into a steady, gentle knocking. Manning's heart sank. It was the soft tap-tapping of Blind Rudley's stick.

Grosman heard it too, and he wheeled. He stood with his head thrust forward to catch the sound; and an angry frown settled down over his brows as he realised what it was. He went out into the main building and stared out among the gloomy shadows. The figure of Rudley appeared, tap-tapping along with the stick out-thrust before him, exploring the pitfalls and obstacles that beset him in the midst of his eternal darkness.

Grosman muttered thunderously under his breath and waited for him. He was so irritated at what was to him a maniacal daylight entry that he did not even go forward to steer the blind man through to the office. Coming in that way Rudley must have come down Gunn Lane and entered via the roof. A suicidal thing to do, with the whole locality alive with plain clothes men.

He came tapping along, heading directly for the inner room. Grosman stood aside to let him pass. But, as though sensing his presence there, the blind man came to a slow halt and his questing stick went feeling out ahead of him, searching for the man he knew was there but could not see.

The high-pitched, plaintive voice came querulously on the silence. "Where are you? Are you there, captain?"

And then Grosman let the vials of his wrath spill over. He cursed him in spitfire, metallic sentences that cut through the air like knives; heaped his vituperation upon him until Manning thought that, in the storm of repressed fury that overmastered him, he was going to spring at him and choke the life out of him.

"Am I here?" he rasped. "Am I here, you maniac? Where else did you think I would be—scurrying for cover like the rest of the rats? What the hell do you want down here? Why did you come here at all, you blind fool? Gunn Lane and all around is stiff with police. Already Manning has found out the secret of this place. I've got him trussed up there—he will be down the trap in two minutes. But how many more are there waiting and watching the approaches to this place? Waiting and watching for some such fool as *you* to come crawling down and give them the trail. How many saw you? You came in through the fire escape. That meant that you climbed the outer stairs—in broad daylight. You've wrecked the last chance we ever had of getting away with the big haul. You've smashed us as surely as you're standing there."

Rudley was slowly coming towards him again, coming slowly and imperturbably through the tempest of cursing that bit at him with all the cornered frenzy of a polecat.

And all in a tense, electric moment Grosman stopped. The stream of venomed bitterness petered out and came to a tingling silence. Manning stared, unable to believe his own eyes. Grosman was backing, trying to get out of the way of Rudley. But Rudley was not being evaded. As often as the mandarin stepped away the blind man turned and followed him, his hands gently fumbling at the air ahead of him.

And then Grosman gasped. A burst of realisation went searing across his brain. Those eyes! They were not the eyes of a blind man. Blind Rudley was looking at him with eyes that saw, eyes that were boring into the man's very soul. Grosman squeaked and tried to move away. But he was too late. Rudley was on him, on him in a single flying leap that took him clear to the throat of the drug runner. They went over in a flying crash with Rudley on top.

Manning felt his eyes popping out of his head. He struggled and wrenched at his bonds, trying to get free to help get the captain under. But Rudley needed no help. He seemed to be suddenly possessed of superhuman strength, and in the same moment he declared himself as a man with no small knowledge of wrestling holds.

With a single mighty heave he got the mandarin over and fastened a scissors lock on his legs. And then, with one swart hand over the instep, he slowly dragged the foot up into the position for the terrible toe-hold. Grosman screamed as the pressure came on, and he tore at the floor in the helplessness of his agony. But the hold was locked and Rudley was not letting him go until the muscles were paralysed.

And then another minor miracle happened. Blind Rudley produced from his pocket with his free hand a pair of regulation handcuffs.

Grosman was beaten. He was screaming for release, yelling that he would do anything, consent to anything, if only the fearful pressure that was cracking his very sinews, was eased. His thigh muscles were cramped up into great knots, and his face was wet with the sweat of pain.

Rudley released him. It would be an hour before the man could walk. He lay there, a quivering mass of violated nerves. Rudley silently lugged his hands behind him and snapped on the handcuffs.

And then Rudley, no longer feeling his way or walking with the testing, timorous gait of the blind, hurried back out of the inner office and cut Manning free of his bonds.

"Better walk about for a bit and get some blood back into your veins," he said. "We have got a mile of work ahead of us yet." And the voice was the sharp, authoritative voice of the Chief.

Manning rolled over and the Chief unlocked the manacles. He tried to stand up, but he was still groggy, and he sat down with a bump.

The Chief grinned. "You asked for it," he said. "It was a daft thing to do to come here alone. You know what happened to Procter."

Manning was vigorously rubbing his arms and legs.

"Couldn't help myself, Chief," he said bluntly. "I got on the tail end of the whole job and I followed it through. There is all the proof we want here, every blessed bit of it. Grosman and Engelberg are one and the same; his disguise is hanging up there. I had a suspicion some time ago that that was how he worked it, but it seemed too tall a story to be true. And when I tested it out it all turned out wrong. That was because I had been caught out over the biscuits. The ones I fed to the birds were all harmless. And I thought my theory had come unstuck. I wouldn't say anything about it because I should have looked such a monumental idiot if things had turned out wrong. Have you had a look round up top, sir?"

"No. I have had a man posted in a building that looks on to the railway siding and he reported activity here today. Then we heard that you had come through on the trail of Engelberg. I had already decided to pay this place a visit. Blind Rudley had been seen in this district—and I copied his make-up. It was the best way to get through their cordon here. There is always someone watching, and I guessed that a warning would go through to Grosman. And," he added grimly, "I guessed you would be standing in need of a bit of a lift."

"You were only just in time, too, Chief." Manning looked up at his superior sheepishly. "He was arranging to dump me down the trap. Some sort of a hole they've got where they can drop a body down and hear no more about it. It's out through there, I think. Anyway, that's where he was trying to drag me when his strength gave out. There's some more of his scum due here at any moment from what he says. We shall have to hurry if we are going to get away with it."

"What is there of special note up there?"

"Enough dope to send half the capital to sleep. Grosman seems to have been having a general clear out. There is a couple of lorry loads of the stuff up there on the railway siding and another heap of it there in the store-room. It looks to me as though he had got the wind up—knew the police were making an intensive comb out right through the district and knew that this place would come in for investigation sooner or later. And so he was trying to get clear with the whole lot before we stepped in. If we can collar the Chinese as they come in we ought to make a clean-up. All the gang is bound to be around here sooner or later, and we can wipe 'em up as they arrive."

"Too late for that now," grunted the Chief. "It would take an hour to get enough men round here to collar all that crowd. We can get them the other way. I want them *all*. And that 'all' includes Lingard and his crowd. You say their stuff is all up there on the railway siding?"

"Yes, sir. Some tons of it I should think. Some of it is still in biscuit form, but they've taken most of it out."

"H'm. That means they are aiming to transport the whole lot tonight. So much the better. It means that Lingard will be wanted. Don't suppose they can manage it all without him. And they have taken the stuff out of the biscuit for ease of handling. Yes, that's it—they were going to clear out of here without a trace. Well, we've got them this time. We can—" He broke off and suddenly leaned forward, listening.

"Hear anything?" he whispered.

"No, sir." Manning, too, had unconsciously sunk his voice to a whisper.

And then Grosman, lying on his back, began to laugh in half-hysterical relief. He was staring at the wall in front of him. And on that wall was a tiny electric lamp—and the lamp was flashing. One—two—three—four—five—six—seven—eight. To him the flashes meant salvation, for they told him that eight of his gang of merciless cutthroats were at the doors and were coming in.

The drawbar was raised. They heard the scuff of it and heard the creak of the door as it opened. And in a moment or two there came the soft scrape of shoes coming down through the building. The door was closed, and the tramp of feet came echoing through the gloomy building, treading out an inexorable message of doom.

"Where is the back way out of this?" snapped the Chief.

"There isn't one," said Manning. "The only way I could find was down the lift shaft. We're trapped. We can't fight that lot—my arms are like jelly. Got a gun?"

"Don't carry one. Come on—quick—there's a way out. Where's that trap?" The Chief was already running silently out through the main building towards the long passage that communicated to the rest of the store-rooms.

"Going to take a swim for it?" asked Manning.

"Nothing else to do. Come on. We shall collar them yet."

The trap was unmistakable; it was right in the centre of the passageway, two great flaps that opened outwards.

"I'll go first," said the Chief, pulling off his greatcoat. "I'll sing out to you when I'm clear of the drop." He wrapped his flash-lamp in the folds of his coat and dropped, all standing, into the blackness below. Manning heard the ponderous splash of his body as he struck the water. Back in the office excited voices were babbling in Chinese, and he could hear the fierce tones of the captain ordering them to rush out and retake the two officers.

Then a light shone out below. The Chief had broken surface again. The water had not had time to get through the thick material of the coat. He had rescued the lamp and let the coat drift away. Manning could see him treading water, holding the lamp high over his head, and the light was drifting slowly and steadily down stream.

"Jump for it," called the Chief from below. Manning lowered himself over the drop, hanging on by one hand as he held up the flap with the other. He let go and dropped like a plummet, the trap falling softly back into place. As the flap fell he heard the rapid padding of feet flying round the comer. The next moment a shearing iciness enveloped him, a coldness so intense that it numbed him. He rose to the surface again, gasping. The Chief was half a dozen yards from him, regarding him with that same humourless smile that was part of his make-up whenever a tight situation suddenly eased.

"How do you feel, old warhorse?" he called. "Damn parky, isn't it?" Manning's teeth were chattering. He gasped out a stifled "Gosh, I never knew water could be so cold and not freeze." He struck out down stream, and the two of them swam on into the blackness.

The course of the underground stream had been bricked in; it flowed through a sort of semicircular tunnel. The tide was well out, for the tideline was marked in thick green slime six feet up the wall, and in consequence they were helped by the flow of the water.

They had been kicking out steadily for ten minutes when a faint disc of light slowly began to shine out at the far end—daylight, where the stream made its outfall into old London River. The torch went out. Water had percolated through and shorted the battery. The Chief tossed it away with a grunt. It didn't matter then; they could see their goal—and his arm had become heavy as lead from holding the lamp aloft.

Twice they had to hang on to projections in the wall for a breather. The water was so cold that it seemed to deaden the lungs. But the tiny disc grew bigger and bigger and finally resolved itself into a great arch of masonry. The two men drifted out through it on the verge of exhaustion. Manning recognised the spot, the long, straight stretch half a mile below the Wapping station. A few yards down stream a slab-sided old lighter was moored. They drifted down to it and hung on to the mooring lines.

"Don't want to excite too much attention," said the Chief. His jaws were stiff with the cold, and he could hardly speak. "When do the boats run?"

"Ought to be one every half an hour, sir. But we don't keep to a timetable. There'll be one along in a minute. I'll give her a hail."

They waited another ten minutes in the numbing cold, and then a motorboat came chugging down river, coming gently down on the ebbing tide. Manning sent a low call over the water, an oddly pitched note that carried with remarkable clarity and was known to the river men.

The sergeant in the boat heard it and wheeled. Manning waved to him, and in a few minutes they were in the boat heading back to Wapping station.

The Chief set about organising the raid before he had got his wet clothes off. He called for forty men from Headquarters to break in and hold the warehouse in Gunn Lane.

"Send them down in Flying Squad vans," he ordered over the telephone. "Manning will meet them at the top of the Lane and will take charge. Arrest every man who enters and hold them till I get there. I'll be through again in a few minutes with full instructions."

But those instructions never matured. He had hardly put the instrument down when there came another violent peal on the bell.

"That the Chief?" said a hurried voice. "About that place in Gunn Lane. The raid's off. They've fired it."

"What?"

"Message just come through from the fire station. Place is a blazing inferno. Nothing can hold it. They've sent out a district call, and there's a dozen engines on the way. But they say it's hopeless. The building's as old as Adam—more than half wood. And the timber is rotten as mush. They will have a fierce time saving the surrounding property."

"Damn!" breathed the Chief. "Are you sure it's as bad as you say?"

"According to the official fire report, it looks as though a general call will go out if a bit of wind springs up. All the buildings round there are just made for a fire. Ought to have been condemned years ago."

The Chief turned wearily from the phone. "Well, what do you know about that?" he said.

He climbed into a spare rig of Manning's that fitted him nowhere and hurried down to the scene of the fire. There was no hope from the first. Long before he reached Gunn Lane he saw the effects. A great column of black smoke was going up to the sky in a high, wide mushroom, and the ominous roar of the flames could be heard three hundred yards away.

The building burned like old tinder. Gunn Lane was choked with pumps and engines, and the water supply, with so many engines concentrated on it, was utterly inadequate. The brigades got through to the railway sidings and fought tirelessly to hold the flames back long enough to get into the main building and search it. But it was in the main building that the fire had been started. Petrol had been scattered round and lit in a score of places. When the Chief got there the warehouse was like a furnace. Thirty jets were playing on it, and they had about as much effect as a toy squirter would have on Etna. The place was doomed. And with it the evidence that Manning and the Chief had fought for.

The Chief watched the holocaust with sullen eyes. The Fire Superintendent came out of the smoke and the grime to tell him that his squads had not found a single grain of drug in the whole place. The smoke-helmet brigade had penetrated as far as the railway sidings before the flames had taken hold there, and so far as they could see there was nothing there. They had felt their way along the whole length of the loading quay and encountered nothing. But the smoke was so chokingly thick that they could not see a yard. And ten minutes later the sidings, too, were involved in the volcano of fire. If there had ever been any evidence there it was now lost forever. Grosman had played him a last savage trump right at the moment of victory.

The Chief went back to the river station. There was just a chance that the trick might be pulled off yet. The post card scheme was up in the air. The evening papers were full of the fire story, for a general call had gone out. For some time it looked as though another Great Fire of London was in its inception, for four other buildings in the surrounding property took fire and the full forces of the Fire Department had to be concentrated on the neighbourhood.

It was impossible that Lingard had not heard of the burning. Even if the newspaper reports had escaped his notice, he was bound to have heard of it from one of his runners. And what would be his position when that post card arrived? He could tell from the date stamp that it had been posted long before the fire originated. But would he realise that Grosman was calling him urgently, that a matter of such seriousness had arisen that his presence was immediately required? And, knowing that the old rendezvous was now a smouldering monument of red-hot ashes, would he decide to go to the *Yangtse?* Certainly he would need to see Grosman. There were obviously a big story behind the burning of that warehouse, and it was vitally necessary for him to get the full facts of it.

It was a long shot, but on that one assumption the Chief based his hopes. He ordered a raid on the *Yangtse*, and in doing so he played the craftiest card of all. The raid was a spoof from beginning to end in every sense.

He knew that Grosman would be openly incredulous if no search was made of his ship after all the suspicions that he knew must have been communicated to the police in the last forty-eight hours, He would suspect guile in his very immunity, and he would shy off like a startled horse.

The raiders came. They put the ship under arrest and they hunted and harried the hull from stem to stern. And they found just nothing. They made a great show of prying into every hole and corner; they went over every bulkhead and superstructure with tap-hammer and test-gauge; they questioned every officer and man for hours; and in the end they retired baffled. Manning himself made a half-hearted apology to the first officer for what he grudgingly admitted was an obvious mistake. It was as though the police fully realised they were barking up the wrong tree, but were rather sorry that it was so. Grosman, the senior officer explained, had not yet returned from a visit to his underwriters.

The Chief allowed the hours to drag. At nine o'clock Lingard received the post card. A detective, posted in the Caverne Diamentée, reported his anxiety when it arrived. Lingard was in the midst of the whirl of what little gaiety was noticeable on the floor at that hour. White puffballs were being flung about. The ones that he caught, with some affectation of hilarity, as often as not contained a five-pound note. The ones he threw in return contained cocaine to that same value. Equally, when he offered a cigarette from his case, the knowing ones knew which white cylinder to take. And when the case was tossed back the payment for that curiously solid cigarette was neatly folded inside. An éclair might, or might not, contain cream; it all depended on the dish from which you were invited to select. He was seen to "lend" a cigarette lighter half a dozen times. None of the lighters ever came back to him—but then, neither did anyone attempt to light a cigarette with them. That detective noted around dozen ways in which cocaine could be passed and payment taken right under the noses of a crowd without arousing the faintest hint of suspicion.

But when the post card arrived even the assumed merriment slid off Lingard's face as though a taut elastic had snapped away a mask. Before the orchestra reached the end of the fox-trot they were playing, Lingard, muffled and overcoated, was speeding dockwards in his car.

Blind Rudley met him at the entrance to the docks. A meeting with Grosman, he said, was dangerous in that crisis. Grosman was on board, disguised as one of his own coolies. The police had searched the ship and had withdrawn. The time was ripe for the getaway. All the dope had been taken away from the ship and from the warehouse. It was all down at the coast by then, being transhipped to a boat on a lonely reach of the Sussex marshes.

Lingard's job was to get down there as fast as his car could take him and get out to sea in the boat. When far out to sea the *Yangtse* would wait on a given rendezvous, beyond the twelve-miles limit. The drugs could then be taken back aboard the *Yangtse* and disposed of elsewhere. It had to be done that way, for Grosman feared another raid on his way out to sea. He was not greatly concerned about the raid, for there was not another grain of drug left aboard, even though they found the hidden compartment, of the existence of which he was positive the police were aware—Grosman having a lurking suspicion that they were playing him like a cat with a mouse.

Rudley gave him a chart showing the exact position on the marshes where the boat lay and giving him the rendezvous. Trusted men were in charge of her, but the captain was not to be given the rendezvous until they were well out to sea. The

Yangtse was slipping her moorings as soon as Grosman knew Lingard had got his instructions.

Lingard pursed his lips. Already he felt the grim, unseen hands of the law reaching out of the blackness for him. But it was neck or nothing now. Rudley heard the car drive swiftly away. And he let out a long breath of relief. He had got both ends on the run now.

He whistled softly and Manning came out of the shadows to him.

"That's all squared," he said. "The *Yangtse* has notified the pilots she's slipping before midnight. Grosman is on board—together with the dope. It came aboard tonight in three loads, labelled up as ship's stores; they cleared it from the warehouse in broad daylight while we were having an underground swim. It's all in the hidden chamber by now, and we will collar them with the lot."

"Shall I phone Mr. Essex now?"

"Yes. Tell him everything is ready for him. He is to come to the Wapping station soon after midnight and pick up me and the squad. In that speedboat of his we can hang down over the skyline till Lingard's boat comes out to pick her up. There are ten other police officers in that hooker, but Lingard will not know that until it's an hour or two too late."

"I'll see to it right away, sir. And the raid on the Caverne? Is that O.K.?"

"Surely. Phone Headquarters and tell them to let it go at eleven o'clock. Lingard will have had time to go back and change and get halfway down to the coast by them. You should find enough stuff there to put him away for years—together with what we get from them when Grosman unexpectedly meets him in mid-ocean. It should be a notable reunion."

It was. The *Yangtse* was given free passage down the old river. Grosman could scarcely believe that fortune could have been so marvellously kind to him. He waited on in momentary dread of hearing that stentor hail come thundering over the tideway, calling on him to heave to. He was in a sweat of apprehension lest a swarm of resolute men came climbing up over the side and chopped and slashed the secret of the hidden compartment out of the ship.

But the miles slipped by and nothing happened. Shore stations bobbed the challenge at him and he answered with the name of his ship. Grey dawn broke, and he was through the worst of the ordeal. He was out through the river, out beyond Sheerness and heading away for the open Channel.

At noon he surrendered the bridge to his first officer. An immense drowsiness was crawling over him. All the reaction of his fierce drugging and the still more powerful reaction of the nerve strain of the last few hours had worn him badly. He stumbled off the bridge down to the saloon.

And a little later a fast diesel-engined boat crept out on a long echelon to meet them from the coast down which it had been running all night.

It put on speed and came alongside. The first mate recognised Lingard and bawled to him that Grosman was down below, sleeping. Lingard grabbed a rope and hauled himself aboard. The motorboat immediately put the helm over and sheered off. Lingard was too anxious to get a word with Grosman even to notice it. And certainly he did not notice the tearing, shearing line of white that was racing up astern, sending up a bow wave that cut into the air in two creaming white arcs, leaving the waters behind her a tumbling seethe of hissing froth.

Then the strident roar of her great engines began to drone on the air, engines going all out in a shining splinter of a hull that was pounding out fifty knots through the smooth swells. The roar increased to an ear-filling crescendo as the long lean shell came snoring up.

Lingard had gone below, but the first officer turned and stared astern at the flying streak. He got his glasses to bear, but all the *Spindrift* looked like at that terrific speed was a whizzing core of white crowned with a central silver sheen. By the time he grasped the situation it was too late. The boat was alongside and silent; uncompromising-looking figures were swarming up over the rails.

As her gunwale grated against the *Yangtse*, Essex held her there till his human cargo was out. Then he pushed his mechanic over to the wheel and went tearing up after them. The diesel boat had closed in on the other side, and the debacle, so far as the Chinese crew was concerned, was complete. Grosman, who had gone through to the Temple of Buddha, did not even know the ship was boarded.

Guns were out, and the crew, dazed with the unexpectedness of it, were standing around with their hands held fearfully over their heads. Essex went racing down to the saloon. The Chief and his squad were in ahead of him. The great sideboard stood gaping wide open, broken and shattered.

He went plunging through. The officers were battering at the second door. It fell in with a crash, the hatchets breaking through the mechanism of the panel with sheer murderous force.

Grossman, cornered, was standing at bay snarling like a rabid dog.

"Get back" he rasped. In his hand was the deadly light-gun.

The sharp crack of a revolver snapped out, and Grosman was dancing round holding a torn hand to his mouth. The gun had been shot clean out of it.

He looked at the hand—and whimpered with a newer and more terrible dismay. The bullet had taken with it the middle finger, taken it off at the roots, the middle finger, with that precious gift of a merciful death in the hollow behind the cameo. And then Essex was at him. Grosman saw the sudden vision of the horror and the terror of the long trial, the black cap... and that fearful last walk from the condemned cell up the steps in the grey of a dawning.

He tried to get his sound hand at the younger man's throat. But Essex slugged him with every atom of strength that was in him. The mandarin went hurtling backwards, knocked off his heels. The whole weight of his great bulk crashed against the Buddha—and the graven image tottered, canted over with a sudden lurch of the ship, and went smashing to the floor. And behind it, trussed up, gagged and bound, her eyes dilated wide with horror, was the girl. Toby caught her as she fell.

The rest was just the inevitable anti-climax of mopping up. A Trinity House tug was puffing down to them when they got up on deck. On her bridge were the Port Authorities who would take charge of her and take out the piledmp masses of drugs that choked the Temple of Buddha. Among the debris of the wood was the piece of evidence that finally hanged the mandarin—the broken hilt of the dagger that was taken from the heart of Ulrich Maxick; and on the inverted V of the break was the Chinese lettering of the word "Dawn." Grosman saw it and shuddered. He was slowly realising that in the West, as well as in the East, Death comes with the Dawn.

* * *

As the *Spindrift* sped homeward, Hillary, wet but almost tearfully happy, was helping Toby to steady the kicking wheel. Toby's hand closed over hers; something crinkled in it. He gently opened her fingers. A piece of paper fell out.

"That was the only mistake Grosman ever made," she said with a tense little laugh. "It—it was what made me know I could beat him if I kept on. That was the note he pinned to my breast when he first locked me in the Temple. He never noticed it was missing when he came in to drug me again; he noticed every single thing but that. Toby, that little piece of paper saved my life."

He took her in his arms and hugged her against the wheel. "It saved a good deal more than that if you think it out," he said quietly. "And why on earth we should be stuck out here in the wet when there is a perfectly comfortable little cabin along there, heaven only knows."

He motioned the girl along. Then he turned and winked at the mechanic.

"Come on, you," he said. "Come and take this darn wheel."

THE MYSTERY MAKER

Colonel Stayne, late of the anti-espionage corps, is the Mystery Maker, and Scotland Yard knows that "where John Stayne is, there big-time trouble is surely coming to the boil."

I

As an individual Colonel John Stayne was unique in quite a number of ways. Even the highly-coloured records at Scotland Yard admitted him as one of their star artists—and a particularly irritating artist at that. He was one who refused to be snared, no matter how perfectly the trap was laid for him, no matter how many brains took a hand in the perfecting of the trap. He seemed to have been mixed up in something more than half the biggest swindles and criminal jobs of the post-war years, and his name and history were definitely involved in the dossier of every international crook in the Yard archives.

And yet... even the higher authorities at Headquarters had to admit that there was an embarrassingly noticeable "And yet" about the John Stayne situation. He seemed to have an "And yet" complex.

To begin with, he was only thirty-one and yet his rank of colonel was genuine, although he had been out of the army some years. He had gained his colonelcy at twenty-two, and yet he had never heard a single shot fired in action. He had done remarkable work in the Anti-Espionage Corps, and yet he had resigned without offering a single reason.

Twenty-four hours later the famous Cottrington case broke in seven-column banner lines in the newspapers. Colonel John Stayne's name was mentioned by every single witness in that remarkable affair, and yet not a single one of them could recognise him at an identity parade; Lord Cottrington repudiated all knowledge of him when he stepped into the witness-box.

He was so good-looking in a quiet, aristocratic way that pretty well every eligible debutante's mother had taken a shamelessly complete fall in his direction; and yet he was a bachelor still, without a single whisper of scandal against his moral reputation. There was no earthly reason why he should exhibit a criminal tendency, for he was an exceptionally wealthy man in his own right, and yet—there were those ineradicable dossiers in pretty well every important pigeon-hole at Scotland Yard.

He seemed to swim around right out on the verge of things, sometimes heading straight into the very heart of the seething whirlpool, with every other subsidiary revolving madly about him, and then, when the crash came, there were all the majors and minors safely under lock and key—and there was John Stayne, a nebulous, unaccusable being, right out beyond the net again with not a tittle of evidence against him. Indeed, such evidence as there was tended to prove that John Stayne had had nothing whatever to do with the unpleasant affair.

The Yard, being human and as wise as they make 'em, had long since ceased to harbour any resentment against him. He was far too useful. As an unfailing guideline, pointing always to where big trouble was brewing, he was infallible. Where John Stayne was, there big-time trouble was surely coming to the boil in the stew-pot of the underworld.

So they gave him his rein, stepped along invisibly four yards astern of his coat-tails, and let him ride. And because of his remarkable propensity for unearthing the big stuff while keeping out of it himself, they dubbed him the "Mystery-Maker," raised their mental hats to him, and breathed a little prayer for his continued well-being.

He lived in a large house in Curzon Square, one of those large, fashionable houses in one of those small, fashionable squares that still carry, on their startlingly ugly facades, something of the unutterably quiet and proper atmosphere of the early Victorian era.

* * *

John Stayne was a tall, military-looking figure, dark-haired, bronzed with the tan of a good many travels under southern suns, and all over him he carried the indefinable stamp of the soldier. His actions were orderly and precise; as were his utterances. So orderly and precise that they implied an orderly and precise brain. His thoughts were co-ordinated and definitely formed before he vocalised them into words. Alene Mathers, his secretary, declared emphatically that she had never taken dictation from a more clear-minded, less annoying employer. And that, knowing the general mudheadedness of a man trying to dictate a letter to a girl with fair hair and speedwell-blue eyes, is a knowledgeable commendation.

Vai Tembridge, a sharp-tongued young gentleman, whom he chose to call his assistant, had thumped the noses of half a dozen individuals who had been incautious enough to scandalise Stayne's general behaviour in his hearing. Scotland Yard had never been able to "place" Tembridge to its satisfaction or to discover in exactly what way he assisted. Except that he had a genuine American accent—one which the disconcerting young pup could switch off at will—and a bewildering knack of bobbing up right in that one spot where they had already conclusively proved it was impossible for him to be, they knew very little about him.

One of the first bright suns of early spring was shining sharply through the windows of 8B, Curzon Square. In the big main room one of the last wood fires of winter burned cheerily in the open grate. John Stayne reached out from the depths of a great leather armchair and thumbed a bell button under the edge of the table.

It was a huge room. The carved mahogany table, eight foot by twelve, looked small. Eight cut-crystal candelabra swung high from the gilded ceiling, and the wallpaper was of stained, chased leather. Stayne relaxed again and re-read a letter in his lap.

Tembridge came in, a sheaf of papers under his arm and a fat red fountain pen behind his ear.

"Tembridge," said Stayne, "I want some information about the Demorval affair. The probability is that there is a case in it for us. Do you happen to know any inside details about it, off-hand?"

"Lady Demorval?"

"Yes, recently widowed. I believe I was in Chicago on that Rutledge business when the case came on."

Tembridge nodded. "Sure," he said. "I haven't all the details, but it's all in the files. Lady Demorval had just left her chateau in Mentone to come back here for the London season. Before she reached London she received news that the chateau had been broken into. Must have done it the same night she left. Thieves went for the jewels. Said jewels were to have followed her to town a few days later under special guard.

"Stones to the value of over £100,000 were taken. Two ropes of diamonds—the Demorval ropes. Fine tiara of rubies. And the whole collection of emeralds. Emeralds not too good. Some good ones among them, of course, but, on the whole, imperfect. Some pretty fine opals went too, but Lady Demorval ranks opals along with coral, cat's-eyes, and coke. The assessors stuck out a reward right away—£5,000 for their recovery. Increased it later to £20,000. Must have been badly stung on the insurance. Plums of the picking were the ropes. A week later Lady Demorval went to Mentone herself to try to hammer a bit of *nous* into the heads of the French police. She had put up at an hotel in London for a few days while the town house was being prepared. All her luggage was stored there pending instructions from her.

"One evening there was a sound of banging coming from the room where the luggage was stored. Hotel manager threw a fright and phoned the police.

They got there in time to arrest Varris in the foyer. He was heading for the street with his hat on his head and the diamonds in his hip pocket—done up in tissue paper. The head bellhop had watched him come out of the storeroom in one peach of a hurry. Varris—Templer Varris—was her private secretary, and was in full charge of her affairs until Lady Demorval's return. Up in the store-room they found half her ladyship's baggage busted open."

* * *

Stayne held up his hand. "Just a moment," he said. "Templer Varris. Have you anything about him?"

"Yes. Unhappy relic of the war. Very good family from one of the shires. A bit county. Joined up as soon as his years let him. Left the army at twenty-two. No more training for a decent job in civilian life than you can derive from four years of loosing off rifles, slinging hand grenades, and jabbing holes in a lot of Jerries with a bayonet. Had two or three years trying to keep up appearances on a couple of pounds a week and then fell fairly lucky. The Demorvals wanted a private secretary and Varris got the job. He'd been with them about three years when it happened. Previous record with them good. No complaint of any sort. Case came up for hearing two weeks ago—just before you got back. Varris got five years."

"Pretty clear case, you think?"

"As it reads, Varris had as many legs to stand on as a puff-adder—and about as evenly distributed. He said he was breaking the cases open because he had lost the keys. Lady Demorval had wired for some papers to be sent on to her out of one of the trunks. He proved that piece all right; and then he said that while rummaging through the grips he came across the ropes wrapped up in the tissue just as they were found on him. He couldn't get away from the fact that the bulls collared him for streaking for the broad highway, with the goods as part cargo. He said he was taking them to the assessors for safe custody. He seemed to ignore the fact that there was perfectly safe custody in the hotel strongroom and that the clocks were just booming 7 p.m. when they stopped him at the door. The assessors close at five."

Stayne was silent for a while and then said, almost to himself: "A great pity about those times. I suppose Varris was aware of the time City offices close?"

"He said he knew all right, but had forgotten to remember. Said he was so astonished and upset he forgot all about everything. Net result—five years for not remembering not to forget. Those ropes were worth £25,000 each."

"Anything else? Did he try to implicate anyone else or hint at other complications?"

"Not directly. He told the judge that there was considerably more than a mere diamond stealing charge at the back of the business, and asked to be allowed to make a statement to the judge privately in his room. The judge told him that except in cases concerning the Crown, blackmail or obscenity, all statements must be made in open court. Any remarks he had to make would be made from the dock or not at all. Varris thought it over for a bit and decided to stay dumb."

"H'm. Very interesting. Very, *very* interesting. So interesting that, I think, before many hours have passed, we shall re-embark on our criminal career. Quite a lot of laws will be broken before we sort out our particular end of this lively problem."

"Varris is innocent, eh?"

"Of any connection with this diamond business—yes. But the diamond affair is only the rash on the surface. The real disease goes a great deal deeper, I think. There should be some quite bright times ahead. I think we have dug our fingers into what you call a real one this time."

A great jade clock began chiming softly on a mantelpiece that was built of solid slabs of alabaster. Stayne had slumped back in his chair again, and was staring hard into the glowing heart of the blazing pine logs. Behind him, on a bracket set in the corner of the room, was a golden idol of incredible ugliness. Gripped in its distorted hands was a tiny silver bell and from its mouth protruded what appeared to be an ivory cornucopia. Suddenly and without any apparent volition the bell tinkled twice on a high musical note. Stayne turned a knob under the arm of his chair, and said, to nobody in particular, "Yes—what is it?"

A minor miracle happened. From the little ivory trumpet in the idol's mouth came a voice of astonishing clarity. It was a male voice, pitched in the natural human key, and its volume was as perfectly modulated as though the speaker was present, there in the comer of the room.

"Front hall speaking," it said; "a visitor to see you, sir."

Without turning round Stayne said: "Thank you. What name, please?"

"Miss Marienne Varris, sir. She says that she wrote you and suggested in her letter that she would like to see you at nine o'clock this morning. If it is inconvenient for you to see her now, would you please make an appointment at as early a moment as possible. She states that her business is of extreme urgency."

"Thank you, Belham. Send Miss Varris up to me here. I will see her immediately." Stayne pushed the knob back and turned to Tembridge.

"That's Templer Varris's sister," he said. "She's in terrible distress about her brother—to judge from this letter here—and says she will do anything on earth if I will help him. The letter of an educated woman going into hysterics through sheer helplessness and despair."

He rolled the letter into a ball and pitched it into the fire, watching it slowly uncoil and burn away to black ash. With an easy movement he heaved himself out of the deep chair and glanced at the clock.

"At least she is dead on time," he said. "I rather like women who respect the hands of the clock. Get me all the data we have about this Demorval affair, will you, and bring it to me here? I want you to be present when we get down to business, because the first thing I want to know from this young lady is how she came to know my name, my address and the exact manner in which she discovered that there was the possibility of getting assistance from me. I don't like it, Tembridge; I don't like it. Somebody is doing a little private talking behind our backs—and Miss Varris is going to tell us who, or my name is not John Stayne."

There was a hard, bitter look in his eyes as he spoke, a look that Tembridge knew better than any man on earth. And for her own sake, he hoped that Marienne Varris would not be too obstinate.

"Will you want the secretary?" he asked.

"No. You and I will see this matter through alone."

Tembridge went out through the communicating door to his own room as Miss Varris was ushered in.

Stayne bowed and motioned her to a seat near the fire. "Won't you please sit down?" he said in his soft, rather deep voice. "The air is quite chilly outside, in spite of the sun. Sit down and warm yourself before you begin talking."

II

The girl stayed at the top end of the table, staring a little wildly at Stayne, as though she couldn't quite realise that this suavely-spoken man with the courtly manners and the grace of a knight was the Mystery-Maker, the man about whom nothing but hinted stories of unimaginable knavery were whispered. She was staring straight at him, diffidently twisting her gloves about in her fingers as though she had not heard a single word of his invitation.

John Stayne regarded her with a half-smile, a smile which could not quite hide a slight reddening of the face—for John Stayne was in process of admitting to his own inner conscience that Marienne Varris was just about the nicest girl he had ever looked at from a distance of less than ten feet. She was one of those gorgeous young creatures one never expects to see in real life. On the covers of the magazines, yes but never in real life.

Her complexion was much too perfect to be all complexion and nothing added but on that point the Colonel had a properly open mind, he holding that it was far easier to look at a face that was nicely assisted with a spot of colouring than one that resembled a slab of dough with a set of features let into it.

Her eyes were average as regards size, but the Demorval diamonds themselves were never brighter or fuller of more varying shades.

Her nose was small and very straight and her mouth was a bewildering series of little curves that somehow melted into lips from her cheeks and chin. What small curls of hair peeped from under her tiny hat were of a shade that was neither black, brown nor fair—but just that bright, happy tint in between. John Stayne continued to smile—and redden.

"Are you—are you Mr.—Colonel—Stayne?" she managed to stammer out at last.

"I am. And you are Miss Marienne Varris? Won't you *please* sit down? You look so unhappy standing there. I've read your letter, and I am most anxious to talk to you—to help you."

"Are you? Are you—*really?*" There was almost a note of entreaty in her voice, and her gloves were rapidly becoming a shapeless ball of horribly twisted kid.

Stayne went round to her, took her by the arm, and led her to the chair. He sat himself down opposite her where the light fell full on that face that was much too beautiful to be true. There, with the sunlight flooding in full from the highlighted windows he saw the tiny worry lines that were crawling, all too wickedly early, into the corners of those bright eyes, saw the slight trembling of the under lip, noted the almost ceaseless twittering of the fingers that indicated a nerve stress of such old standing that it was working up to a breakdown. And he knew then, if he hadn't been definitely certain before, that there was something pretty terrible behind the burgling of the Chateau Demorval in Mentone and the theft of the Demorval diamonds in London.

The communicating door opened and Miss Varris looked up with positive fright in her eyes at the sudden sound.

It's quite all right, Miss Varris," said Stayne gently. "This is Mr. Valdon Tembridge, my assistant. Impolite folk refer to him as my accomplice. Mr. Tembridge, this is Miss Marienne Varris, who has come to see us about a very private affair."

Tembridge bowed slightly from the hips, and stuck there. He was gazing at Marienne in sheer unbelief, and it seemed age-long minutes before he prised himself upright again.

"I'm delighted to see you, Miss Varris," he said, and mentally informed himself that he had never spoken a more touchingly true sentence in his life.

Stayne took the portfolio from Tembridge's limply extended hand and briefly glanced through the contents. There were printed cuttings of every phase of the story, taken from the various papers, verbatim reports of the magisterial proceedings and the full agency reports of the trial. Here and there were such notices, proclamations and private statements as Tembridge had been able to get possession of by means best known to himself.

Stayne looked up to see Marienne eyeing the accumulation in wild alarm.

"Miss Varris," he said quietly, "I trust that in explaining the reason for your visit to us you will deal with the matter as frankly as possible. You will notice that we have here quite a full résumé of the whole matter in so far as it has yet become public property—and not a few other documents that not even the judge has been privileged to see. You have hinted in your letter at a good many other matters of far greater consequence than the theft of a couple of ropes of diamonds and—if I may put it brutally—five years' penal servitude."

The old frightened look, a hunted look, came back into her eyes and she plucked nervously at the torn fingers of a glove. Then, after a little silence, she seemed to screw all her courage up into a single sentence. Looking him straight in the eyes, but with lips that all the courage in the world could not keep from twitching, she asked:

"Mr. Stayne, if I promise to tell you something of what I know—enough for you to discover the rest yourself—will you promise to get Templer out of prison, to get him out in such a way that nothing of this terrible business will become public?"

* * *

The words came tumbling out of her mouth in an uncontrollable stream—as fast as though it were part of a set speech she had already prepared and rehearsed and was determined to make before she gave away a single line of her own story.

"Will you? Will you?" she rushed on, a light of feverish intensity burning in her eyes. "I know Templer has been indiscreet—has been a perfect fool in some respects—but it has been the foolishness of loyalty. He is absolutely innocent—he no more intended to steal those diamonds than I did—and *I* wouldn't wear the beastly things if I were paid a thousand a week to do just that and nothing else. Those diamonds should never have been in London at all. It was a terrible blunder on Templer's part. Templer didn't want them—he was only getting rid of them so that he could save a brace of Demorval skins. Yes! You can look. I said a brace and I mean a brace. If I could tell the full story that lies hidden behind those two footling ropes of diamonds suddenly appearing in London there would be more trouble on the Continent than all the European Chancelleries put together could put right. But I can't! I can't until Templer is out of prison. Templer himself could be free inside an hour if he chose to put what he knows on paper—but he can't do that any more than I can. Oh, what am I to do? What *am* I to do?"

In an access of helplessness she wrung her hands together and her head fell forward in a fit of half-stifled sobbing.

"There's been murder done already over this terrible business," she said in a strangled voice, "and there will be murder done again unless somebody with a cool head gets at the head of things to stop it."

Stayne leaned forward and gently touched her arm.

"Miss Varris," he said, with quiet incisiveness, "you are already saying a great deal more than you intended. You made me a condition just now, a condition which stated that, before you would tell me anything, I would promise to effect the release of Mr. Varris without further publicly compromising him in this business. Before you go any further, I wish to tell you that I, too, have a condition to make."

The girl looked up quickly, her face draining a shade whiter under its nervous pallor and her hands gripped together till the knuckles shone.

"A—a condition?" she whispered, and looked timidly from Stayne to Tembridge and back again.

* * *

Stayne did not give her a chance to think. "Yes, a condition—but a very simple one indeed," he went on smoothly. "I only wish that yours to me had been one-thousandth part as simple. It is this: What is the name of the person who sent you to me?"

Marienne looked down into her lap and covered her eyes with her hands. Stayne noted that those hands were trembling badly.

"No—nobody sent me—I just came," she muttered.

"That is the first lie you've told for many a long day—and you told it badly," said Stayne. The hard glitter was back in his eyes. He had risen and was standing over her.

"Who sent you?" he demanded. "Listen, girl: there is not a soul in England who knows that I am capable of getting a man out of jail, not a soul in England who knows that Stayne, the Mystery-Maker, makes mysteries for others to fall into and get themselves entangled in webs of their own weaving. Only Tembridge there knows the extent to which we have broken laws—knows the extent to which we are able to break them further. You have been to someone. That someone, at his wits' end, has sent you to me. Now, who was it?"

She shook her head helplessly.

"How do I know anyone to go to?" she said.

"Then how did you know to come to me?" He put his hand on her shoulder and pressed her upright. "Miss Varris," he went on, "would it interest you to know that I am not unaware of some of the facts behind this case? Until recently my duties took me a good deal to the French Riviera. As a brother member of the Diplomatic Corps, Lord Demorval was known to me. And the Secret Service, my dear, travels along byways that are not even known to Scotland Yard. Would it surprise you to know that I could go straight to France this very day and challenge Monsieur Flocard, the French waiter, his right to his French name—to ask him why he widowed Lady Demorval so recently, to ask Lady Demorval herself why her diamonds were not in the Mentone chateau, to arrange a prison meeting with Templer Varris and to ask him point-blank why—"

But the girl had risen and was clinging to him desperately. "No! No!" she gasped. "Please—*please!* There is no need—Templer is—"

"Yes, yes, I know that too. Now—who sent you to me?"

"Lord Demorval himself." The girl looked at him blankly for a moment and then collapsed over the arm of her chair.

Stayne, with two deeply-drawn furrows down the centre of his forehead, sank slowly back in his seat, and his hands were trembling. Tembridge was staring at the girl as though she had suddenly gone mad. Then he caught John Stayne's eyes boring into him. There was a flood of newer—and greater—understanding blazing in them and perhaps just a hint of the fear a man gets when he gazes full face at something that transcends the credible.

"Tembridge," he said, soberly but with deadly conviction in every syllable, "we have got to get Templer Varris out of that cell within forty-eight hours—*and without the permission of the authorities*! We've got to abduct him from under their noses! Quick—some brandy for Miss Varris—she's fainted."

III

Tembridge was already on the way to Marienne Varris. In a minute or two she had recovered sufficiently to sit back and try to force a little shamefaced smile. A mountain of relief seemed to have toppled from her shoulders the moment the Mystery-Maker decided to take a hand in the fate of Templer Varris.

Stayne slipped out a little notebook, and, while Marienne was dabbing her eyes, he jotted down a few questions, taking meticulous care to verify certain names and dates from the cuttings in the dossier.

"Do you feel like concentrating on a few of the finer points of this unusual story?" he asked at last.

For a few moments her fingers wandered nervously over her forehead, and then she said quietly: "I will answer any question you care to ask me—provided my answers don't implicate my brother any further. You probably realise already that there is one aspect of this matter on which I can shed no light at all."

Stayne nodded grimly. "I understand," he said. "It is possible to clear a man of one serious charge only to get him into worse trouble than before, isn't it? Please don't look so unhappy. Your secrets are safer with me, perhaps, than with his own lawyers." A reminiscent chuckle came into his voice. "The same sort of thing might have happened to ourselves any number of times during the past few years. Templer, to my knowledge, might have cleared his good name at the expense of his neck. Let us not refer to the matter again. I'll promise not to embarrass you any more than I can help. At the same time, we can hardly break through granite walls without tools of some description. Now then"—he tapped his teeth with the butt of his pencil—"I'm taking it for granted that, at the time of his 'death,' you knew that Lord Demorval was occupying a high position in the Corps Diplomatique? Perhaps the highest of all the continental appointments."

"I knew that—yes. He was also a very important Secret Service agent."

Stayne's eyes narrowed. "We don't usually publish that sort of information to the world," he said. "How do you come to know that?"

"I was Lady Demorval's companion, and I could hardly help knowing. A great many code messages came to the house—both here and in France. And all sorts of queer people called—tramps and beggars and mechanics and street vendors. I've seen Lord Demorval himself leave the house dressed up as a telephone linesman, as a clergyman, as a lascar sailor, and—all sorts of things."

"H'm. Was that before your brother became private secretary to Lord Demorval?"

"Yes. It was through me that he got his appointment."

"Are you still in Lady Demorval's employ?"

"No. I resigned some months ago. I couldn't stand the strain of it any longer. I could see something dreadful happening like this—I could see it coming."

"Why? What made you suspect a crash was coming?"

Marienne looked away into the fire. "I—I'd rather not answer that question," she said after a long pause.

* * *

Stayne smiled, just a little wisp of a smile that flitted across his mouth for a moment and was gone. "Does it occur to you that you have already answered that question?" he asked.

The girl shot him a quick glance of apprehension. "I don't think I understand," she said hurriedly.

"You, as companion to her ladyship, would know considerably more about her affairs than his," came the quiet rejoinder. "If you resigned it would be in consequence of something you feared on her account. It would seem that all is not well with Lady Demorval's affairs. Still, we will let that matter slide. Now, tell me, when did you last see Lord Demorval?"

"Three days ago, in Paris."

"That was when he recommended you to come and see me?"

"Recommended is a very weak word. He begged me to."

"And where was this?"

"At the Credit Lyonnais. It is one of the many pseudo-appointments he holds in Paris. I think he was acting as a bank clerk at the paying-in grille. At least, that was where I saw him."

"And now about Flocard."

"Emil Flocard? I've never seen him personally. All I know about him is that he, too, is attached to the staff in Paris. He is a waiter."

"Where?"

"At Monsieur Sebillon's cafe in the Boulevard Periere. It is a very fashionable restaurant a little way out of the main centre of—"

"I know it. Expensive, too. But the cuisine is perfect. Let me see now. Lord Demorval has been 'dead' now nearly three months, has he not?"

"Nearer four. Lady Demorval was in mourning for over three months at the Mentone château."

"And Lady Demorval actually believes him dead?"

"Yes. So did I. So did we all. He went into a private nursing home and died there. It was as perfectly arranged as only the

Secret Service can possibly hope to arrange such things. I went to the funeral. I went over specially for it when I read of his death in the English papers. It happened about a month after I had left the Demorval employ. I remember thinking he had found a happy release from the crash that was coming. The coffin was buried at Chantilly with full official honours."

"Just one more question, Miss Varris." Stayne leaned over and eyed her keenly from under his dark brows. "Where did Lady Demorval go for her little gambling flutters?" He pitched the question directly at her and his eyes never left her face.

She started badly, and the old hunted look leapt back into her eyes. Her body tensed and she crouched back into her chair.

"I never said she gambled!" she said breathlessly. "I never mentioned it—never even hinted at it!"

"Probably not," said Stayne dryly. "It isn't necessary to have facts written down in headlines before they become visible." Suddenly his manner changed and he became a hard, masterful figure, dominating her attention by the very menace of his attitude.

"Miss Varris," he said, with the cold bite of steel in his words, "your brother is in prison with five years between him and liberty. He can clear himself only at the expense of uncovering one of the biggest scandals that ever endangered the financial stability of this country. Now listen carefully. A little while ago a man was murdered in one of the private gambling halls in Paris. The whole matter was one for the French police, but somehow it was fiercely hushed up. No one on this side, for instance, ever knew exactly where it happened.

"We do know, however, that there was a terrific fight going on at the time, and that it was only through the mad heroism of an unknown man in the room that a certain Englishwoman of title escaped before the gendarmerie broke in. He held the whole place single-handed till the lady got clear. He did it at the expense of a smashed skull—somebody else's skull.

"When the police forced the doors the lady was gone and her honour was saved. Also there was a dead body on the floor, its head battered in with a champagne bottle—and the valiant unknown was hauling himself out through the window with a clear twenty-foot drop to the ground. He made it and got clear.

"That Englishwoman of title was Lady Demorval, and the man who pulled her through was Templer Varris. Varris is now in the sweet position of only being able to clear himself of a five years' sentence by offering his neck to the rope on the murder charge. Now—I want that address, and I want it now! Where did Lady Demorval go for her little gambling flutters?"

Marienne had been listening to Stayne's grim recitative with eyes that slowly filled with fright. The extent of his inside knowledge appalled her. For some time she could not speak.

Stayne pacified her.

"Dear lady," he said, "I assure you that until you came in here I did not know one-tenth of what I've just told you. You tell me a little and I infer a lot. I knew there had been a scandal in a roulette club over there. I knew that a man, at the risk of his life, had saved a lady's name. I knew that Lord Demorval was dead; in common with the rest of the world I honestly believed it. Then you tell me that you resigned her ladyship's employ because you could not stand the strain of the anxiety. You tell me that Lord Demorval is not dead—that he quietly withdrew out of life and left nothing but a faked funeral behind him. You tell me that Templer Varris is your brother, and that he is incapable of such an act as stealing valuable diamonds. You tell me that it is impossible for him to clear himself without seriously implicating others. And that the moment he tries to he is letting himself in for worse trouble than before.

"Dear lady, isn't it rather a simple effort of logic to unite the details and to assume that one is the direct cause of the other? Who else would your brother risk his neck for but the employer who had befriended him when he was down and out? What else would keep his tongue silent when nothing but five years of prison misery stared him in the face?

"No, Miss Varris, you need not be frightened. Your secrets are not quite such public knowledge as you might think. I know, for instance, from your own reluctance to give me such a simple piece of information as the address of that club that you are frightened of having the place investigated. Your agitation precludes any other conclusion. That means that there is something far worse than murder going on there. Consequently I know that Lady Demorval is seriously implicated in that too. One affair is simply the outcome of the other. Now—please!"

Marienne Varris opened her bag hurriedly and with trembling fingers, as though too frightened to listen to more of that cold logic. She took from it a small visiting card and passed it over with a hand that shook. It bore the neatly-printed inscription:

CLUB TABARIN,
Rue Pigalle.
Laisser passer

"Thank you," said Stayne. He glanced at it and handed it back. "I don't know the place, and I didn't know that gambling clubs were beginning to appear in the Montmartre district. Still, we live and learn. Tembridge, are you getting tired of London?"

"Passports are all O.K.," said Tembridge shortly.

The Mystery-Maker nodded. "As soon as we have arranged about Varris we will run over," he said. "There should be some interesting hours in the Rue Pigalle. Show Miss Varris out, will you, please?"

IV

Stayne turned to Marienne as she rose with a look of surprise and relief on her face. He was smiling.

"It's quite all right," he said. "You can now get out of the dentist's chair. Not a very pleasant quarter of an hour for you, was it? But most troubles have to get a little worse before they get a little better. Let me see now; today is Tuesday. If you come round here on Thursday afternoon Templer will be here to meet you. Mind—not a word of this to a living soul."

"Oh—I—I promise," she said with tears of emotion starting to her eyes. "Mr. Stayne, I don't know how to thank you. My heart is nearly bursting with gratitude. You'll never know what—"

Stayne took her by the arm and piloted her gently to the door. "Let's not talk about it until it is all over," he said soberly. "Believe me, there is a lot more in this affair than even you dream—and I think you have a pretty shrewd suspicion. There are quite a few hectic hours to be lived before this matter passes out of the danger zone. Don't forget now—Thursday, about teatime." He squeezed her hand and opened the door.

She dabbed her eyes with a handkerchief as she went down the stairs. Belham, most impeccable of butlers, was waiting for her at the foot of the stairs. Stayne watched her go, deep lines of thought creasing over his forehead.

"Miss Varris," he called softly, leaning over the balustrade. "Just one more thing. Did you come here by taxi?"

"Yes," she answered. "From my hotel in the Strand."

Stayne waved his hand. "Keep smiling. Goodbye," he called.

Back in the big room Tembridge was studying a shorthand note he had been taking of the whole conversation. Planked in front of him was a silent typewriter. Stayne glanced at him. "I wouldn't worry about that, this time, if I were you," he said. "What we heard we will just keep in our heads. Burn that lot—quickly."

Tembridge looked up. "Bad as that—eh?" he jerked.

Stayne inclined his head, once, very deliberately.

"Probably worse," he muttered. "That distracted little fool came round in a taxi. That means the Yard will be nosing around inside five minutes. Still, we shall know what the Yard thinks of it from the size of the man they send. Get that dossier put away." He pulled the knob on the armchair and said: "Has Miss Varris gone yet, Belham?"

"Yes, sir! A moment ago," came the uncanny voice from the golden idol.

"Very good. If a gentleman should call—a gentleman who will prefer not to give his name—warn me and bring him straight up, please."

"I will see to it, sir."

Stayne turned and eyed his assistant critically.

"Well, Tembridge," he said, "what did you think of her?"

Tembridge stuck his fat red fountain pen back behind his ear and glanced up dreamily at the massive ceiling.

"I'm glad," he said to the furniture in general, "I'm glad to think that you're too old to marry—and that I am just of the right marrying age."

Stayne didn't smile. For a man who had only just turned thirty he looked even younger—except, perhaps, for that deep dominance of will and strength of character which were visibly present even when lying dormant.

"What I mean is," said Tembridge, tucking the dossier under his arm, "colonels never marry. It's against the ethical code. They either marry before they become colonels or they just stay uncles to their own nieces. And very good uncles they make, I hear.

"Marienne—I make no excuse for calling her by her Christian name—is a delightful blend of a duck and a darling and a dear and a delicious little Dresden Shepherdess all dolled up in short skirts, silk stockings—*black* silk stockings, bless her—neat little patent shoes, and bobbed hair. I rather think I like England. You never—"

He stopped short, made one lightning dive for the communicating door. and shot through it like a stone from a catapult. The golden idol had suddenly said: "A gentleman on his way up to see you, sir. He gave his name as Chief Superintendent Hawker, the head of the Criminal Investigation Department at Scotland Yard."

* * *

Then Stayne smiled. But it was a smile that had not the remotest bearing on the last observations of his assistant. There was a grim line of determination about it that wiped it clean of any trace of humour. It was the gargoyle grin of a man who realises that two lifelong adversaries were coming face to face—the smile of a man who smelt battle ahead and was unafraid of the issue.

Tembridge returned, lighting a cigarette.

"Did you hear that?" he asked, with an unholy glee glittering out of his eyes. "Hawker! The Chief of the whole circus! That's what the Yard thinks about it. Somebody is going to get the cane."

The door opened and the butler announced the detective. Hawker came in. For once, he was a detective who almost looked his part. His eyebrows were greying and shaggy, and the eyes that burned beneath them were slaty-grey, morose and unfriendly. He had a hard mouth and a disconcerting way of pursing it up as though he didn't like you on sight and wasn't taking any pains to hide it. There was antagonism in his very presence and he stared you hard in the eyes as though he knew you were going to come out with a pack of lies before he spoke a single word.

"Good morning, Chief," said Stayne, pushing forward a chair. "Rather early for a call from you, isn't it?"

Hawker grunted. "Midnight wouldn't be too early for some people," he growled. He stood in the middle of the room and peered round, his cold, metallic eyes boring into every hole and comer. "Well? Where's the gadget?" he demanded.

"The what?"

"The gadget. The doohickey. The tiddy-falah that your butler chatted to you on?"

"Oh, that? The little Cupid up there in the comer." And not even Hawker's probing eyes saw the tiny action of Stayne's right hand under the arm of the chair.

"Belham?" said Stayne, almost to himself. "You might bring up a decanter and some glasses, will you, please?"

"Certainly, sir," belled out from the golden idol, "Coming in one moment, sir."

* * *

"Pretty good," said Hawker, staring appreciatively at the tiny ivory trumpet. "Yes, that's pretty good."

"Good in this respect," admitted Stayne, "that Belham might be asked to bring up revolvers for two just as easily as whiskies. It goes one better than the detectaphone, that's all. Same principle. Works both ways."

"Yours?"

"Not this time. Tembridge worked that one out."

"Neat. Neat, I must say. Care to give me the prescription?"

"No reason why we shouldn't. Tembridge will no doubt give you a copy of the blueprint. Quite simple. And now, Chief, what's the reason for the visit? Tembridge hasn't been wangling his income-tax returns, has he?"

"You know perfectly well the reason for this visit, Colonel."

"I regret to say that I haven't the haziest notion."

"You haven't, hey? That's why Belham announced me right away, having only asked me my name. You hadn't whispered down that doodah that I was on the way, hey? That's why you let the girl out of the front door. Unless you'd known that we were already waiting outside and had watched her come in she would have been gently whisked out of that other exit that even we haven't been able to discover yet. That's why that fire there is half choked with ashes—paper ashes. That's why there's a brandy bottle and a single glass on the table. Say, which of you has suddenly taken to brandy nibbling at nine o'clock in the morning, hey?"

Stayne was laughing quietly. "All right, Chief," he said. "I just wanted to see if you'd lost any of the old *flair.* That lot wasn't left about by accident. What do we do now?"

Hawker glowered at him. "Still the same old Smarty," he snapped. He eyed his man steadily for some seconds, and his eyes were like twin drills boring Stayne's slightly amused nonchalance. "Well?" he demanded at last, "what are you going to do about it?"

"Candidly, I think I shall have a try at it."

"You do, hey?"

"I certainly do. I told Miss Varris so."

"D'ye think I don't know that? Hey? D'ye think I didn't see her step into that fool taxi with a face that looked as if the weight of the whole earth had suddenly slid off it? D'ye think I didn't see her almost laughing with relief through eyes that were still wet with tears? D'ye think I didn't know how much you had managed to worm out of her in that quarter of an hour she was up here with you?" His eyes strayed to the brandy again. "Enough to make her throw a flop, anyway," he added.

"We thought about going over to Paris on Thursday," said Tembridge, as though anxious to get off a subject that was not untempered with embarrassment for them all.

"You did, did you? Well, you won't. And another thing, my son—when I'm talking to the organ-grinder I don't want the monkey to butt in. When I want you I'll rattle your chain."

Tembridge cocked an owl-like eye on Stayne. "I think it's the cold air," he said solemnly. "The cold air on a naughty liver, too early in the morning. Mr. Hawker, you oughtn't to get up until the streets are properly aired and warmed," he advised, "you oughtn't, really. 'Tisn't fair, Chief, 'tisn't fair to old and valued customers."

Hawker growled far down in his chest like Stromboli working up for a demonstration. He favoured Tembridge with a malevolent glare.

"Finished?" he barked.

Tembridge folded his hands in his lap. "Oh, quite," he said.

Hawker turned back to Stayne. "Listen," he said. "You are not going over to Paris on Thursday. And you are not mixing up in this Varris job any more than you are going to run round the equator or square the circle. You are going to back out of it just as fast as you know how. Both you and your tame goat."

"But why?"

"Because there's bigger brains than yours working to straighten out this tangle. Bigger—and more of 'em."

"Bigger—maybe. More—maybe. But certainly not so humane."

"They're on it now, anyway—and they don't want you!"

"Meanwhile, I suppose, they haven't the faintest objection to Templer Varris doing five years for their amusement?"

"That's just his bad luck. Somebody's got to hold the buck. And Varris is a good plucked 'un. He won't give the show away."

"I'm sure he won't. And I'm equally sure he won't do five years."

"Oh? And who says so?"

"I do. I told Miss Varris so. I promised her."

"What's the new move, Colonel? Turning Good Samaritan, hey?"

"A cross, I think, between that and Sir Galahad."

* * *

Hawker suddenly leaned forward across the table and took Stayne by the wrist. His face was deep-set and more serious than Stayne ever remembered seeing it.

"Candidly, Stayne," he said, "you've got to lay off this one. It's not up your street and there won't be any pickings for anyone. You're on a bad egg. There isn't a bob in it—anything you spend on it, you'll be that much out of pocket. And you'll be prevented, by force if necessary, from trying to queer the pitch. That's orders from the man up top—and you know who I mean. Now you're no fool. You've been mixed up in some pretty smart shows one way and another, and I'll hand it to you that up to now you've always been able to wriggle clean at the last moment. Sometimes you've been so slick that you've sent me back home gnawing my own gums. But this time you're up against the whole box of works. You won't get away with it. That's *orders*. I'm telling you for your own good."

"Nice of you. I always had a soft spot for you, Hawker. You fight fair—or fair enough—and there's no humbug about you. But this time I think you're out of your depth. Even you don't know just what's been happening over in Paris. Neither does the man up top. He's only feeling his way. And he's being made a tool of, too, by The Man Higher Up Still—just like Varris.

Know who I mean? No, I don't suppose you do. Used to work with that crowd myself once. They're smart, believe me—too darned smart for belief sometimes. The chances are that if you interfere with me you will only be putting your own foot in it. That's all. Good morning. Here comes your whisky. I'll leave you with my tame goat. He's got a little blueprint to show you. Don't be surprised if there is a hiatus in Varris's cell before long, will you?"

He pushed out through the door, leaving Hawker staring after him, chewing morosely at his clipped-off bristle of moustache.

The Chief grinned again and reached out for his hat.

Tembridge peered at him over the top of the decanter as he poured out a couple of stiff pegs. "What's wrong, Chief?—Going? So soon?"

Hawker let out a bass rumble. "I don't drink any man's whisky who won't drink with me!" he said, with a dismissing jerk of the hand.

Tembridge frowned. That was a declaration of war. And Hawker had not troubled to be polite about it, either. He shrugged. Well, if it was going to be a war, it would be a good lusty one—and the odds wouldn't all be piled on one side either.

V

Stayne went upstairs into his own bedroom. It was a room in keeping with the rest of the house—large, autocratic; a room in which only a man of wealth could have slept in any comfort, for an oppressive air of opulence hung over it like a heavily-brocaded pall.

Against a wall was a massive ebony library, its shelves lined with richly gilded leather-covered volumes that are only published by private subscription at so many guineas per copy. They were reminiscences of great soldiers, lawyers, sailors, politicians, and men who held high office in the inner councils of the nation. There was nothing there by Colonel Stayne, though his, with perhaps one exception, would have been the most interesting of them all.

He silently locked the bedroom door and crossed over to the great library. That library could only be manipulated when the bedroom door was locked, and Stayne alone held the queer oddity of a key that snapped over the wards of that lock. He pulled out two books and thrust his arm down a cavity behind where an oiled bolt lay concealed. Then he pushed the books back with a jolt. From somewhere inside the packed shelves there came an audible "click!" and the whole of the great library swung away, revealing a locked door behind it. It was a private telephone cabinet, the existence of which was not known even to Tembridge.

It controlled one line only, a direct wire to another telephone at the other end, and beside it was a little dial housing a magnetic needle that tick-tacked infallible information the moment a leakage came on that wire. It was as private as the ingenuity of humankind could make it.

Stayne went in and closed the door behind him. He picked up the receiver, and a remarkable conversation began almost as soon as the instrument was to his ear.

* * *

"Hallo—is that you, Number One? Number Three here. Were you expecting a call from me—or have I been sitting on a mare's nest?"

"No—no mare's nest, Number Three. I've been waiting at this end for over an hour. Miss V.'s letter to you was intercepted and read. I knew you'd answer in the right way. You have seen her, of course?"

"Yes, I've only just left her. Couldn't get to you before. Hawker called. He was stepping on the back of her taxi, and he nailed me the moment she left."

"Damn!"

"Bit unfortunate, I admit. But I was looking to you to clear him off the scent."

"Can't do it. Our hands are tied. This matter had got to be done—and without even the Yard knowing how or why. It's a case for a lone hand. And you'll have to play it without any official help whatever. If you get caught out you will have to stand your own racket. The Government will repudiate you and wash its hands of all responsibility whatever. You understand that, don't you?"

"H'm. I do now!"

"It's as serious as that. If it wasn't, I'd have the Yard in on your side from the moment you left your house. Number Four has had to die. If everything breaks all right for us he will be found wandering in the Bois de Boulogne woods. A case of loss of memory. The funeral will be a shocking case of bad management on the part of the nursing home—mistaken identity and a changeover of the patients concerned, etc. The nursing home is going to close down at the end of the month, anyway. We are reopening it at Auteuil. Address and date will be sent you later. You realised where the call came from, I presume?"

"As soon as I connected the diamonds with Number Four's wife."

"Where is Hawker now?"

"Down with Twenty-two drinking my whisky. He's going to make a fight."

"Can't help it. You'll get no help from us. If anything goes wrong and the thing is discovered it—it—means war, nothing could stop it. You've just got to go your own way—and may the gods go with you."

"The girl?"

"Knows nothing. Suspects a great deal, but it's all away up over her head. She's frightened. Too scared to speak. Got your line of action?"

"Mapped. Varris comes out first thing. With not a soul implicated except Twenty-two. He will be my chauffeur. If the storm breaks he is hidden."

"Good man."

"Number One—there's just one thing you might do for me. Don't cross a rail anywhere. Do it through the prison surgeon. Or the Governor. He's one of us. And it will just make the thing possible. Just—and that's all."

"Well?"

"Arrange to have Varris transferred to the outside working party. He's in Scrubs, isn't he?"

"Yes."

"Well, get him moved to the gardening section. See that he is trimming the grass or weeding the beds down by the main gate on Thursday afternoon. That's all I'll ask. The rest I will arrange myself."

"Varris will this afternoon put in a request to the Governor to be allowed to join an outdoor party on account of his health. There is every possibility that his request will be granted."

"Many thanks. Is there anything more?"

"You have quite enough in your knapsack already."

"Then I'll get to it. I'm going to tour the police courts till I find a drunk and disorderly who hasn't a bob in the world and wants his fine paid."

There was a puzzled silence at the other end for some seconds, and then a gentle exhalation of breath came floating over the wire. "Oh-h-h. I see. Oh, very clever, Number Three." There was a soft chuckle and then: "Oh-very good in-dee-ed!"

"You're very bright this morning, sir."

"*Et vous, m'sieu.* Anything more to report from your end?"

"No—er, yes. I think Number Twenty-two comes off the bachelors' list very soon."

"What—already? That boy's a trifle sudden, isn't he? What a pity. Another good man off the risky-list. But she *is* rather sweet, isn't she?"

"Sweet? Listen, sir. That young hound has got to step out quick and lively and leg it all he knows or you will be rubbing another number off the bachelors' list—and Number Twenty-two will only be best man to him."

"Hell!" said a startled voice at the other end, and the receiver went on with a bang.

* * *

Stayne left the cabinet, locked it, and went down to the garage for his car. He had several there, from a zooming great limousine that had no engine at all, but just an enormous car-bonnet-shaped steel hive with a single, faintly-buzzing bee in it, to a rackety old two-cylindered taxi that proceeded in the midst of a noise like a boatload of old tin cans in a gale.

He selected a trim-looking sports model, one that looked as though it had a heady turn of speed under its bonnet. The garage hand filled her with petrol and oil and in a few minutes Stayne was purring down the road heading for Marlborough Street.

Hopes were dashed there. For though there were two charges of drunk and disorderly on the chargesheet, neither delinquent was present, both having been admitted to bail earlier on in the morning. That meant that both would be able to pay their fines, or, at the very least, that they would not be committed to jail out of hand. Stayne went back on the road again. It was not till he got to West London that he found what he wanted.

He walked by the officer at the door, who looked at him inquiringly.

"Witness," muttered Stayne untruthfully, and the officer nodded as he wandered through. Along in the charge-room he found an unhappy wight who looked as though he had been hung out in a thunderstorm all night. He was bleary-eyed and heavy-lidded, and all the evidences of a hectic steaming-up in alcohol hung about him. He appeared down and out, and his clothes might have done duty on a scarecrow. From the very look of him, his was a hangover that had been hard earned.

* * *

Stayne took a good long look at him. The man was so miserable and so full of last night's aches that he did not even resent the continued scrutiny. He just sat on the wooden side bench with his head in his hands and resigned himself to his own red-eyed misery.

Stayne walked across and spoke to him.

"Feeling bad?" he asked.

The man gulped and blinked. There was no show of anger in his eyes, nothing but the sheer animal history of a man who has just emerged from a long bout with devils of alcohol and realises that he is hard up against it.

"Feeling bad?" he growled at last. "Listen, mister. I'm feeling so bad that if I was feeling good I'd be feeling bad. I've had a terrible night, I've had—a terrible night. And now I'm going to get it in the neck—right in the neck."

Stayne pondered the thought.

"Been out on the razzle, eh?" he queried.

"I certainly have," grunted the man. "Drew me pension, see? Drew me pension and got blindo—abserlutely blindo. Socked a copper's helmet over his ears and lorst me barrer. Lorst it. And now I'm going to get it in the neck. An' serve me damn well right, too."

"That's one way of looking at it. Who's your lawyer?"

"Lawyer? Me? Me have a lawyer? That's a good 'un, that is, mister. I couldn't pay for a packet of fags, let alone a lawyer. And, anyway, a lawyer wouldn't do me no good—not this time. The Beak knows me, see? Promised me a turn in the clink next time I showed up. The lawyer don't breathe who could do me any good. The Beak has had it waxed up for me for months."

"Bad luck, that. You've been here before, then?"

"Reg'lar." The man was positive about it. "Once a month I shows up here—every time I draws me pension. I draws me pension and then I gets blindo. But larst night was the limit. A copper came up to me just as I was showin' folks how Jack Dempsey could have knocked the 'oly 'ell out of Tunney. He got argufyin' with me and I bumped his helmet down past his eyes. And the next thing I knew, I was on me back in a cell with 'arf the 'Ammersmith police force sitting on me chest. And they don't half sit heavy, them coppers."

He broke off mournfully and regarded a set of burst knuckles and tenderly massaged a lump on his head the size of an egg.

"You've no money at all?"

"Not a bob. Ain't got the price of a cup of tea about you, I s'pose? Strewth, I'd give me soul for a mug of tea—strong and hot."

Stayne signalled to the jailer and slipped a note into his hand. "Get him a hot one, will you?" he said. "Get one for yourself with the change."

VI

Stayne was smiling inwardly, Tom Dobey's case was made for him: made so perfectly that it fitted into his plans like a foot in a well-built shoe.

"Well, look here, Tom Dobey," he said. "I don't think you need be too despondent, I'm feeling rather tender towards my fellow human beings this morning—and I'd like to do something for you. If it's a case of a fine I'll pay it for you."

Dobey looked up with a start. There was a burst of incredulity in his eyes, and his eyelids shivered as though with a sudden fear.

"D'ye mean that, mate?" he said huskily. Then he relapsed again into his attitude of bunched-up moodiness. "Very nice of you—and thank you," be muttered. "But you hadn't better do it, mate. It'll mean an awful lot of money—a terrible lot of money—maybe twenty pounds, what with costs and all. And I wouldn't ask anyone to pay that much money just to keep me out of quod. Thank you—and thank you kindly. But I don't reckon you ought to do it."

Stayne laughed cheerfully and held out a cigarette case.

"Have a smoke," he suggested. "You're too good to spend a few useless months stitching mail-bags. Twenty pounds or so won't hurt me—and I'll be more than pleased to be able to help you. More pleased than you think," he added grimly. "What time does the Court sit?"

"Sitting now, sir. My case will be on in about an hour—so the jailer says."

"Very well; here's my card. If your luck's in and you get the option of a fine, get into touch with me here at this address and I will see that the whole fine is paid immediately."

Dobey gulped and he tried to stammer his thanks through a throat that had suddenly turned fiery.

Stayne waved the thanks aside.

"Wish you luck," he said. "I can't wait to see you through—got an urgent appointment elsewhere—but I only hope you get the option."

Stayne hurried out as the jailer returned with a great steaming mug of tea. A welter of thanks and blessings assailed his ears as he went down the corridor.

So far things were good. Angels couldn't have planned it better for him—or made the running smoother.

* * *

Dobey's good luck was tempered with just a spot of bad. For Stayne hadn't the remotest idea of paying that fine out of hand. There was a little ceremony to be enacted first, and it entailed Tom Dobey's temporary presence in Scrubs Prison. Stayne had got his man and got him planted. If the presiding magistrate wasn't feeling up to extending further lenience to the persistent drunk the whole scheme would take a disheartening fall earthwards. But there was just the chance that, as Dobey described, he would pass the usual sentence with the option of a fine which he knew the man was financially unable to pay. It would be a lesson to Dobey and a sop to his own conscience at the same time.

Stayne hung around for a while and then kept his urgent appointment. That appointment was at the West London Police Court. He went into the public well of the court and squeezed himself into an out-of-the-way corner where Dobey would not be likely to see him unless he deliberately turned round and searched for him.

* * *

The magistrate glanced at Dobey. Dobey looked sheepish and apologised to the Court for having been rough with the constable. The rest of it, apparently, was all in the game. Stayne's heart gave one gentle bump against his side.

The luck held. The magistrate adjusted a pair of pince-nez and focused a disapproving eye on the delinquent.

"Thomas Dobey," he said, "you have excelled yourself. You've broken even your own wretched record. The last time you were before me I threatened you with prison. Not satisfied with ordinary drunkenness you have added assaults on the police to the tale of your misbehaviour. I had intended sending you to prison without the option of a fine. But in view of your apparently sincere apology to the Court and to the officers concerned I am going to offer you one more chance, realising, as I do full well, that you will not except by exercising a beneficial drain on your financial resources, be able to pay the fines.

"Five pounds or one month for being drunk and disorderly. Five pounds or one month for assault and battery. Twenty pounds or three months for assaulting the police while in the execution of their duty. The cost of the broken window and the price of the constable's helmet will be added to the general costs of the case. A total in all of eighty-five pounds ten shillings. Stand down."

Stayne breathed a sigh of mental relief.

He saw Dobey flinch as though he had been hit. Dobey swayed to the back of the dock, realising that, even though he had found a friend who was prepared to stand for him up to ordinary limits, eighty-five pounds odd was asking too much of any man, no matter how well-intentioned he might be.

The jailer called to the prisoner, who meekly stepped down from the dock and vanished through a side door. Stayne waited till he had gone and then slipped out too. He penned a short note:

"Please tell Thomas Dobey that if he gets into touch with me his fine will be paid"—passed it to the charge-sergeant and hurried out before the officer could read the note. Outside he vanished round the corner like a shadow.

He didn't want to be called back to explain himself. The address on the card he had given Dobey was the name of a big hotel in the Strand, and he didn't intend calling there until the next day.

* * *

Scrubs Prison, that forbidding great fortress of red and white stone that sits on the edge of the almost countrified road on the edge of London, is one of the most difficult prisons in the world to break out of. Its outer walls are twenty feet high, two feet thick, and are under constant surveillance from two angles at once by sentries in the comer watchtowers.

Stayne had early come to the conclusion that the only safe way to help a man break out of that grim stronghold was to break *into* it first. And before he could break into it there had to be a decoy duck at the other end—a sort of reasonable excuse for being allowed to penetrate that first outer wall. The rest would have to depend on the elements of speed, surprise and accuracy.

He rang up Curzon Square, and Tembridge came on at the other end.

"Number Three here," he said. "Anything happened?"

"Yes—just what you expected. Hawker was on your heels when you went round to the garage."

"Indeed? I looked for him and couldn't seem to single him out."

"He did a bit of fast work, Chief. Must have had one of the Yard cars with him. Did you notice that coster standing on the corner of the street—man hawking ferns?"

"Yes, come to think of it, there was someone standing there—had his arms full of aspidistras."

"That was our little sweetheart. I was about fifty yards behind you. He trailed you down to the garage, hung around there for a while, shed his palms in a refuse bin and called a taxi to follow you when you came out."

"Did you head him off?"

"Yes, but not till after you had called at Marlborough Street. He drew up on the other side of the road to you and I came up in the old sedan. Got my nose in just in front of him and let her drift back till the taxi-driver yelled that my back fenders were kissing his radiator. So I stalled the old bus and cut out the ignition. Then you came out and went streaking down the road—beading for Bow Street, I guess. Two jumps behind you out came Hawker, yelling for me to get out of his road. I climbed out to start the old tank up on the handle. Hawker swore at me beautifully. So I hopped back at the wheel because he was howling for his man to back away and chase you.

"I got my bus going on the self-starter, edged out in front of him as he turned to clear me, and stalled the old boat again. Language! I think the police force wants a vacuum cleaner over it. By the time the taxi-man had pulled his bus clear again you were well out of sight."

Stayne grunted. "Pity," he muttered. "He knows that car number now. That means there's another perfectly good *alias* gone west. Still, couldn't be helped. Luckily you were able to head Hawker off. I didn't think he would get his teeth so far in. He's going to be troublesome."

VII

Soon after eight o'clock the next morning Stayne called round at the Strand Hotel. He drove up luxuriously in a vast and shining limousine. Tembridge, neat, smart, and infinitely composed in his dark blue chauffeur's uniform, sat with professional poise at the wheel.

Stayne crossed to the inquiries grille and addressed the clerk with a familiarity that franked a friendship of long standing.

"Any letters for me today, Arthur?" he asked. "I'm especially solicitous about one that looks like a family skeleton."

The clerk smiled and dived for the pigeon-hole marked "S."

"Here it is, sir," he said. "Came first post this morning."

Stayne read it, a poor, ill-written scrawl, covered with much ill-spelling and corrections. It was addressed to Mr. J. Stemdale, Strand Hotel, London.

Dear Sir,

I am the man you spoke to this morning in West London Police Station about the fine. I got the option, but I never knew I was having it waxed up so *hot. They got me for eighty-five pounds ten. Or five months in here where I am. I think you had ought to let me do the five months. The jailer gave me the note you sent round, but after that they couldn't find you. So they sent me round here to start my sentence meanwhile I write to you at the address you sent.*

If you can pay the fine, which I shouldn't if I was you, I shouldn't straight, you can get me out as soon as you like. If you bring this letter to the Scrubs and ring the bell the gate jailer will read it and let you in. Then you can pay him and he will give you a receipt. After that they will give me my clothes back and let me out. And I must say I am very much obliged to you, even if you don't pay the fine. Hoping it finds you as it leaves me at present.

Yours respectably,
Thomas Dobey.

It was written on the official prison-letter form, and the envelope bore the black inscription: H.M. Prison Service.

* * *

Stayne caught the clerk's eye as he looked up.

"Birthday greetings from an old friend," he said with a wink, and the clerk laughed outright.

He swung round and headed for the exit, thoroughly pleased with the outlook. That document represented his passport into the prison. Armed with that he could penetrate at least the outer defences and, knowing something of the inside organisation of the prison, he knew that by one swift stroke, deftly carried through, he could get his man out and away in the car before the alarm could be raised.

Stayne climbed in as Tembridge gave him the signal that everything was clear. In order to keep Hawker off that particular piece of the trail neither of them had slept at Curzon Square that night. They had gone out of town in the car, and criss-crossed about the open country lanes until they shook off the inevitable shadowing car. Then they struck out across country to Maidenhead, where they put up for the night, coming back into town in the early morning by a roundabout way.

Less than an hour later they were heading into the great tree-lined courtyard that gives on to the prison entrance.

Tembridge swung the car round and backed it up so that it was no more than a yard or two from the huge prison doors themselves—all ready for a quick getaway, its bonnet pointing for the open highway.

On the way down Stayne had opened out a suitcase. In it was a dark brown lounge suit as near as he could get it to Templer Varris's size; a fifteen and a half collar, a tie, underclothing, socks, soft felt hat, and a pair of brown shoes, size eight—a complete rig-out according to the plans and specifications supplied by Marienne. The various articles were laid out neatly on the seat, covered by a travelling rug.

* * *

Tembridge remained unconcernedly sitting at the driving wheel while Stayne got out, fishing in his pocket for the letter. By that time he was wearing a neat little white moustache and beard, clipped down almost to nothing. Astonishingly enough, even though it was the beard of a man of fifty, it seemed to fit that young-old face as naturally as though the years had grown it there.

He rang the bell, a great, ponderous bell-pull, as old-fashioned as the penal code itself, and stared up at the massive double gates. A brassy clanging echoed to life inside and there came a jangle of keys. A little grille was pushed back and the gate jailer looked out.

"Well?" he asked.

"I have called in respect of the payment of a fine," said Stayne. "The man concerned arrived yesterday from the West London Police Court."

"Have you a warrant—or a letter?"

"Yes, officer. I have it here." Stayne held it up.

A key rattled in the lock and a small door, so small that Stayne had to stoop to enter, opened like a panel in the main gates. Stayne went in and presented his letter.

"Wait there a moment, please," said the jailer, and entered a guardroom on the right.

Stayne found himself in an enormous lock, a kind of gigantic tunnel with locked gates at both ends. The right wall of the tunnel was the jailer's guardroom, the left was the waiting-room for those who had business with the authorities or had called to see prisoners. The entrance doors were of stout oak, painted green, but the gates at the other end were made of two-inch steel bars and extended right to the top of the tunnel. By a flickering gas-jet a notice board hung, on which were pinned notices to warders going on and off duty, new prison regulations, and fresh orders from the higher authorities. That second pair of gates had still to be forced before he could get through to his man.

Beyond the gates lay the gardens, with trim gravel paths running round the perfectly kept flowerbeds. The rest of the view was taken up by the fine outlines of the prison chapel, with its high curving roof and stained-glass windows: a vast lump of a building that blotted out the rest of the view.

But it was neither the gardens nor the chapel that held John Stayne's critical attention just then. His eyes were focused on a working party of four men who were busily weeding the great central flowerbed. Twenty yards from the gate they were, their backs bent laboriously over their task, taking no great hurry over the matter and seemingly chatting together quietly while working.

They appeared to be in charge of a "trusty"—a prisoner dressed in a cocoa-brown garb with a band on his arm on which were three white chevrons. He, at least, seemed to be directing their operations. And John Stayne's heart gave another little bump when he saw that the man on the extreme right was Templer Varris.

There was no mistaking the trim, smart young lines of him. His obvious awkwardness and newness to his surroundings marked him out. From Marienne's description and from the photographs she had supplied no one could possibly have mistaken him.

"Mr. Sterndale, please." He heard the unhurried voice of the jailer calling from the guardroom and went over. The jailer was a solid, kindly looking fellow, one who had seen so much of the unhappiness of life that he was long since case-hardened to it.

"Is the prisoner a relation of yours, sir?" he asked, slowly reading over Dobey's letter.

"Oh, no—just an acquaintance. He was in a spot of trouble and I offered to help him out. He was at West London and I happened to be there at the same time. Unfortunately it was not convenient for me to pay the fine at the court—so Dobey was brought here pending the arrival of the money, I suppose."

VIII

The jailer nodded cheerlessly as he turned to check off some particulars in a record. This was routine stuff to him. He had gone through the ritual hundreds of times before. Many times in the course of a week an unhappy wife would arrive with the two or three pounds necessary to secure the release of an erring husband who had fallen foul of the law on minor counts.

From outside came the soft purr of an engine being gently accelerated in little bursts—a danger signal from Tembridge not to start work yet. Val had seen some unsuspected danger looming up and he was sending out the delay action warning.

Then a klaxon hooter sounded, discordant and imperious, outside. The jailer muttered, "Just a minute, sir," and pulled back the grille. Then he opened the great main gates, Stayne watching keenly to see which one of the great bunch of keys hanging by a chain from his belt he used. He photographed it on his mind as the two huge doors swung open.

A long motor Black Maria pulled slowly into the lock and stood panting smoothly there while the jailer checked the entries. The doors were closed and locked again behind it. Then the second pair of gates were opened and the prison van passed through. Again Stayne fixed his keen eyes on the key used to open the second gates, and he knew that when the time came he would make no mistake.

The jailer came back to his room and entered a note in a book.

"This fine's a bit heavy, sir, you know," he said.

"Yes. Dobey, I'm afraid, misbehaved himself rather thoroughly. But I have all the cash here. Can I pay it now?"

"If you please, sir."

Stayne took the money from his pocketbook in an envelope and counted it out on the desk, nice new notes, easy to check back. While the jailer was re-counting it Stayne stepped quietly aside and laid a white capsule on the desk by his elbow. The jailer finished counting and said, "That's right, sir, eighty-five pounds ten. And very lucky he is, I'm sure, to find such a friend. Generally, if it's anything over a tenner they stays in. Do you want to take him back with you, sir?"

"Oh dear no," said Stayne hurriedly. "I don't care two jigs if I never see him again."

"Then if you'll just wait while I phone the Governor's office I'll see that he comes out straight after dinner, sir—thank you."

* * *

He turned to pick up the letter again and stopped suddenly to stare in a puzzled way at the white capsule on the desk.

"'Allo!" he said. "What's this? Is this yours, sir?"

Stayne eyed it curiously as the jailer held it out between his finger and thumb.

"No, nothing to do with me," he said with an off-hand smile. "I don't go walking around with bantams' eggs in my pocket. That's what it is, isn't it? A blown bantam's egg."

The jailer scrutinised it oddly.

"No—'tain't a bantam's egg, sir," he said.

"There's a little ridge running round it—like as if it had been joined together." He rattled it against his ear, trying to divine its contents, if any. But there was no sound from it and it felt astonishingly light in his fingers, no heavier than a ping-pong ball and ever so much more fragile.

"Well, that's a funny thing, sir. Where'd it come from? It wasn't here two minutes ago. I cleared that bit of the desk off this morning and it wasn't there when I put that letter there. H'm. Very odd."

He held it to his nose and sniffed at it hard.

Stayne turned away as though the affair no longer held any interest for him. "Probably one of those puff-ball things one gets in the eye at cabarets and dance places," he said. "Open it and see. Squeeze it."

Stayne said it as though the pettiness of the affair nettled him slightly.

He took a couple of paces to the doorway and slowly turned. Then, all in a hurry, he leapt. For from behind him there had come the faint sound of the capsule cracking, a tiny crackling like the soft breaking of a blown eggshell. The jailer, with the capsule still close up under his nose trying to get his nasal organs to discover some recognisable quality in the odd little object, had pressed his thumb too firmly upon it. The tightly prisoned gas came out with a malignant hiss, and its amazing volatility did the rest. The jailer gasped, a sudden indrawn contraction of breath that cut short the moment the vaporised acid struck the lungs.

His face went dead white with the rapidity of a fogged photographic plate, and his eyes shut tight, the muscles of his face flexing up into white, stiff knots of agonisingly unexpected pain. Stayne, with a wet silk handkerchief pressed up over his nose, leapt forward with an arm outflung to save the jailer's head, for the officer, crumpling up and toppling backwards, was collapsing like a boxer knocked out in the ring. Consciousness had left him in the same instantaneous second that the gas hit the lung tissues. He did not know, either then or afterwards, that he had taken one deep-drawn sniff of the same deadly gas that a veterinary surgeon uses to put a broken horse out of its pain, the bitingly powerful hydrocyanic gas, which is nothing more nor less than prussic acid in vapour form.

Stayne got to him in time. The man was going down like a house of cards, the back of his head a foot away from the massive desk. Stayne reached him with a "hand-off" that sent his skull sheering away from death by a couple of inches.

Stayne grabbed the broken capsule and pitched it into the crackling wood fire, where its foundation of dried creamed rice burned up whitely and faded. Thereafter Stayne worked with the speed and precision of a machine in top gear. He cut the jailer's heavy chain with a pair of powerful steel nippers and seized the huge polished keys.

Running outside he opened the outer door.

"Quick," he said. "He's out—won't last more than two minutes. It was a small dose. Stay here and see that he doesn't raise hell if he comes to."

Tembridge was already by the door. He was through in a second, with the door partly pulled to behind him. Stayne ran to the inner gates, opened them, and in a voice of cold authority called "Varris—Prisoner Templer Varris!"

Automatically Templer Varris straightened his back and looked round. The "trusty" stood up and stared across. The sight of a man in civilian clothes at the gate was nothing new to him indeed, everybody except the warders wore their own clothes in the prison, and he had not the slightest suspicion of anything wrong. Unauthorised persons don't usually open the inner gate and call a prisoner by his name.

Varris looked round inquiringly at the "trusty." and the senior prisoner nodded. "Go on, you damn fool," he barked. "Want to keep him waiting all day? It's a visitor for you—or your lawyer bloke." The "trusty" did not realise it, but he had absorbed something of the outlook and psychology of a warder himself since he had worn the chevrons.

"Varris, come here. You others carry on." The firm commanding voice sounded a little impatient. Templer Varris dropped his trowel and walked tiffly to the gate. Stayne passed him through, relocked it, and passed down the lock.

Tembridge hurried out of the guardroom.

"O.K., chief," he said. "Varris, this way," and hurried through the outer doors. Varris, bewildered and puzzled, hesitated for a moment and received a push in the back of the neck from behind.

"Forward. You are wanted at Bow Street," crackled a voice in his ear. That sounded reasonable enough, and Varris went forward again, out through the doors into freedom.

Tembridge was standing by the open door of the limousine. As soon as Varris was in he dashed to his own seat, Stayne slamming the door as he climbed in beside Varris. In less than six seconds from passing through the outer doors the car was in motion racing down the courtyard. At the bottom it pulled sharply to the right—away from London.

IX

The car went droning on past the outer limits of the vast open common, careering past the outer confines of the last battlemented outer wall.

A brazen bell began to sound its clamorous summons to the skies. It welled and swelled to a whanging cacophony of sound, taken up here and there at various points from the watchtowers. A bull-throated howl of surprise and anger.

Stayne realised what had happened back there at the Scrubs. An officer had come down to the inner gates on some duty or other, possibly in connection with the release of Thomas Dobey, had called to the gate jailer, called again and got no reply. The jailer inside that double lock was the only one who held the key to the inner gate, and for the first time in Scrubs history there was no reply to the summons. Followed a hurried look around, a hailing of the "trusty" in charge of the gardening hands, an excited telling of what had happened—and a quick sounding of the alarm.

The car was now four miles away and safe from any hope of being overtaken from the prison. The telephone was the only thing that could serve them now. He knew that Hawker would have taken the numbers of every car in that garage. Under pressure the garage foreman would readily admit that the big limousine was out, and, furthermore, had been out all night. Inquiry along the Dobey line of approach would rapidly connect the incident of Stayne's visit to Marlborough Street

Police Court and the presence of that same sports car outside West London while the Dobey case was on trial. An inquiry at the Strand Hotel would unfailingly provide the rest of the evidence. J. Stemdale of the Strand Hotel was no other than Colonel John Stayne of Curzon Square, the Mystery-Maker, now abroad with Templer Varris in a big blue limousine of a certain make and register number that would, within an hour, be circulated to every constable and point policeman in and out of London.

Stayne pointed to the clothes.

"Dress!" he said shortly. "And hurry!"

"I'll see you in Scrubs yourself first," replied Varris quietly.

"You probably will unless you do. And not only me, who does not matter a tinker's cuss either way, but also Lord Demorval, Emil Flocard, yourself, Marienne—everybody, in fact, except our graceful friends Perrigo and Canning. Dress, you damned fool—and jump to it."

* * *

The secretary's eyes opened wide in sheer unbelief, an incredulity that anyone living could, in one sharp sentence, betray such a seething knowledge of the inside facts of his distressing affair.

"I—I just want to know that—that this is all square and above-board," he said defensively. "You come to the Scrubs and shanghai me out—when I've only gone in to save others—and you expect me to accept it all and act as though I understood all about it and acquiesced in everything that happens to me. How do I know that this thing is on the level?"

"Of course you don't, you blithering fool! A man with your infantile intelligence couldn't be expected to. You think you were brave, don't you? You think you did a noble and a self-sacrificing thing in going to jail?" Stayne's eyes almost crackled at him. "Let me tell you, Varris, you were not only a fool, you were a coward. You funked it. You dived into jail like a rabbit into a hole. You went in because you couldn't face the issues outside. Listen, man. By this time tomorrow night I hope to be in Paris. And not only in Paris but talking to Lord Demorval! Why, man alive, Marienne has got more courage than you. And those clothes, by the way, are from her, not me. The fact that I'm here all springs from her too. Now climb into those clothes while the road is still open. Tembridge out front there has got all he can do to keep this car on the move without running it under a policeman's eye. For God's sake don't make his job any worse than it is!" He snapped his fingers in growing irritation. "I never knew it was so hard to help a man to help himself," he snorted.

Varris flushed a deep crimson.

"You might be a little easier on me," he said at last. "Your end of this case is all up in the air to me. What do you think I am—a thought-reader?"

"No. Just a loyal fool. Very loyal—and very much of a fool."

"How do I know that you aren't one of the Perrigo crowd?"

"You don't. You don't have to. Except that you should know that Perrigo wouldn't shift a finger to save a friend."

"Perrigo would only be saving his own oily skin by getting me out of jail."

"Would he? Now think in terms of Standard Two. You had already elected to go to prison rather than spill the beans. A good fat sentence, too. Why in the name of beauty should he risk his neck getting you out of a place into which you had voluntarily thrust yourself?"

* * *

Varris relaxed. He was half convinced, but resentful still, and as ferociously on guard as a wild animal that has just been captured and is being offered a tempting morsel from a hand that it still suspects.

"How can you prove you are all you say you are?" he demanded.

"I'll take you to Marienne. Marienne can do all my talking for me."

Varris thought that one over for some seconds. He was dressing rapidly, glancing out of the window now and then furtively, as though the window of every suburban house they pased sheltered a watchful enemy eye.

Halfway through the operation of tying his tie he hauled himself round from the mirror and suddenly asked:

"Well—what do you want me for, anyway?"

"I want you to tell me the full story of the Lady Demorval affair—from the Paris end," said Stayne.

Varris stopped dead and his hands went back limply into his lap.

"I'll see you damned first," he said.

Stayne seemed indifferent. "All right," he said casually. "Finish your dressing. I want to get rid of that prison rig. Perhaps even you can see reason in that." Stayne took the heady course of mailing it back to the prison whence it came.

"Anyway," he muttered grimly, "we shan't have a charge of stealing? Government property added to our list of criminal offences."

He reached for the speaking-tube. "Stop at the next General Post Office, so long as it isn't under the nose of a point policeman," he said.

X

Varris sat with his hands on his knees for a long time, staring out unwinkingly at the long, drab streets as they flashed by.

"How are you fixed for cash?" asked Stayne suddenly.

Varris seemed to pull himself to with a jerk.

"I—er—I've several hundred pounds in the bank," he said, "but—but—"

"Awkward to draw it out, eh? Of course it would be. And dangerous too. Make me out a cheque for five hundred and I'll pass it through one of my private accounts. Meanwhile, you'll find a wallet in your inside coat pocket. There's money in it. Also visiting cards in the name of Harris, with a quiet little Bayswater boarding-house underneath. Tembridge booked the rooms yesterday by phone, so there will be no suspicion about that. You could hardly have booked your rooms before you broke out of prison, could you? Also a cigarette-case with the name 'H. T. Harris' engraved on it. Also a season ticket made out in that name from Bayswater to Bishopsgate, where you will be in charge of an office I have there. The season ticket is a month old already. It is valid for two months more. It's one of Tembridge's various decoys. He has several others going permanently. You'll have one of those if that one gets dangerous. You'll find a couple of letters waiting for you at the Bayswater address. Also a post card referring to certain conversations you had with the signatory last week. Boarding-house landladies have been known to glance through post cards; and that will help to put her off the scent again."

Varris, throughout the quiet recital, gazed at Stayne with eyes that slowly grew wider and wider with astonishment.

"You're—you're pretty thorough, aren't you?" he said with a long exhalation of breath.

"Also efficient—and speedy. If any of those arrangements break down during our running of this case we shall have others that you can slip into at a moment's notice. You see we have already come to the conclusion that it will be safest for us—and for a great many other people too—if you remain at liberty while this problem is being flattened out. Just a moment, here's the post office."

He stepped out of the car with the tightly-tied parcel. Tembridge had gone on past the post office and had turned down the first side street, where he jumped out and covered the radiator with a blanket that reached right down over the front number-plate. He himself stood round at the back, masking out the other number-plate with his own body till John Stayne returned.

Stayne came back and beckoned Varris.

"Come along," he said, "here's where we get out and walk. Tembridge, take the car round somewhere handy and garage it. Say it will be left for a week. Pay a deposit covering that length of time and then leave it. We can recover it when everything is cleared up. Get back home as soon as you can—and use the private entrance. I wouldn't use the front door again. Hawker is bound to have a squad there. Come on, Varris."

* * *

They walked quietly for something over a mile and then took a series of buses to Bayswater.

"You'll be all right at that address," said Stayne. "Some of your luggage was sent along yesterday. Three hand-grips packed with underclothes and thingummyjigs. The rest you can get yourself. Tell me, what else can you do besides secretarial work?"

Varris paused for a moment and rubbed his chin.

"Well—um—m—I've dabbled at a variety of things and made a pretty fine mess at most," he said ruminatively.

"Motor mechanics?"

"A little—but not too good."

"Wireless?"

Varris brightened. "Hobby of mine," he said.

"Understand it?"

"Know it inside out."

"That'll do, then. I'll put you on rigging up the office with communicating telephone lines. If you understand wireless you can get the hang of telephone wiring inside two jiffs. Pair of dark-blue dungaree overalls, second-hand stepladder. Bag of tools. Cloth cap. Face none too clean. That'll be all you'll need for that. Get the idea?"

"I don't think I do," said Varris. "You move a bit too fast for me."

"Keep that disguise locked in a drawer at your office. Everything bar the dirty hands and face. You see, Hawker is no fool. He's good. And he's out on this job like a stoat on the trail of a rabbit. And he's every bit as persistent. The chances are a hundred to one that he will ferret out my Bishopsgate dead-end. He's like that—the old rat!"

"I see," said Varris, not too happily.

"Ring me at home every two hours. Then I'll know everything is O.K. If you once go over two hours without calling me I'll know something radically wrong has occurred round at the office. Then I'll come around and rescue you. I think I can handle Mr. Hawker all right. Tonight at ten o'clock I'll come along to Bayswater and see you. Together we must piece this thing out and get it all square. As soon as I've got the details fixed I can start for Paris. Not until. It's my way to plan every move out ahead. And no man living can plan in the dark. Here's your place. See you later, Varris. Keep your pecker up, don't play the fool—and good luck!" Varris found himself being ushered out on to the step of the bus in a semi-daze by the most remarkable man he had ever met in his life.

At the Marble Arch Stayne climbed off the bus too. As he stepped on the kerb a newsboy went streaking by, yelling "Prison Escape!" at the top of his high-pitched lungs.

Later in the day the story was added to. There came the cryptic phrase that inferred quite a lot but gave no real information at all. "An arrest is hourly expected." The inference was that Scotland Yard officers were on the trail of the outside conspirators—were aware of their identity and knew where they could eventually locate them.

Stayne allowed himself a satisfied smile at that. It meant that, without giving away a ha'porth of information to the outside world, Hawker was informing him, through the medium of the public Press, that he was perfectly aware of all that had happened and that the best thing Colonel John Stayne could do was to keep out of it, for he would be arrested on sight.

As an even darker hint, an official notice from Headquarters appeared in print. It was headed "Have you seen this car?" And underneath ran the information: "It is known that two men in a car were concerned in the escape of Templer Varris from Scrubs Prison this morning. Both of them are known to the police, but for reasons of State their names are temporarily withheld. The car is a Silent Six limousine, 1927 model, coloured dark blue, nickel fittings, upholstered inside in dark blue leather. The register number is GG 4012. For some months it has been garaged in a mews off Curzon Square. Anyone seeing this car should immediately inform the police."

The next edition informed the world that the car had been found, located in a garage on the western outskirts of London. A chauffeur had taken it in and left a deposit on it for a week's garaging. Stayne was secretly pleased at the construction put on that revelation. The report went on to state that it would appear that the three men were heading out of London. Apparently another car, with a chauffeur, had met them at that prearranged spot—a car that could not be known to the police—and in it they were making their escape from the Metropolis.

Motorists, for the next few hours, complained bitterly of the inconvenience they experienced in trying to get through on the main roads. Traps seemed to exist at every mile, and even those who chose to go by circuitous routes through the by-roads fared little better. At every post they had to undergo a critical scrutiny and questionnaire by the police patrols, and no sooner were they through one cordon than they were into another.

But there was no further news of the supposed flying motorists. Hawker had to admit that the patrol system, for all the miraculous speed with which it was organised and put into operation, had failed.

XI

John Stayne entered his house by the secret way. It led in from a cellar in a little house at the back of his own. He owned that house, and the passageway had been cut, laboriously, yard by yard, by his own hands. The earth had been removed, load by load, in the early hours of the morning, with the aid of a builder's cart. Val Tembridge, the epitomisation of every corduroy trousered carter that ever lived, poised half asleep on the top, with the limp reins in his hands.

Stayne passed through and let himself into the cellars of his own house. He removed the lid of a whisky keg and lifted a small telephone from its interior. In a little while a voice, suppressed as to be barely audible, came down from upstairs.

"Is that you, sir?" it asked.

"Yes"—Stayne himself was hardly more than whispering—"has anything happened while I've been gone?"

"Yes, sir. That Mr. Hawker came back—half an hour ago. I told him you weren't in and he wouldn't believe me. He said he was coming in to find you: or, if you were out, to wait till you got back."

"Yes, yes—is he there now?"

"I couldn't help myself, sir. I told him I could not possibly let him into the house without your permission, but he told me if I didn't mind my own business I would find myself under arrest. I knew he was from Scotland Yard and I didn't know what to do. He demanded admittance and I had to let him in."

"Has he searched?"

"Yes, sir. He went all over the house and finally said he was satisfied you weren't in. But he sat himself down in the dining-room and says he won't budge till you come back—not if you stay away for a month."

"All right, Belham, don't worry yourself; you did quite right."

"But that's not all, sir. Ten minutes ago another detective came in. I believe Mr. Hawker telephoned for him. The two of them are in there together. One keeps answering every telephone call that comes, and the other is sitting by the window watching everyone that calls at the house."

"Well, that won't matter. I'll see them myself presently, but I want to get up into my bedroom first. Is the way clear?"

"Just a moment, sir. I'll see."

* * *

There was silence for a little while, and then the butler's voice came on again. "Yes, sir; it's all clear. I've listened at the door. They're still in there, talking. Are you coming up now?"

"Right away."

He slipped off his shoes and noiselessly crept up through the trapdoor into another cellar above, and up the stairs to his room.

In a few minutes he was in through the library panel and talking on the private line.

"Is that Number One?" he asked.

"Yes, beautiful work, Colonel," came the quietly appreciative voice from the other end. "Have any trouble?"

"Not a piece. Everything went along like ball bearings running in an oil bath. Sorry about the jailer, but it couldn't be helped. Better than bumping him on the head with a spanner, though."

"I can't see how it could be avoided."

"It couldn't, short of bribery. And they're not that sort. It was only a little whiff, anyhow. He would be as right as rain five minutes afterwards."

"Have you fixed Varris?"

"Yes. That end is all right. But I want your help. Hawker is here. He seems to have anchored himself at the telephone and refuses to budge an inch until he has got his hands on me."

"You rather expected that, didn't you?"

"It was inevitable. That's why I'm in the house without his knowledge. Will you do the necessary? Three should be sufficient. Any more would make it too obvious."

"They will be ready by the time you get down to Hawker. He may not wait, of course. He may choose to take you straight off to Bow Street. In that case you will have to do it from there."

"I'll see to all that, Chief."

"Then they will be numbers Eight, Ten and Seventeen."

"Thanks. Goodbye."

"Goodbye, and congratulations."

Stayne relocked the cabin and went down into the dining-room. He pushed the door open carelessly and walked through as though he was doing nothing more exciting than going in to dinner.

Hawker sprang up as the door opened and he stared at Stayne in grudging surprise. He had expected him back, but not nearly so soon and not nearly so undramatically.

"Hallo, Hawker, how's tricks? Belham told me you were in, comfortable?"

Stayne took a cigarette from a big silver box on the table and lit it with delicate precision.

"So you made it, did you?" said Hawker sourly. "I'll find that damned secret dive of yours if I have to tear the house down stone by stone."

"And that wouldn't help either," replied Stayne cordially. He noted with a slight amusement that the other detective had risen too and had crossed round to the door; he now stood between him and it.

Hawker eyed his man grimly, "Well, are you coming quietly?" he snapped.

Stayne affected a mild surprise, "Coming?" he said vaguely. "Coming where?"

Hawker snorted. "Oh, don't play the fool," he growled. "I've had a cell specially washed and scrubbed for you ever since midday. It's waiting for you now—round at Vine Street."

"May I ask what for?"

"Colonel, that's not funny. I expected a better one than that from you."

Stayne sighed patiently. "Hawker, you might at least extend me the usual privileges of the law of the land," he said. "I am legally entitled to know what the charge is."

"You can have it any way you like," retorted Hawker hotly. "If you want it all dolled up with the fal-de-lahs according to Cocker, here it is. John Stayne, I arrest you for complicity in the escape of one Templer Varris from Scrubs Prison today, and I hereby warn you that anything you say may be used in evidence against you."

"Thank you: I just wanted to know what idiotic trick you were up to now." Stayne seemed relieved. "Now, let's stop acting the goat. Candidly, what do you want me for?"

Hawker blinked. "Eh?" he said, and there was a faint shock of surprise in his voice.

Stayne did not seem to notice it.

"Honestly, Hawker, do you really think I had any hand in that fool affair?" he asked.

Hawker staggered. He gaped at the ice-cool man in front of him and swallowed hard. He thrust his head forward to stare at him through a luxurious cloud of pale blue cigarette smoke that was coming idly down Stayne's nostrils. He seemed unable to believe the evidence of his own ears. For some seconds he stared at his man, incredulous. Then he pulled himself together with a tremendous effort, and there was a ring of sheer bad temper in his reply.

"Do you mean to say you dare to put up a denial?" he snorted.

"Dare? Dare?" Stayne turned the word over on his tongue as though to get its full mental quality. "Of course I dare," he added gently. "Why on earth shouldn't I? You know perfectly well that I have nothing to do with such a silly business. When you read out that charge I thought you were joking."

"Joking!" Hawker was nearly inarticulate. "Say, Stayne," he managed to strangle out, "are you trying to get my goat?"

"Don't be a fool. Hawker, my son, you're losing your nerve. Arrest me by all means, but I'll promise you that by this time tomorrow you'll be the sorriest man in London. And not only that, but you'll admit that you've made the biggest blunder in your career."

"Is that so?" Hawker had so far recovered himself as to be almost sarcastic.

"I fear it is. I can definitely prove to the satisfaction of any court in this country that I had not the slightest connection with that particular affair, that I neither knew nor saw Templer Varris, and that it was impossible for me to have assisted in his escape from jail."

"You can do all that, can you? Yes, you can! And then some! Now listen to this little lot. Yesterday you were traced from this house to Marl borough Street Police Station. You were driving a sports model car the number of which is known. An hour later that same car was parked just round the corner from West London Police Court.

"At West London there was a man up on several charges, a man whose name is Thomas Dobey. You saw Thomas Dobey. The jailer has identified you from several photographs submitted to him. You bought Dobey tea. And you offered to pay his fine. Then, for obvious reasons, you refrained from paying the fine right away. You did that in spite of the fact that you were present in court and heard the sentences passed. You were recognised and identified in that court. That manoeuvre insured that Dobey would go to Scrubs Prison. On your way out you scribbled a note and gave it to the charge sergeant. He, too, will swear to you. And—"

"The note?" asked Stayne levelly.

"The note is in my office now. It is in your handwriting. Also the card you gave to Thomas Dobey. J. Sterndale is the name you gave him, and the address was the Strand Hotel, London. Dobey wrote you from prison. That letter is also in my possession. You left it on the bench in the guardroom when you drugged the gate warder. At the Strand Hotel the inquiries clerk identifies you as the man who called in there this morning and received a letter from Scrubs Prison. Tembridge was driving you, dressed as a chauffeur. Your blue limousine is found, the car is registered to J. Sterndale, of the Strand Hotel. Now disprove that little lot to the satisfaction of any court in the country—and I'll resign."

XII

Stayne softly rubbed his chin. "Fast work, Hawker! Fast work and good," he admitted "But on the wrong tack, old man. You've got yourself badly tangled up somewhere."

"Yeh?"

"I'm afraid so. You've got me mixed up with someone else. This Sterndale chap—he's the boy you want to go after. Now, before you make a fool of yourself do you mind if I do a little phoning?"

"You're not going to touch that phone again for some years," said Hawker flatly. "What you're going to do is to put on your hat and come right round to Vine Street with me—now!"

"You're very trying," said Stayne sadly. "I'm attempting to help you. You've made rather a bad mistake and I'm trying to assist you in avoiding a worse one. Just let me telephone. I promise you that I will only put three calls through. They will be to men whose names are beyond reproach—men who, except in the service of their country, would not stoop to the violation of a single law. You can hear every word I say. It wilk simply be to ask them to come round here and make a statement to you. If, after what they tell you, you still think you'd like to take me round to Vine Street, believe me I shall be only too willing to accompany you."

Hawker looked uncertainly from Stayne to his assistant. Then he took out his handkerchief and mopped his forehead.

"You're up to your old tricks again, you rascal," he muttered, "but I'm blest if I can see what the game is. Are you going to pull an alibi?"

"Most certainly I am. And when you've heard it you'll realise how nearly I you came to making the most perfect *faux pas* you ever made in your life."

Stayne rang the bell and the secretary came in.

"Miss Mathers," he said, "I want you to ring up Mr. Calhoun, Major-General Stonehaugh, and Sir Ardleigh Powers. Tell each of them that I would esteem it a great favour if they would call here at their earliest convenience. Say that I much regret having to trouble them, but that the matter is of such grave import to me that I have no other alternative. If any of them should not happen to be in, please inform me."

The secretary departed, and Stayne turned to Hawker.

"It is better that she should do it," he said evenly. "It leaves me no chance of coding them a message or doing anything utterly impossible like that. When they arrive I will simply ask them to tell you what I've been doing today in their company. One could hardly be fairer, could one?"

"You beauty! You're pulling another line of bull on me, hey?"

Stayne shrugged. "Glance at the names," he suggested. "Mr. Calhoun is private secretary to the Prime Minister, General Stonehaugh is the head of the Army Ordnance Department, and Sir Ardleigh Powers is Undersecretary of State for India. You'd hardly question their credentials, would you?"

Hawker was obviously perplexed. He mopped his forehead again, and grunted.

"I'll wait and see 'em," he said at last, and sat down sullenly.

"Of course you will. You would only be making yourself look supremely ridiculous if you didn't." Stayne seemed to dismiss the whole affair with that thought, and he sat down to wait for his callers.

The secretary came in again to say that she had got into touch with each of the gentlemen concerned, and that they were on their way.

* * *

Hawker smoked on in a restive silence. He seemed to sense already that Stayne had beaten him again. He saw him wriggling out of the coils he had thrown around him, although for the very life of him he could not define the nature of the particular wriggle employed.

Templer Varris was cheap as the price to be paid for John Stayne. Hawker would willingly have given a year of his life to have put the Mystery-Maker safe behind the bars. Stayne had pricked his official pride too long: and now, just when it seemed that he had got his man on the inevitable march up to the dock, there was another convulsive wriggle coming and, equally inevitably, he could see Stayne slipping out of his fingers again.

He jammed his cigarette butt savagely into an ash-tray. It was unfair, unjust! Stayne was blatantly as guilty as any man ever was in his life. That chain of evidence had not been built up on surmise! Every single link of it was definite, a concrete fact that was proven and re-proven. Stayne had actually warned him at that first meeting that he would have Varris out of jail within forty-eight hours. He had done it, had made good on his boast, Hawker and his men had traced his every movement. It was imbecile to say that Stayne was guiltless.

"How are you going to get clear of the evidence of that car?" he suddenly demanded.

"It was probably stolen from outside my house," said Stayne imperturbably. "That sort of thing is constantly being done in London. I should think it was one of those abnormally frequent cases of borrowing a car. The fact that it was a chauffeur who garaged the car adds credence to that view. The less scrupulous of them borrow a car occasionally and take young ladies of their acquaintance for joyrides. You must have come into contact with many such cases yourself."

Hawker's eyes glittered and he looked as though he was ready, there and then, to get up and have a stand-up fight with Stayne.

XIII

One by one the visitors arrived. Calhoun, tall and thin; Stonelaugh, unmistakably a soldier of the old school; Powers inclined to portliness.

Stayne said nothing whatever until the last of them arrived. He just rose and received them as they were announced, with a formal little bow and muttered greeting.

When they were all in and seated, not without a feeling of embarrassment, Stayne addressed them. He himself was not in the slightest way nervous of the outcome. He knew perfectly well that the Chief would have drilled them into their parts and made them word-perfect. And besides they had played that part before at the sudden quick call of duty.

"Gentlemen," he said, "I want first to introduce you to our friend here. This gentleman is a police officer; you probably all know him quite well by name. He is Mr. Hawker, of the Criminal Investigation Department at Scotland Yard. Mr. Hawker, this is Sir Ardleigh Powers, the parliamentary head of the India Office; this is Mr. Calhoun, to whose bodyguard you were attached during the General Strike, and this is General Stonehaugh, the present head of the Army Ordnance Department.

"Now, gentlemen, I am not in a position to be able to enlighten you as to the reason for this rather hurried conference. Such an act would, I feel, be a breach of faith with Hawker. But I will say this much, that it is a very serious affair for me, very serious indeed, and I must ask each of you to weigh your words with the utmost care when you reply to such questions as Mr. Hawker may care to put. I deeply regret the inconvenience to which you have been put, but when you understand the reason for this abrupt call I'm sure you will realise that there was nothing else for me to do.

"Mr. Hawker here is anxious to trace my movements from an early hour this morning up to, say, one or two o'clock. Why he wishes this information is for Mr. Hawker to tell you, or not, as the case may be. At that point, gentlemen, I must leave it. General Stonehaugh, would you mind telling Mr. Hawker, please, at what hour today you first met me and when we parted?"

Stonehaugh set about the business as methodically as though he were back on the barrack square.

"I can give you that information with a certain degree of exactitude," he said in his queer, ponderous way. "For official reasons it is my invariable custom to keep a somewhat fully written diary." He produced a monthly diary from his pocket.

"I first met Colonel Stayne at my house at ten minutes to nine," he said, opening the volume at its most recent entries. "Here is the note. 'Stayne called 8.50. Left 10.35. Matter discussed: Gun Calibrations for the Alder-shot Manoeuvres. See also letter files under that heading.' "

"And where was this?" asked Hawker.

"At my house in South Audley Street. I had a telephone message from Colonel Stayne overnight, and I suggested that he should breakfast with me while we discussed the matter in hand."

"Was Colonel Stayne phoning from here?"

"No; I think he said he was at an hotel in Maidenhead."

Hawker turned inquiringly to Stayne. "It was at a little place just outside Maidenhead. The 'Old Bell' at Hurley;

you probably know it. In any case you can verify. I signed the visitors' book."

"And he stayed till 10.35, did he?"

"He did. I was due at the War Office at eleven, and we cut our discussion short."

"General Stonehaugh, this man Colonel Stayne was at the Strand Hotel talking to the inquiries clerk at ten o'clock," said Hawker coldly. "That fact can be proved. Do you still say he was with you at that hour?"

"I most certainly do," said the General with some asperity.

"Would you repeat that statement on oath in the witness-box?"

"I should take the utmost pleasure in doing so, and I might add that I am not in the habit of being asked questions like that."

"Maybe not, sir, but when you are trying to clear up a particularly unsavoury mystery, questions like that have to be asked—and answered. I know that Colonel Stayne did not sleep in this house last night, and he isn't fool enough to say he did. Not only was the house under observation all night, but the servants were questioned today. The fact that he came in from Maidenhead fits in with other information I have concerning his movements."

Stonehaugh frowned. "I regret, officer, that I have nothing to add to, or retract, from my previous statements," he said severely. "Colonel Stayne was at my house at the time stated, and he left at the time stated, as noted in this diary. Also he was never out of my company from the minute he entered the house until he left it. That is all. I have nothing further to add."

"Did anyone else see him there?"

"Naturally. The butler who opened the door to him. My wife, who entertained him. The maid, who waited at table. And I'm not sure that the nurse didn't look in for a few minutes."

Hawker looked round at Stayne again in bitter exasperation. "You've got this thing pretty closely knit up, haven't you?" he grated. "Do you mean to say you actually sent someone round to impersonate you? You didn't bluff the General—and he's not bluffing me! But there was someone sufficiently like you around there to get the servants to corroborate what the General says."

"That individual must have come from the Man Higher Up," said Stayne cheerfully. He had only just realised how perfectly the Chief had helped him through. He had gone a jump ahead of Stayne every time, and had made his alibi watertight for him by sending a man round in advance.

Hawker began to see the true nature of the wriggle.

"Well, who's next?" he growled. "Where did he go after that, hey? Who was he with when he was pumping hydrocyanide into the lungs of the gate jailer at Scrubs Prison?"

XIV

"I should think I was the next one to see Colonel Stayne," said Calhoun quietly. "That is, he was with me at the Treasury at eleven o'clock. If he left General Stonehaugh's at 10.35, that would give him twenty-five minutes to get from South Audley Street to Whitehall."

"And he was in your office, I suppose?" There was a sneer in the question.

"Undoubtedly. He was with me till a little after one o'clock."

"And he was arranging who was to be the next Prime Minister, hey?"

Calhoun smiled. "Oh, no. I don't think his powers run quite to that—yet. He was giving me a résumé of the purport of his discussion with Stonehaugh. The P.M. has to answer certain questions connected with ordnance at the next sittings—there was a lot of private matter as well that I cannot discuss now. The whole of it is now in writing and in the P.M.'s hands. So there should be no difficulty in verifying that."

"How many others saw him?"

"Quite a dozen, I should think. I can get you their names if you wish."

"I don't wish. I know when I'm being framed up. And when was he with you, sir?"

"Immediately after," said Powers. "I called for him at Calhoun's office, and together we went out to lunch. We lunched at 'The Ship.' He left me soon after three o'clock."

Hawker chewed savagely at his lip.

"And I suppose all you gentlemen are perfectly willing to stand up in open court and reiterate all that—on oath?" he said.

"I for one would not hesitate for a single moment," replied Sir Ardleigh Powers. "There is not the slightest reason why the others would. I am quite sure that on the day you require us to appear we shall be at your service."

Hawker reached for his hat and made a sign to his assistant that the conference was finished. "Well, that's enough for me, gentlemen," he said, and Stayne's heart warmed towards him, for his voice was not without a hint of a grudging admiration somewhere in its timbre. "I know when I'm bested, and I know when all the loopholes are sealed up. Valdon Tembridge has definite evidence that he was up at the North Pole when Templer Varris broke jail. Eh? I bet you've got that end all nicely fixed up too."

Stayne laughed silently.

"You left the garage end open too long, old friend," he said. "Within ten minutes of your man being hauled off to watch this house Tembridge was in the pit under one of my cars cleaning out the gearbox and readjusting the hydraulic brakes. He's never left the job; you'll find him there yet. The garage hands can testify to the truth of that. In two minutes from the time he began he would be black as a stove with axle oil and whatnot. Run around and see him, Hawker."

"All right," he said. "I know that piece of it. I could smell it out a mile away, down-wind—on a cold day. It's the *real* Tembridge round there in the pit now, hey?"

"I sincerely hope so," said Stayne fervently.

Hawker jammed his hat hard on his head. "Good day, gentlemen," he snapped. "I only wish I could get gentlemen of such unchallengeable integrity as yours to frame up jobs like this for me now and then. I'd have half the criminals in London slammed away in cells inside a month. Come on, Morby, this wants talking out with the Chief. Maybe we can get authority to go all out for it and risk the arrest." He turned and flung back over his shoulder: "I hope so, Colonel. I'd like the chance of banging seven bells out of that alibi of yours." In a morose silence the pair of them went out.

Stayne called Tembridge on the phone at the garage. "It's all right now," he said. "You can stop pretending to do a decent job of hard work. I'm sure it must be breaking your heart. Hawker has gone off in a sour mood. Wash off the dirt and come round here. I want to see you."

The three guests departed without so much as a further word about the incident that occasioned their visit. The only thing they did was to make definite notes of times and places according to each other's story.

While Stayne awaited the advent of his assistant the little golden idol in the corner announced "Miss Marienne Varris to see you, sir."

Stayne's eyes clouded, and a fleeting frown of annoyance shadowed rapidly across his face. Then, with a half-sigh of regret, he said, "Very well, Belham, I'll see her. Show her up to me in here, will you, please?"

She came up and entered the room hurriedly, a torrent of half-articulate thanks on her lips. Stayne rose to greet her. She was a different girl from the pitifully-distressed, cowed little thing that had pleaded for help in that room a few hours before. She was radiant, and her eyes held a glow of warmth in their depths that was almost a reflection of worship. At that moment it was sheer hero worship that lit up bright lamps of thankfulness and sent their rays boldly gleaming out.

"Oh, Mr. Stayne," she said breathlessly, "thank you so much—a thousand, million, *million* thanks—how can I ever be grateful enough—how can I ever show you my gratitude—how"

Stayne took her impulsively outstretched hands in his and firmly led her to a chair.

"By keeping that pretty little head of yours as firmly on the horizontal as you possibly can," he said. "You have—"

"But—Mr. Stayne, I've seen the papers—I read them all—positive eaten them! I don't think I've ever read so many papers in my life. And I think it's wonderful—absolutely wonderful! I got so excited reading about it that I wanted to jump up and yell with delight. I wanted to tell the people in the hotel that I knew who had done it, and that he was the bravest and best man whoever lived. And I—"

"Miss Varris," Stayne's voice had the rumbling note of distant thunder in it, "please get a grip of yourself. And—*please*—get this very firmly plan in your head. Neither John Stayne nor Valdon Tembridge went within a mile of Scrubs Prison today. We neither assisted in his escape nor do we know anyone who did. That fact has been definitely proved to the satisfaction of the authorities at Scotland Yard. It's awfully nice of you to come careering round here with bouquets and all sorts of nice things to say, but you must—not—do—it! You are acting unwittingly, unthinkingly. And in this affair you must use every grain of intelligence you have. You are running us all into serious danger by rushing round here like this."

In a moment all Marienne's keyed-up excitement vanished. It evaporated into thin air like an early morning mist before the heat of the sun. Stayne wasn't being gently remonstrative; there was nothing in either his voice or his manner that suggested an indulgent father shaking a finger at a well-meaning but thoughtless daughter. There was a positively angry ring in his voice and the glint in his cold eyes was definitely resentful. She looked unhappy, full of contrition, a girl who had only come round because her heart was bursting with gratitude and because it was part of her generous, emotional young nature to pour out her thanks to anyone who had offered her a kindness. Her lips trembled.

"Do you know," Stayne went on in his icily deliberate way, "that Scotland Yard has been treading on your heels ever since you first decided to bring your troubles to me? A detective followed you here the first time you called on me. One of the slickest detectives in the world, too. He was round here and in this room five minutes after your taxi left my front door. A man has been specially detailed off to watch your every movement."

Marienne looked round with a half-frightened little turn of the head.

"But, really," she gasped, "I didn't know: I only came round to thank you—and to find out Templer's address. I *do* want to see him so badly. If you knew—"

"Yes, yes, I do know. But you have got to realise that though we're all on the side of right and justice in this matter, Scotland Yard is against us—and they're doing their utmost to get us trapped. Every movement you make is a pointer to them."

"But, Mr. Stayne, what can they find out from me? I haven't done anything wrong."

"You've done wrong in coming round here at all. Can't you see how suspicious it is? The moment Varris is out you come flying round here again. Correspondence of yours—letters you have written—have been opened in the post. They *knew* you were coming here the first time, and they knew what you were going to ask me. Within forty-eight hours of that Varris has broken jail and you come tearing round again as fast as a taxi can bring you. And now—of all the imbecile things on this earth, you want your brother's address! Candidly, Miss Varris, what do you think would happen if I were lunatic enough to give it you?"

"I—I don't know," whispered Marienne. She felt so shocked and so bitter at having offended the man who, at that moment, was the greatest hero her mind had ever pictured, that she wished she had been stricken with paralysis rather than have left that stodgy hotel.

"Your shadower would have taken up a position about ten yards behind you, on the opposite side of the road, and followed you round. And if you a hundred eyes all round your hat you would never have seen him or suspected his presence. It might have been the man sweeping the gutter, or the teamster driving a lorry—or the beggar with a tray of studs to sell. But you would have directed him to Varris's sanctuary as surely as though you laid a paper trail all the way."

"Does that mean that—that I cannot see Templer?" she faltered.

"It means that you will see him when and where I can arrange a meeting," said Stayne grimly. "And it won't be here—or at his place either. And it also means, young lady, that you will wait for instructions from me before you either come here again or even ring me on the telephone. For all I know, my very phone wires may be tapped. Now, is all that perfectly clear?"

"Yes," she said very gently. "I promise I'll never even move from my rooms without permission. I'd—I'd rather die than make things any more difficult for you."

"Then we'll say no more about it. You're the weakest link in our chain. They know it. And they'll hammer at you till they break you. Although Varris is out of jail it does not follow that he is free. He will go back the moment he is discovered. And we have a long job ahead of us. Getting him out was only the first step in a long and difficult business. I'll ring you tomorrow morning early at your hotel and tell you if I can arrange for you to see your brother. I may be flying over to Paris tomorrow night—but I will do what I can. But until then don't make a single move without thinking out first what the consequences will be."

He patted her cheek and added: "That's all. Terribly sorry I've had to be so blunt—but bluntness pays when the other fellow is so sharp." He led her to the door and Belham showed her down.

Stayne stood at the top and watched her go. He caught sight of his own reflection in the glass and silently, but viciously, he swore at it.

"John Stayne," he growled, "you're a brute and a bully—and one hell of a specimen of a big damn fool. You aren't fit to live in the same town with her—yet just to please your own sticky chunk of vanity you dam nearly made her cry again." He thrust out his jaw at himself and said "Bah!"

With his brows deeply knit in hard thought he went over to the balcony window and looked down. He looked down—and swore again.

Marienne, with one foot on the step of the taxi, had been stopped by a tall, slim, rather elegant young man who wore a smartly cut brown lounge suit extremely well, and evidenced a marvellously unselfconscious manner. He raised his hat, a soft brown felt of unquestionable taste, and gently disentangled her hand from the handle of the door. Stayne knew from that trim back view that it was that cavalier young gentleman, Valdon Tembridge.

The girl turned, in some slight surprise and confusion. Then when she saw who it was she smiled and coloured delightfully. The masterful young gentleman, apparently without further argument or permission, thrust his hand into his pocket, presented the driver with a bunch of small change and airily waved him on his way. Stayne saw him transfer his gloves and stick to the other hand and, as though he had been keeping an appointment dead on time, calmly pick up a position by her side, and walk coolly off down the street with her.

Stayne, without troubling to find a reflection at which to address his remarks, decanted a further load of vitriol over himself.

XV

The man who owned the house at the back of 8B, Curzon Square was a dry goods exporter, which is sufficiently vague to mean anything. He was only very occasionally in residence there, his purchasing of dry goods apparently entailing a good deal of travelling about the country.

He was exactly Stayne's height—exactly, to a millionth of an inch. His hair was exactly the colour of Stayne's hair—exactly, to the millionth of a shade. Only in those two features, however, did they resemble each other. Apart from the fact that they were one and the same man, their dissimilarities were wholly remarkable.

The dry goods exporter had a decided inclination to an ageing spread of adiposity under the waistcoat, in startling contrast to Stayne's own athletic lines. Swathes of *crêpe de Chine* deftly wound into a bulbous curve accounted for most of it a natural stooping of the shoulders and a consequent relaxing of the muscles of the diaphragm served for the rest. The merchant was at least fifty, and his deportment was that of a man of at least sixty. His gait was heavy and slow, and the springs of youth had long since snapped in his insteps. His voice, too, was querulous, and he rarely entered or left his house except by taxi. Grease-paint and pigment, artfully applied, had improved the facial appearance till it suggested the bloat of a life lived over well. All that, and the neat brass plate outside the front door, announced to the world that the dry goods exporter was S. G. Daleson.

Not even Belham, the silver-tongued and impeccable Belham, had ever seen his employer in that disguise, for Stayne never emerged on the upper floors wearing it. It was too perfect, and the two identities were so exclusively necessary to his continued ownership of that secret passage into his house, to risk it being suspected even by Belham.

Stayne's dressing cabinet for his disguises was down in the lower cellar. Down there he changed before going out and again before coming in. And it was by this devious route that S. G. Daleson, Esq., finally emerged on the night.

Darkness had fallen an hour before he wheezily rang for a taxi. He drove to Piccadilly. From there he changed taxis and went on to the far end of the Strand, where he changed again before directing the driver to the Bayswater boarding-house address.

He knocked and asthmatically inquired if a Mr. Harris had arrived yet.

"Yes, sir," he was informed. "He arrived today."

"Indeed?" Stayne affected a semi-senile surprise. "He wrote me last week saying he would be here two days ago. Not that it matters, my dear lady," he rambled on, "but it would make business so much less complicated if the younger generation would only evince a regard for correct statement—so much less complicated, my dear lady, so much less complicated. Still, don't let it worry you—just send and ask if it would be convenient for me to see him."

The landlady, with a patience born of a generation of serving all types and conditions and ages of the human tribe, ushered him into a neatly furnished little reception-room. "Tell him", said the maudlin voice in her ear, "that I would prefer to see him in his own rooms, and that I hope he has a fire going. I can't stand these chilly, draughty waiting-rooms. Tell him, my dear woman, will you?"

The landlady withdrew, and returned in a minute or two to say that Mr. Harris was at liberty and would he please follow her upstairs. He did. And all the way he kept up his high-pitched, querulous complaints about the ways and methods of the modem generation, of life in general, and of boarding-houses in particular.

Varris heard him from halfway up the corridor, and he looked across in a puzzled way as the door opened.

"Ah, there you are," wailed the staccato rotundity. "Do you know, I've been four days trying to get hold of you, young man, and that you broke your last appointment with me without the slightest hint or warning? When you wrote me from Manchester you said you'd be here two days ago. Since when—nothing but a profound silence. And while you dally, big business is slipping through your fingers. It is not equitable treatment, young sir, it is not equitable treatment."

Varris was on his guard from the moment the old fool entered, like an animal cornered, with the pack at his heels. He pulled his fascinated eyes off Stayne and turned to the landlady.

"Thank you, madam, that will be all," he said. And the fat old gentleman stood polishing his heavy pebbled glasses as the door closed.

There was a tense silence during which Varris stared at Stayne, visions of all sorts of unimaginable catastrophes whirling round in his brain.

"Who the devil are you? "he asked at last.

"Phew!—Thank the Lord that's over," said Stayne with a long breath of relief. "I thought you were going to give the show away as I came in."

Varris literally gaped at him with his mouth open in sheer amazement. He passed a hand nervously across his forehead and sat down limply in a chair.

"I still don't believe it," he said thickly. "You're—you're trying to trick me."

"And if I was a detective, you'd have stood a fine chance, wouldn't you, making a damfool remark like that?" Stayne grunted. "I've just set a precedent here, that's all! I've impressed the landlady with the fact that you were in Manchester four days ago. Next time I come I shall be in a different rig, and, I hope, in a different voice. And I'll do the same trick again. She must never suspect, never even get the start of a suspicion. Well, I don't think she will now. That's all. I'm Stayne all right. Take another look at me—perhaps you'll see."

Varris started and stared again. Doubt and conviction were warring within him.

"Well, I'll be damned!" he exclaimed.

"Still can't see it?"

Varris shook his head. "I'm blest if I can. And I'm blest if anyone else could either," he said.

"It's a hundred to a hayseed that Hawker would have done—if he had seen me in your company. I was trying out your powers of observation, Varris. You'll need them pretty well sharpened on this racket. I'm apt to turn up in any old guise, and if you don't get me the first time you'll be spilling the beans with a vengeance. Now, look again. You should have had me fairly well fixed in your memory after this morning. It isn't every man who suddenly steps in and recovers an unknown prisoner from jail."

"Yes—I see it now," said Varris slowly. "You're wearing the same tie."

"And more than that," replied Stayne. "Every bit of colour on me is the same as I wore this morning. This silk handkerchief. This shirt and collar. The socks, too. Also this blue stone ring. It's an uncommon piece of jewellery. One would have thought you'd have noticed that without much difficulty."

Varris fingered his chin ruefully.

"All right," he said. "You're Stayne. But there's only one way in which I could ever recognise you. And I think I could always do it now—no matter how you tried to disguise yourself."

"Oh, yes." Stayne's ears pricked up.

"By your thoroughness. Not even you can disguise that."

Stayne was thoughtful. "'M, well," he said hopefully. "Perhaps even old Hawker himself hasn't thought of that yet. Seen the papers, I suppose?"

"Yes."

"Means you've got to lie pretty low. I didn't think they'd give the Press so much news. Your picture is in all the latest editions. Everybody knows it on sight now."

"Shall I grow a moustache?"

"Not on your life. These people in the boarding-house would be the first to notice the change. No—they might start thinking. It wouldn't be wise. You'll be all right here for a bit. I want you to talk to me tonight. There are certain details I want before I can tackle the Paris end. The fox is air on the jump. I see in tonight's paper that Lady Demorval has left unexpectedly for Mentone again."

"She was to have been here all the summer," said Varris quickly.

"Well, she's packed up and gone back. That shows it's time we tackled that end of it before trouble breaks."

"Well, I don't know why she's gone back," said Varris listlessly.

"I think you do. Now, to begin with, I want to be sure of certain things in connection with you. Don't think I'm doubting your honesty, Varris—you're too much of a natural born fool to be anything more than completely trustworthy. But there is one thing I want to clear up in my own mind. Now why did you take those necklaces from Lady Demorval's bag?"

Varris stirred uneasily in his chair. "I've told the judge all about that," he said.

"I know you have! I've read every report of the trial, including the shorthand notes. And I still don't believe your reason."

"I—I was all upset and bothered. I was—so—surprised at seeing them there that I hardly knew what I did. I just did the first fool thing that came into my head."

"You went out with them in your pocket?"

"Yes—I—I wanted to get them round to the assessors."

"At seven in the evening?"

Varris flushed. It was obvious that he was as uncomfortable as a man sitting on an ant-hill. And he was stalling all over the place.

"I—I didn't stop to think about the time," he muttered. "Put yourself in my shoes and see how you would have acted. But then you are about the one man in the world who would have sat down quietly and thought things out. Unluckily for me, I'm not mentally constituted that way. I just breezed off. I wasn't trying to steal the rotten things."

"I know that. Otherwise you wouldn't have been raising hell with a mallet, trying to open the locks of those trunks. Why on earth didn't you send for a locksmith—"

"Lady Demorval wanted an envelope of private papers. The last post was going out and time was urgent."

"Then you *did* realise that it was seven o'clock."

Varris licked his lips and looked away. "Oh, I don't know," he said. "I don't know what I knew—or thought—or did."

XVI

"I suppose all you knew was that those diamonds shouldn't have been in London?" Stayne asked sarcastically.

"I *know* they shouldn't," Varris replied. "I was the man who made all the arrangements for bringing them to London. I packed every piece of jewellery separately in the boxes and saw them officially sealed by the insurance agents. They went straight into the safe. I alone held the key."

"What you are trying to tell me, then, is that the diamonds you were found running away with were fakes, and that sooner or later an insurance swindle was to be worked on the ones stolen?"

Varris looked steadily at Stayne for a moment, and then slowly shook his head.

"No," he said dully. "You've got it all wrong. So did we—at least, I mean so did Lady Demorval. She was pulling the swindle at Mentone. She was up to her ears in debt. Perrigo and Canning had got her by the throat on the other matter. She planned the burglary to be done by some of Perrigo's paid thugs. The trick failed because, unfortunately for her, *real* thieves broke in a few hours before the fake burglars. Perrigo had schemed to get possession of the Demorval jewels and leave Lady Demorval with the insurance award."

"Well?"

"The stones I found were the real ones. She had double-crossed Perrigo. She had left him with the fakes. And I'll swear

I locked the real ones in the safe that night. Perrigo went mad. That's why she's gone back to France. Perrigo must have sent her the call. Maybe he's in London himself. I don't know. All I know is that nothing will stop Perrigo now. He will pull the whole bag of tricks."

Stayne was seriously thoughtful. That was an aspect of the affair that had never occurred to him. He had sensed the possibility of the insurance swindle and was quite prepared to have discovered that the ropes stolen from the London hotel were imitations. But the double shift added a new piquancy to a dish that was already over-seasoned.

"Did Lady Demorval invite you into the secret of the faked burglary?" Stayne asked.

"No. But I knew it was coming off. Lady Demorval was so insistent on the jewels going into her bedroom safe. That safe was about as secure as a petty cash box. It was only meant as an emergency measure anyway. Usually it contained nothing but furs—and not very expensive ones at that. The real safe was down in the library, let into the wall."

"Was that a really strong one?"

"One of the best on the market. Blowpipes wouldn't have cut through it. And there was an electrical equipment on it, too, that would have electrocuted anyone but a person holding the right key. Nothing short of dynamite would have opened that one. But, in spite of my advice and protests, she insisted on them going into the one upstairs."

"Did she offer any reason?"

Varris sniffed his indifference.

"Said she wanted them near her on the last night she was in the villa," he said.

"Any other reason why you suspected her?"

"Yes, she was always taking out the insurance documents and re-reading the terms. She asked me for the plain English definitions of many of the more complicated legal phrases.

Then the fact that she didn't travel with the jewels herself, though I begged to be allowed to bring them along with us. They were deliberately left there to be stolen."

"And Perrigo?"

"I'd seen him nosing about the villa several times. He and his friends used to stroll in and pretend to chat to Lady Demorval about this and that—and all the time they were taking measurements of the rooms and the window—and things. And then again she had never let me hold the key of the jewels before. On that occasion she was insistent, as she said she feared she might lose it in travelling." He sniffed again and smiled faintly—"as though she hadn't travelled that key herself hundreds of times before."

"Lady Demorval was gambling?"

"Very heavily indeed."

"At the Casino in the Rue Pigalle?"

"Call it a casino if you will. I suppose it is really—there's every murderous gambling game under the sun going on there. They call it the Club Tabarin."

"Who owns the place?"

"Perrigo and Canning."

"Do they indeed?"

"Yes. It's a sort of headquarters—the centre of all their operations in Paris."

"Were you responsible for the murder of the man found dead there on the night you got Lady Demorval out of the place?"

A reminiscent smile flickered for a brief moment over the drawn face.

"You mean the man whose head was bashed in with the fizz bottle? No. I had no hand in that. It was a case of the biter bit. I saw what was coming. Four of the blighters were all edging towards me. They were doing their best to look nonchalant—but I saw the hands go out and grip on the necks of the champagne bottles. Another son of a gun was strolling over towards the electric light switches. I got over quietly to one of the refreshment buffets and pretended I knew nothing of what was in the air. They were mad at me—and I knew it."

"Why was this?"

"I'd been into Perrigo's raising hell with the bunch for enticing Lady Demorval in there. They had stripped her of every penny she possessed—and of Lord Demorval's money too. That's why he was supposed to have committed suicide. You can't stay on in the Corps Diplomatique unless you've a bank balance the size of a multiplication table. I kicked up the devil of a shindy. They flung me out on my neck and told me to go to blazes. I went to the police. The next thing they knew I was at the private telephone telling the *Sûreté* enough to bring the gendarmery round. That caused it. Some of the gentlemanly-dressed bandits inside were detailed off to scalp me and get the debris cleared away before the raiders arrived."

"But the raiders were too quick for them?"

"They were round almost immediately. They came in from a local station and I heard them thundering at the door just as I got to the refreshment buffet. The lights went out and I ducked. I was out and away from them as they came at me. I s'pose they all swung at the spot where my head had been the second before the lights went out. Something made a most horrible crunching sound behind me and I knew they had hit one of their own number on the head. The women had all gone into hysterics the moment the police began pounding the door down. They were shrieking blue murder and I don't suppose they heard me at the window. Neither did they hear the groaning of the man they had dropped. But in the darkness they finished him off. Ugh! Those champagne bottles were full too. They must have given him a terrible beating up, because next morning he was unrecognisable. They honestly thought they had got me. Their mistake was only discovered when the absence of one of their own number was discovered—and when news got through to Perrigo that I was travelling with Lady Demorval to London."

"That is the truth?"

Varris relapsed again into sheer indifference.

"Take it or leave it," he said. "I don't care a hoot either way. You just told me I was too big a fool to do anything else than tell the truth."

"Then why did you remain silent in the dock?"

Varris began to colour again.

"There was no need to rake up old scores," he said defensively. "The French police had hushed up the murder, and I didn't see why I should blurt it all out."

"Not at the expense of five years' penal servitude?"

"That wouldn't have helped me. I got five years for pinching diamonds; not for being implicated in the raid on the Club Tabarin."

Stayne leaned towards him, and Varris noted, with a bit of a shock, that he was commanding, dominant even in that absurd make-up.

"You kept your mouth shut in there for a great deal bigger reason than a raid on a gambling hell, or a diamond robbery—or even than the shielding of Lady Demorval, didn't you?"

Varris nodded with a single stiff jerk of the head.

"What was it? I want to know, Varris, and I want to know right now. Otherwise you can look out for yourself now that you're out of jail—and I warn you that a letter concerning the whole of the case goes straight to the authorities concerned; not here—but in France. Now then."

Varris had blanched. And the last threat drove him over his breaking point.

He fidgeted nervously in his chair and his fingertips drummed an unconscious tattoo on the edge of the table.

"It's—it's not a story I can tell in a single sentence," he said with hesitation, as though hunting about for the words he wanted.

"Well—tell it in your own way. I won't hurry you."

Varris fixed his eyes on the table-runner and his fingers picked uncertainly at the braiding.

"Mr. Stayne," he said, "there is the biggest bank swindle blossoming to life over in Europe that you've ever heard of in your life. It's not just a matter between England and France—but all Europe is involved. Operating centres have been established in Berlin, Madrid, Rome, Paris, Lisbon, Vienna, Amsterdam and Oslo. That is, you'll realise, every country whose currency has the slightest claim to stability. The whole thing is as intricate and involved as a crossword puzzle in Latin, and I can only give you the baldest idea of its scope and organisation.

"It's a matter of securities for loans now being raised by the various banks concerned. The totals run into incredible figures: millions and millions. Perrigo and Canning are raising the loans—ostensibly for huge commercial exploitation schemes in the still only half-civilised States of South America. But the reason for the loans does not trouble the banks an iota, and the reason is that the securities which Perrigo and Canning are putting up are as gilt-edge as any securities could well be. For every pound raised they are depositing securities worth thirty shillings—it's one of the finest deals a big bank could wish. That is—if the securities were genuine. But they're not. They're fakes from beginning to end. They are some of the most beautiful forgeries I've ever seen. The banks haven't questioned them. And the simple reason is that most of it has been worked through Lady Demorval. You see what it means? Lord and Lady Demorval have the privilege of ambassadorial immunity. They are beyond arrest, and therefore, as our ambassadors are and have been all over the world, above suspicion. The Perrigo crowd, having got Lady Demorval into their clutches, have built up the whole organisation round her.

"It began in a small way at first: well, smallish, considering the totals it has now attained. A hundred thousand, or something like that, was the original idea of the haul. Then the thing grew as the possibilities began to dawn on them. Fresh countries were involved, new confederates drawn in, till finally it was so big that it almost got out of hand.

"Railway stocks, mining shares, controlling interests in all the biggest motor industries in England and America, vast holdings in some of the finest and most prosperous commercial concerns in the Empire—those are the stock with which Perrigo and Canning have stuffed the Continental banks. Stuffed 'em tight. And every single one of them is forged. Forged in England and smuggled over to Paris and then distributed with the guarantee of our Embassy on them to every capital in Europe.

"Perrigo and Canning have taken out their loans in the currency of each country concerned, banknotes and bearer bonds, things that can be cashed in any bank in the world. They are aiming to make their getaway soon and then they will vanish, leaving the whole affair to drift gradually to light.

"By that time the whole crowd of conspirators will have got clear away to one of the South American States where all the hunted criminals go; one of the States that allow no extradition warrants to disturb the equanimity of its inhabitants. It will take months before the banks even begin to be suspicious. Interest on the loans will not be due for a year at least. Meanwhile, the forged securities are locked away in the vaults, apparently as genuine as actual cash. All Europe is salted with millions of them. And up till now the Perrigo crowd are as safe as houses.

"There is just a chance to pull things together before the crash comes. As yet all their notes and money are still in Paris. Where, I don't know. For all I know they may have begun to send it over the Atlantic already. But when I was last in Paris they had not then made a move. If those two devils can be collared before they close down—if the money can be rescued and returned to the banks before they get away with it, there is just the chance that the crash can be averted. But from what you've told me tonight it looks as though they're already at work."

"It does!" cut in Stayne harshly. "And from what I can see of it, it's all your own lunatic fault! You'll have a lot to answer for, Varris, before this affair is cleared up."

XVII

Varris looked at Stayne then with just a glint in his eyes.

"That tone doesn't scare me, Mr. Stayne," he said bitterly. "You're only seeing half the case—the half you can see with your own eyes. I'm looking at the rest of it too—and I've nothing to reproach myself with. I've done my best from first to last. In some things I may have acted foolishly. I certainly have never acted criminally, or even played the fool willingly. I couldn't help myself. I was caught up in the whole web of it myself. Being private secretary to his lordship almost made me part of the thing."

"But you could have acted before," protested Stayne.

"Could I? Tell me how! With all that kettle coming to the boil. The moment I opened my mouth to the authorities the whole thing would have been exposed. The crash would have come inside an hour. I would have been the cause of the very thing I was trying to prevent.

"Besides—put yourself in my shoes. To me it was all unbelievable, incredible. At first everything seemed straight and above board. Then; even when I did begin to suspect, I couldn't believe it. The magnitude, the daring, the reckless daredevilry of it was beyond credence. And by the time I realised the thing really was crooked it was too big for me. It had already passed into the realms of the tremendous menace it now is. Think of it, Mr. Stayne. Instead of vilifying me, get your brain to bear on it and work out what it all means, reason out the possibilities.

"It will be one of the most terrible scandals that has ever confronted the country. As it has all happened through the co-operation of one of the ambassadorial staff—or the wife of one, which is tantamount—we can't prevent it becoming a national affair. It could no longer be regarded as a private thing—something for the French police to settle and squash. There would be the Government stamp all over it. British securities in Europe would topple with a crash, and British currency values would fall through the floors. With the touchy state of things in France, not to mention some other countries, there is not the slightest doubt that we should be in the midst of another war before we could look round.

"Perrigo and Canning are English, the Demorvals are English, the forgeries are English, and the whole conception of the idea and the lesser members of its executive are all English. The fact that Lord Demorval committed suicide would only inflame the Continentals the more. They would know from that that he knew all about it—and kept his mouth shut. That's not true, but it's obvious to see that that's what they would think.

"You see, Mr. Stayne, every country of any stability at all in Europe would be holding the baby, as the saying goes, to the tune of millions—millions; with not a bob of real money to cover it. If we wanted to keep out of war—and if we wanted to save our honour at all—England would have to refund every penny of it to subsidise some of the biggest criminals our underworld has ever turned out. With the value of the pound sterling gone in Europe all our huge commercial enterprises over there would be bankrupt overnight. The whole thing is so tremendous and so unparalleled that my head swims when I try to think of it—"

"You damned fool—is that any reason why you couldn't have opened your idiotic head about it weeks ago—before the thing reached these enormous proportions?"

* * *

Stayne was boiling over. In that three minutes Varris had shown him the whole magnitude of the plot that was slowly coming to the explosion point over there in the Bourses of Europe. He realised, all in a lightning flash, a great deal more than Varris had suspected, the workings and machinations of a foreign Power to overthrow Britain's credit abroad.

This was not merely the work of a pair of super-criminals. It went far deeper than that. No gang of criminals on earth could have designed, invented, and put over such a gigantic swindle as that unless someone far greater than an Ambassador's wife franked the guarantees. The whole weight, authority, and credit of a foreign Power stood behind it. Criminals alone could not have got through immune.

Perrigo and Canning were merely the executive tools. As criminals there was no doubt they were of an extremely high order; brilliant, subtle, daring, and with all the ice-cold courage of their own knowledge. And it was evident that they would get away with the loot. Such pickings as were to be made would go into their pockets, and theirs alone. That would be their reward—and a colossal one—for the far greater prize of having wrecked British credit in the great markets of the Continent.

And it could all have been prevented by anyone with the sense of a hen. Stayne could see how the man felt about it and could visualise the ease with which the thing had progressed beyond his imagination. But even so, no one but a coward, or one who had lived for weeks in a cold panic, would have acted as Varris had done. If he was scared of going to the police—and Stayne admitted out of hand that Varris was right there, for there were graver risks attending such a course—if he had only gone to his own bank manager and communicated his knowledge, the manager would have had such inquiries set afoot as would have scotched the whole business, and without publicity.

As it was, the crash was imminent. It might come that night—or the next morning. And the crash was inevitable the moment the Perrigo gang got away with the money. While the money still remained in Paris there was a hope. All that would be necessary would be to return the cash, to each bank its own share, and to leave the financiers behind Perrigo and Canning with nothing but an enormous expense sheet to show for their labours, and no loot to meet it with.

Stayne had gone white beneath the pigment and his cold eyes were glittering ominously. There was a frosty atmosphere about his whole attitude. Varris sat back, bolt upright in his chair, and ran his fingers nervously through his hair.

"Why fly off at me?" he questioned resentfully. "I've told you all I know, haven't I?"

"No, you haven't—not by a mile!" retorted Stayne. "Maybe you think Perrigo and Canning are the real villains—maybe you know a lot more yet than you've told me. But to anyone with half a grain of sense it's obvious that Perrigo and Canning are not working alone, isn't it?"

"Of course it is. I've already said so. They've got their confederates firmly established all over—"

"Confederates—pish! I'm talking about men bigger than Perrigo and Canning ever knew how to be. Men big enough to put up the preliminary capital required. Men who could organise such a vast scheme and bring it through the various exchanges and banking federations immune. International crooks can't bring off such a scoop as that—a scoop that must have taken months to mature. There are bigger fish behind Perrigo and Canning. Men who have the power to rope in their own Government's printing works. Nothing but a combine with the whole printing resources of a Government behind it could have run off enough of those false share certificates, scrip, etc., to have done what that crowd has done."

"Well? What has that got to do with me?" demanded Varris petulantly. "I didn't engineer the wretched thing, did I? If I did I wouldn't be here being snapped at by you. I'd be hitting the outward bound with several millions stuffed in my suitcases."

Stayne was wriggling his fingers in an attempt to hold his patience.

"If that was all there was behind it," he said, "you'd have opened up about it weeks ago. Now—what was the big motive that bound you to silence? You'll tell me or I'll have half Scotland Yard round here within ten minutes."

Varris chewed at his underlip. "I think you might let me off that one," he said at last. "I think I've told you enough to assure you of my honesty in this affair. Why ask me to break faith on a matter that is, after all, only a secondary consideration?"

"There is no secondary consideration in a danger of this description," Stayne rapped back. "This is an occasion when the part is as great as the whole."

"Well—anyhow, I've told you enough for you to get to work on. You can find out the rest for yourself as you investigate."

"Varris"—Stayne's tone was bitingly smooth, but there were blue, hot daggers darting about among the syllables—"in comparison with the enemy I'm only half armed—but you can take it from me I'm going to carry every weapon I can possibly get my hands on. And you've got one that I want more than anything on earth just now. Now—out with it."

* * *

There was a silence between them that slowly ticked on into a whole minute, a minute of palpitating battle, challenge on the one side, defiance on the other. The minute lengthened into two, and still Varris stared Stayne doggedly between the eyes.

"Bring in your Scotland Yard," he said at last, almost inaudibly.

Stayne scarcely heard him. His brain was working at lightning speed, and on a new track. When he spoke his eyes were looking on beyond Varris as though his words were the vocalisation of thoughts far ahead, thoughts on which every atom of his concentration was centred.

"To have brought this deal through successfully," he said, "they must have been in possession of at least one original copy of all the shares they duplicated. That stands to reason, doesn't it?"

"Y-yes," said Varris.

"I mean—they could not possibly have produced those marvellous forgeries, so perfect in every line and letter that they deceived the heads of big Continental banks, without having at least one genuine original to work on."

"I suppose—yes, they must have."

"Some of the designs of those share scrips are most elaborate, are they not?"

"I—I—don't know."

"Pardon me—you do. You could not have been mixed up in this business so long, or have become possessed of the amount of knowledge you betray, without actually having seen a great many of the actual documents concerned. I think you'll agree that some of the documents to be forged were of exceptionally intricate design?"

"Yes—some of the engraved backgrounds were a bit ornamental."

"And they would not easily be forged?"

Varris ran a finger round the inside of his collar. It was sticky and little pin-beads of perspiration began to damp his forehead again.

"Some of them would be a bit—be very difficult to copy," he said.

"Knowing as we do that the photographic process is now hopelessly out of date—the damning word 'counterfeit' comes out inerasibly on the sensitised negative if anyone is fool enough to try forgery with a camera—only an artist of first-class merit—extraordinary merit—could have engraved the plates from the originals. Isn't that so?"

"It—it seems so to me." Varris seemed to be talking as though his mouth and throat were choked with red-hot dust. Stayne paused for a moment in his smooth flow.

"Who was that perfect artist? "he suddenly demanded.

Varris swallowed, and a lump seemed to stick in his gullet.

"Why ask me?" he whispered. And Stayne saw that his fingers had recommenced their nervous plucking at the braiding of the table-runner.

"I *am* asking you!"

"Well, I don't know."

"Varris, you're a liar. An absolute liar!"

"I tell you I don't know," repeated Varris hopelessly.

"And I tell you that no man ever yet told me a lie that I couldn't recognise as soon as I looked at his eyes."

Varris, hardly knowing what he was doing, pulled his eyes off Stayne as suddenly as though they had been snapped away on elastic bands.

Stayne whirled on him. "That action alone betrays you, you poor fool," he shot at him. "Varris, you're as poor an actor as you are a liar. Over and above which, you're the most obstinate maniac I've ever encountered."

Suddenly his eyes narrowed and he changed his tone completely. Reaching over the table he grasped Varris by the wrist and slowly pulled him towards him.

"Tell me," he said, looking him straight in the face. "Are you in love?"

Varris, unexpectedly released from a brainstorm of doubt and fear, opened his eyes wide with astonishment.

"What—me?" he asked. "Me in love? What the devil do you ask me that for?"

"Never mind why I'm asking. Just take it for granted that I am. Are you?"

"Good Lord, no! What a silly ass thing to say."

"Are you engaged?"

"Of course I'm not."

"Have you ever been in love in your life?"

"Not to my knowledge. A spot or two of calf-love perhaps when I was a kid, but I wouldn't rely on it if I were you."

"Then it's someone connected with your sister," said Stayne deliberately.

XVIII

Varris flared up again. "You leave Marienne out of this," he stormed. "Leave her out of it—or *I'll go* round to Scotland Yard—and damn quick." His face was red and his knuckle-tips, clenched on the table, were fixed till they were all white and shiny.

Stayne relaxed, and his head was nodding in tiny little half-inch jerks of satisfaction.

"So—so!" he muttered. "Touched the sore spot, eh? Well, well. That's nice. That brings us so much nearer the bone. Tell me, Varris, you're very fond of your sister, aren't you?"

"I'll—I'll brain the man who says a word against her." Varris was half rearing up on his feet.

"That's as it should be." The bulbous figure opposite was all acquiescence. "Please don't get excited on my account. I myself think she is an extremely nice girl. We won't get at loggerheads over that angle of it. On the contrary, I admire your taste. Believe me, I think Marienne is one of the sweetest girls I have ever met."

"Well, then, leave her out of it," demanded the secretary hotly.

"I have every hope that we shall be able to. Although, as I'm sure you will admit, she is already very far in it. But I've noticed, Varris, that when brother and sister develop family affection to the degree that you two undoubtedly have, it becomes a bond that is as strong as, and frequently lasts longer than, the more common love of husband and wife. I'm simply taking the points as they come now. Marienne was the first to approach me on this affair. She was terribly agitated—as you were. She, too, kept stalling when it came to particular points in the narrative. It was obvious to anyone who has had any experience at all of human nature that she was shielding someone.

"Not unnaturally I presumed it was you. I judged that either you *had* intended taking the Demorval diamonds or that you were directly responsible for pulping the skull of the man found murdered in the Club Tabarin.

"Now I find you doing exactly the same thing. Every time I've asked you a direct question that leads to a certain line of investigation you hedge, you vacillate, you back and fill—and finally you tell deliberate lies. Even a fool would realise that there is a reason behind it all. You're both trying to shield someone. As there is no particular entanglement in your own life we must look for the answer in connecting with Marienne."

"Why there?" snapped Varris.

"Because you have already told the truth about everybody else concerned in the case. You've shown up Lord Demorval in a bad light—or, at least, in a poor light. You've painted Lady Demorval in her undoubted colours, although I'll everlastingly hold it to your credit that you made more than one effort for her. You have admitted to being something of a fool yourself in the way you've handled your end of the case.

"It all boils down to the theory that you are shielding someone very dear to you—or, if not that, a very great friend of someone who is dear to you. As we know it is not Marienne herself it must be someone very dear to *her*. It's all very simple, isn't it?

"Now then, Varris, who originally provided the Perrigo gang with the forged plates?"

Varris reached out a shaky hand for another cigarette. He lit it with studious care, though the flame trembled badly.

Stayne regarded him now without malice.

"You'll tell me," he said, "or I'll tackle Marienne herself on it."

"Only a cold-blooded brute like you," said Varris distinctly, "would think of doing that."

"This is a serious business, my dear Varris. And now that I know so much; I don't think she would hesitate to tell. Marienne has, I think, considerably more firmness of character than you."

Varris winced. "The man who forged the share certificates was Arthur Raymond," he said quietly.

"And who is Arthur Raymond?"

"Marienne's fiancé."

Stayne did not move. The ash on the end of his cigarette glowed red in a long intake of smoke. He blew it out in a long pale stream that came slowly through his lips.

"Indeed. How very interesting," he remarked. "I would hardly have thought it." Varris did not notice that the muscles of his face had suddenly gone stiff.

"Probably not. But you can't get away from facts."

"Is—she—is she very much in love with him?" Stayne was not even looking at him. The matter appeared to be too petty for serious attention.

"Madly. Ask yourself, Mr. Stayne. Would a girl of her character risk her own freedom to shield an obvious criminal unless—pah, what's the use of talking to you? You'd never understand if you lived to be a hundreds. London's Perfect Bachelor, aren't you? Half the scheming mothers in Mayfair have traipsed their daughters through Curzon Square, haven't they?"

Stayne indifferently struck a match and flicked it across the room.

"Happen to know where Raymond is now?" he asked.

"Yes, I do," growled Varris. "He's located in a mansion flat on the coolest side of the North Pole. Go on—why not cut the heart out of her? Why not telephone her and chortle out the news that you know who committed the forgeries? There's a phone there. Tell her. Go on. Tell her you'll get him into jail with the same ease that you got me out of it."

Stayne inspected his fingernails. "I was going to phone her—but I don't think I will now. I—er—I rather think I've got all the information I want. Thank you for what you've told me, Varris. It'll help me; help like hell. Let me see now, what was I going to say? Oh, yes. About yourself. You'd better go to the office tomorrow. Yes, you'd better begin at Bishopsgate at, say—er—ten o'clock. That's the usual office hour in that neighbourhood. I'll be there myself to see you started, and to explain the various bits and pieces you can do to give an air of verisimilitude to your presence there. Tembridge and I will be going over to Paris later in the day. Use this place as long as it is safe. I'll arrange about further funds for you at the office. Excuse me a moment, I must phone Tembridge."

He picked up the instrument and put the number through.

"Hallo! Is that Belham? "he called.

"Yes, sir."

"Put me through to Mr. Tembridge, will you, please?"

"I'm very sorry, sir, Mr. Tembridge is out."

"Oh! Did he leave any message?"

"Not with me, sir—there may be one in the usual place."

Stayne was nettled. It was disturbing to have carefully prearranged plants blown up by an unexpected move on his assistant's part. That sort of thing generally spelled trouble. Tembridge, by hook or by crook, would always manage to get word through to his chief before embarking on a move of his own. There was valid reason for his not using the telephone, for Stayne had already hinted that Hawker might have a tapper on the wire—and if that call were traced the Bayswater retreat would be knocked off the earth. Stayne felt more and more convinced that there was something in the wind.

"Have you any idea where he was going?" he inquired.

When Belham's voice came on again it was tinctured with a hint of surprise at the nature of his own information.

"I can't say precisely what his destination was," he replied, "but—ah—he was wearing full evening dress. And he requested me to put all his—ah—nightclub membership cards on his dressing-table."

"Did he?—Damn him!"

"He did, sir."

"Thank you, Belham. How many did he take with him?"

"Four, sir. The Merry Andrew, the Burnt Wings, the Avalon, and the Dead Rat."

"A noble assortment. I'll be home myself as soon as I can get a taxi."

"The police are outside, sir. He partakes of the nature of a gentleman selling hot chestnuts from a barrow. Looks quite odd in Curzon Square, sir."

"I'll come in the other way. Thanks."

Stayne took his adieu of Varris and let himself out of the boarding-house, still protesting in a high wheezy voice against the general inutility of all boarding-houses that were not provided with electric lifts.

Out in the street he heard a newsboy shouting something utterly incoherent from the contents bill of one of the late extra editions of the evening newspapers. He bought one as he hailed a taxi. His heart gave a great bound as he read the flaring placard, "Escaped prisoner recaptured."

The news paragraph was brief but illuminating. "An official message this evening states that Templer Varris, the prisoner who, with the connivance of two men in a blue Silent Six limousine, escaped from Scrubs Prison this morning, was recaptured at an obscure address in Wapping. He was emerging from a tavern when two detectives closed with him. Varris offered but a brief resistance and afterwards said that he was glad to have the matter over. As in the dock, he stubbornly refused to say anything about himself. The reason for his reckless breakout from jail remains a mystery. Chief Inspector Hawker was responsible for the tracing and arrest of the escaped man."

Stayne was actually chortling when he reached the end of the message. Three possibilities presented themselves to him at that moment. Either Hawker had committed a gigantic blunder—a thought which was ruled out almost as soon as it was made—or Hawker was playing a deeper game than ever Stayne imagined him capable—or someone higher up was putting in some fast work.

XIX

By the time he had arrived at the home of Mr. S. G. Daleson, Stayne had thinned the matter down. Hawker could gain nothing by publishing false news to the world. The utmost good he could hope to do would be to still public criticism of the ease with which a prisoner could escape from a prison and get clear away. And from what he knew of Hawker that was very unlikely. That bull-headed, dogged old thinking machine was impervious to public opinion. Public opinion was fickle anyhow; and what the public thought today would not necessarily be that same public's opinion tomorrow. He had seen too many good men go wrong because their nerve shook under pressure of public criticism—men who tried to force the game along too rapidly in order to reinstate themselves as quickly as possible in public esteem.

Hawker was cast in a different mould. He let the storm of public clamour break over him without turning a hair; and certainly without allowing it to deviate his chosen course by a single inch. He knew, like all seasoned warriors, that storms spend themselves out sooner or later, and that the waves return eventually to the sea that gave them birth.

No. It was no move of Hawker's that had occasioned that cheering paragraph in the newspaper. And yet, at the same time, something pretty slick must have been done. Hawker would not authorise such a communication as that to the Press unless he had got his man under lock and key. And he wouldn't be fool enough to put a man under lock and key unless he was convinced he had got the right man.

Someone, some high-souled young adventurer in the service of Intelligence, must have voluntarily gone back to prison in Varris's stead. It was curious, to say the least of it. Varris would not be very difficult to duplicate in a physical sense. He was one of a type of Englishmen of whom there are several in every crowd. Tallish, slim, fairly good-looking—one of the type that comes down from the 'varsities every year in dozens. Properly primed with knowledge of his part by the higher units of the Secret Service, he could pass muster for a little while anyhow. And, having got their man, with his confession, and such other proofs as he himself could furnish with a bit of well-simulated acting, it would not be a very difficult job to carry through.

There remained the problem of the fingerprints. It was inconceivable that the prison authorities had not yet taken Varris's prints. That would be one of the very first ordeals he would have to undergo as soon as his decision not to appeal was filed. With that action he passed into the ranks of convicted criminals, and his fingerprints would be added to the records with all dispatch.

If the authorities did not again take the fingerprints and compare them, all would be well. But to Stayne it seemed that there would be very little possibility of that. As soon as the newly recaptured man's prints were recorded there would be a holy flare-up in Scrubs Prison. The cat would be out of the bag with a vengeance.

So that, viewed from all points, it appeared that, whoever was responsible for Varris's rearrest, it was only intended as a temporary move; one to covet something else that would require to be done during the time that police suspicion and watchfulness for Varris himself was lulled to rest by his recapture. And Stayne wanted to know, urgently wanted to know, what was at the back of the brain of the Man Higher Up.

He entered his house and hurriedly shed the guise of S. G. Daleson. In a few minutes he was up in the private cabinet and talking to Number One.

"Hallo, Chief—fast work, I must say," he warmly commented. "But how long will it last?"

"Long enough for you to get Varris through the Customs at Dover, we think."

"You do, eh? What makes you think the necessity will arise?"

"Varris would be extremely helpful to you over there, surely?"

"Well, he would and he wouldn't. He's as loyal as a dog. But he hasn't the happy knack of quick thought. You have to hit him on the head with it before he notices it."

"Still, it would save you time."

"Maybe—but I think it would be risky. He isn't one of us, Chief, and I wouldn't rely on his nous in an emergency. If Perrigo and Canning, or any of that bunch, spotted him over there, I should be in a lively hole. And, candidly, I don't think he has the natural speed to avoid detection."

"You're tired tonight, Colonel?"

Stayne detected a faintly bantering note in the softly modulated voice at the other end. His mind performed a lightning back somersault and landed him back at the beginning of the job. It raced over the affair point by point and phase by phase. He arrived right along the line of reasoning, back to where he stood—and still failed to get the Chief's hint.

"Feel a bit muggy tonight," he apologised. "Perhaps I'll—"

"Had some bad news?"

"No—oh, no. Just a bit depressing and—and all that. I—oh, by gosh! I've got you, sir. That's to cover the Paris end, isn't it?"

"That's as we thought. Time is pretty short and the Perrigo crowd might take the bit between their teeth. That would be pretty fatal. They would cut and clear—and the fat *would* be in the fire. As it is the news is bound to get to Paris. In all probability they already know that Varris has been recaptured.

That will put their minds at rest, and if only the man in Scrubs can keep his head and not arouse suspicion you may be able to get away with it before the sky bursts."

"Thank you, Chief. I'm all right at this end. I'll be crossing over tomorrow night. Have you heard from Twenty-two?"

"No. Had no news here."

"H'm. Well, you might do a little thing for me, will you, please? Get the scouts on him. He left here some little time ago all dolled up in glad rags, and taking with him four nightclub cards. Those cards are the Merry Andrew, the Burnt Wings, the Avalon, and the Dead Rat. He's in one of those clubs, and I want to know which."

"I'll do it now, Colonel. Hold the line, will you? It's only a phone job."

In less than five minutes Number One was back on the other end of the line.

"That you, Colonel? "he asked. "Number Twenty-two is in the Avalon—arrived less than ten minutes ago from the Ritz Park. He has a lady with him."

"I rather guessed as much."

"The lady is Marienne V."

"And I guessed that much too. All right, sir. I'll go round. I think there's something pretty big smouldering up round there. Good night."

"And good luck," came softly over the wire.

Stayne hurriedly changed into evening dress and let himself out.

As he walked down towards the taxi rank an itinerant vendor of hot roast chestnuts on the opposite side of the square crawled laboriously to life and began plodding along in his wake.

Stayne waited for him at the corner, fumbled for some coppers, bought a bag, and said: "Shouldn't worry about following me, old son. It's a coldish night and you'd have a miserable time if I felt like playing hide and seek tonight.

I don't. But here's my address for the next hour or two. 'The Avalon Dance and Supper Club.' It's a nightclub—one of the posh ones—on Dean Street. Tembridge is there too. I'm going to meet him. Good night. Here, take these fool nuts back; I don't want them."

He walked off towards the rank, leaving the plain-clothes man, hot under the collar, staring after him.

Stayne arrived at the club, paused for a while as though hunting for change, and with a smile saw another cab drive up on the other side of the road and wait there stationary. The Mystery-Maker walked over, stuck his head in at the window, and said: "Suspicious lot of devils tonight, aren't you? Now watch me go right in. You'll be all right there, officer—this is the only entrance."

He swung over and entered the club, nettled. It was so dam silly to keep shadowing a man so obviously. But Stayne guessed he was one of the underlings who had been given a job to do and was determined to see it through, though Stayne tried a thousand ruses to throw him off the scent.

He went in through the wide swing doors and on into the cocktail lounge. Late suppers were being served on that floor—a big low room, rather loudly appointed, seen dimly through more glass doors at the far end. From downstairs came the faint sounds of a jazz orchestra playing the plug number from the latest musical comedy hit.

He ordered a drink and glanced swiftly through into the long supper-room. So far as he could see there was nobody in there he knew, certainly neither Tembridge nor Marienne. Nightclub habitués are apt to change clubs three or four times in a night, but he was loath to think they had departeds already.

"They're probably downstairs, dancing," he mused. "In that case Marienne is going to be perfectly sweet and come over to my table—and she will ask me to dance. And if she does that I shall get up and yelp. I know I shall. It *would* be just my wretched luck to have to run across her tonight after—after that confounded rogue Raymond. What in the name of all that's good and beautiful does a charming creature like Marienne want to get tangled up with a criminal for? Blest if I know. Women beat me—beat me flat. John, my son, you've done quite right to stay up on your little bachelor shelf."

He drank his whisky-and-soda and glanced round as a newcomer entered and passed through to the supper-room. The stranger nodded affably as he went through and muttered a polite "Nice evening." Stayne nodded back and felt his instincts rearing up and warning him against the man. He frowned a little, but knew that he had subconsciously taken an instinctive dislike to him. For the life of him he couldn't tell why, but over a long course of years he had come to have a ferocious faith in the rectitude of his instincts.

The man seemed all right. He was well groomed, and even a perfectly dressed man might have been excused wondering who his tailor was. For if Stayne himself was perfectly dressed, the stranger's clothes were super-perfect There was not a line wrong with them; he seemed to have slipped into them without disturbing a single button. And there was nothing wrong with his quiet "Nice evening." That was nightclub etiquette. All were members, and it was understood that all members knew each other. Formal introductions were just plain bosh, and for the sake of the general gaiety of the evening the usual assumption was that everybody should be as friendly as they felt inclined to each other.

And yet he would willingly have laid a thousand to one that there was something wrong about him. Nothing flashy—but just wrong—psychologically wrong. It stood out around him like an aura.

XX

Through the glass Stayne could see the stranger sitting down, carefully ordering his meal from the ornate menu.

The waiter hovered over him very attentively and seemed to know him well. At any rate there was a pleasing familiarity between them. Stayne could see the waiter dissuading the guest from ordering a certain item, recommending another as being especially good that night.

Stayne argued that if the waiter knew him, that veritable encyclopaedia of knowledge of human faces, the commissionaire, would undoubtely know him.

He finished off his whisky and went back to the head of the stairs leading down to the dance floor. The commissionaire was there, getting a telephone number for a member. Stayne approached him and said: "Excuse me a moment, sergeant—who was the member who just came in—the one who went through to the supper-room. It's very stupid of me; I'm always forgetting faces. And it's so awkward when you want to speak to a member and you can't recall his name."

"Who—that one there, sir, the gentleman sitting down ordering? He's a real stranger here, sir; no wonder you didn't know him. Hasn't been here for months. His name's Perrigo, sir. Gabriel Perrigo."

"Who? Perrigo? Never heard of him." Stayne grunted. "Must have made a mistake. Still, thank you, sergeant."

He moved away, hectically conscious of the knowledge that if he stayed there much longer he would have betrayed himself. The nape of his neck was crawling and a little red-hot elevator was whizzing up and down his spine.

So that was Perrigo, was it? Now what on earth did his presence there portend? Had he heard the news of Varris's escape from jail earlier in the morning and rushed over from Paris to investigate? Had he suddenly taken a dose of cold feet and decided to get as near as possible to the source of immediate danger? Or—and this was the biggest question of all—had his tremendous coup reached that point of maturity when it was now safe to launch out and begin picking the plums? In other words, had Perrigo already begun to shift the money from Paris?

Why else had he come to London? Lady Demorval had gone back to France some days ago. He must have known of her presence there. So his sudden arrival in town could have had no connection with her end of the affair.

One thing was certain, he was taking no pains at all to hide his identity. On the contrary, he was going to some lengths to show himself where he was well known. The commissionaire for one knew that he was in the Avalon that night. The waiter, too, would be able to swear to it—and doubtless before the evening was out the head waiter would be roped in for a chat. It certainly looked as though he was out to establish an alibi. In that case things looked very black indeed. It implied the sinister fact that the last phase of the gigantic plot was already happening in Paris.

* * *

Stayne looked gloomily at the wall and hid his agitation behind a blank wall of seeming indifference. The brighter spots of the situation brought a brief ray of satisfaction. Tembridge was there in the building anyhow: he would not be working, single-handed, trying to keep up half a dozen ends at once. And, since Perrigo was here in London, he could not be hastening his devilries in Paris. If Perrigo wanted to get back to his headquarters there were only two routes open to him—either by boat or aeroplane. And Stayne assured himself that whether Perrigo went by sea or air he would have company on that return trip. Mr. S. G. Daleson would be there with him, every inch of the way.

Stayne moved over to another cabinet and put in ten minutes' rapid telephoning. He emerged with the old chilly glitter back in his eyes and the determined line of his mouth was set and grim. If Mr. Perrigo wanted an alibi he should have it all right! But not in the way he expected.

The chances were a thousand to one that Perrigo would show himself down there on the dance floor when he had finished his supper. Doubtless he would make his alibi complete so far as the Avalon was concerned. There would be waiters to chat to, friends to nod to and fling streamers at, a bottle of "the boy" for the orchestra and a request for a couple of his favourite tunes to the leader.

Stayne made his way downstairs, having first waited to see a man with a tray of wet violets take up his position on the kerb outside. He was a dirty, dilapidated-looking specimen. His hat was bedraggled till there was neither shape nor stiffness left in it. His face carried the grime of many days and a four-day straggle of beard stuck out in a raggedy bristle from his cold jowl. He was swaying mechanically, first on one foot and then on the other, in an effort to keep a torpid circulation moving through his chilled limbs, the while he chanted in a monotonous sing-song drone: "Vi'lets, lady? Vi'lets, lady? Sweet vi'lets? Vi'lets?"

But as he came to the swing doors of the Avalon and stuck his broken boots against the kerb, Stayne saw the secret sign pass, a sign so simple and natural that it would have passed without notice among a dozen trained watchers—the hard drawing at a cigarette which had gone out and the tossing of it away with just the tiniest frown of annoyance. It was the interrogation sign of the Secret Service from one unknown man to another. It implied the unspoken question: "Are you the man I'm told to look for?"

Stayne answered by flicking an imaginary speck of cigarette ash from his coat sleeve—and made for the stairs.

The unkempt wreck scarcely seemed to have noticed. Stayne heard his droned out, hopeless monody: "Vi'lets, lady? Sweet vi'lets? Vi'lets?" as he made his way down to the lower floor.

A brisk foxtrot was in progress and the floor was full. The Avalon was, for the time being, *the* fashionable rendezvous among the smaller Soho nightclubs. In the queer way of changing and waning fashions the Avalon was at the height of its popularity, riding the crest with a swing and a glitter of tinsel. Packed on the restricted floor were over a hundred dancers, the men all in formal tails and the women in dazzling frocks.

Stayne caught a waiter's eye and inquired for a vacant table: "A small one if there's one going, just enough for myself."

"There's one over in the corner, sir, by the palms there. It's not very good and you can't see much of the floor—but it's the best we can do, sir we're pretty full tonight."

"Thanks, I'll go over after this dance. A bottle of Lanson—fifteen, please."

While he was talking he caught sight of Tembridge, dancing smoothly and easily in spite of the absurdly crowded floor with Marienne. He waited till they had swung round and were hidden by the crush of dancers at the far end. Then he slipped along by the wall and reached his table.

Twice he saw Tembridge and Marienne swing past him. They seemed supremely happy to be dancing together, she laughing gaily at his whispered comments in her ear, he swinging her out of danger from thrusting elbows and awkward feet with the neat skill of the born dancer.

Stayne would have sworn that he had not been noticed, yet the third time they passed him Tembridge definitely gave him the sign—"Do you want to be known?" Stayne returned the affirmative, and when the trot was finished Tembridge came over, alone.

"I guessed you'd be around before long," he said. "I left enough bait at Curzon Square to have hooked a whale."

"Where's Miss Varris?"

"We're right away over in the other corner. I left her attacking an ice the size of a tennis ball."

Stayne was in no free-and-easy mood.

"Is there any reason why you couldn't have left word about your movements?" he asked.

Tembridge nodded. "Yes—sure—a good one," he said.

"What?"

"Marienne. I told you, Chief, you'd have to step along lively." Then he caught the cold, fish-like stare in Stayne's eyes.

"Honest," he said in an altered tone. "I've had the devil of a job shaking off Hawker. Thought I'd never get anywhere where I could get in touch with you. We've been right out on a long tour through the wilds of Highbury trying to get clear. There has been two of them this time—on my boot tags from the time I left home."

"What's wrong now?"

"Hawker's mad! He's hoppin' mad. Says he never authorised that statement to the Press. Says we've given away information that should never have been divulged without Headquarters' sanction."

"He blames us for it, does he?"

"All the time and always."

Stayne frowned. "Hawker must be losing his touch," he muttered. "Why—he's only got to go round and see the papers concerned. There isn't an editor in London who wouldn't tell one of the Yard chiefs the origin of a statement like that. Have you seen Hawker?"

"Yes. He's out for blood. Says he won't have us dancing around on his stamping ground. And what d'you think now?"

"What?"

"Says he's going to search Curzon Square."

Stayne's eyes narrowed.

"He said that, did he?" he growled.

"Sure. Says he'll be along there before midnight with a search warrant and a squad of men. He was so catty he could hardly speak. Who have they got in Scrubs?"

"One of the S.S. men. Hawker doesn't suspect, does he?"

"Hasn't an inkling. He was crowing over it like a hen that's just laid an oversize egg. Said he swore to the heads that he'd have Varris back under lock and key inside twenty-four hours. And he chortled at me for having done it. And he's almighty nasty about it. He swore he'd have Varris on the grill and roast him till he squealed."

Stayne smiled.

"He won't have much chance of making *that* lad squeal," he said. "He doesn't know himself who got Varris out of jail. All the grilling in the world won't make him cough up.

"It relaxes the watch at the ports. We shall be able to get through. See that everything is ready for a quick getaway tomorrow afternoon. I've just left Varris. He's all right. And I've got the rest of the information out of him. It's going to be a sticky business—one way and another." He sighed and turned with a breath of relief as the waiter arrived with the cool green bottle in its silver tub of ice.

"Does Marienne know?" he asked guardedly.

"No. I've kept the papers from her."

Stayne watched the waiter disappear.

"She may find out before the night is through. If she does, tell her. Tell her it's just a move on the part of the police to allay public uneasiness. Varris is safe with me. Have a spot?"

"No. I'm not drinking tonight."

"Well, if you should notice I've got very drunk as the evening wears on, don't be too surprised. If Marienne notices it, tell her anything you wish. Tell her it's a little failing of mine, and that it only happens very occasionally—otherwise I'm almost respectable."

He paused a moment and then asked quietly: "Do you think Hawker was in earnest about that search party?"

"He certainly seemed to be. Gosh, he was mad. He says we've been riding the high horse over him too long—and now we've started doing it roughshod. He says he's going to put a stopper on our game if he has to take 8B to pieces stone by stone."

"I don't mind him doing that so much," said Stayne thoughtfully. "There are one or two little arrangements at 8B that all the searchers in England couldn't find. But I'm worried about that cellar entrance. If he finds that, we are going to be in the very devil of a pickle."

"Think he will?"

"It's fairly well hidden. But he's bound to ferret down to the fact that there are only three secret ways of getting into, and out of a house: over the roofs, through the walls or from a passage underground. If the first two draw a blank he will concentrate on the third till he's got it. After all, it's only a matter of shifting the right barrels around and not being put off the scent by the other smaller cellars."

"It will be a nasty smack for us if he does find it!"

"It will alter every plan I've made. Bluntly, what it means is that we shall have to find a new place—one with equal facilities. And I don't think that's humanly possible at short notice."

"That's why I thought it necessary to see you. I couldn't stay on there; I had to shake Hawker off. I reckon we had best get back to Curzon Square and hold the fort from that end. Maybe we can bluff Hawker out of it."

XXI

"The devil of it is that I can't move from here," said Stayne.

"Can't? Why not?" asked Tembridge in surprise.

"Perrigo is upstairs."

"*What?*"

"Saw him as I came in. He's up there now, feeding his ugly face and making himself affable all round. He will be down here before long. For Heaven's sake don't let Marienne see him. She will give the game away as sure as the band is going to play 'Hallelujah' another dozen times tonight."

"Well, where do we get off now?"

"You hold on at that end. I've an idea about Mr. Perrigo. And if it happens to be right we shall have him nicely sewn up in a sack."

"I'd like to rub his nose up and down his spine," said Tembridge fervently. He rubbed his hands softly together.

"Nice thought, but it wouldn't help much." Stayne chuckled right down in his chest. "I'd got something fixed up for you!" he said darkly. "Something to teach you not to take Miss Varris out to nightclubs and think you can get away with it on an old warhorse like me. However, it will serve its turn here just the same. If Perrigo starts yelping, go for him, pretend you've made a mistake, do anything, but keep him from getting up those stairs. You'll see what I mean when the shindy begins. Now you'd better go back to your little friend—and I wish you joy."

"Marienne is quite all right for a few minutes," said the other with an airy wave. "We understand each other perfectly."

"And that's not the first time I've heard that," said Stayne. "You had better bring her over here when the next dance comes on. They're just getting ready for it now. She will be fairly out of sight here behind these palms. I want to talk to her for a few minutes before our friend upstairs puts in an appearance. See if she has finished yet with that tennis ball."

Tembridge, self-assured and apparently as carefree as a schoolboy out on the spree, went off practising a new Charleston kick all to himself as he went. Stayne watched him go. Suddenly he stopped his skylarking and hurried across the floor. Just for a moment Stayne watched him in mild surprise. Then he saw what was behind his assistant's urgent move. He had placed himself in a few swift strides in the direct line of vision between Marienne, sitting demurely at her table, and the slope of the entrance stairs.

Coming leisurely down the stairs, humming a snatch of song to himself, and looking round the floor pleasantly, was the immaculate figure of Perrigo. He nodded to the manager, smiled cheerfully at his profuse greeting and passed along within a yard of Marienne's table. Tembridge, leaning with his hands on the table, kept himself between her and the man she hated, the while he talked and chatted and pulled her leg gracefully about her capacity for absorbing vanilla ices.

Stayne could only follow the action by craning his neck round the great tubs of palms that shielded him from the now busily playing band. But he saw the swift play of it and the neatness with which it was done.

That knack of doing things on the spur of the moment, of taking an awkward situation in his stride and of wriggling out of it by some twist or other was only one of the qualities that bound the two together in a bond that seemed careless enough on the face of it, but which really had its roots very deeply planted indeed. Marienne had not the slightest idea of what had happened. She just sat and laughed at his cheerful antics. Then as the band struck up he whisked her out of her seat.

"Come along," he said, "let's have a swing while we can. The floor will be stiff with blighters in a minute." They went circling away to a quick one-step, Marienne unconscious of the fact that her back was turned the whole time to the side table where Perrigo sat, beamingly watching the waiter fizz the cork from a magnum.

They only went round once. As they tripped by the orchestra platform Tembridge whispered: "There's a friend of yours here I'd like you to meet—would you care to?"

"Why, of course," she said. "I haven't recognised anyone here—who is it?"

"I'll show you. Break off when we get round the palms again. It's a he. And he wants to see you urgently."

They swung out of the ruck on the fast-filling floor, and Marienne found herself face to face with the Mystery-Maker.

He rose and pushed the only other chair clear of the table for her.

"Delighted to see you again so soon, Miss Varris," he said. "Won't you please sit down?" Then, turning, he said: "Tembridge, you'll have somebody collaring your own table if you don't grab it yourself. Hurry, my son, before you're right out in the cold."

Tembridge passed him an eyeful that was neither polite nor respectful. But Stayne just failed to notice it. He was swaying ever so slightly, and a suspicion of a hiccough escaped him. "Waiter," he called, and there was an expansive thickening of his voice, "another bottle of Lanson—fifteen."

Marienne eyed them in undisguised surprise. Tembridge caught her hands and, helping her into her chair, whispered: "It's all right, Miss Varris—he gets that way at times. Just a little squiffy. He will get worse during the evening, but don't take any notice. I'll be back in a minute or two." He was off and away before she could reply.

She sat and stared after his retreating figure, with her forehead knit with puzzled lines.

"Well!" she thought. "This is a queer sort of an evening. Stayne squiffy?" Her hero, the acme of polish and correct behaviour—squiffy in front of the poshest crowds of London's night life. And taking no trouble to hide it either. What did Tembridge want to leave her with him for, knowing he was half tipsy?

"Miss Varris," said a voice beside her that was having a slight difficulty in making itself distinct, "I'm awf'ly pleased to be—that is, for you to be sitting here because, if y'know what I mean, s'nice to have you around. See?"

"Yes, I see," said Marienne, nervously diving into a tiny handbag in a frantic effort to appear unconcerned.

Stayne drank deeply of the bubbly wine.

"Seen th' evening papers, th' final editions?" he asked.

No: she hadn't. She'd seen them all except the finals. And the news was so marvellously wonderful that she didn't want to see another paper again as long as she lived.

Stayne opened a late extra and laid it on the table before her. "Thass why I asked you," he said. "An' I wanted to tell you, before you saw it, s'all a lot of rot. See? S'all a lot of abs'lute rot. Templer was sitting down all nice and comfy in his sitting-room when that was in the press. Talking to me, he was—s'large as life. They got wrong feller. See? Got the wrong feller and s'all a lot of rot."

* * *

Marienne hardly knew what to make of it. Definite statements from official sources were not to be doubted. And there it was in black and white, as authoritative a declaration as anyone could ask. But then, if it had been so, surely Tembridge would have broken the news to her. They had been together nearly three hours now, and he must have known. He had bought papers himself. Surely he would have said something about it. It was all very unsettling and confusing.

"An' there's another thing I wanted to see you about, m'dear," the bibulous voice went on. Stayne took another swig and filled up his glass to the brim. Marienne's was still standing untouched. She made a pretence of sipping at it, mostly because her throat had gone as dry as a sandstorm.

"Yes, there's cert'nly another thing I want to see you about, that feller Perrigo. That ruffian—that out-and-out scamp—y'know the feller I mean? Perrigo, the blighter who got Raymond into trouble."

Marienne started as though she had been stabbed and the colour drained from her cheeks. She looked quickly round at the extraordinary man beside her with a wild look of dismay on her face. But Stayne wasn't even looking in her direction. He was peering across the room, with an eyelid half drawn over one eye and an alcoholic squint in the other. Tembridge, in his free-and-easy way, was whirling round the crush with a newly-found partner his hands.

"Perrigo. Thass th' feller, m'dear. Want to tell you about him. Want to tell you not to start playing a lot of feminine antics if you should sudd'nly catch sight of him. See? Keep your head. Don't make a scene with the blighter. He's here, m'dear. See? He's here, right here in this room. And he's going to get the s'prise of his life in a minute. So's Tembridge, the young pup. So's you, my dear. I'm sorry about that. But I can't—ho! Help myself there. You're included in the crowd. See?"

Marienne laid a hand on his arm. "Do you—did I hear you say Perrigo was here—in London?" she asked unbelievingly.

"Thass right, m'dear. He's here—in this club. And I'm just going to toss a wrench into his works while the wheels are going round. Got an idea we shall upset his plans long enough for us to get to work over in Paris. If his passports are made out in a fictis—fisch—in a false name, he's going to bat me one in the eye. But I don't think he's fool enough to try that game. He's only just landed, and I reckon we've got him where he belongs. All I want you to do is to stay right here in this corner and keep out of sight. See? Don't let him see you. There's going to be a bit of a rumpus in a minute—but as soon as thass all died down you wait around for Tembridge to get you out of it. I shall have to make a run for it."

In spite of her fears, her mystification, and her downright unhappiness, Marienne could not help a fleeting smile at the thought of that more than half-inebriated man in full evening dress "making a run" for anything.

He turned to her and eyed her with the absurd seriousness of more than half-seas over.

"Don't forget what I said," he begged her solemnly. "Stay right here and keep out of sight. If anything happens, don't get frightened, an' above all don't help yourself to a dash of hysterics if you should suddenly catch sight of Perrigo in the crowd. Thass all, m'dear. Here goes the balloon.

The manager, who had been upstairs receiving guests, suddenly reappeared down the entrance stairs, white-faced and agitated. He made frantic signals to the band, the leader of which, not understanding him, opened his eyes wide in mute interrogation and called for a *fortissimo* effort from his instrumentalists.

The manager, flinging all the tenets of correct M.C.-ship to the winds, dashed on to the floor, wriggling like an eel among the press of dancers.

"Stop! Stop!" he called to the leader, but above the blare of the band and the scuff of feet on the floor his voice did not carry.

But those around had heard him, and from his mere appearance they sensed that something was wrong. They ceased dancing. The conductor, turning round to see what was going wrong, saw the manager frantically paring to him. His baton slowly dropped to his side, and he cupped a hand to his ear to hear what was being shouted to him.

"A raid! A raid!" Slowly the music died away and the dancing stopped. The word went round in a flash. "A raid—the police were in."

"Ladies and gentlemen"—the manager was up on the orchestra rostrum—"I must ask you, please, not to get excited. For some reason best known to themselves the police are raiding this establishment." Perrigo's magnum went over with a crash. "Ladies and gentlemen, please remain just where you are and carry on as usual. Nobody here is violating the law, for the Avalon is licensed up till midnight. There is no need for—"

The rest of it was drowned in a wild scramble for wraps and furs and handbags in an effort to get out before the police arrived. In a valiant effort to restore normal decorum the band broke out once more into the lively syncopations of "Hallelujah," and, for the first time in her excitement, Marienne noticed that Stayne was up and standing away from her. With one hand out unsteadily against the wall he was keeping his balance, glaring through the hurry and bustle with a baleful eye on Perrigo, who was bawling lustily for his hat and coat.

He began walking towards him, hiccuping gently to himself.

XXII

All in a moment the hurry and the bustle ceased. New arrivals were entering, coming down the stairs with unfamiliar but purposeful tread, wearing evening dress clothes with an unconscious but resolute air. Two—four—eight—twelve—sixteen of them all told, a stalwart crowd, not one of them under six feet, a bunch tough enough to have held the exits to the shadiest dance hall in London. "Hallelujah" died stillborn.

"Ladies and gentlemen, *please*!" squeaked the manager in an unhappy voice. "It's quite all right. The management regret it exceedingly, but if you will just answer the few questions that these police officers will put to you, it will be all over in a few minutes." Perrigo was halfway across the floor on his way out. Stayne was within a yard of him.

An awkward, constrained silence settled over the crowd as the officer came down. The man at the lead was a tall, well-cut figure. He earned air of high authority all over him, and it was obvious from the first moment that he was in charge. He played his part admirably. Among the whole sixteen he was the only one who looked as though he really liked wearing evening dress. Two others who had been sitting down at different tables all the evening got up and joined the party. They passed written notes to the man on the fourth stair, who thrust them into his pocket without reading them.

"I must ask you all to remain exactly where you are—and this little matter will be over and done with in no time." It was the leader, speaking formally and casually. "I am a police officer attached to the Criminal Investigation Department of Scotland Yard, and these officers here are acting under my orders. This is not a raid in the usual sense of the word, but I would inform you that we are looking for a certain individual, one whom we have every reason to suspect is present in this club tonight. There is no charge made against this club, or, indeed, against any member of this club, but we have certain inquiries to make. I wish to add that anyone refusing to give such particulars of himself as my officers will demand will be liable to summary arrest."

There was nothing else to do than to accept the situation with as good a grace as possible. One by one the various guests were taken aside and a few simple questions put to them regarding their identity. Each was required to show evidence in proof—visiting cards or letters, or some such concrete evidence. The women were not troubled at all.

Stayne recognised in the leader of the raid a detective named Lynton. He had had dealings with him before, and knew him for a shrewd, capable officer. Lynton himself tackled Stayne.

"Name?" he asked, a ghost of a twinkle in his eye.

"John Stayne." The answer came through a fog of alcoholic muzz.

A little whisper of curiosity rustled round the floor when it was known that the notorious Mystery-Maker was in their midst. Heads turned to inspect the man who had figured so largely in the news of the day. The majority of them immediately jumped to the conclusion that this was the man for whom the search was being made.

"Is that your correct name, sir?"

"You don't think," said Stayne foggily, "that I would be admitting to that name if it was anything else, do you?"

Stayne pulled a fistful of papers from his pocket, a telegram, a couple of letters addressed to himself at Curzon Square, a tailor's bill, and a first-class pass over all the British railways.

Lynton glanced at them, entered the particulars in a notebook, and nodded his dismissal.

"All right, Colonel," he said pleasantly. "That passes you out."

He turned to Perrigo. "And you, sir," he asked; "what is your name, please?"

"Perrigo—Gabriel Perrigo." The reply was surly, tinged with doubt.

"And the address?"

"I have no permanent London address. At present I am staying at the Grand Embassy Hotel. I shall be there at least for another fortnight."

That satisfied Stayne. He knew from that moment that Perrigo was planning to get to France immediately. He had probably chartered a special aeroplane from one of the cross-Channel companies and was aiming to get to Le Bourget that night, as soon as he was satisfied that his alibi for that night would hold.

"Thank you, sir. Have you any proof of identification?" Lynton was politeness personified.

Perrigo reached into his pocket.

"Yes," he growled. "One doesn't usually carry one's birth certificate around in evening dress. But I happen to have my passport with me. I was at the passport office today, having it renewed."

Stayne offered up a little prayer of thankfulness. That was all he wanted to know. Perrigo was actually going back that night. Men don't carry passports around with them in evening dress any more than they do their birth certificates. Even accepting the fact that he had been to the passport office that afternoon, it did not follow that he would normally have transferred that passport to his evening clothes when he dressed.

Lynton noted down the details and proceeded to the next.

"All right—you other gentlemen: you are at liberty to proceed as you wish as soon as the officers have taken your particulars."

Perrigo muttered something under his breath and made for the stairs. At the same moment Stayne lurched forward. He tripped half tipsily over his own feet and cannoned heavily into Perrigo.

"Clumsy brute!" snarled the swindler, roughly disentangling himself from the drunken embrace.

"S-So sorry—so sorry, ol' feller," burbled Stayne thickly. "Damn nearly over that time. Th-th-thanks—'scuse me."

He walked unsteadily to the stairs and went up while Perrigo stood rumbling stormily under his breath. "Disgusting beast—drunk as an owl—what the devil are the management doing in allowing such pigs in a decent club!"

The manager hurried up to pacify him.

"Awfully sorry, Mr. Perrigo," he said mollifyingly. "I wouldn't have had you annoyed for worlds. But to tell you the truth I didn't know he was in that state or he would have been asked to leave."

"The clumsy wretch—he's flattened out half my toes."

"I certainly saw him crash into you, and I apologise for such a thing happening. He seemed quite all right when he came in. He must have been hitting the champagne bottle pretty heavily. Funny thing, that. I've never seen Colonel Stayne pickled before."

"Colonel my hat!" snarled the other. "He's no more a colonel than I am. He was fired out of the army years ago—chucked out, bag and baggage."

At that point Gabriel Perrigo let out a startled howl—a yell in which astonishment, shock and blazing anger were equally blended.

"My passport! My passport!" he cried. "Stop him! Somebody stop him! Hi! That blighter has stolen my passport."

The manager looked his amazement.

"Mr. Perrigo!" he expostulated, thrusting out a detaining hand on the enraged man. "You must be mistaken. Please wait a moment and look for it—you must have put it back in another pocket—please don't shout things in the club."

"Damn the club!" barked Perrigo. "I know when I've been robbed and I know what pocket I put my passport in. Let go of me, curse you—that devil is getting away with it." The manager still clung to the man, striving to smooth over a scandal, and Perrigo was doing his best to shake him off. Stayne had already reached the stairhead and was passing through the vestibule.

"Let go," he shouted. "I tell you that man has robbed me. The passport was in my inside pocket. I put it back there after the Inspector had examined it. Stayne cannoned into me—deliberately cannoned into me—dammit, you saw him do it yourself. And he grabbed my passport while I was trying to save myself from falling. Get out of it!" With a violent shove he rid himself of the agitated manager, and went pounding up the stairs, Lynton himself only a jump behind him.

When they got out through the vestibule they saw Stayne swaying dizzily on the pavement, waving an erratic hand at a passing taxi.

"Excuse me a moment, sir," said a polite voice at his elbow, "but would you mind stepping back into the club?"

"Eh?" said Stayne, and cocked a leery eye at the detective.

"This gentleman here, Mr. Perrigo, has made a statement that he has lost his passport, and he accuses you of having stolen it. I sincerely hope he is mistaken, but apparently he is sure of it. I must ask you to step back into the club and allow him to satisfy himself."

"Passport? Whose passport?" hiccuped Stayne. "I've seen no passport. Cert'nly I'll step back into the club. Jolly good idea. I can do with a spot of bubbly. Have all those bobbies cleared off yet? If not, ask 'em—hic—ask 'em to have a bottle with me."

XXIII

Perrigo, red-eyed and teetering with indignation, was behind him, seeing that he didn't drop that precious passport. Together they hustled the semi-helpless figure back through the vestibule and into the manager's private office.

"Mr. Perrigo, you realise that you are bringing a pretty serious charge in this business, I hope? You have made a public accusation against Colonel Stayne, one that seriously impugns his honour."

"What the devil do you mean?" demanded Perrigo, whirling round.

"I mean that if you demand Colonel Stayne to submit to being searched, and if the passport is not found, you will be in a very serious position. Colonel Stayne will be in a position to sue you for heavy damages. And he would get them. You realise that, I hope? Your accusation was made in front of a great number of witnesses.

"Damages, fiddlesticks!" stormed Perrigo heatedly. "The man's a crook, and you know he is. Turn out his pockets. I demand it."

"Very well, sir," said Lynton. "I just wanted you to understand the position. I must say that I can't see any other explanation myself."

He turned to the Mystery-Maker. "Colonel Stayne, will you please turn out your pockets?" he asked.

Stayne looked uncomprehendingly at the detective.

"Do which?" he said throatily.

"Turn out your pockets, sir. Mr. Perrigo suspects you of having misappropriated his passport."

"Cert'nly," said Stayne, with an affable nod. "Turn 'em out any time you like, officer. Have a cigar?"

He pulled out a cigar-case and flopped it on the table. There followed a thin gold watch on a black silk fob, a key purse containing four keys, a wallet containing money and private notes, a silk handkerchief, a few coins of silver change, a platinum matchbox, and a small private diary written in a cipher of his own.

And that was all. He dived flabbily into various pockets again in a bibulous effort to discover something more, but finally gave up the effort and sat down with a bump.

"He's bluffing," protested Perrigo. "Of course he's not going to produce it. He's got it stowed away somewhere. And you know it."

Lynton fingered his chin ruminatively.

"Well, there's no passports showing up as yet," he mused, "and he seems to have gone through every pocket bar the hip."

"Search him yourself. You're within your rights. You're supposed to."

"I don't know so much about that, sir. I've only got the right to search him at the station. You can insist if you like—and if Colonel Stayne is willing."

"Willing? Of course he's willing. He's already turned his own pockets out, hasn't he? And you know he's got the damn thing. He hasn't been able to dispose of it. He hadn't had it in his possession more than sixty seconds when I was chasing after him. And if it hadn't been for that perfect fool of a manager I'd have been after him in less than ten."

Lynton hauled Stayne up to his feet and began a systematic search of his pockets. He did it as thoroughly as only a trained searcher can, going over the seams and the cloth with fingers that were as sensitive to the unusual as a photographic plate is to the light.

But there was nothing there, not a single match end, let alone a passport. And Perrigo realised, with something of a shock, that there was nowhere on that elegantly cut suit where a passport *could* have been hidden without being obviously noticeable.

"Well, what do we do now, sir?" asked Lynton helplessly. "He can make things pretty nasty for you if he chooses."

"Bosh! I tell you he took it!"

"That's as may be, sir. But you've got no proof—"

"Proof—what greater proof do you want than the fact that I haven't got my passport? And I shall need it, urgently."

"Proof that you haven't got it isn't proof that Colonel Stayne has. I'm sorry about it, sir, but this argument isn't getting you anywhere. You'd better have a look around on the dance floor, sir. I think you must have dropped it."

"Don't be a fool," shouted Perrigo vehemently. "I can't drop a book as big as a wallet out of my inside pocket, can I? I tell you he—"

"Yes, yes, I know, you've said all that before," said Lynton patiently. "The fact remains—you accused Colonel Stayne of having stolen your passport—and I've proved to my own satisfaction that Colonel Stayne hasn't got it. If he's got it stowed away in that suit I'll eat my hat—and yours. Also, a further fact remains, that I shall have to make a report about this to my chief. Mr. Stayne is a bit too tight to understand much about it right now, but I'll bet that in the morning he's going to feel almighty cross about it. He'll phone the station and get corroborative details—and we daren't refuse them. It was a public defamation, Mr. Perrigo, and you can't get away from it. You brought it on yourself and you wouldn't give him a chance to explain or deny. And where you look trouble in the face is that you are liable in heavy damages to Colonel Stayne."

Perrigo was nonplussed. He neither knew what to say nor to think. In that sudden flash of realisation he saw all his cloud castles falling earthwards. Everything had gone violently and unbelievably wrong in one brief minute. Without that passport he could not get back to France—couldn't get out of England except to some place where he could be hauled back as soon as the warrant was out. And it would be days before he could get that passport replaced—days of delay that would be fatal.

He had to get back to Paris within the next twenty-four hours or see all his perfectly prepared schemes crumble to dust. And what a crumbling it would be. The hue and cry would be out for him: in less than an hour the police net would be spread for him in every corner of the country. And that would be the end of it. All his friends were in Paris. Without money he could not hope to compete with Scotland Yard. He would be under arrest within twenty-four hours—with half Europe going dancing crazy about him.

"I—I must think this out," he muttered at last. "Lord—I want some air—this place has gone as clammy as a hot-house!"

He went out, slamming the door behind him. Upon the pavement, hatted and mufflered round the neck, he stood signalling for a taxi. From the kerb a broken-booted, ragged-clothed flower hawker looked across appealingly at him and held out his tray of wet flowers. The chant of his monotone came to Perrigo—"Vi'lets, sir? Sweet vi'lets, sir? Vi'lets."

He edged the tray a little nearer, almost sticking it under Perrigo's nose.

"Oh, go to the devil with your dratted violets!" snarled Perrigo, clambering into his cab.

A few minutes later Stayne came out and signalled a cab. His semi-drunken stupor seemed to leave him as he passed the flower-seller. As he drifted by, the ragged arm lifted with an action that was incredibly smooth, flicked the little heap of flowers aside, picked up the passport, and slid it deftly into the pocket of Stayne's coat, a pocket which he was holding wide open with a crooked thumb.

No word passed—not a nod or a sign. The flower-seller passed on down the street and the chant of his wares grew fainter on the night. "Vi'lets, lady? Sweet vi'lets, lady? Vi'lets?"

XXIV

Next morning Stayne was early astir. The events of the previous evening had followed in quick succession. Perrigo had gone direct to Bow Street adn had lodged a formal information covering the whole affair. He did it in the hope of recovering his lost passport more than from a desire to indemnify himself against possible risk of prosecution by Stayne.

The result was swift and urgent. The matter naturally reached Hawker's ears. And when Stayne reached home Hawker was in possession. He had landed in with a swoop, presented his search warrant, and proceeded about a systematic search of the entire house with all the bitter thoroughness of a crew of Custom House searchers going over a ship suspected of carrying contraband.

Hawker, before arriving at Curzon Square, had long since negatived the possibility of a runaway over the roofs or a secret passage throw the walls. To begin with, no one but a man with the tread of a cat—and cat wearing air-blown rubber shoes at that—could have made the passage over the roofs night after night without creating suspicions in the minds the householders beneath.

In a big town noises are continuous. They are outside and all around from long before dawn till long after dark. Then come the silent hours, when every sound carries with remarkable clarity. The rattle of a train half a mile away is distinctly audible—Big Ben booms his brassy clamour around for five or six miles in the stilly silence that falls after midnight. Sounds even in adjoining houses, come through with disconcerting clearness. So what chance had men of coming and going over the roofs without the people beneath hearing them sooner or later—when even a bird twittering in the eaves almost drives one to distraction?

No. The roof theory was ruled out—as was the possibility of a hidden outlet through the connecting walls. A few inquiries as to the character of the people living on either side had settled that. Both his neighbours were citizens of unchallengeable integrity. They were people who were known in the City, people whose ways of life and whose methods of living were as open as the day. There was no question as to their credentials. They would not have the slightest hesitation in informing the authorities if they thought anything was going wrong in their immediate locality. That was one of the reasons why the Mystery-Maker had chosen to take up his abode at 8B, Curzon Square. He had planted himself in the very centre of law and order as exemplified in the householders of ultra-respectable Curzon Square, an address for which there was competition among people of undoubted substance.

Hawker was in as sour a mood as Stayne himself. The night's activities had left Marienne in Tembridge's hands.

XXV

Hawker glared at the man whose genius was baffling him. "For two pins," he said viciously. "I'd like to smack you twice round Curzon Square."

"At your disposal," murmured Stayne, "are three things—the time, the place—and the man. Care to have a rummage round the house? I'm sure you'll find something of interest. Built in eighteen-forty by the chief accounting clerk in the office of the Adam Brothers. You may have heard of them. Modern improvements by the Sanitary Board Limited, telephone instalment by the National—since taken over by the State—running water in all the upstairs rooms even when not required, stairs by Rise and Tread, disinfectant by Cigar Smoke out of Virginia Cigarette, furniture by Instalment, colour scheme of the general *décor* by Accident, cork lino—"

Hawker let out a snort that made his moustache shiver.

"Damn funny," he growled, "oh, damn funny. Think you're going to get my goat, eh? Well, you're not, see? You can bluff some of the other poor stiffs over with that slick tongue of yours, but you don't get me! I'm going to bust into this secret runaway of yours if I have to do it with a charge of dynamite. D'ye get that, my cocker, hey?"

"Oh, yes, I get it," said Stayne with a dangerous glitter in his eyes. "Step this way, will you, please? I'll show you over. The rent is only £600. You'll go crazy over it."

"You'll stay right here where you are!" yelped the detective heatedly.

Stayne sat down resignedly and reached out for a current magazine. "As you will," he agreed. "On your way, officer, and may the luck hold. But I do hope you don't get lost in the perfect labyrinth of secret passages that infest this house. If you do, ring for Belham, will you?" He pushed over the little button under the arm of the chair.

"Oh, Belham," he said, "you might bring up that whisky that Mr. Hawker wouldn't drink the other day—thank you, Mr. Hawker seems in difficulties."

"Coming now, sir," said the little golden image in the comer.

Hawker went out in a temper that would have done credit to a Billingsgate fishwife after a passage-at-arms with the man about the instalments.

But Stayne had done what he wanted. In spite of Hawker's declaration, Band without Hawker realising it, he had got Hawker's goat. The Yard man was in such a spite that his extraordinarily keen deductive faculties were dulled. No man can fill his head with two different lines of thought and expect to function with a hundred per cent efficiency on each. That's what Hawker was trying to do. He could not entirely rid his brain of the vitriolic thoughts he harboured against Stayne, and it was just on that impaired reasoning faculty that Stayne caught him. Anyone had to think pretty deeply to get under Stayne's own thoughts—and Hawker was just a little too bad-tempered to be able to think down beyond Stayne.

The Mystery-Maker caught him on the filled barrels. Among the dozens of casks down there in the second cellar were two or three that were kept permanently filled. They were big ones, hogsheads, the height of a man. And it took two or three hefty men to shift them. Hawker was certain, the moment he saw those great heavy barrels, that they hid the secret of Stayne's hidden passage out of the house. So they did, but not in the way Hawker thought.

Had he given himself time to think, had he obliterated from his mind the boil of raspy thoughts that cluttered it, he would have pulled up short and got down to Stayne's own depth of ingenuity. As it was he want for the almost immovable barrels bald-headed.

"Shift 'em!" he ordered to his search party. "Shift 'em and get 'em out of the way. His secret trapdoor is down under one of those. If he thinks he can skull-drag me off this cellar he's mistaken. We'll have Mr. Stayne at Vine Street inside an hour or my name's not Hawker."

If he had given himself time to think he would have gone on inevitably to the fact that Stayne would never have been fool enough to mask his secret exit under a full hogshead. To do so meant that at least three others would have to be let into his secret, for before they got the first great barrel clear four great pairs of brawny hands were heaving and straining at it. And Hawker knew as well as any man breathing that Stayne went by secret ways—he did not placard to the world the methods by which he worked. To have let three others into the private confidence of that secret exit would be the last thing he would dream of.

* * *

The real entrance was there, open to view, but so perfectly amalgamated with the rest of the flooring that in artificial light it was imperceptible. With much grunting and straining they lugged the first hogshead clear. As its weight came off the circle whereon it rested, the tiniest of "clicks "sounded from under the flooring. And neither Hawker nor a dozen like him could ever have opened that trap from that side of the cellar.

Oiled bolts on powerful springs had slid across under the panel and the door was fast closed to anyone unless he approached from the house at the back of 8B, Curzon Square.

Two hours in all Hawker spent with his men down there in the humid closeness of the cellars. Then they gave it up in sullen disgust. They knew, better than anyone in that house except Stayne himself, that the secret of the passageway was down there in those cellars. And they knew that they had been fooled again.

Upstairs they found that Stayne, weary of waiting, had gone to bed. Bellam, imperturbable and irreproachable, was waiting up to let them out. He had hot coffee, whisky and, close up behind his eyes, the glint of a smile waiting for them.

They ignored all the three, also his solicitous hope that they had spent a pleasant evening, and went out into the night.

Stayne heard Tembridge arrive later. In the morning the assistant imparted the information that Hawker's men had followed them round all night for that reason he and Marienne had gone on from club to club and then taken a long motor run in the cool of the early morning through the outer suburbs.

"Came back through the West Road and got up by the Scrubs Prison," he said cheerfully. "Hawker's men got all steamed up about it. They didn't know we had spotted them hours before. We loitered around and made fake signals with our headlights till we had their eyes nearly popping out of their heads. One went streaking back in the shadows of the prison wall—either to warn the Governor or to get on the wire to Hawker, I guess. I'll say we had one beauty of a night. Marienne was tickled to death. She's a great little kid, a good-plucked 'un all the way. Too bad you were too drunk to dance with her last night."

"She objected to my condition?" queried Stayne absently.

"Said she thought it was rather odd. Seemed a bit surprised, and said you never can tell with men. I assured her that her last remark was as true as anything she had ever said—and that you were as sober as she was."

"You told her that?"

"Sure. Why not? I knew you were playing a deep game, and I knew she wouldn't spoil it. Gosh! That was a neat one.

I've never seen a professional pickpocket fish out a wallet as smoothly as that passport came out. Where is it now?"

"In the post back to Perrigo. He can have it now. We held him up for twenty-four hours, and that was all I wanted. We've caught up with him now—and he still doesn't even suspect that we know anything. He thinks I really wanted a passport to get myself out of the country surreptitiously. Tonight we go to Paris. You didn't get tangled up with Hawker's men, did you?"

"Nothing serious. They tackled us, of course. Made a concerted dive, and fired a Gatling gun of questions at us. But I said something had gone wrong with my lighting installation. A wire had broken or crossed or something. I still kept jigging about with the thing, and they went nearly crazy. Whoopee! It was a great night. Say, Chief, how did you get away with that passport after all?"

"Took advantage of the raid I had already fixed."

Tembridge blinked and eyed his superior with a baleful eye.

"The raid you had already fixed?" he repeated. "What was the idea?"

"To teach you a lesson, you young pup, that you can't take Marienne out night-clubbing without letting me in too. I got the raid fixed and I was going to take her off your hands."

"Land sakes!" breathed Tembridge, and then let out a loud guffaw. "Well—if that don't take the whole bakery," he said. "Chief, I'll hand It to you."

"And then the Perrigo complication arose. I guessed he had only just landed in London and would be going back that night. Guessed right, with the gods on my side—and he had his passport with him. Number One got busy, bless his bones, and the idea of the raid was shifted. I got my hands on the passport and handed it on outside. It came back to me later. That passport never left the kerb outside the Avalon. And if Perrigo kicks up rough I'll bring an action against him that will keep him in London for Says."

Stayne finished his breakfast in a grimly pleased silence.

"I'm going round to Bayswater and then on to Bishopsgate with Varris—sorry, Harris," he said. "I shall be Mr. Daleson. If anything happens, ring me either at the boarding-house or at the office. I ought to be in Bishopsgate soon after ten."

"Righto—I'll stay in till you're back."

Stayne hurried down to change into his portly disguise. As the cellar door closed behind him Tembridge's voice came through the speaking tube, "Hurry, Chief; Hawker is just arriving—looks fierce."

And it was at that moment that Stayne realised that the second cellar trapdoor was locked against him. Hawker's overnight activities had shot the bolts across and he could not open it.

XXVI

Stayne took in the position in a flash. It was impossible for him to shift that great hogshead back single-handed. It had taken four of Hawker's men all their time to move it. And until it was back on its springs those bolts would remain immovable. The only other way to open them was from the passageway through from the house at the back.

And between him and the house at the back stood Hawker. If he attempted to get round there he would be followed and the game would be up. The Daleson identity would be exposed and the secret way through into 8B, Curzon Square laid bare.

And another meeting just then with Hawker was the last thing he wanted. Not that Hawker could do any more than he had done last night—unless he had got hold of a mass of fresh evidence—but a hold-up with the detective again would be highly inconvenient. He wanted to be out and at work, squaring things up before he left for Paris.

He jumped back to the speaking-tube.

"Tembridge—quick—hurry," he said, his voice vibrant with urgency, "Get round to the other house and open the trap. I'm penned in down here. Those fools last night shifted the counterweight and the bolts have shot."

"I can't make it, Chief. Hawker's in the house already—coming up the stairs"

"Well, for Heaven's sake give him the slip. I want to get clear."

There was silence at the other end.

Upstairs Belham was escorting Hawker through to the breakfast-room, assuring him on the way that it was useless to see Colonel Stayne just then, as he was out.

"Stuff and rot," retorted Hawker. "He's in. Saw him myself only two minutes ago from the house opposite, drinking a second cup of coffee. Saw him pouring it out myself. Tembridge is in there too."

"I quite agree, sir, that Mr. Tembridge is present," replied Belham. At same time, I must ask you to believe that Colonel Stayne has gone out. Mr. Tembridge, however, is at liberty. It was he who said he would see you."

"I don't want Tembridge. I want the big noise."

"Well, sir, all I can say is that I regret he is not at home."

Hawker glared at him. "How long is it since he went out?" he snapped.

"Barely a few minutes, sir, I handed him his hat, there in the coffee-room."

"Which way did he go?"

"Through the front door, I presume, sir."

"You presume, do you? Well, let me tell you, you don't, Stayne never went out of the house a few minutes ago, and he never went out of that front door. I've had a man stationed out there since two o'clock this morning. And no one has been either out or in since he's been there. You lead me into the breakfast-room. I want Mr. Stayne, and I want him now.

Belham sighed and pushed the door open.

"Mr. Hawker to see you, sir," he announced, and then looked slightly surprised. The room was empty. Not even Tembridge was there. He turned back to the detective.

"Just a moment, sir," he apologised. "He must have gone through to his bedroom. If you will wait a moment I will fetch him."

Belham went on through the big reading-room into Tembridge's bedroom. The assistant, at lightning speed, was making up his face at his mirror. He looked white, pasty-skinned, and, under his nose was a small ginger moustache. A huge wardrobe stood open at one end of the room exposing a multitude of queer dresses. Tembridge's lounge suit lay scattered over the bed together with his underclothing. At that moment the young gentleman was wearing a pair of blue jean trousers and a porter's long-sleeved waistcoat. A dirty blue shirt was open at the neck and he wore neither collar nor tie. Round his waist was a leather safety belt with a big steel hook in the middle. With a very draggled cap on his head, pulled over sideways, he looked a not very healthy, not very interesting specimen of a general cleaner.

On the dressing-table was a small red bucket, with a screwed-up washleather.

"Quick—put some water in that bucket!" he said as the butler entered, "Fill it just over halfway and rinse the wash-leather out thoroughly. It's full of dust, and I want the water to look as though it had been well used. Keep Hawker there, whatever you do—till at least five minutes after I've gone."

"Yes, sir. I understand perfectly, sir." Belham was already busy with the bucket.

"Tell him that I will be along to see him in a minute or two. Say that he caught me halfway through dressing."

"He's already seen you in the breakfast-room, sir—from the house opposite."

"That's all right. Say I had a sudden telephone appointment—an engagement that necessitated formal morning dress. I'll be with him in five minutes. And, Belham, get him a drink of some sort. Time your entrance so that you get in as you hear me opening the door into the breakfast-room. Then when you see me tell me that you want the pantry windows done next. Get me?"

"I quite understand, sir. You wish to get down on the ground floor."

"And out of the house without exciting suspicions. It'll look bad if I go out through the front door. Even a dam-fool shadower might take it into his head to think it funny for a window-cleaner to come out of the house without one going in previously. But I'll go up through the tradesman's entrance and leave my pail at the top of the area step. They'll think I'm one of the inside servants—hand me over some of those self-addressed letters. I'll be going out to post."

Belham dried his hands, deposited the bucket of dirty-looking water on the floor and departed, leaving Tembridge to finish his rapid preparations.

Hawker was eyeing him suspiciously when he returned.

"Is he in?" he snapped.

"Yes, sir; he will be with you in five minutes, sir. In consequence of an unexpected telephone engagement he has to change into morning dress. But he is more than halfway through now, sir—he will not keep you long. Meanwhile, 1 am desired to ask you what you will take to drink."

"Is Stayne in there with him?"

"I've already informed you, sir, that Colonel Stayne is out."

"You saw him go, hey?"

"I did not, sir."

"Then how the devil do you know he's out?"

"I cannot, of course, make that statement definitely. But I gave him his hat five minutes now and Colonel Stayne immediately went downstairs.

"As he is not in the habit of waiting about in the front hall I must presume that he has gone out. You yourself, sir, came in that way and you must have seen that he was not there."

"I did. I also saw that he didn't go out."

"What will you take to drink, sir?"

"Nothing—without soda."

At that moment the inner door opened and a stoop-shouldered figure entered, with a red bucket in one hand and a flabby wash-leather in the other. A cigarette stub was behind his ear.

"Where to nah, sir?" he asked, with a noticeable Cockney accent. "These here's the ones, ain't they?"

Belham turned ponderously to him and regarded him with half-concealed disdain.

"As this room is occupied it will be inconvenient for you to clean these windows now," he said. "You will please do the pantry first. Then the staff-rooms, and then you can inquire if this room is available."

"Thank you, sir. I can git some clean water dahn there, can't I?"

"The cook will show you where."

The anaemic-looking figure shambled out. In a few minutes he was going up the area steps with several letters held ostentatiously in his hand. The pillar-box was just round the corner of the square, and he took his time, pausing on the way to light the cigarette stub, drawing the smoke down in enormous lungfuls.

Once safely round the corner he hurried and a few seconds later Stayne heard the welcome click of the bolts going back.

Hawker got restive after a couple of minutes.

"Dam queer," he muttered. Then he jumped to it. If Stayne hadn't gone out through the front door he must be making his getaway now—through the cellars. That was why Belham wouldn't definitely say he saw him go out. He was up and on the run. He raced downstairs and into the cellars. And there was nothing there: not a thing other than the crates and bottles and hogsheads, exactly as his men had left them overnight.

He hurried back upstairs again and did a bit of rapid thinking. The breakfast-room was still empty and he barged through incontinently. The bedroom, too, was empty. The big wardrobe was shut and locked, but the clothes on the bed told their own tale.

On the way out again he saw the figure of the window-cleaner coming down the area steps. Halfway down he stooped and picked up his little red bucket, bringing it into the house with him. Hawker turned and his eyes followed him, glinting, ominous. He did not immediately penetrate the disguise the make-up was too good and Tembridge carried it off too well.

"Where's them pantry winders, miss?" he asked of his own housemaid—and she did not recognise him. If Tembridge could carry the bluff past his own servants it was small wonder that Hawker did not see through it at a jump. But to his ever suspicious brain the whole incident was suspect. It reeked of suspicion.

With a determined air he went out and up the steps, giving the sign to his man as he went. The man came over, a tall, fairly well-dressed out-of-work, delivering tradesmen's handbills.

"Did you see anyone come out of here recently?" Hawker demanded.

"Yes, sir—a window-cleaner."

"What did he do?"

"Went out to post—he had a sheaf of letters in his hand."

"Which way did he go?"

"Down there, sir. There's a letter-box just round the comer."

"How long was he gone?"

"About six or seven minutes, sir."

"Didn't that strike you as a damn long time to be gone to a letter-box just round the corner?"

"It—it does now you mention it, sir."

"I should dam well think it does." Hawker had just realised from the time lapse that the window-cleaner must have come straight downstairs from the breakfast-room and gone out. Neither the pantry windows nor the necessity for getting clean water had mattered to him. Hawker did not know it, but that same cleaner was eyeing him intently at that moment from an upstairs window.

"Was he hurrying?" asked Hawker.

"No, sir, he seemed to be walking quite casual like."

And Hawker grunted and went off down the road. Burning in his head was the knowledge that when the window-cleaner spoke to the housemaid he was slightly out of breath.

He turned the corner, noted the letter-box and knew that a man merely going to post letters would be back in sight of his watcher in less than thirty seconds. Fifty yards down the road turned again, and he stood on the corner indecisively, trying to puzzle it out in his head.

A taxicab passed him, heading from the rank higher up the road. It was empty, but the flag was down. That meant that it was ordered. He watched it half unconsciously. It stopped outside a door and a portly-looking old gentleman with slightly flat feet came out, gave an address to the driver and entered.

All in a second Hawker jumped to it. That house was immediately behind No. 8B, Curzon Square. That window-cleaner would just about have had time to get round to that house and back. He ran forward, but the taxi was fast gathering speed. He yelled, but the cab was too far away. Accelerating into top gear it was off and away round the corner. Hawker just had time to note its number. He jotted it down and went back to the house, banging the knocker on the door.

There was no answer. He knocked again and knocked repeatedly. It was inconceivable that a well-dressed, portly old gentleman like that should be inhabiting a house alone and unattended. He was sure he was on the right track now. He hurried back and phoned headquarters, asking for the net to go out in search of the taxi and to get from the driver the address to which he had taken the portly old gentleman. Outside the door the window-cleaner listened and made rapid notes in his book.

All Hawker needed now was a search warrant for that mysteriously empty house, and he knew that the secret of Stayne's secret runaway would be laid bare.

Stayne got to Bayswater and was shown up to Varris's rooms. He had scarcely been in two minutes talking when the phone bell rang violently.

It was Tembridge on at the other end, Tembridge in quick and urgent mood.

"That you, Chief? Better get out of that place as fast as you can. Hawker has seen through it. He knows about that house at the back and he's getting a search warrant. And he knows the number of your taxi. He's coming after you right now. Clear quick—he's on your heels!"

XXVII

The knowledge that Hawker was on his track was a grim piece of news for Stayne, but just then even Stayne himself did not know how swiftly events had passed and new situations arisen in his twenty minutes of absence from Curzon Square.

Hawker had stumbled blindly on a devastating piece of information, and his single-track mind was beginning to hammer it down into its rightful groove even while a fast car carried him towards Bayswater.

It had all happened quite naturally, without any fuss or excitement. At the end of his phone conversation with headquarters when he was asking for an urgency call to go out for the taxi, the inspector at the other end had said: "Just a minute, Hawker, someone else here wants a word with; you hang on a minute and I'll plug you through."

Hawker waited, and in a little while Maybury, the Chief at the Yard, came on.

"That you, Hawker?" he said genially. "Glad you were handy. There is an interesting little piece of news just come through from Scrubs Prison. At least, it should be interesting to you."

"Oh! Nothing gone wrong, I hope, Chief?"

"Well—yes and no. But it's most confoundedly upsetting. You remember that man you arrested down at Wapping yesterday?"

"Of course I do. You mean Templer Varris."

"That's the name we're holding him on. Well, the Governor reports that he has been acting most curiously since he returned."

"Uh! Trying to pull a bluff to get into the infirmary," grunted Hawker.

"What's his line? Malingering heart or just going slowly daft?"

"Not that—quite. He just didn't know a thing about the prison routine.

"Had to be told everything all over again like a new arrival. Odd for a man who has been in for several weeks."

"Rot!"snorted Hawker.

"He definitely did not know how to roll his bedding up this morning, and even after he was shown he made a most ghastly mess of it. Didn't know how to clean his cell utensils and looked utterly amazed when he realised that he had to scrub his cell out, not only that morning, but every morning."

"Say, Chief, that's a new one. Lapse of memory, eh? Couple of days on Number One diet would shift that, once and for all."

"Several other little things happened too, Hawker. Such as leaving his breakfast. Only new arrivals do that. They find it unpalatable. But next morning they're hungry as hounds. Varris, however, didn't even trouble to hide his bread ration. Any fool would have done that. There were other things, so curious that the warder reported them to me. And I passed him on to the doctor. The doctor reported the case as genuine. The man isn't malingering. He doesn't want a soft job. He doesn't want to leave prison and he genuinely doesn't want to make trouble, either for himself or for us."

"Somebody's pulling wool over your eyes, Chief."

"I think not, Hawker. If there's any wool coming down, it's over your eyes, old scout. The doctor naturally turned up the man's medical sheet. The following interesting facts were disclosed. During his absence of twenty-eight hours from Scrubs Prison he lost nine pounds in weight, gained an inch and a half in height, came into possession of an old war-wound scar, three inches long, on his left shoulder-blade and acquired a hammer toe."

"Good Lord!" muttered Hawker.

"I should think so too. Not only that, he managed to change the colour of his eyes from hazel to a very definite shade of slate grey."

"It—it couldn't be done!" gasped Hawker.

The Chief's voice was mild and acquiescent. He knew the extraordinary ways of criminals and was prepared to allow for their unexpected idiosyncrasies of behaviour at all times.

"I quite agree," he said. "And it hasn't been done. For some odd reason best known to himself, this man wants to stay in jail, Scrubs Prison preferred. We retook his fingerprints. The intriguing fact emerges that Number A320 in Scrubs Prison is not Templer Varris. The two sets of fingerprints varied at every point. At no single number were they alike."

"But—but where do *I* get off at?" asked the detective in a puzzled voice.

"That, my dear Hawker, is but another of the interesting problems facing you in this quite unusual case. You seem to have laid your hands on a man quite as well bred, quite as well educated as Templer Varris in every way and one who resembles him physically in no small degree. But for some reason this gentleman also wishes to remain out of the public eye."

"Have you any record of him there, Chief?"

"The Records Office have been on him all the morning and have drawn a depressingly decisive blank. His fingerprints are not known, and there's nothing out for him in the 'Wanted' section—neither does his description tally with that of any other prisoner who has passed through our hands. He would appear to be someone who very much wishes to hide—and, when you rushed him at Wapping, tumbled on the bright idea of hiding in prison. He's interesting, Hawker. I'll keep you posted on events. Varris is still out—and it's time he was roped in."

* * *

Hawker's voice was harassed. "But I'm all at sea, sir," he said. "I got my information from the best source imaginable. If that man isn't Templer Varris there's been some almighty dirty work going on behind my back. Three different men squealed on the man I arrested. And I got my first intimation from the friend of a man high up in Government service. The amount of knowledge disclosed about Varris's whereabouts, movements and intentions was too great and too sound for any man to pass over. One of them actually knew how Varris got out and who helped him. If I got my hands on the wrong man, someone has laid a plant on *me*!"

"That is for you to investigate. You know the source of your own information. I'm afraid I cannot help you there, Hawker. You see my difficulty, don't you?"

"No, I don't," replied Hawker, angry with himself.

"I cannot hold this man in prison, that's all," came back the quiet voice. "He is not a criminal; there is no sentence out against him, and so far as we can trace there is nothing known against him. He apparently does not want to go, but I'm afraid he'll have to. We could bring a case against him of criminal personation—but where would it land us? Right at the top of the newspaper columns—with all the world having a merry giggle at our expense. No, Hawker, it can't be done. The crux of the issue is that we're still waiting for you to get Templer Varris. That's all. Good morning."

There was a click at the other end and Hawker found himself straining his ears at an ominous silence. He put the receiver down and mopped his forehead. His head was filled with a bewildering complexity of thoughts, and at no single angle of them could he see a ray of daylight. That was the most staggering blow he had been dealt yet.

How was it done? And why? And what was the idea behind the men he had paid for their information? The whole thing baffled him. That friend of the man high up in the Government service had never sent him a false scent yet. His information had been as reliable and as authoritative as though it had come from the official dossier itself. It was through him that he had got on to this mystery at all. He was the individual who had slipped him the guarded intimation that, during the past few months there had been a vast leakage of Government paper—the almost unduplicatable paper on which banknotes and Treasury notes are printed. Those papers are of such quality and the secrets of watermarkings so perfectly contrived that it is utterly impossible to copy them.

Yet it had been known for some weeks that the banks had been receiving notes back from the Continent of such perfect workmanship that even the banks themselves could not tell the difference. They answered to every test. The sensitised plate told them nothing—except perhaps that by some extraordinary oversight the Bank printing press must have issued some thousands of notes in pairs. Whole series of numbers appeared to have been duplicated on the numbering machine. And the banks shook their heads, for they knew that that mistake was mechanically impossible. The system of checking and rechecking and counter-checking was so involved and complete that the whole system would be automatically thrown out of joint if the numerators went wrong.

The banks were more worried over that case than over any for fifty years. It was not the extent of the financial loss, heavy though it undoubtedly was. It was the fact that the secret processes by which the papers were made and marked were no longer secrets. Both Treasury notes and banknotes had been reproduced with such perfection of detail that they were in fact one and the same papers.

* * *

An international police conference was called. The French police came over in force. It was the French banks that were the greatest sufferers in the case. British banknotes are currency all over the world, and, by an oddity in the workings of commerce and exchange, are much better known and in far greater circulation in Europe than in Britain itself. In Britain the Treasury note rules. But across the Channel the big clean white bill with the neat black copy-hand writing is honoured in any little café, where in England it would be suspect even to the extent of requiring the vendor's written name on the back before it would be changed.

And the counterfeiters seemed to have plagued the banks of the big French towns with thousands of them. Many drifted in from cities far afield; the Black Sea ports sent back quite a few. But they bore the marks of weeks of travel and had probably landed out there in the ordinary course of a note's travels. It seemed that, for the time being, the forgers were centred in and around Paris.

The international cordon was drawn. For two months the police of the Continent pretty well drove every known forger to distraction. And they finally arrived at the unsettling conclusion that each and every one of them was innocent. A new gang, of supreme skill, a coterie of past-masters, had arisen in their midst, unheralded and unsuspected—until the fruits of their marvellous labours began to appear in the cash-tills of Europe, to baffle the police and evoke vague fears in the souls of the banks.

Even under the most searching tests there was only one way in which the experts could say that a note had been forged. And that was when two notes came back to headquarters each bearing the same number. And even the bank experts could not detect the forgery from the genuine. The Bourses of the world gave a little shiver when the news leaked out that the British Bank of England paper had at last been copied.

And then Hawker had been able to weigh in and allay all fears with the knowledge that the Bank's secrets were secrets still. The paper had not been reproduced—it had been stolen: the actual paper on which the notes were printed had been spirited away from storage in huge quantities. How it had been done was not yet known, but a grave scandal was bound to arise in connection with it—for *someone* in high authority must have connived at its abstraction. Still it was grand and comforting news to be able to bring. And the man who was responsible for it was the same man who sent him the information about Varris. Now what on earth was his idea in pulling a deliberate blind over him like that?

XXVIII

Hawker gave it up, but as he settled down in the car, whizzing to Bayswater, he began thinking pretty hard. The wrongly arrested man would go out; but he could rely on the Chief having him attended to satisfactorily. There wouldn't be an hour of the day or night when a slinking figure wouldn't be flitting along on his tail. But that didn't help so far as Varris himself was concerned.

The thought brought him down to another idea. Why had Stayne been so confoundedly anxious to get out without being seen that morning? Why had he disguised himself up so completely and gone haring off in a taxi? Why else but to see Varris?

Ten minutes after the call had gone out the taxi was found. The driver described his fare accurately, and remembered the address in Bayswater to which he had taken him. Hawker set his teeth and went out for it bull-headed. Inquiry showed that the address was a boarding-house, and that convinced him more than ever that Varris was there and that Stayne had gone to see him.

Hawker rang the bell with the firm conviction in his own mind that S. G. Daleson was the Mystery-Maker, and that whoever he was interviewing was positively Templer Varris.

He met the faded, patient woman who ran the establishment and stepped inside as soon as the door was opened.

"Good morning, madam," he said brusquely. "I am a police officer, Detective Inspector Hawker, of Scotland Yard. Would you be good enough to answer a few questions? I require certain information, and I think you can supply it."

The landlady blenched. Her thin frame, at the mention of Scotland Yard, seemed to draw into itself and become rigid. She eyed the detective with acute disapproval. The police! Her very select boarding establishment invaded by the police! Throughout all the years of her experience as a caterer for respectable boarders of high-class character the taint of police inquiries had never once soiled her record. Such a thing was damning enough to keep custom away for months. At all costs the nature of this man's business must not become known in the building.

"I will see you immediately, sir, in my private office. Will you please step this way?" she said with regal dignity. She swept ahead of him to the little, primly furnished office beneath the stairs. Hawker followed, with his muzzle down to as hot a trail as he had ever scented in his life.

She turned on him like an offended aristocrat, her hands clasped primly before her.

"And what," she asked, with studiously primmed lips, "can I do for you?"

"I'm making inquiries with regard to a Mr. Daleson, a Mr. S. G. Daleson. I will be quite frank, madam, and tell you that so far as you are concerned, and so far as this establishment is concerned, I haven't a single thing against you. It just happens that someone is in the habit of calling here—and I am in the process of making a few inquiries about him. Daleson is the man I refer to." The landlady bowed ever so slightly in acknowledgment of the official absolution.

"How long has this man Daleson been coming here?" Hawker asked.

"Daleson—Daleson? I don't think I know the name. At any rate not well enough to recall off-hand." The landlady was only faintly helpful.

"He just came in, madam, less than half an hour ago. A stoop-shouldered, rather fat old chap of between fifty and sixty. He walks as though he suffered slightly from fallen arches; and he wears thick, heavily pebbled glasses."

"Oh, that old gentleman. Yes, I know him. But he never stays here, Mr. Hawker."

"But he calls here?"

"The first time I ever saw him in my life was yesterday evening. He called to see one of my guests."

"And he has been here again today?"

"He is here still, sir. He came, as you say, about half an hour ago. He went straight upstairs and has been here ever since. Look—that's the gentleman I mean, the one going across the hall now to the front door. Is that the gentleman you are inquiring for?"

Hawker glanced through the glass panels and smiled inscrutably to himself.

"Yes, that's the gentleman I'm referring to," he said, and was silent for a few moments. He watched the bulky old gent with the rounded shoulders waddle laboriously across the hall, calling plaintively for a taxi, puffing and blowing with a slight touch of asthma.

"A taxi, please," he bleated. "Will somebody please get me a taxi? I want to go to Curzon Square. Will somebody please get me one? Bless my soul, where's the page?"

Deliberately Hawker watched him go. And had his surmises been correct, Hawker probably never did a more brilliant thing. By having the old gentleman trailed back to either Curzon Square or to the house behind it, he could establish the dual identity of the Stayne-Daleson combination beyond dispute. Also he could go up and tackle Varris, leaving Stayne in the dark about anything that might have happened to him.

All Stayne would know would be that Varris would just vanish completely out of the weft of his scheming. The landlady could be sworn to secrecy. He knew her type; knew it well. For the sake of the honour and select standing of her establishment she would raise horrified hands at the mere mention of the presence of police in the house. Daleson could question her till she was blue in the face. She would stoutly deny any knowledge Varris's movements.

Her knowledge of him would break off short at the bare statement that he called for his bill, paid it, and walked out of the house. Even his luggage would be left behind.

Stayne would be left with a notable problem to face—and the gnawing suspicion in his heart that Varris had gone back on him—turned him down just when things were planning out well for him. The escaped prisoner would be quietly spirited away to jail again, face the visiting magistrates and receive another three or four years on his sentence for his temerity in daring to escape from prison. The other man would be released and a shadower set to follow him wherever he went, an infallible pointing-finger to an eventual connecting-link with the main thread again. And Stayne would be left in a blank ignorance of the whole matter.

Up to now—so far as he knew—Stayne did not suspect his presence there: did not even know that the Daleson alibi had blown up. And Hawker was a man who believed in the first of the tenets of crime detection—that of playing on the other man's ignorance. Stayne, without Varris, would be in a fierce predicament. He wouldn't know where he stood or what had happened. The silence and the mystery of it all would be bound to lead him into making a false move.

And meanwhile Varris was up there, alone and unsuspecting, a fit subject for as neat a recapture as the Yard had ever brought off. Varris would be as far off his guard as a hibernating bear. The paragraph in last night's papers—repeated again authoritatively in the great morning dailies—would have lulled every breath of suspicion. Also the fact that Stayne was free to come and go to him as freely as his fancy dictated would also smooth out any waking fears in his mind.

The door swung close behind the shambling figure, and Hawker smiled again. Outside his man would be waiting and watching. Daleson could take his taxi as far as he wanted; there would be another taxi rolling along in the fumes of its exhaust.

The landlady seemed rather surprised that he made no move to accost the man he was seeking—surprised but intensely relieved. Ever since Hawker's entry she had been dreading the possibility of a "scene," or even the bare whisper of scandal that would bring her house into disrepute. She turned to the detective with distastefully raised eyebrows.

"Don't you require to speak to him?" she queried.

"Not just yet, madam. He will be attended to outside. I don't think you will be troubled with Mr. Daleson again. I rather fancy he has paid his last visit to this establishment. What I do want to know is the name of the man he has been coming to see. It *is* a man, I suppose?"

"Oh, yes. It's a Mr. Harris. I think he comes from Manchester."

"Madam," he said, "if you will permit me, I will go up and see this Mr. Harris."

She put a hand appealingly on his arm. "You—you're not going to arrest him?" she asked breathlessly.

"I'm afraid something like that will happen," he answered bluntly.

"Oh, but, *please*, not here! Not in public—where my visitors can see. You won't bring him down in handcuffs?"

"Sorry about that, madam, but this lad happens to be about twice as slippery as a greased eel. I prefer handcuffs on a fellow like him. Don't worry yourself. They won't show unless he makes a fool of himself and cuts up rough. There won't be any scene. We shall just walk down those stairs like two old friends. Get me a taxi ordered, will you, please? We will go right straight through. The only thing you'll notice is that a thousand to one I shall have my arm linked in his. Thank you so much: up here, isn't it? What's his number?"

"Suite Number Two on the first floor," said the very nervous landlady.

Hawker went up, feeling for the pair of steel bracelets in his hip pocket.

The landing was broad and fairly spacious. Number Two suite, consisting of a bedroom, a sitting-room, and a bathroom, was on the left. Hawker entered what he took to be the sitting-room without knocking.

He looked round for a moment uncertainly before catching sight of the man he wanted. Wooden shutters outside the windows were half drawn against the strong flood of early spring sunshine, and on the inside heavy curtains were draped across the panes. The light was none too good, and it was not until he got used to the dimness that he saw the figure in the corner.

A loosely-built form was sitting in a chair by a big bureau, leaning over, tying his shoelace. He glanced up at the unceremonious entry and stayed there staring, the ends of the lace held taut in his hands.

Hawker closed the door behind him and advanced into the room.

"Coming quiet?" he asked crisply.

The figure in the chair straightened up and regarded the detective with a puzzled frown.

"I—I beg your pardon?" he said.

"Yes, I'll bet you do, you beauty," retorted Hawker softly. "But what I want to know is, are you coming quietly, or do I have to get rough with you?" He pulled out the cuffs and let them dangle, glinting dully, from his hand.

The man stared at them. "What's wrong?" he asked vaguely. "What have I done? Do you mean that you are going to arrest me?" There seemed to be genuine surprise in the half-bewildered voice.

Hawker nodded. "That's about the size of it, son. You're not going to deny your identity, are you? Don't mean to say you're going to be fool enough to say you're not Varris—Templer Varris?"

The other regarded him blankly. "Varris," he said. "My name isn't Varris. You've got the first letter wrong. My name's Harris—Geoffrey Harris."

"And then some. You're Templer Varris, my son. You've just been speaking to Mr. S. G. Daleson, otherwise Colonel John Stayne. Yesterday morning, with Stayne's connivance, you broke out of Scrubs Prison. I'm re-arresting you right here and now. And I warn you that anything you say may be used in evidence against you."

Varris scratched his head and held his end up magnificently.

"I haven't the least idea what you're talking about," he said, "but I can't help thinking you're making a pretty hopeless mistake. Who are you and what are you, anyway?"

Hawker nearly giggled. "Not bad, but just damn silly," he said. "I'm Hawker, of Scotland Yard, that's who I am; and well you know it, my son. I s'pose you'll be telling me you're a private window-cleaner next. Come on, hold 'em out!"

Obediently, but with a palpably worried look, the man held his hands out. Hawker suspected a flash move from the first. The darbies looped over the wrists, and with a quick push the locks snapped to. The young man dropped his hands into his lap and regarded them as though they were some strange new insect that had just settled on him. He seemed palpably mystified by the whole proceeding.

Hawker sat on the table, swinging a leg idly. He had got his man, and now he had time to spare to lay a trap to get the others. He eyed his capture, well pleased with a good job of work well done. The expected resistance hadn't materialised, but he was still trying to guess what Varris had up his sleeve.

The detective canted the other man's head back and inspected it keenly in the dull half-light. He rubbed a finger over the upturned cheek and then laughed.

"Pigment!"he chuckled. "Gosh—that's good. The poor simp has been play-acting around with a grease-paint set. What's the idea, Varris? Thinking of going on the stage?"

Varris sighed. "I've told you I haven't the least idea what you're talking about," he said. "If you'd only be a little more explicit I might be able to help you."

Hawker sat back and smiled. "You're not doing yourself a great deal of good," he said. "Not that I care a hoot. I'd like to see you get another six years on top of what you've got. You pulled a raw deal on me between you—you and your friends. That was a hot one, that volunteer prisoner stunt, and I'm still sore about it. Bet your sweet life, But if you take my tip you'll come clean. It's up to me to get you a long stretch tacked on to your sentence—or to recommend you only to receive a merely nominal punishment. But, as I say, it's in your own hands. I don't care a damn."

The other looked round helplessly. "But what—what do you want me to do?" he said. He made an unthinking attempt to get a hand into his pocket for a cigarette, but the handcuffs dragged, and he looked up sheepishly. "Forgot about these," he said. "Get me my cigarette case out, will you, please?"

"Not on your life," growled Hawker. "You'll get a smoke when I've got what I want. And I haven't got it yet—and you've made a bad start."

XXIX

Varris sighed and relaxed. "Go on, then! Do whatever you want to do," he said. "I'm perfectly willing to help you all I can, but I'm blest if I know what it's all about."

"I want you to make a full statement of the manner in which you made your prison break yesterday morning from Scrubs Prison, also the names and addresses of those who assisted you."

"Me?" said Varris weakly. "I never broke out of prison yesterday. I was never in prison yesterday."

Hawker rubbed his moustache patiently. "Come on, son, don't be a mule," he said. "It's no use acting green like that. That game blew up years ago. Come out with the story, and it will be easier for you. We know who it was, and we know where we can lay our hands on them any old time of the day or night."

"Well—what do you want me to say?"

"Just tell me all about it. How you did it. How it was arranged. Who helped. Their names. And *why* they helped. It's not much use you pretending to be in a fog about it, because I can jog your memory for you. We know who it was. All we want is the definite admission from you. You tell the yarn, son. I'll write it down and then you can sign it. Do that, and I'll recommend you for all the leniency there is knocking about."

Varris looked down at his manacled wrists, and the fingers were clasped together in a fierce grip.

"But I—I don't even know how to begin," he said.

"Varris, I'm trying not to get exasperated with you," came the ominous rumble from Hawker. "Colonel John Stayne fished you out of Scrubs. Stayne and his runner, Valdon Tembridge. That's right, isn't it? They had a car at the gates. Stayne entered to pay a fine for a man named Dobey. He drugged the gate jailer with a fast anaesthetic, cut the keys off him and opened the inner gate. You were out in the gardens with a working party. Stayne called to you. You went over. Next thing you knew the job was done. You were outside and into the car and away. You see we know the whole story—what's the use of being such a dam fool? Come over with it!"

Varris clicked the cuffs together unhappily and his brows were furrowed.

"But I—I read about that chap," he said. "They got him back again. It was in the paper this morning. There's a paper there on the desk. Look—see for yourself."

Hawker's mouth cracked into a humourless grin.

"Sure—it's in the paper all right. But Varris isn't in prison."

"Well, I'm afraid I can't help you in the matter, much as I'd like to be able to. You see, the trouble is, that I don't know a thing about it. I read bits in the papers this morning, and I read bits yesterday when the man got out—but that's all I know."

"You're going to stand by that attitude?"

"I can't help myself. I can't invent a story for you."

"You know what it means, I suppose?"

"No. I haven't the loosest idea."

"It means that you needn't ask for favours, that's all, when you get back. You'll have the thinnest time you've ever had in your life. What you had to put up with when you went in before will be just heaven to what you'll get when you go back. *And*, you'll be lucky if the visiting commissioners don't give you just as much as you can swallow."

Varris cupped his chin moodily in his hands and stared at the wall. Hawker didn't rush him. He let him have a good long think. The man knew what prison was like inside; knew that, though the life could never be desirable, it could either be made bearable or intolerable.

"Well? Have you thought it all out?" asked Hawker at last.

"Yes, I have," said Varris, with the light of a bright idea in his eyes.

"Well, out with it, son," said Hawker, flipping open his notebook.

"It's this," said the other, looking earnestly at the detective. "If, as you say, you've had the man Varris in prison before, it stands to reason that you have a record of his fingerprints, doesn't it?"

"It does. We filed Varris's prints away as soon as sentence was passed. What's the game now?"

"Well then. If you take me to Scrubs Prison, take another cast of my fingerprints and find that they don't coincide with the ones you already have—that will prove that I'm not Varris, won't it?"

"Yeh!" grunted Hawker. "And it will prove that black's white and that the opposite to five o'clock is a piece of cheese."

"Well, that's what I think you'd better do," rejoined Varris, standing up "I'm sorry about the inconvenience of it, but I suppose it can't be helped, You've got to do your duty. I'm perfectly willing to come with you, Mr. Hawker, as soon as you are ready."

Hawker's brows came down over his eyes like window blinds. A vague suspicion that all was not well began to burn to life in his breast. He had never come into close contact with Varris himself. He had seen him once or twice in the dock when he was present in court giving evidence. He could not definitely swear to the man. His real lack of personal contact accounted for his being landed with a likely-looking substitute when he made his raid down at Wapping. And he didn't intend having the laugh handed to him again.

He strode to the windows and pulled the curtains wide, letting in a flood of light. The better to make sure he pushed the outside shutters flat against the wall, and the accretion of light in the sitting-room was so strong that it hurt the eyes.

Varris was standing up, a limp smile on his face, holding out his hands.

"Come on, Hawker, we've had enough of this," he said. "I think Varris has had time to get clear by now. Take these fool things off."

Hawker knew, in that sudden flush of realisation, that he had been bluffed again. The figure was the figure of Varris, but the voice was the voice of Stayne. He came back and stood point blank in front of the impostor, his face dark with incredulity. The few deft touches of brown and grey flesh-paint had altered the features out of all recognition. A tiny layer of modelling wax had given him a completely different cast of nose: and the crimping up of the hair had actually altered the curve-line of his head at the back. In the white glare of light the deception was obvious, but in the dim shadows of the semi-darkened room it had passed without question. Knowing what he did of the movements of both men, Hawker had never for a moment suspected.

He just stood and stared, while the anger in his breast rose to boiling point. With something of a physical effort he got a grip on himself.

"Take these off, please," repeated Stayne, pushing his manacled arms out under Hawker's exasperated nose.

The Yard man snorted. "I'm not so damned sure that I will," he retorted.

Stayne smiled, a little deprecatory flutter of amusement, that scarcely moved his features. "Think it out, Hawker," he advised. "It's no crime to put on a little grease-paint and alter the contour of one's nose. I break no law if I do my hair in a slightly different way from the style in which I wore it yesterday."

"I'm holding you for aiding and abetting," rasped the detective. "And I'm warning you that anything you say will be used in evidence against you. Not only did you assist in the escape of Varris from jail, but you planned this layout for him. You got the whole thing fixed up by phone even before you found Tom Dobey in need of someone to pay bis fine. You pulled wool over the landlady's eyes, and you bluffed her pretty successfully. But you don't get away with it all the time, Mr. Stayne. That landlady will swear that you're not Harris. She will prove that you are not the man to whom she rented rooms in the name of Harris."

"Well? What of it?" queried Stayne respectfully.

XXX

Hawker was nearly bubbling over. He was so mad that he could not see even then that Stayne was still fighting for time, bluffing him still. "What odds will it make?" continued Stayne. "The fact that Harris rented these rooms and gave me permission to be here is a matter between Harris, myself and the landlady. We have broken no law. You might as well rope in the poor old girl downstairs and include her in the business. You're ageing. Hawker, that's what's the matter with you—you're losing your old close contact."

"I don't care a hoot about that," snarled the thoroughly angry man. I'm holding you. You're coming with me to Vine Street. Drop those darned hands. Those handcuffs don't come off till I've handed you in front of the charge sergeant."

Stayne dropped his hands and sighed.

"Ah, well," he muttered. "Have it your own way. It'll make a pretty tale for the papers."

And at that Hawker stopped dead. He realised in a tremendous burst of understanding what a charge against Stayne meant. Not only Scotland Yard, but he himself would be held up to the whitest glare of ridicule and obloquy. The story of it would make great newspaper reading. One of the most cleverly contrived prison escapes on record: the quick and urgent search for the missing man, followed by one of the smartest and quickest recaptures in the Yard's history. Then the gorgeous bit of news that, after taking their man up and locking him away in his cell again, the authorities discover that they have arrested the wrong man.

Fingerprints prove that, whoever the mystery man is, he is certainly not Templer Varris. Who then is the mysterious man in Scrubs? Why didn't he prove his innocence to the Governor before having the cell door slammed upon him—a perfectly simple thing to do?

They would make great play with the items of the official statement from headquarters, stating definitely that Templer Varris had been recaptured. And then the most priceless jape of all: the clever tracing down of the real Templer Varris, the actual appearance of a detective at his retreat while Varris was still in the building—the arrest of Varris by Chief Inspector Hawker under dramatic circumstances, only to discover that Templer Varris was none other than the notorious Colonel John Stayne, the Mystery-Maker.

Once more Colonel Stayne would blaze in the news headlines. Once more his name would be on the lips of amused but perplexed people in bus and tram and train. And once more they would see the remarkable individual wriggle out of it, leaving the police standing, with an empty case in their hands.

Hawker relapsed into a savage silence. All his boiling anger and spitfire resentment cooled away. This was a job that needed a bit of quiet thinking out. He had had quite enough liquid acid from headquarters for that day. True, the Chief had been very nice and suave and polite over the phone, but only Hawker knew how much concentrated caustic there was in those gently restrained sentences. He had whipped Hawker with verbal rods till he was mentally sore. And he was in no mood to take a second dose. He turned away uncertainly, chewing at his lower lip.

"That's better," said Stayne softly. "You've got to see reason in these things, old scout. You know as well as I do that your case wouldn't stand two minutes' cross-examination by a good lawyer. He would eat your ears, singe the hair off you. One can't aid and abet a man who is officially under lock and key at Scrubs Prison."

"Go to hell," said Hawker rudely, making for the door.

"Oh—Hawker," called Stayne, as the stocky figure passed through. "Leave me in peace for the next hour or two, will you? I'm going over to Paris tonight and I want to get a lot of packing done and odd jobs finished off?"

"Going to Paris, are you, my beauty?" said Hawker over his shoulder. "Now you just watch your step and see how far out of England you get tonight. I'm going right back to the Yard to have a consultation with the Chief about this business." Stayne rubbed his hands as he watched him go.

Stayne sat himself down at the mirror and rubbed the paint off on a towel. Then rapidly he applied some more, rubbing it with his fingertips till it was all evenly distributed. A little touch of powder whitened his eyebrows, and then he took from one of the silver tubes a neatly trimmed little grey moustache and adjusted it on his upper lip. He listened at the door for a moment. Down below he could hear the quiet murmuring of voices, and he knew that Hawker was having a final talk with the landlady before leaving.

Hurriedly he stripped off and tipped the contents of his pockets out on to the table. In the bedroom were all Varris's suits, hastily left when the order to fly came through from Tembridge. He changed into one, and, because it did not fit any too well, climbed into a fairly full-chested tweed overcoat. From a half-dozen pairs of gloves he carefully selected a pair of dull lemon hue. A final pat at the moustache to fix the gum and he sauntered idly to the stairs. Marbury, head of the Yard, to the life.

At the first big haberdasher's he stopped and purchased a black ebony cane, one with the largest ivory knob he could find. Lemon gloves and that famous ebony knobbed cane were the signs-manual of Marbury, autocratic ruler of Scotland Yard.

He lunched at a swagger restaurant and received a respectful salute from the *maître* as he took his place at table. Three others in the room recognised him and smiled. He nodded politely and retired into a brown study, an intimation that all his friends understood. Marbury was not "mixing" today. There was something on his mind and he was going to puzzle it out over lunch. They left him severely alone, merely whispering his identity to the intensely interested people at their own tables.

From there he took a cab to the bottom of Curzon Square and idly walked up to 8B.

XXXI

Hawker jumped into his car and drove rapidly back to Scotland Yard. Marbury was in and hinted that he would see him as soon as Hawker cared to appear. The detective went up, sourly aware that he was getting the raw end of the deal. He had worked day and night on the case and had honestly done his best, conscious of the knowledge that he was getting very little help or encouragement from the higher authorities. He was working against handicaps that were intolerable. Facts against John Stayne were sticking out a mile, and yet he hadn't a scrap of real evidence on which to base an arrest. As often as he spoke of arrest to Stayne, as often as a new opportunity presented itself of forcing the issue, Stayne came back with a completely unexpected reply that effectively checkmated him and broke up any hope on his part of lodging him behind prison bars. And all he got from the gods was a hoot and sarcastic reference to the fact that even Varris was still at large.

He entered the room and laid his hat on the table. Marbury was writing and he did not stop as his man came in.

"Well, Hawker? What's the alibi this time?" he asked gravely. And Hawker chewed his lip.

"Chief," he said, "I want your permission to knock Stayne off. He's running wild, playing the very devil. I know for a fact that he's up to his eyes in this business—and I just can't lay my hands on him. There's enough evidence against him in this last two days to put him away for twelve years—and he's still running around as perky as a sparrow. And I'm fed up with it. I can't get any further ahead while he stays out of jail. All I want is permission from here."

"Asking us to hold the baby, eh?" Marbury kept on writing, but the acid in his voice was chilled with ice. Hawker reddened.

"It isn't that at all," he said. "I just want to feel that I'm not playing this hand alone. I want to feel there's someone standing back of me."

"David Hawker, you have eight men detailed off to assist you. That is a team of nine, with you at the head. How many more do you want?"

"You can have the lot," said Hawker bluntly, "for two good shadowers and permission to arrest John Stayne."

Marbury dabbed his pen in the ink.

"It occurs to me," he said smoothly, "that the arrest of John Stayne is the sole object of your present labours. What you mean is that, up to now, you have not succeeded in getting sufficient evidence to warrant arresting him yourself?"

Hawker hesitated. That, in a nutshell, was exactly what it amounted to, but it was phrased about as coldly as one could well do it. The inspector bridled. That was about as much consideration as he had ever had on this case. The Chiefs wanted results, all the time and always. Nothing but success, and quick success, seemed to interest them.

"It's—it's a bit difficult, Chief," he muttered. "The blighter seems to be able to get news ahead of me. Just when I've got him all set for an arrest somebody sends him a mental wireless and he's ready for me—and Heaven alone knows where his scouts get the information from. I've got every end blocked up, none of my men is giving a word away. But he seems to tap in every time."

XXXII

The Chief referred to his notes.

"Up to the present moment," he said, "spurious banknotes to the value of fifty-two thousand eight hundred and seventy pounds have been received back at Threadneedle Street. More are coming in every day. The matter has now become so serious, and the forgeries so difficult to detect, that a special staff is now employed at the Bank of England to deal with it. The average return of fake notes has now swelled to five hundred and ten pounds a day. Of all the danger points in this affair, Stayne's is by far the most menacing. Once he became embroiled in it we knew we had a real fight on our hands. For that reason alone we roped in our best to handle it. And for that reason alone you were put in charge of the men on the road. It's your fight, Hawker."

Hawker looked diffidently at the empty fire-grate. "That means I don't get the warrant, eh?" he asked.

"Not necessarily. You know Stayne's end of it better than I do. You know where he stands. You have already told me the line he intends to adopt if we swing a charge against him. It seems to me that as fast as you collect new evidence against him he ripostes with alibis that prove conclusively that he was not there. When I say 'conclusively' I merely refer to a judge and jury, of course."

The intonation was as moderately regulated as though the Chief were discussing the merits of various holiday resorts for that year's vacation, but Hawker was not deaf to the bitter, accusatory note of failure that bit through it.

Hawker plunged. "Chief," he said dispassionately, "let me put it this way. I can't do much while he remains at liberty, checkmating every move we make. I say 'we' because I mean that I am not alone in this fight—Stayne is twiddling you round his fingers as much as he is me. I can do a hell of a lot once I get him cooped up in a twelve by eight. Once let me get him isolated away into a cell and I'll have all the evidence you want. I'll bust up his alibis inside forty-eight hours. I'll get my witnesses lined up so that the Lord Chief Justice himself couldn't pick a hole in their depositions. I'll have the whole layout fixed against him so that Lloyd's would bet ten to one on a full conviction."

"Yes?" said the Chief gently.

"I certainly will," declared Hawker. "You know as well as I do that Stayne alone planned the escape of Varris from jail. He alone put it through. He alone has kept him out of my hands ever since. That's crime enough to sling any man into the jug for a good long stretch. You know as well as I do that he worked that passport business, and you know—better than I do—that he is up to his ears in this banknote swindle. Marienne Varris went to him right away. Demorval has killed himself. Lady Demorval doesn't know which way to turn. The Embassy over there is at its wits' end, yelping to us for help by every post. Both Varris and his sister were employees there. They know the full strength of it. If they were on the straight, why didn't they come to us? No. Being crooks, they prefer the crook course. Marienne goes to John Stayne for help, and Varris himself takes five years' penal rather than open his mouth. That's the evidence, Chief—and it ought to be enough. You know it's the truth, and I can establish it up to the hilt as soon as I get Stayne shut away. On top of that Stayne tells me he is going over to Paris tonight. Once he gets over there, where will I be? Hey? In the name of God, tell me where I'll be!"

Marbury looked up and his eyes met Hawker's.

"Stayne goes to Paris tonight?" he repeated.

"Told me so himself. Boasted it. Chief, you've got to give me that warrant. You know what these French police are. If I've got to hold up this business, Stayne has *got* to go under lock and key."

Marbury reached over for a new pad. There was neither hesitation nor diffidence in his voice.

"You get it, Hawker," he said. "I'll stand by you, if I have to get remands till the cows come home. Why the devil didn't you tell me about Paris before? Heavens, man, things have moved too fast even for me. Get him! Arrest him on sight."

Hawker did not pause for thanks. He saw the brief order written and signed. He saw the Chief bang his thumb on a bell-push and pass the order over to the messenger who entered; and he saw the messenger depart. Without a further word he went out, a rankling sore simmering hotly in his breast. If Marbury had only done that two days ago—when all the fingers of common sense and logic pointed avidly in that obvious direction—the whole job would have been over and done with by now,

He went down to his own office and waited for the order, discussing the entire case with his team. His own pointed belief was that as soon as he had roped in the Mystery-Maker the whole problem of the continental banknote swindle would be laid bare. And at last he had got the Chief round to his way of thinking. No longer was he harassed with the knowledge that he was working alone and in the dark. The Chief was in with him and the whole power and resource of the Yard was now lined up behind him. He knew the signs: he knew what it meant when the Chief dropped that assumed air of courteous suavity. The mask was off, and the Chief was out for a fight. He would stand by now to the last clang of the bell.

Hawker made his dispositions, apportioning his men where they would do most good in this new drive. He phoned the house opposite, where he had taken the front rooms.

"Anybody arrived?" he asked pointedly.

"Yes, sir. An old gentleman with a slight paunch and a stoop to his shoulders, heavily pebbled glasses and walks badly; fallen arches or flat feet, I think. We let him go through."

"Good!" breathed Hawker to his crowd. "Varris is in. We get 'em both together. How long ago was that?" he asked.

"A little under an hour, sir. Nothing further has happened. Three men arrived soon after and sent word through. They're operating at the back, in the house behind 8B. They're dressed up as decorators, You'll notice them in long white coats. We haven't heard from them for half an hour, but I reckon they've tapped that tunnel by now. They were to report back here again inside half an hour if they ran up against a snag. Looks to me as though they've got through."

"Fine! Hold on there. We've got 'em now by the scruff of the neck. Stayne himself will be along soon—in a few minutes now. He may take some fool disguise, but tabulate every man who goes in. The boys round at the back will safeguard that end of it. Arrest out of hand any man who comes *out*! Get that? Make no bones about it. Arrest 'em, and I'll stand for it all. The warrant for Stayne is coming through right now: and we've got the blighters where we want 'em. They're making a break for the Continent tonight, and our job is to grab 'em all before they can get to Victoria. If you let me down on this I'll rub your faces out. Has the window-cleaner been out again?"

"No, sir. I've seen him in the breakfast-room again in his ordinary kit. He's changed back again."

"Well, don't risk him again. If the butcher boy calls, haul him back to the shop and get him identified before you let him go. That brute could get his living as a quick-change artist in vaudeville. Shadow everyone who goes through, if it's only the rate collector."

"I'll see to it," came the cheerful response from the other end.

"And another thing—has anything come through from our man on the Exchange?

"Yes, sir. That's how we knew here that they were making a break for it. Tembridge has telephoned through reserving two firsts on the boat train through to Paris."

"Two? Sure it wasn't three?"

"No, sir; two. They booked right through. And a couple of district messengers were sent for later on to see to their luggage."

"Great stuff, Tom. Which messenger office was called?"

"Victoria, sir; just by the station."

"Well, don't even trust *them*! Question 'em when they arrive and make 'em show their credentials. Bind them to silence and then let them through. We'll have this business fixed up and exploded before the sun goes down. I'll be along there inside half an hour. Keep your end up."

"You bet."

Hawker banged the receiver down and hurried through to the great main yard, where his car stood panting against the kerb.

In twenty minutes he was round in the front room, the whole atmosphere electrical with expectation. Tom, his subordinate, was waiting for him.

"The Exchange man has just been through again, sir," he said. "It was Tembridge on the line. He's ordered a taxi to connect with the boat train."

Hawker rubbed his hands. "Planning out fine," he breathed. "Pity that Exchange man wasn't put on before," he said. "How long has he been on the board?"

"Something under an hour. Couldn't get headquarters' permission before. There's been a bit of love-spat between us and the P.M.G. over it."

"Do they suspect us yet at 8B?"

"Don't think so. Calls come and go just the same."

"It doesn't matter, anyway. We've got 'em cooped up inside. Varris and Tembridge are there: Stayne is on the way. As soon as they are all in we'll go up and raid. I've got men posted at Victoria and six have gone down to Dover—just in case they work another miracle—which they won't curse 'em!"

"Are you going out, sir?"

"Yes. Your orders are to watch—and wait. And act on instructions. Don't argue about it. Just grab 'em off as they come out. I'm going round to see what's doing at the house at the back. Keep me informed of anything happening by phone. Daleson is on the phone round there: got the number?"

"Sure I've got it. Our man is attending to our section of the switchboard. He's guaranteed me a seven seconds service."

"Great stuff. See you later. I'll be back again in a quarter of an hour. We may be able to make a surprise entrance from round there and take 'em in the act. I'm just itching to get Stayne napping. He's had it all his own way up to now. But I've got the backing from the inside now—and I'll roast the liver out of him."

Hawker hurried down the stairs and out into the bright sunlight. He strode swiftly down the square and crossed over the road. All of a sudden his pace slacked and he stared. His heart took a violent jump into the region of his throat and little imps of joy began dancing about in his soul.

Coming towards him was his Chief, Marbury, head of the C.I.D. Marbury, the ice-cold block of logic, the terror of the wrongdoer, the man who held in his hands the swift direction of all the vast authority and power of Scotland Yard—Marbury come to take charge himself!

Just for a moment Hawker paused indecisively. There was no mistaking that elegantly groomed figure in the smart raglan and the soft grey hat. Never a detective on earth looked less like his part than the slim, neat figure walking quietly up that square.

But to those who knew him, the look, the walk, the dress, the air of quiet assurance and that indefinable, unanalysable air of authority that grows round a man in high State employ, all betrayed him, "Marbury of the Yard." If a further hallmark was required it was there in the slim black cane with the big ivory knob, carried slantwise under the arm at just that well-known angle and the pale lemon gloves slipped casually into his left hand crooked over the stick.

XXXIII

Marbury came on, approaching without even a sign of recognition. He took Hawker, flat-eyed and square in the face—and looked not at him, but through him, sheer through him as though he either did not exist or was as dirt beneath his perfectly-shod feet.

Hawker thrust a pipe into his mouth and fumbled for a match, taking a cue long since known between them.

"Got a match, sir?" he asked affably as Marbury drew alongside.

"I have—yes." The Chief stopped and the box was handed over.

"Varris is in there. Stayne hasn't turned up yet, but he's on the way." Hawker was talking through lips that were stiff and motionless. Marbury turned away indifferently.

"Oh, yes?" he said in the same odd, ventriloquial way, "and what else?"

"They've booked through to Paris. Next train from Victoria. Two of them. They're aiming to park Varris somewhere on the way. Two district messengers arrived to fix their luggage through. They'll be in disguise, and won't risk bobbing up at the Customs. An old trick—but it doesn't get by this time."

Hawker puffed away stolidly at his pipe. Marbury carefully flicked a speck of non-existent cigarette ash from his coat-sleeve.

"Are you going in, sir?" he asked in between puffs.

"Yes. I'll hold it from inside. Wait for my signal before you raid. A blind will be pulled down in the front room. When that comes down, step into it lively. But that won't be until Stayne appears. We can rope in the others and put them on the grid. Tembridge may stay dumb, but I can make Varris recite his piece. Are you going round to the back?"

"Yes, sir. I was on the way. Three men are already round there."

"It will be a cellar entrance: bound to be. You'll find the trapdoor and station your men underneath. Then wait for a signal. Any sort of a noise in the cellar above will do—knocking over a barrel or loosing off a gun. When they hear that, let them come swarming up. The Dover end all fixed?"

"Six down there. With photographs of them all. Stayne they know on sight."

Marbury nodded, slightly bored, and held out his hand for the matches.

"Thank you very much, sir." Hawker touched his hat in polite salute and passed on down the road.

The Chief continued his quiet stroll up the square. At 8B he paused, walked up the steps and knocked. Belham the imperturbable opened the door. What sign passed between the two was not visible, but it went over to perfection. Marbury stood for a moment, idly swinging his cane, chatting away as though discussing the advisability of waiting for someone who obviously was not in. Eventually Belham bowed, held the door wide, and the Chief entered.

As soon as the door was closed behind his back he made a leap for the stairs, going up them two at a time.

"All ready, Tembridge?" he called through to his assistant on the first floor.

"All ready and waiting, sir. There's a thousand pounds in notes in your wallet and your passport is in your pocket." Stayne was pulling off his moustache as he went up, refolding it back into its tiny silver case.

Up in his room he got through to Number One again.

"More trouble?" came the soft voice from the other end.

"All fixed now, sir. With a bit of fast work from you I think we can make it. Perrigo goes over tonight. We're on his trail all the way."

The soft voice cut in gently. "There must be no arrest, Number Three, you understand that? This matter must never come up in the courts."

"Obvious. Perrigo and Canning will not trouble any judge in ermine. They go the way of Kuhlmann, Velpan, Murdis, the Little Dancer, and a good many more we needn't mention. I will see to all that. Best they should die in Paris, I think. It will look like suicide—and the French police will stand in. Their end is already fixed—and they'll do it of their own free will!"

"One day," said the Chief softly, "you shall tell me how. I've yet to hear a story from your own lips—and I think it's time we met. Kuhlmann was a stroke of genius; Murdis was an inspiration. Yes—one day we must meet. We owe it to each other, Number Three."

"That will be when *you* are out of harness," said Stayne with almost a hint of an old-standing grievance in his voice. "I've had perfect help from you up to now—and now I want some real fast stuff, Chief."

"I know." The voice at the other end was tolerantly good-humoured, but somewhere in its fibres was that ring of steel, that undercurrent of deadliness that marked the man who dealt continuously in matters of life and death.

"I know—our man has been listening in too."

* * *

A gentle chuckle came over the wire, and the level voice said: "Well? Anything you want from our end will be delivered at your door, in plain vans, *tout suite*. What can I do?"

"If you've been tapping in on the line there isn't much in me telling you, is there?" said Stayne.

"To begin with, I believe you want two long-service district messengers. Yes?"

"Never wanted anything more urgently in my life."

"Don't worry. They're arranged for. They're here now dressed and waiting. It is not necessary for you to know their numbers. Commissionaires. I thought they would be better than district messengers and they're nearer to your own height. On a quick job, I think, they will pass all right."

"And a taxi-driver."

"Certainly. I couldn't see how else you were going to work it. Suitcases are in his cab right now. He shall be at your door in thirty-five minute—that is, ten minutes after the commissionaires arrive. Your own order for a taxi has already been cancelled by hand. I couldn't trust the phone. The rank number is on your exchange, and the Yard man might have got it. Was that what you wanted?"

"Perfect."

"Anything more, then?"

"No. Except to tell your two men that they will be questioned by Hawker's men. Their job is to get our luggage, take it to Victoria, and book it right through to Paris—register it. The two big suitcases go into our carriage. We already have a whole first-class compartment booked. When Hawker hails them, just tell them to play up to surprised innocence. They'll get through all right. Just one more thing. I think you had better send a second taxi to wait for us. The two commissionaires will go off with our luggage in the first taxi. Then the second one drives up a minute or two later. Hawker will let the first one go: only too glad to get the commissionaires out of the way."

"Agreed." Again the amused chuckle floated over from the other end.

"That's all then, Chief. And—thank you!"

"Please don't. I hope the Channel's flat. To our first meeting."

"Not, I hope, for years. You are much too smooth to work with."

Stayne hurried out and relocked the great library into its place.

Tembridge he found down in his own room. He was already dressed for his part, looking the capable, dependable commissionaire to the life. His get-up was perfect, even to the thick-soled, industriously polished boots. The pouch hung across his back at just the right angle, and his cap was as square on his head as though balanced and held there by straps.

"There's yours, Chief," he said, pointing to another complete suit on his bed. "They're watching us from the house opposite. Better change in here."

"I'll go and show myself in the breakfast-room first, just to satisfy Hawker that I'm moving about unmolested. He won't raid till he gets the signal. That will be just five minutes too late for him to get to Victoria. Where's Varris?"

"In the breakfast-room, for the same reason. Showing himself."

"How does he feel about it?"

"Beginning to like it, I think. He's all primed and knows just what to do. His taxi-driver's licence came through this morning in the pocket of a suit that had ostensibly just been returned by the cleaners. I'll say Number One certainly knows how to get things through. The Post Office detectives would never have dreamed of examining that parcel. It actually carried a genuine cleaner's label."

Stayne went through to the breakfast-room. As he entered Varris looked up and started badly. His face drained white and he half rose from his chair.

Then he said: "Oh—it's you, is it? Gosh, you gave me a fright."

"Keep it up—keep it up," said Stayne quickly. "They're watching you from opposite. How did you spot me? I got past Hawker with it just now—and he knows Marbury well."

"That tie," said Varris grimly. "It's the same one you were wearing this morning. You don't trump the same trick twice, Colonel."

For the benefit of those across the way, Stayne raised an imperious hand. "Come with me," he said, and Varris, the much-wanted jail-breaker, went meekly out.

By the time they got back to Tembridge's room the assistant had got Varris's disguise ready. The great wardrobe was wide open and from it Tembridge had taken a taxidriver's dress, complete right down to the obvious signs of long usage and the short-peaked vap.

"Quick, jump into that lot," he said. "I'll fix your face up as soon as I've seen what the real taxi-driver looks like. You take his place on the wheel. And you carry on driving a taxi round London till we get back with the job done. As a taxi-driver you can get digs anywhere you like. Better take some clothes out into the cab with you; leave them inside with our luggage and then carry them off with you when you leave the station. Fresh number-plates will be in the cab. Change them quickly. The driver will tell you where you garage—somewhere in one of the Government Service garages. The changed number-plates won't excite any interest there, it happens too frequently to that bus."

* * *

Both Stayne and Varris were rapidly changing, while Tembridge was rummaging about in the bottom of the wardrobe among a heap of leggings, trying to find a pair to fit Varris. Stayne, halfway through making up his face to a dull, weather-beaten red, tapped Varris on the arm.

"Are you all right for your piece?" he inquired.

"All set and ready," replied Varris cheerfully. "But you'll have to give me a minute or two at the wheel before you come out. I've never driven a taxi before."

"You'll fall into it all right. The gears are simple. Now get this, and don't make a slip, for God's sake! You will be waiting down in the front hall. The commissionaires will arrive and enter the house. That will give us time to put the finishing touches to our make-up. Then the taxi arrives. The commissionaires—Tembridge and myself—begin carrying out the luggage while the real commissionaires are downstairs waiting in the servants' hall. The taxi-driver stays at the wheel."

"Yes, I've got all that."

"Belham appears at the front door and asks the taxi-driver to give the commissionaires a hand with a particularly heavy steamer trunk. During that time of waiting I shall have had time to finish off your make-up to get you as near as possible to the Secret Service driver. The driver enters, thirty seconds elapse and you reappear, helping us with the trunk. We fasten it down with ropes beside you. You get up on the seat and wait for us. You'll have time to feel your gears and clutch them. The real driver accompanies Belham down for a drink. Tembridge and I climb into the cab and you drive off just as the second taxi arrives. Got it?"

"Fine." Varris rubbed his hands together and his eyes shone.

"You'll be as safe as houses. No one would ever suspect the man wanted for breaking out of Scrubs Prison to be tooling round London on the seat of a fully-licensed taxicab. Licences aren't obtained as easily as that, and there's a devilish stiff road knowledge test to be passed. Know your way round London pretty well?"

"Well enough on all the main points. But I reckon I can get away with it. What I don't know I can ask. And, anyhow, I shan't be too particular about picking up fares."

XXXIV

Tembridge had been watching at a curtained window on the landing. “Here come our two men,” he called. “A plain-clothes man is giving them the who-which-and-what down the road. Better hurry up in there.”

The two commissionaires appeared to satisfy their interlocutor, for in a minute or two the plain-clothes man nodded and they continued on their way.

Belham received them and they came upstairs to Stayne.

“All ready?” asked the Mystery-Maker.

“Yes. The second taxi is waiting round the corner. He flagged us as we came along. He will come around as soon as the first taxi pushes off. By the way, Number One sent this to Varris.” He held out a little parcel. It was Varris’s licence number.

One of the commissionaires had his hand bandaged. Tembridge pointed to it.

“Camouflage?” he asked.

“Yes. It’s noticeable, and I guessed it would help a bit.”

“You bet it will.” Tembridge rapidly wound a piece of bandage round his own hand and clipped a little sandy moustache down to resemble the natural one of the commissionaire. Having made their last preparations, they moved off downstairs, the two commissionaires going down to the servants’ hall with Belham.

The whole plan went off with the smoothness of a boat floating in oil. The taxi arrived and hooted outside. Belham opened the door, and Stayne and Tembridge emerged with suitcases in their hands. They piled a succession of portmanteaux into the cab, and then Belham called to the driver.

From the corner of his eyes Stayne could see Hawker, now back at the window, watching their movements critically. Hawker was not worrying. He knew that Marbury was inside and that anything that was happening there was happening with his full knowledge and compliance. And in any case Stayne had not arrived yet, and he was not expecting that window-blind signal till the big game was in the net.

The driver climbed off his seat and entered the house. Tembridge took his place at the door so swiftly that the back of the driver's coat was not lost to the view of the watchers opposite for more than a split second. It seemed as though he went in and a moment later was staggering out backwards with the steamer trunk, the commissionaires grappling with the other end of it. With their appearance together the crux of the scheme arrived. Stayne stumbled on with his heart beating faster. But not a sign came from the house opposite. A baker's roundsman drifted by. Stayne recognised him. But the man did not even raise a querulous eyebrow. He cocked a look up at the window, made the faintest of O.K. signals, and passed on.

The transference of identities was complete. Varris climbed up on the driver's seat and spent the next couple of minutes surreptitiously trying the clutch and gear lever. He found the reverse and backed the cab a little nearer the door, to get the "feel" of the wheel. Then he waited stolidly for the reappearance of his fares.

Stayne and Tembridge emerged with their final load, an assortment of magazines and travelling rugs. They entered the cab, wiping the perspiration from their heated brows.

Varris drove off, feeling gingerly for his second gear. As the cab disappeared up the road the second taxi drifted up and stopped at the door. The driver clambered down and rang the bell. Belham answered it, spoke to the man for a moment or two and closed the door again, while the driver went back to his cab and settled himself down to a period of waiting.

Varris drove fairly slowly. The cab was awkward in his hands. He had never driven a car before that possessed so abnormal a lock. The merest touch on the driving-wheel seemed to send the car swooping across the road-and Varris was not out to attract police notice. Neither was he particular about catching that boat train.

He drove to a garage out beyond Catford, where much of the luggage was transferred to a big waiting hire car. Stayne paid the owner in notes, and the owner asked no questions. He had done many quiet jobs for the Intelligence in a minor way, and the full facilities of his garage were at Stayne's disposal.

Varris ran his taxi into a little lock-up and climbed on the seat of the big car. Stayne and Tembridge ware already inside with the lights on and the blinds drawn. In a minute or two the big saloon was out and heading away rapidly for the Dover road while all hell seemed to be breaking loose at 8B, Curzon Square.

The showdown came through a simple fluke: simple but devastatingly effective. The phone bell rang in Hawker's room. The detective picked up the instrument and a smoothly-accented voice said: "Is that you, Hawker? The Chief here. How are things going? Have you made a move yet? I've been expecting a ring from you."

"Eh!" said Hawker blankly. He stared at the receiver as though it had suddenly tried to bite him. "Hey! Did you say you're the Chief? How in Hades did you get out of Stayne's house?"

"I beg your pardon?" Marbury's voice sounded as though it had just come straight off the frozen Pole.

"I said how in the name of miracles did you get out of 8B, Curzon Square? I've been waiting for your signal to step in and collar them."

"I regret that I haven't the faintest idea of what you are talking about."

Hawker let out an explosive breath of sheer disbelief. "But, Chief," he protested, "when I saw you, less than half an hour ago—when you were going along to see Stayne yourself — when you fixed up about the window blind—"

"Hawker—are you ill?" Hawker winced at the metallic chill in the tones.

"Ill? Me? Of course I'am not ill. What's the matter, Chief? What's gone wrong? Are you pulling my leg—having a bit of a joke on me?"

"Don't be a fool, Hawker. When I start joking on duty I'll recommend my successor to the chair."

"Do you mean to say you weren't around here less than half an hour ago? Are you telling me that I didn't speak to you out there in the street?"

"I haven't moved from this desk since you left me with the search warrant."

"My God!" breathed Hawker. Then he leapt into action. Without waiting to offer explanations to his Chief, he slammed the receiver down and ran for the door.

"Come on, you fellows," he yelled. "We've been toasted. Staynes caught us again. Jump to it. In you go and search the house from top to bottom."

The four of them pelted down the stairs and across the road.

Belham admitted them with an air of slight bewilderment. In two minutes the trick was revealed. Hawker went mad. There were the two commissionaires, looking as innocent as a couple of maidens. There was the taxi-driver, looking as perplexed as the rest of the household at the unceremonious entry. They had a perfectly lucid story to tell. They had been invited down below to have a drink until Mr. Stayne was ready to go. As he would be ten minutes or so, Stayne had sent them down to the servants' hall. They were still waiting. And that's all they knew about it.

Hawker raced to the phone and got on to his squad at Victoria.

"Hey! They've made it!" he cried. "The blighters have got through! All three of them. Two dressed up as commissionaires and Varris as a tax-driver. They left twenty minutes ago, Should be on the train by now. Two commissionaires and a taxi-driver. Grab 'em. Hold 'em and haul 'em off the train. Keep 'em till I get there. I'm coming right along now."

"Too late now, sir, there's no commissionaires on the train. I've seen every man go through the gates. Neither Stayne nor Tembridge nor anyone has got through here."

Hawker nearly squealed with impatience.

"Don't stand there bleating," he yelped. "Do as I tell you. Get on that train and find them. They're there. Question anybody who even looks as though they might be Stayne and Varris."

"Too late, I tell you, sir. The second half of the boat train left two minutes ago—and neither Stayne nor Varris was aboard it."

Hawker swore, definitely and vitriolically, as he banged the receiver arm for Exchange. "Quick—give me Trunks," he bawled. "I want Dover police—hurry."

When he got through he handed out long strings of orders, as a result of which a tough-looking squad set out for the landing-stage. The inspector in charge roped in all the railway and jetty officials, and together, while the boat train sped down the miles, they laid their plans to search and identify every single passenger as they boarded the boat.

And as the boat train steamed on, Varris was giving his car all the gas she could take. He whizzed down the open arterial road with the accelerator jammed down on the floorboard. Only once he stopped, and that was to change into Tembridge's neat blue chauffeur's livery coat. And as he drove, Stayne and Tembridge inside were changing from their commissionaire's uniforms into the dark green corduroys of station porters.

They arrived at the other end with twenty minutes to spare. Half a mile from the station yard the car stopped and two business-like, capable railway porters climbed out. In their crumpled peak caps, long-sleeved waistcoats and worn red ties they looked as much their part as any of the swarms of other porters that stand ready to meet the boat trains in and transfer passengers' luggage from the trains to the boats.

Walking separately they reached the station, timing their entrance to be on the platform as the giant train steamed in.

In a few seconds they lost themselves in the hurry and bustle of arrival. Stayne got a job at the first hail—carting four big suitcases on board for an old lady who knocked his tip down to sixpence because she was so exasperated at the long police inspection on the gangway head.

Number One had booked Stayne's cabin in a name that was sacred. The shipping office knew it as an accommodation name, used by a good many of the bigwigs when they crossed the Channel incognito. As Stayne hurried back down the gangway, grumbling angrily under his breath at the paucity of his tip, he caught sight of Tembridge, staggering along with a Noah's Ark trunk on his back.

They passed and Tembridge gave him a nod. It was the signal that their own luggage had arrived. Varris had brought in five portmanteaux and had stowed them down by the money-changers' booths. Stayne grabbed a couple and yanked them aboard. The scheme was working perfectly. Already Varris was on his way back to London; and the police watch on the gangways were reporting a definite blank. After a hurried consultation with his squad the inspector surmised that either the wanted men had decided not to risk the passage or that they intended trying to make it by a later boat.

In a little while Tembridge appeared with the other three cases. They closed and locked the cabin door, while the last of the passengers came abroad.

Tembridge grinned. "I'll say I'm getting pretty fed up with this changing business," he said. "I reckon I've been everything today except a royal duke. Where's my blouse?"

The last odd remark was occasioned by his hunt for the disguise that was to get them ashore at the other end. The passport trouble was the difficulty—Stayne decided that he would not risk trying to get through on the false passports in their possession. The cancel stamp could be easily forged later on, but the passport officer might ask questions, and Stayne decided that the safest plan would be to stay in the cabin throughout the trip.

They heard the dull boom of the siren as the bridge called for the right-of-way, heard the clatter of the winches as the last of the cargo was hoisted and lowered into the holds, heard the smack of the gangway going out on the jetty, and then the first deep rumble as the propellers began to thresh the water.

Stayne heaved a sigh of relief. "That's the first leg to us," he said. "I think we shall get through all right now. Did you see Perrigo at all?"

"Not a sign of him. I fancy he's gone over by air."

"Doesn't matter. We've got him now. How's your French?"

"Filthy. If any old dame comes cackling to me in correspondence school French she's going to get a streak of New Yorkese from me that'll startle her off her toe-nails. I'm going to stay dumb on this racket. I'd never get by the *douane*."

Stayne laughed. "You'd better fail in your efforts to get a job at Calais," he said. "Got your straps? Good. Grab your own bags. Give the crowd a couple of minutes to get on board and then we'll both go through together."

"What do we do with the railway rigs?"asked Tembridge. "Can't take them through the Customs. Gosh—that would blow the lid off."

"Out through the port, piece by piece," said Stayne. "You'll find lead sinkers, with tie-cords attached, in that grip there."

"Lead sinkers, are they?" muttered Tembridge. "They felt to me as though you were bringing over a museum collection of old typewriters."

Before they were halfway over the Channel the two Southern Railway men had disappeared. Their essentially English atmosphere had faded and re-emerged in the guise of a couple of French Customs *porteurs*. In their dark blue jean trousers and billowy blouses that came down to the knee and were washed sky-blue they absorbed something of the volatile French character. Over their shoulders their broad leather straps, on which, by some extraordinary feat of legerdemain, the real French *porteurs* can attach anything up to a dozen suitcases and go staggering off with them to the gaunt Customs sheds. On their heads they wore a kind of rakish semi-shako, crushed in on the top, and their shoes were of dirty white canvas with rope soles.

They stuck pungent Capitan cigarettes in their mouths and remade the make-up on their faces. Then, piece by piece, they jettisoned the railway clothes. Tembridge tied the sinkers to them and dropped them through one port while Stayne screwed his head up out of the other and signalled when the upper deck rail was free of inquisitive faces.

The packet was running into Calais Harbour in just over the hour, and as soon as the gangways were hoisted the old hustle and bustle began again. Fifty or sixty shouting, gesticulating *porteurs* came swarming aboard, yelling "Baggage? Baggage, m'sieu? Spik Engleesh."

Stayne gave the horde a minute or two to get thoroughly humming, and then he kicked the door open. With the fag-ends of cigarettes in the corners of their mouths they made their way through the press of passengers at the gangway heads, Stayne with three cases as his quota, Tembridge with two. Stayne was bawling out with the best of them, "*Attendez! Attendez!*" which is the French equivalent for "Mind your backs! Gangway!"or anything else that will secure a quick passage.

They scrambled ashore and headed for the Customs sheds, Stayne piling all five cases in front of him. They were unlocked and he opened them all with a disarming *naïveté* that charmed the heart of the Customs official.

"Where is your passenger?" queried that dignitary. Stayne intimated that he was at the booth changing money into French currency. The officer took a pull at his truly magnificent moustache, nodded indifferently, ran his fingers through some of the articles in a couple of cases, and dismissed him, chalking his weird little hieroglyphic on each.

Tembridge and he passed along to the train, Stayne with his eyes roving furtively along the streams of hurrying passengers. At last he caught the signal, a long delicate hand that carefully tapped the ash off a cigarette and then as carefully flicked the cigarette on to the track.

"Lord Demorval?"

"Yes. Come quickly. The landings are being watched from this side. Word has come through that you were not seen at Dover, but the authorities have reason to believe that you managed to get on the boat. The car is outside. Come along."

Demorval looked an aristocrat, and about him there was a faint, indefinable atmosphere of the highly-bred Gaul. His clothes were French, his neat little dark moustache was pointedly French, and the tiniest little strut in his walk suggested the full-blooded Parisien. They passed through the *Sortie* without notice. Out on the cobbled courtyard of the entrance a big car was drawn up, with a chauffeur sitting placidly at the wheel.

"This is Burdy," said Demorval under his breath. "He will see you through to Paris. There are inside blinds which will not be liable to spring up. And there is food in the locker. The old address?"

"Yes. Aren't you coming along?"

"I'm waiting to see if Perrigo follows by the night boat. He has not landed yet at Le Bourget—I've been on the phone. I must be back in Paris myself before dawn: you will get through all right. Meet me when you wish at the Café Sebillon. As Emil Flocard I have the end station inside. God speed."

The two *porteurs* had entered the car with the luggage. The blinds were pulled down, and as soon as Demorval was sure that no curious eyes had watched two third-class porters enter a first-class car—and stay there—he gave Burdy the signal and they were off, long before the last of the passengers were through the *douane*.

XXXV

Evening shadows were drawing in over the city of Paris as the car drove in through the *octroi*. When it drew up at a little hotel in a quiet side street off the main boulevard two very English-cut gentlemen stepped out of it. The blue jeans were carefully packed and stowed away in the luggage, and Stayne and Tembridge were dressed in Savile Row lounge suits.

The proprietor was English and knew them well. He had sheltered many a member of the Intelligence Department when they arrived in the gay city on errands that remained discreetly private.

They arranged for their rooms, ate a hurried meal, and stepped out into the cool night air. Through the Arc de Triomphe, at the beginning of the Bois de Boulogne, streamed the blaze of light of the great Paris Exhibition, and above it floated the great illuminated balloon that advertised it. Stayne gazed up at it, swaying gently above the sea of light.

During the day it was hauled up and down on a powerful winch, taking up relays of passengers for sightseeing trips aloft. Tembridge promised himself the modest thrill of a run up in that giant gas-bag when the more pressing affairs of the moment were settled. He never got that trip, and just then he never even suspected the dramatic part that swaying monster of silk and gas was to play in the lives of the two men they were hunting.

They paid a visit to the *Sûreté Générale* and had a long interview with the Chef de Police. The Chief had already been advised of their coming by Number One, and the coded letters that had passed hinted at the nature of their business. Stayne told him enough to rope him in urgently on their side.

"Monsieur," he said, "I am investigating the activities of a new company that has just been formed in London. I refer to the powerful combine which trades under the designation of the South American Development Corporation. You probably know of it."

The Chief nodded vehemently. "Yes—yes." He certainly knew of it. A very powerful combine indeed, with a capital of milliards of francs behind it. Milliards. It was a splendid company—one doing a fine work for the trade and commercial markets of Europe. Its aim was trade expansion with the practically undeveloped States of South America—a vast market as yet untapped. The company had floated loans in the countries to which they proposed to carry this tremendous new influx of trade. Only that week a big Paris road-making company had subscribed a million—all with the very best of securities behind it. Oh, yes, yes, he certainly knew of the South American Development Corporation.

Stayne hedged a little. The Chief was far too biased in favour of that obviously popular concern to stampede him into a panic.

"Well, the facts of the matter are these, Chief," he said gravely. "I am not in a position to question the *bona fides* of the S.A.D.C.—for all I know they may be a perfectly sound body and their aims beyond criticism. But this much we do know. Operating from London is a bogus company which is not only stealing the S.A.D.C. thunder, but is actually raising heavy loans on their account. What I mean is this: these swindlers come over here to France and Austria and to the capitals of pretty well every country in Europe, armed with perfect forgeries of the letterheads and stationery of the S.A.D.C. You over here are not to know that you are not dealing with the genuine people. They trade on your natural trust."

"You mean that money has been raised in France by people who are no way connected with the firm they allege they represent?" asked the abruptly.

"I don't say they have, sir, but I do distinctly say that that is their intention. I am over here to prevent it if possible—and to cut the matter short if they have already commenced operations. Almost any corporation in the world will lend money to the S.A.D.C., but certainly not to the precious coterie of high-class swindlers who are personating them."

"Do you represent the genuine company?"

"In a way, yes. I am working on their behalf—but principally in the interests of British credit abroad. You realise from letters written to you from the Treasury that we are in British political employ?"

"Yes, yes." The Chief certainly realised that the moment he read the letters. They were discreet, but, to one of perception, perfectly clear. He highly commended the action of the British authorities in endeavouring to cut short the nefarious enterprise of two of their own nationals in a foreign country. It was a magnificent gesture. With France almost bleeding to financial death, the mere thought of bloodsuckers at the arteries of French trade was intolerable. *Violà!* In what way could he assist? The entire resources of the *Sûrété* were at his command.

"This is what I want you to do, Chief," said Stayne, thanking the effusive little gentleman. "Attend the conference of bankers tomorrow and get from them a list of all the moneys raised by them for loan to the S.A.D.C. The full totals should be available with a little diligent research at the clearing houses. It will not be too easy, for the money is split up into francs, lire, guilders, marks, pesetas, and goodness knows what else. They will have to make it a mutual benefit task: but, no matter what labours it entails, I must have the full list in my possession at the earliest possible moment. The matter is grave."

"Monsieur, I will do my utmost," said the Chief.

"You must do more than that, sir: you must promise success. Every item must be found and the full amounts noted against each. I have in my possession a detailed account of the exact moneys raised by the company. I know to a penny what their commitments are and where the loans are placed. Any items additional to my own list will be false. They will be deliberate swindles and we shall find our own way of checkmating the criminals. Not a single bank nor a society in Europe shall lose one penny-piece over this matter. You will help?"

"With all I have, monsieur. The information you want shall be in your hands tomorrow afternoon. Special telegraph lines shall be cleared and the whole matter put on the priority list."

"Thank you, Monsieur le Chef." Stayne rose, and the ardent little gentleman bowed them to the door, raining a shower of benedictions on the heads of two foreigners who were magnanimous enough to assist him in cutting the claws of criminals in his own capital.

"That's fine," breathed Stayne, when they got outside. "The old boy doesn't suspect any more than we have told him. And he'll discover nothing from the banks. All we wanted from him we're getting—and that's that list. Perrigo and Canning are going to suffer a shocking hiatus in their own treasury before very long."

When they got back to their hotel they found a telegram awaiting them. It was in cipher and came from Lord Demorval. Decoded, it said simply:

Perrigo arrived on night boat. Left immediately for Pans by fast car.

"That means that this is where the balloon goes up," grunted Stayne—and he did not know how literally true the simile was.

Tembridge nodded and put a match to the flimsy, watching it slowly burn to ash which he powdered in his fingers.

"And where to now?" he inquired.

"The Club Tabarin," said Stayne grimly. "We beard that crowd in their own den."

"Anything you say suits me, Chief," said Tembridge simply. "But I guess this is where little Valdon totes a gun along." He reached into his grip and fished out a dull and deadly-looking automatic. "After what that guy Varris got in the buffet there I reckon you darn nearly want a machine-gun with you. Well, if they want a piece of rough stuff, no doubt we can carve them off a slice. Haven't had a scrap for weeks. Tails are bad form in Paris, aren't they?"

"Dinner jackets will do," Stayne replied. "I'll wait for you down in the hall. Are you going to disguise at all?"

"Nothing very exceptional. Don't think it's really necessary. Neither Perrigo nor Canning knows me from Adam. Think I'll go as a typical American tourist? How do you tog up a typical American tourist? I'll stand for the fairly tightish trousers and a slight cut in at the waist: I'll stand for a saw-edge straw hat with evening dress and a pair of gogacks, but I'll be everlastingly disintegrated if I'll stand around chewing gum." The young gentleman retired, cheerfully and emphatically removing the safety-catch from his gun.

Stayne dressed and very carefully rubbed a little deeper bronze on to his tanned skin, and put a slight suspicion of a sag under his eyes. He gave the faintest greying of his hair at the temples and added a perfectly cut grey moustache under his nose. The moustache was a work of art; it was slightly bunchy in the centre, thinning out at the edges, and so perfectly threaded on the tiny bits of webbing that it looked as natural as a real moustache, even at close range.

When he stood away from the mirror he looked exactly what he set himself out to be, a tall, cultured man of the world, slightly matured in years, something, probably, in the Corps Diplomatique, a quiet-voiced emissary whose integrity could not be questioned—a man who had served his Government perhaps a little too long in tropical countries, and on whom malaria fevers had left their mark. He looked anything but strong, rather on the fragile side, and the exquisitely fitting dress suit accentuated the deception.

Downstairs he found his assistant had contrived, in some totally inexplicable fashion, to suggest the American travelling for pleasure. There was nothing of the caricature about it, nothing that implied exaggeration, but he was "it" all right, the cheerful, youthful American, in Paris on his maiden trip, and thoroughly enjoying himself, bent on just one thing, and that was having a good time.

He had a taxi waiting, and together they travelled out to the long sloping hill that lies in the shadow of Sacré Cœur, Montmartre, one of the poorest districts of the city, but where it costs ten francs an hour to breathe plain air, and where even cold water goes down on the "addition."

They drove to a semi-deserted little café almost opposite the Club Tabarin. Night life on the hill does not begin until the real, hardworking Paris is in bed and asleep, and the night was still young. At midnight the theatres would empty and the big restaurants close. Not until then would the overplus of humanity begin to drift out to Montmartre—and Montmartre does not close its doors till the dawn is high.

The Club Tabarin hid its light under the guise of a squalid little *épicerie* shop, one that remains open all night to supply sudden urgent demands for supplies from the myriad cafés and nightclubs around. But on through the dim-lit shop a passageway led through to a lift. A certain signal on the bell brought the lift down, and not until that signal was given would the lift move. Habitués of the place knew the signal, and new visitors, having been approved, were apprised of it.

XXXVI

The café proprietor seemed surprised to see visitors out that way so early, for it was scarcely ten o'clock yet and the hill was dead. Stayne spoke to him in the polished French of the Elysée, and the proprietor seemed more surprised than ever. Tembridge sat himself opposite a vile concoction of Amer Picon and simulated a keen relish in a new drink.

"Your friend," said the proprietor."I would suggest that he does not drink too much of that Picon. It is not good for him—spoil the stomach for him."

Stayne smiled a little tolerantly.

"My friend," he said, "is enjoying himself. You understand? He is in Paris for the first time, and he wants to try everything once. He has also visited the Casino de Paris and the Folies Bergère, and the several other interesting places that most young men like to sample in this charming city." Stayne lowered his voice and glanced surreptitiously round the café. "Now he is looking for something a fit tie more exciting," he said suggestively.

The proprietor eyed him shrewdly. "So many things in Paris are exciting," he said guardedly. "Paris caters for many tastes. What is it monsieur wishes to do?"

"He had thought about having a little flutter with the shoe. Or perhaps a few francs on the wheel." Stayne glanced away off-handedly and added, "A little turn at *roulette* or *chtmin* does no harm, monsieur—I thought perhaps some little quiet place might be found—somewhere where the *gendarmerie* will not spoil a little evening's entertainment with a raid."

"Does m'sieu wish to gamble heavily?"

"Oh, no—he's just out to see what it's like. What are the limits?"

"Some are as low as ten francs a minimum."

"Well—somewhere where it's not too high: and where they serve a bottle of champagne that actually came from grapes. The charges don't matter: he has all the money he needs. That's all, m'sieu; somewhere with a reasonable minimum, where it's pleasant and the wines are good, where there is no risk of a raid—and handy." That's all he said, and smiled disarmingly. "If you can find one that covers all that I'll be eternally indebted to you."

The proprietor smiled too. Stayne's conditions were reasonable enough, but he did not realise that in making them he had penned him down to the Club Tabarin.

"I will telephone," he said. "I'll not be long."

He disappeared into a room at the back of the café, and Stayne could hear the soft rumble of his voice over the wire. He was gone about five minutes, and when he returned he was smiling and nodding.

"You see the little *épicerie* three doors down," he said, coming out to the door. "Walk straight in and through to the back. You will be quite all right. No one will question you. You will see a lift with a bell-push by the door. Ignore that bell-push; it simply informs the owners that an unauthorised person is attempting to gain admission. Behind the frame of the lift shaft you will find another button. That is the one. Your signal is two long rings, a long pause, and then three short rings. Use that whenever you go there. And they know who it is before the lift is sent down. Thank you, *au revoir*, m'sieu—and good luck to your friend."

Stayne gave him a hundred-franc note for the drinks and waved away the change. "I am deeply obliged," he murmured as they headed to the little shop.

* * *

Two steps led down to the dismal little store. A smell of old stale foodstuffs assailed their nostrils, and through it came the reek of an oil lamp. From behind the cluttered counter an old woman looked up at them through thick steel-rimmed glasses, squinting horribly.

Seeing the flash of white shirt-fronts she bobbed her head in a grotesque apology for a bow, and without a word her attention dropped back to the perusal of an evening paper which was held a few inches from her nose.

They passed through to the passage and found the lift. Stayne fumbled down the woodwork behind the shaft for the hidden button. His fingers encountered it, and he pressed it, giving the signal, two long rings, a few seconds' pause, and then three short rings. There came the soft hiss of the lift gliding down.

It was empty, but as soon as it touched the bottom the gates opened automatically. They entered: at the pressure of their feet on the flooring the gates quickly closed again and the lift went up.

"Reckon this is why Varris went out by the window route," muttered Tembridge, slipping his automatic into a side pocket. "Got your gun with you, Chief?"

"No," said Stayne gently, "but I have something else, equally efficacious and less noisy."

Tembridge grunted."Let's hope we shall need it," he said. "I'd like a good smack at this bunch. Gang-work: don't like it. Doesn't give a man a chance unless you've got half Woolwich Arsenal packed in your carcass. Personally, I prefer my champagne in glasses. And I like to drink it. When it comes to presenting it, in bottles, on your head, then I take leave to slip the safety-catch."

The lift slid to a standstill and the doors opened. Just in front a perfectly groomed man was waiting to receive them, a smooth smile of welcome on his heavy face. "Canning, for a million pounds," muttered Stayne to himself as they stepped out.

"I am delighted to receive you, gentlemen," said the man, stepping forward with extended hand. "We are always very pleased to receive English and American friends here. May I hope for the pleasure of your company as often as you care to come?"

"Thank you, indeed," returned Stayne. "This is my friend, Mr. Woolmer, of New York."

"How do you do? My friend at the café opposite has already given me information of your requirements. If you'll just step along here I'll show you the various salons and then you can get your own bearings. You'd rather be alone for the first half-hour, I suppose? Yes, of course, most us do."

Stayne bowed and politely intimated that perhaps a bottle of champagne would not be amiss as a preliminary to a little tilt against Lady Chance. The manager was all acquiescence.

Suddenly, as Tembridge stood handing over his hat and light overcoat a brilliantly uniformed young black page-boy, two deeply sonorous rings came on the lift bell and then a quick one. It was more like the deep-throated zoom of a buzzer than the strident note of a bell, but it made both men prick up their ears.

"If you'll excuse me just one moment, gentlemen," said the manager, smiling. "Another guest arrives."

He stepped back to the lift and operated a series of buttons on a brass disc and the lift went sliding down.

They heard it reach the bottom, heard the lift gates open and shut, and in a moment or two it came winging up again.

A young man stepped out, a handsome, nervous-looking young man, who glanced uneasily at the two strangers. Canning hissed in his ear as he passed him: "Go through, Raymond, and keep out of sight—*she* is not here yet"

Tembridge smiled enigmatically at his chief.

"Something doing," he whispered. "Come along, let's go through to the gilded haunts of vice."

They found themselves in a suite of apartments in striking contrast to the dismal hole they had just left down below. The furnishings were luxurious in every sense. Beautiful tapestries hung from the walls, interspersed here and there with oil paintings that were genuine works of art. Miniature marble statuettes and pieces in bronze and jade were scattered through the rooms with prodigal hand. Real old brass braziers, bearing in their finely hammered lines the stamp of the greatest craftsmen of India, diffused the faintest of alluring perfumes on the air. Their feet sank ankle-deep in carpets as soft as silken floss.

The actual gambling salons opened from a sort of central hall that was built in a wide-swinging circle. The ceiling was vaulted and heavily gilded, the panels between being painted with all the French eye for perfect colour and worship of the human figure in the nude. Heavy velvet curtains, of a deep plum purple, draped the arched entrances to the salons, from which, even at that hour, came the buzz of voices, the soft click of the celluloid ball and the ceaseless drone of the croupiers' voices.

The buffet was away to the right, a sumptuous counter of green marble and waxed oak. Two iced-water fountains trickled musically, one at either end, to cool the humid air. The place was very hot, centrally heated, and, with the braziers going, both felt the immediate stuffiness of the atmosphere.

Tembridge gave a nod to the white-coated servitor behind the counter, and in a moment a couple of fat magnums were thrust down into a silver tub of crushed ice.

"Those two rooms there are for roulette—the near one has a maximum of ten thousand francs, in the other the sky is the limit," said the suave voice of Canning at their side. "You can take your choice. We do not like our clients to go too high unless they wish. Hence the special tables with the limits. In those two rooms there, baccarat only is played. In that one fantan, and in that one poker, but I shouldn't advise you to risk poker; they play pretty high and fast in there. And I'd rather you got your land legs here first. Goodbye—wish you luck."

Canning withdrew with easy grace.

"Too darn nice to be true," growled Tembridge, lighting a marvellously pungent stogie.

Stayne hissed a quick warning. "Look—coming through the *portière* there, Lady Demorval!"

Tembridge puffed away at his native cigar and cocked an eye along at one of the great gilded mirrors with which the walls were hung. In its reflection he could see the figure of a tall, hard-mouthed woman, gorgeously gowned, coming in through the hanging draperies. She was wearing one of the latest creations from the Rue Rivoli, cut daringly low at the top, but modestly low at the bottom to hide her thinning legs. Round her neck was a rope of pearls, and across her shoulders one of the most beautiful ermine cloaks that ever came out of the Paris ateliers.

Stayne stared at her reflection. In spite of her magnificent toilet she seemed listless and dull. She walked as though walking were a burdensome duty, and her arms hung listless at her side. Her eyes were heavy and there were dark rings round them. Her neck was almost skinny, and there were sunken cavities round her collarbones. Her hair, beautifully coiffured though it was, was lustreless. She walked to the buffet, draped her cloak round her as though she felt chill, even in that heated atmosphere, and ordered an absinthe.

The forbidden drink was served and she began straining it through the square of sugar with unsteady fingers.

"God—how that woman has changed," breathed Stayne. "She—she used to be one of the most beautiful women in London. She was ravishing. When Demorval married her every club in Piccadilly toasted 'One of heaven's lucky men!' And look at her. Why, she's a gawk—a bony scarecrow."

"Dope," said Tembridge laconically. "Seen 'em before. Know the signs. Some of 'em go that way. Seen others that run to fat. Had a lot of that sort of thing out in God's Own since prohibition came in. Just dope. She's waiting for her shot now. Going crazy for it."

With the acute sensitiveness of the dope addict whose anodyne is denied, she seemed to realise that the two men out in the centre were talking about her. She gave them a malignant stare and looked with dull surprise when she saw that they had their backs turned towards her.

She was having a sharp and acrimonious conversation with the server behind the bar. Stayne could follow it. She was demanding to see Canning, and the server was assuring her that Canning's last orders to him were that he was not to be disturbed on any account. Apparently the altercation was one of old standing, for the server accepted the situation with philosophic patience, scarcely paying any attention at all to the woman. Lady Demorval had lost her last vestige of dignity. She argued with the attendant like a semi-drunken slut at a public-house bar pleading with the barman for just one more glass of beer. There was something of a malignant smile of contempt in the barman's eyes.

The two men sat down at a little ebony table as the champagne was brought over, deliciously cold and invigorating after the breathless tepidity of the air.

"There's the whole crux of the tragedy there," said Stayne slowly. "It's dope all right. Cocaine, I should think, with about five per cent heroin. She'd need heroin by now to give anything of a kick to the cocaine. There's the whole root of it. Why on earth didn't Varris tell me about this? He must have known. Ah! See, here comes Canning. Watch! He's been keeping her short in her dosage."

As Canning entered Lady Demorval seized him by the arm and poured a hot string of vehement sentences into his ear, shaking him by the sleeve and protesting shrilly when he tried to disengage his arm. Canning was bluntly refusing to comply with her demands.

Stayne shivered."This is dreadful," he whispered. "Canning must have been playing her along for months to have got her into this state. Why, she's half animal. And a year ago that woman was one of the shining lights in the Chancelleries here, a dazzling magnet to any man's attention. What on earth can have happened to bring about this terrible change?"

"When she married—was it a love match?" asked Tembridge.

"On Demorval's side, yes. But I'm not so sure about her. It was a brilliant affair, and nothing finer could possibly have been arranged from either side—regarded as a purely social union. One of those sort of marriages that *ought* to be. Know what I mean? The thing seemed just 'right' from every point of view. Demorval, I know, was madly in love with her."

"That's put the finger right on the spot," said Tembridge decisively.

Stayne raised his glass and smiled.

"It's a thousand to one," went on Tembridge solemnly, "that that woman simply made it a marriage of convenience when she married the peer. She was in love with someone else—madly, violently, I should think—the type who take to drugs always are: they've never got their emotions properly under control. And that someone else had other ideas. He must have turned her down stone cold. She tries to get an opiate out of the high lights, the glitter and the excitement of marriage with the Diplomatic Corps. It suffices for a year or two: the constant change, the travel, the entertaining, the close association with the keenest brains in the land, the Royal parties and all the rest of it: it all acts as a narcotic for just a little while. And then the old gnawing hunger breaks out again, all the more virulent for having been kept in suppression so long. Hidden fires burn deep. And a woman like that would simply let every damn thing slide once she realised she was treading a hopeless road. And that's what she's done, Chief. She's kicked right of the traces and she doesn't care a brass sou what happens. She no longer cares, because she no longer feels. Something has gone dead inside, and only dope can get the misery out of her soul for a passing hour of forgetfulness. She needs that artificial kick in order to keep off the poison bottle."

Stayne inspected the effervescing liquid thoughtfully.

XXXVII

"I believe there is something in what you say," said Stayne. "Ever since Miss Varris first brought this matter to us I've been puzzling out why Lady Demorval suddenly, from the very heights of grace and charm, stoops to placing a concoction of villainess and vamp. Canning and Perrigo must have introduced her to cocaine, given her a kick in life to which she had been dead for years; gradually increased the dose until it took hold and she couldn't break it. From then on the rest was easy. The foundations of decency and dignity were cut away, and all that remained was the screaming demand for more of the fire that had burned her. Drugs had undermined her, and drugs alone could keep her going. They've got all they wanted out of her on the promise of more supplies."

"Yeh—and now they're holding up on her to get a last final demand out of her. Canning's holding back till Perrigo turns up. He should be coming in soon. Seems to me it was through the victim that they got hold of the banknote paper. She'd be able to get into touch with people in London, be able to wangle things that no one else could nose into."

"It's clearing, certainly. But to me the most tragic figure is Demorval. She has flattened him out for life. Poor devil—didn't you see the misery in his eyes—at the station there, in Calais? Terrible. Just dumb misery and hopelessness. And being perfectly charming with it all, too."

"What are we going to do about that woman, anyway?"

"I'll get in touch with Number One in the morning and give him the full facts. It looks to me like a nursing home for life. One of those private homes that are all of a lunatic asylum and almost a prison. There's nothing else for it. That sort of thing has to be pretty well hushed up. But medical certificates from this side should do it. The rest will be easy, over in England."

"And Demorval?"

"I think he will prefer to remain just Emil Flocard, waiter at the Café Sebillon. His real identity will be gone forever. He can do great work still for Intelligence—and his heart and soul are bound up in the work. It would be by far the best way out for both of them. Demorval is above me in the Secret Service. He won't let go of that. It's his life blood. His keeping of this affair till London got busy is just another feather in his cap. Demorval was the first to find out about the forged script. And that brings us down to the subject of Arthur Raymond."

"It damn does!" said Tembridge raspily. His underlip was thrust out and he was reddening.

Stayne chuckled quietly. "Oh! So you've found out about that, have you?" he murmured.

"Yep. The rat! Marienne told me."

"Perhaps you rather—rushed her?" The voice was infinitely solicitous.

"Did I hell! I wrote her a perfect little note and sent it around—with flowers. Never rushed a word. Took four pages to do it. And she called me up on the phone."

"And turned you down?"

"Flat as a busted tyre. Aw, shucks! I only stand third on the list."

"Third?"

"Yep, third. She said that she knew exactly her feelings in the matter and that they were not open to change. Said she was very much in love with Arthur Raymond—the mouse!—And would marry him, no matter what he had done and no matter what happened. And next to Arthur Raymond—the pop-eyed hop-toad—she said she liked you! Drat you."

"Me?" Stayne's fingers shook ever so slightly on the stem of his glass.

"She said so. So now, both of us being in the same boat, we have the pleasurable privilege ahead of us of finding the cleverest forger of this or any other generation, keeping him clear of the twelve years' penal servitude he undoubtedly deserves, the mud-brained dimwit, and marrying him off to the sweetest kid in this or any other hemisphere. Jam for everybody, bar us!"

Stayne rose. "Come on—you're supposed to be a young blood out on the loose, mad to fling your monthly allowance on the wheel. No use mopping fizz all the night."

"Where away?" asked Tembridge, crushing out his cigarette.

"I'm going to get hold of Lady Demorval. You must get fixed up first at a roulette table, or it will look suspicions. We'll take that end room. You can cover my movements from there. I'll get hold of her and confront her personally, if necessary. But I must get hold of the address of the office where Perrigo and Canning are conducting their coup. I can force it from her, I think. Also Raymond. We *must* find out where that boy stands. The rest will depend on the information we receive."

They strolled into the roulette-room, the biggest salon of them all. This was the one where, in Canning's words, "the sky was the limit." Play was running pretty high. Gamblers were standing round, gazing in a kind of fascinated apathy at the little white ball spinning and bouncing about in the whirling wheel.

Lady Demorval was out at the end of the table, regarding the whole business with the keen, watchful gaze of the spectator forced by circumstances to be out at the touch-lines and not mixing in with the fun and excitement of the game.

"Madame is not playing?"

She turned swiftly and her torpid eyes made a rapid survey of the man who spoke. She saw a tall, well-dressed man, with a deep tan on his face and a neat grey moustache that somehow put him into the category of the fifties: a complete stranger to her.

"No—I am not playing tonight. This table is unkind to me."

"Going through one of the bad spells?"

"Rotten. I haven't picked a franc off that table for twelve consecutive nights."

The affable stranger nodded. "It's wise if you have the willpower to let the table sleep for a while. A night or two may see the luck change. Never back a real bad run."

"My trouble is that I can't," said Lady Demorval, with all the frank bluntness of the real gambler. "I'm broke for a day or two—waiting for further remittances from England."

Stayne bowed. "Perhaps, madame, you would permit me to—?"

Again that quick, furtive look swept him up and down, a look that was dead, fish-eyed, and yet penetrating with the subtle instincts of the drug addict.

"I am staying in Paris for some time," went on Stayne imperturbably. "If I can be any slight assistance to a countrywoman, the privilege and the honour will be all mine."

Lady Demorval hesitated for a moment, then, gathering her wrap about her, she swept towards the door of an ante-room leading out at the back of the salon. It was a private room where debts were settled and such little matters arranged between temporarily embarrassed clients and the management. No one would disturb them in there once the little panel in the slot was turned to the word "Occupied."

Stayne followed her in and quietly closed and locked the door.

Softly as the action was performed, she heard it and turned with surprised challenge in her eyes. But Stayne was fumbling in his wallet, pulling out a sheaf of English banknotes of high denomination.

"How much was Madame thinking of requiring?" he asked courteously, and her eyes gleamed.

"Why—why do you wish to assist me?" she suddenly asked.

"It has been done before. You look a good gambler—and roulette breaks through the conventions. My action is perhaps a little unusual, but, of course, I shall require security if you need a large amount."

"My usual reserve before staking a bet is two thousand pounds," said Lady Demorval flatly.

"That sum is quite reasonable. I have it here. What security can you offer?"

Demorval's wife swept the magnificent ermine from her shoulders. "This cloak," she said, without the slightest touch of arrogance, "cost seven thousand four hundred pounds last week in the Rue Rivoli—and many of the skins were supplied by myself."

Stayne smiled. "I would not dream of so embarrassing you," he said gently." It would look odd indeed for a gentleman to be seen walking out with an ermine cloak over his arm—a cloak which but a few moments before had graced the shoulders of a charming lady."

She unfastened the collar of pearls from round her neck and tossed them on the surface of a perfect buhl table. They lay there shimmering in the down-beating blaze of a great candelabra overhead, like imps' eyes shining in a woodland sunlight.

"Those are not quite so valuable," she said simply." The centre row is not all genuine. It was impossible to match them properly, but the matching is being done by slow degrees. The outside rows are all perfect gems, though. It should fetch over three thousand at open auction."

"Put them back, madame. Suppose we deal in a simple note of hand? What you have told me is quite sufficient—and a signature is so much nicer and—easier, shall we say?"

Lady Demorval inclined her head the merest fraction of an inch.

"If you require to know my name," she said, "it is Lady Demorval. Until recently my husband was attached to the Embassy here in Paris. You may remember that he died recently under an anaesthetic."

"I recall the matter, madame, and so far as I am concerned your signature will be ample for me."

He put the notes on the table beside the pearls, and made a little gesture inviting her to replace the gems round her neck. While she did so he prepared a little slip of paper—"I O U £2,000 (two thousand pounds)," and she signed it with scarcely a glance.

"You are not even asking who I am?" Stayne asked with a smile.

"It is hardly necessary, sir. The money shall be left here for you within a week. Will you make it convenient to call?"

"It may not be necessary, Lady Demorval."

There was an odd significance in the simple sentence, a queer note of warning that rang instantly on her high-strung nerves. She was in the act of counting through the notes. There were twenty of them, crisp and white and new. Each for a hundred pounds. The movement of her fingers ceased abruptly as a flood of suspicion swept over her. It was as though a strident warning had sounded in her ears, and the general suspicion, the whole outlandishness of the transaction, struck her with full force. This affable, courteously-spoken man held her signature for two thousand pounds. For what? She stared at the notes again. They seemed genuine enough. There was no mistaking that perfect, crisp feel of the genuine English banknote.

The feel of that note is not, and never has been, duplicated. But Lady Demorval was too intricately bound up in the affairs that were happening back in the locked rooms of the gloomy Old Lady of Threadneedle Street to take much stock of the feel of banknote paper. She agitatedly looked at the numbers. But they gave her no clue. She did not know what series numbers Perrigo and Canning had used on their spurious notes. Then her eyes dropped to the signature.

Stayne saw her eyeballs jerk, and what little colour there was in her face drained away, leaving it white and ghastly, save where the rouge clothed its nakedness with a bright dab of colour that only added to its stark display of staring artificiality. For in place of the signature of the Governor of the Bank of England was the neatly written name—ARTHUR RAYMOND.

Lady Demorval threw her hand up over her eyes. She staggered to a low, heavily-cushioned divan and collapsed upon it, moaning as though stricken. The notes fluttered from her limp hand and cascaded in a black and white stream over the carpet.

There in that signature she read the end. Discovery and the inevitable showdown had come. Who Stayne was she hadn't the vaguest idea. The only thought that was searing through her brain just then was that the man *knew*. He had planned that approach. He had inveigled her into that room. He had prepared the false notes—*somehow* he had actually got hold of some of their stolen paper. And he *knew* their king forger's name. He had actually forged Raymond's own signature.

XXXVIII

Lady Demorval realised that this stranger was fully aware of the whole plot: that he was aware of her connection with it. And now she was trapped like a rat in a cage. She was alone with him in a locked room—and he the man of mystery, held her signature on a bond for two thousand pounds.

Her drugless brain cursed Canning. Fool! Why hadn't he given her that shot of snow? With the virulent fire of that potent drug pouring through her veins she would have known how to deal with this new menace. Her torpid brain would have reacted to its exhilarating stimulant and she would have had that meddling old fool at her mercy. As it was she couldn't think, she couldn't even begin to scheme for a way out. Her brain was dead, dead as blown leaves scurrying along in the icy blasts of winter. Small beginnings were gone from her.

Next moment Stayne was over her, struggling madly with a woman who, with all the strength of mania, was fighting to get a tiny blue poison bottle to her carmined lips.

Her bony fingers, no longer feminine, but clawing with all the bony harshness of a vitalised skeleton, gripped the bottle, her thumb pressed tight over its mouth.

With her free hand she clawed at him like a fiend. Stayne turned his shoulder on her and fought for possession of the bottle. But even his steel-fingered strength could not break the hold of those bony talons.

Suddenly he took the drastic course. He whipped his left hand away and clamped it hard over her mouth and nostrils.

Her eyes began to roll wildly. The seconds dragged on, and she fought frantically against his grip. But the slow strangulation of air from the lungs began to tell. Blood was suffusing her neck to a dull beetroot colour. She was flat on her back, and against Stayne's weight helpless to do anything except hold that vixenish grip.

Sudden as her startling accretion of strength was, its desertion was equally swift. The superficial power in her muscles cracked out as rapidly as it had formed. She relaxed completely and lay back, as though in a semi-faint, moaning almost inaudibly, her bosom rising and falling to the storm of emotion that shook her. Stayne found himself standing above her, wet at the temples, pouring out a bright amber liquid from the wicked little blue glass phial. Where it struck the carpet it turned the rich purple colouring to a sick, unhealthy green.

He wiped his forehead and straightened his crumpled clothes.

After a little while she opened her eyes and stared up at him, heavily, like one just waking from a long sleep.

"Why—why have you come here to me?" she asked weakly.

He pulled up a chair and sat down beside her. "I want the address of Perrigo's office," he said directly.

"I don't know it—I've never been there," she moaned.

"Lady Demorval, you are lying. You've been there many times. You must have done. Perrigo has supplied you with cocaine from there."

"Don't torment me—please. Why don't you see Perrigo? Why—" A slow, puzzled look crept into her eyes. "Who—who are you?" she asked dazedly. "You're not a policeman? You're not from Scotland Yard?" She passed a hand nervously across her forehead.

"No, madame—you should know who I am. I belong to the other Service. That should imply a great deal—to *you!*"

She seemed to go limp again, pondering another stunning blow. Her used-out brain refused to function. It neither thought out facts lucidly nor held them once they formed.

"Canning's outside," she said with a faint show of defiance.

"That is why I came to you, madame. With me you have a chance to get clear of this awful mess. But not if I go and challenge Canning. That would, as one might say, burst the whole box of tricks. And then neither the Secret Service nor any other power on earth could prevent the affair coming out into broad daylight."

"I know nothing, I tell you," she gasped.

"That is why you nearly fainted when you saw Arthur Raymond's signature on those false notes. That is why you tried to get that filthy acid down your throat when you reasoned things out."

"It—it wasn't that. I'm sick of life: sick and weary of it."

"Lady Demorval, that statement is a witness to its own truth. I want that address and I'm going to get it. There is yet time to avert the calamity that threatens. Let me tell you a few of the facts in my possession. We know how the banknote paper passed out of the vaults and we know who was responsible for its withdrawal. We know who is responsible for the forgeries. We know on what banks the spurious scrip has been unloaded, and tomorrow afternoon we shall know to what extent each country is involved. The *Sûreté Générale* is working on that now. We know your intended plans as soon as the coup has gone through. We know that somewhere, in an office here in Paris, currency notes and bearer bonds to the value of millions of pounds sterling are lying packed away ready for shipment. I know that Perrigo is on his way here by the fastest car he can command. Which tells me that you are aiming to cut and clear out tomorrow with the loot. It is time that I told you that one word from me will close the ports and frontiers of all France against you. The *Sûreté Générale* will be only too willing, believe me."

Lady Demorval shivered at the mention of the *Sûreté*.

Stayne touched her arm, and there was a newer, more dominant note in his voice.

"And I know that murder has been done, here in this club, for your sake," he said grimly. "Both murder and suicide stand to your account. I know that you were going to swindle the insurance companies out of a hundred thousand pounds on that fake diamond robbery. On that trick you double-crossed Perrigo himself—and that was the beginning of your falling out with the two men who got you into this awful mess, wasn't it? That's why they've been punishing you—they've been keeping you on the rails by making you wait for your periodic dose of cocaine. You need not trouble to deny it, madame, the facts are all ready for publication. You were actually prepared to let a man—the man who saved you from dishonour when the *gendarmerie* broke in—go to prison for five long years, without raising a hand to prevent it. Madame, you are one of the foulest things I have ever seen in my life. The very least you can do is to make what amends you can before it is too late."

Lady Demorval climbed painfully into a sitting position. She looked at the man in front of her and there was dumb misery in her eyes.

"That sort of remonstrance has lost its power," she said in an odd, flat voice. "Once it might have hurt. Once—but long ago. It doesn't seem to matter now. I've been living with thoughts like that for longer than you've ever known the name of Demorval. I could tell myself worse things than you could ever dream of. I just don't, that's all. I've grown used to loathing myself. A year ago I would have died rather than be seen arguing in public with a man like Canning as I was, out in the buffet just now."

She stopped and caught her breath. Stayne was sitting there, the gleaming sheen of a silver hypodermic syringe sparkling in his fingers. She clutched out at it wildly, her eyes white and distended. But Stayne evaded her clawing fingers and thrust it back into the small leather case whence he had taken it.

"Madame, that is the wickedest and yet the kindliest action I can do," he said. "There is cocaine in that cylinder! Not quite so big a measure as you by now require. But enough, and more than enough to give you a little relief from the craving that gnaws you. You shall have it—when you have told me what I want to know."

The change in Lady Demorval's attitude was magical. She sat bolt upright, stiff as though every muscle in her body had suddenly flexed to marble, her eyes turned fiercely on the inside pocket where Stayne slipped the leather case.

"What do you want to know, eh?" her nervous voice broke querulously, "What is it you want to know? Why shouldn't I tell you, eh? Why shouldn't I? Do Perrigo and Canning care a hang about me?" She rushed on as though thinking her own thoughts aloud. "What have they done for me? They got me into this mess. Ruined me. Ruined my husband. Smashed my every chance of happiness. Made me a drug fiend—and out there Canning even denied me the little pinch of snow that keeps me from utter misery. What do you want to know?"

"First I want the address from which Perrigo and Canning are operating."

"Forty-five Rue Paysanne. It's a big suite of offices on the first floor. They've rented it in the names of Martin et Bruyère, Société Anonyme." Staynes made a note in his pocketbook.

"Thank you. And now I want to know how you came to be associated with these foul swindlers. Tell me your story, frankly and truly, madame, and I will see what I can do for you. Candidly, I can't see a way out. But the authorities in London may find a way."

A hunted look came into Lady Demorval's eyes, and her fingers were twisting nervously into each other.

"The story goes—goes back a long way," she said, and for the first time her voice sounded human. Actually a fine touch of the sweeter feminine sounded in it, the feminine with the power to love and love till all hope is lost, the feminine with the divine gift of self-sacrifice.

"Yes—a very long way back," she said slowly. "It began when I just played the fool—once, I'd done everything and seen everything and been everywhere, and I thought there wasn't a thing left for me. Then one night I came here just for a little flutter—a new sensation. I wish to God I had lost heavily that night and burned my fingers so badly that I'd have been frightened off for life. But that isn't Perrigo's way. He lets them win the first night—win heavily. Then they come back for more, and they don't get it."

A sad smile twisted the corners of her mouth. "Go out and tell your friend that," she said. "Tell him to whack it down in lumps. He will win tonight."

"The wheels are all crooked, eh?"

"Every one. You get your big win, and then you come back to collect the rest, thinking you've got into a lucky vein. You lose, and then you come back hoping to recoup your losses."

"So Perrigo was running this place even then?"

"Yes. This was their first beginning. The other things came later—when they had got me into their clutches."

"Knowing the game is not on the square, why did you want to borrow from me?"

"For any number of reasons. One is that I saw a stranger here tonight—another pigeon for the plucking. I knew they'd let him win. I could follow him and win too. Or I should normally have played baccarat. You can't fake the shoe—unless Perrigo was in the bank. He'd fake anything. Another is that I would borrow from anybody on earth. I've sunk as low as that."

"Just how much do you owe then?"

"I don't even know. Thousands. They've taken every penny I had and they've robbed my husband of every sou he possessed. Through me, of course. I bankrupted him. Then, when they had me at their mercy, they forced me into the bigger swindle—this terrible bank business."

"How did they come to find this forger?"

Lady Demorval checked herself abruptly. She thought hard for a long while, and then shrugged.

"You may as well know it all," she said, with another bold attempt at bravado. "You know such a lot there's no use me holding back on that. And, anyway," she broke off and looked away, "anyway, it will save that poor little devil from what's hanging over him. No one will be more pleased than he will to see this matter cleared up. For God's sake give me a shot of that tube."

"Later on, madame. From what you say, this fellow Arthur Raymond, the man who committed the actual forgeries for the syndicate, is something of an innocent victim?"

"Yes. He never dreamed that what he was doing was being put to criminal use. He was in Government service here in a minor capacity. But once Perrigo took the mask off he resigned, and he has been more or less living on Perrigo's money ever since. I know it all sounds foolish and absurd, to some it will be utterly incredible but they got their first plates from him by a trick—and then he had to carry on. He did not even know it was a criminal offence to make an engraving of currency."

"Oh, I see!" breathed Stayne. "They caught him on the jump?"

"Yes. He was doing some little sketches one day of the heading of a newspaper and I saw them. He said he couldn't do an original drawing for toffee, but that, right from a child, he had always been able to copy other people's drawings with extraordinary fidelity. It was a natural gift, I suppose. Anyway, I thought they were marvellous. If you examined them through a pantograph you could not find even the thickening of a line anywhere that was not in strict conformity with the original.

"He came here one night with me, just to see what the place was like. And I got him to do something for Perrigo. Perrigo and I were good friends then. Raymond did a copy of the menu card, with the crest and the scrolls and—and everything. He did it on a menu blank, and even Perrigo himself couldn't tell which was the copy. Perrigo said it was marvellous. He called Canning over, and together they pulled the finest piece of bluff on Raymond I have ever seen in my life.

"Perrigo, speaking in a jocular, self-satisfied way, as though he himself had found an eighth wonder of the world, said, 'Here, Canning, remember that sister of yours you're always bragging about, the one who goes to the art school and does all the clever reproductions? '

"'Sure,' said Canning, lying like a hero—I had never heard him even mention a sister. 'Sure, I remember her what about it? '

"'Well, I've got a young friend here who will knock her stuff into a cocked hat.'

"'Have you?' said Canning, bridling. 'I don't think you have.'

"'Well, he happens to be right in at this moment. And I'll bet you a level fifty that he will do a drawing of anything you like so accurate that even you will admit he's a marvel.'

"'All right,' growled Canning. ' I know what my sister can do, and I'll back her against anybody who is likely to come in here.'

"'That's a bet,' said Perrigo, jovial as though he had caught his friend for fifty pounds. 'What shall we get him to draw?'"

XXXIX

"Canning planked down his fifty-pound banknote. 'There's my money', he said. "If he's such a wonder, let him copy that so that I can't tell the difference.'

"Perrigo eyed it a bit dubiously. 'H'm,' he said. ' That's hardly fair. You could easily tell the difference from the quality of the paper. He can etch it, though, and I'll get some deckle edge paper that is as near the real banknote stuff as makes no difference. Then I'll take a couple of copies off and I'll defy you to tell the real one from the false.'

"'All right, that'll suit me,' said Canning. 'Where's this miracle-maker of yours?'

"'Right by your elbow,' said Perrigo. And Raymond, looking a bit embarrassed and self-conscious, was introduced. That was the start of it. A complete stranger in a strange place, he felt he had to comply to be agreeable. He did the thing and brought it along the next night. It was a marvel.

"Perrigo made him a club hero and made bets about other members being able to tell which was which. Canning, too, admitted that he was something right out of the ordinary, and paid over his fifty without a murmur. Then Perrigo suggested that he should do some more notes of all denominations, and they were going to stamp the words 'Club Tabarin' all over them and use them at the tables instead of chips. Raymond fell right into that. And before he knew it they had him by the throat. On the threat of exposure they made him copy all the bonds and share scrips with which they have packed the European banks. Arthur has had to do it all—with the threat of twelve years hanging over his head. They've actually made him pass counterfeit notes himself in shops, hotels, restaurants and places. They tightened their hold on him till I thought the poor boy was going mad."

Stayne was silently thoughtful. This woman's story, blatant though it was, held something of the pitiful in its context. It had given him a new and unexpected slant on the whole business. Right from the first he had marked Lady Demorval down as the crook, the spendthrift cause of all the misery. Admitting that Perrigo and Canning were the real powers behind the scenes, she was really the root cause, for without the pull of her social position and influence the arch-conspirators could never have begun their nefarious machinations. There was food for hard thinking in all she had said.

And somehow, in spite of the terrible change in her outlook on life, there was the ring of truth through it all. Stayne could not blind himself to that.

And somewhere, veiled away behind it, was the hint of a deeper tragedy still. She had not even indicated it in direct speech, but it was all there, in her manner, in the inflexions of her voice, in the very way that she left the bigger things unsaid.

It flashed across Stayne suddenly, in an overwhelming burst of understanding. He saw it all, in that one brief, thunderous moment, the major tragedy, in all its humiliation and pathos. Tembridge, in his direct way, had been uncannily right.

"Aren't you going to give me that jolt?" Her voice was shaking, and her flesh was shivering as though with an ague.

Stayne took out the little black case and balanced it in his fingers. "This man Raymond," he said. "You seem extraordinarily anxious to clear him and put him in a good light. Why?"

She looked up at him, and there was a fleck of blood on her lips where she had bitten them: her eyes were almost glassy with suppressed emotion.

"Because I loved Arthur with every atom of my being," she said.

That was all. Lady Demorval said it as quietly as though she had just confessed to a saint, but the words seared Stayne to the core. She was staring fixedly at the silver head of the syringe, and her handkerchief was chewed to a rag in her fingers.

Silently Stayne handed her the case. The syringe was out and the dose forced home in the quick flash of a single second. High up under the upper arm she took it, where it would not show—and she took it to the last drop.

Stayne sat back and regarded her. And there was nothing but pity in his heart. This woman, going to the last depths of depravity and degradation for the sake of a love that was hopeless, her heart torn and battered, wrecking herself body and soul in quest of a man who was already passionately in love with someone else—and that someone else Marienne Varris.

Without doubt Tembridge had put his finger on the canker. On her side the brilliant Demorval marriage had been a loveless affair, the last wild resort of a woman whose deepest longings had been thwarted, whose very love, overflowing and spilling over, had been thrust aside. Stayne realised—and understood; for Stayne himself was not unburned by those fires.

She pulled herself together with a little shudder. The vitalising, spurious life-force of the coca leaf was beginning to course through her, and she felt the thrilling tingle of it. The lifeless lethargy, the dull apathy began to retreat into the furthermost recesses of her brain. A keener sense, a newer appreciation of the magnitude of the thing she had done began to crawl across her waking faculties. She stared at Stayne with something of horror in her gaze.

Stayne was slowly tearing the I O U into tiny fragments, flicking them on to the carpet in a tiny white rain. This man, this dominating, quiet-voiced, searching-eyed man held every key to her secrets. He had pumped her dry of every vital piece of information she had to give. And he had admitted he was an emissary of the Secret Service! A mental spasm of anguish shot through her. That meant that London was in full possession of the facts; the authorities knew every detail of the coup! Perrigo would shoot her stone dead for this.

She pressed her head into her hands. Why on earth had she been such a heaven-deserted fool as to tell this utter stranger the secrets she had been even too frightened to think about? What in the world had made her open her heart to this man—whose very name she did not even know? Stayne carefully replaced the empty hypodermic syringe in his pocket. The confounded snow again! Always these beasts had tricked her with cocaine! First they had undermined her with it, then they had kept her going with it—and now the other side had stepped in and caught her again by the same foul means.

Anger flamed within her, a deep bitter anger that sprang from no wells of calm reasoning, but had its roots in a wild surge of blind feminine passion—the fury of the woman caught out on a trick. Her eyes glittered bright. An appalling steadiness came over her tormented nerves and the colour came back to her face with a rush. Her features held the stiff glaze of a set resolve. Her fingers groped carefully into the inner lining of the ermine cloak for the long, thin, pointed stiletto concealed there. Stayne stood up and turned away, his brain buried in a welter of thoughts in conflict. His chin was thrust deep on his chest and his fingers tightly interlocked behind him.

The long groping fingers found the weapon, slipped caressingly over its shiny ivory handle and softly withdrew it. Quietly as a cat she crawled to her feet, stood for a moment to flex for a spring and then something went wrong with her eyes.

The lights seemed suddenly to recede to the uttermost distances of space. They became mere pinpoints of bright, searing white in a world that was going intensely black. The blackness began to whirl, revolving madly in her disorganised brain; then with a crash even the blackness vanished. She uttered a short, breathy little hiss and toppled back on the ottoman. Stayne had put something more than cocaine in that shot of snow.

XL

Out in the saloon Tembridge waited with a patience born of knowledge.

"Ha! Monsieur wins again!" The croupier pushed out another respectable mound of notes to the young American. He was now winning seventeen thousand francs, and realised with much amusement that they were being planted on him.

And all the while his super-sensitive ears had been tuned for sounds emanating from the ante-room. Twice he had heard Lady Demorval's voice raised in anger or heated argument. If the others heard they took no notice. Either they were too intent on the game, or they knew, of old experience, that financial matters were not always apt to go through in that room without acrimony.

He had seen Stayne go in, saw the signal he passed him, and he stayed, winning hand over fist and never enjoying a win less in his life. Once Canning came up and congratulated him, and he felt like knocking his back teeth out.

It seemed hours before Stayne came out. When he did he came slowly, and so quietly that no one at the tables knew the door had opened and closed. They went out to the buffet and took another sip of champagne.

"Fixed?" asked Tembridge softly.

"Got it all. With a spot of luck I think we can get through the scrum without raising a single squeak."

"Where's Lady Demorval?"

Stayne indicated the ante-room. "In there. Having a little sleep. She won't wake for twenty-four hours—maybe longer considering the state of her tissues. That should give us a margin to spare. The whole thing can be cleaned up before then."

"A smooth run?"

"Fairly. I'm only interested in one thing here, though. And that's young Raymond."

"The ass-eared camel!"

Stayne smiled, but it was a humourless crack across his face, a smile bereft of amusement. "He's in here. I'd like to speak to him—just once."

"So would I!" muttered Tembridge with spiteful emphasis.

"Remember that young fellow who came up in the lift just behind us?"

"Yeh. Nice-looking, handsome kid."

"That's Arthur Raymond."

"Was it! Well, I'd still like to park a tank on him—sideways."

"He's O.K. Did you notice where he went?"

"Yes. Through to the baccarat."

"Let's go. And in case anything should happen in there, the address we want is 45, Rue Paysanne: upstair suite: held in the name of Martin et Bruyère, Société Anonyme. Which last, if you don't know, means Limited Company. Which same is darn comic. Come on."

They passed along into the baccarat salon. The atmosphere in there was less humid. There were barely half a score gathered round the shoe, and there was less tension in the air. They were a hardier crowd, longer in the tooth at the gambling game than those in the roulette-room, and their emotions were under better control. One or two glanced up and scrutinised the newcomers.

Raymond was standing away from the actual gamblers, idly turning the pages of one of the illustrated periodicals. It was obvious that he was uninterested in the luck of the cards—probably only waiting for Perrigo. And Stayne was anxious to get away before Perrigo put in an appearance.

Tembridge's hand slipped unobtrusively into his coat pocket. His job was to cover the crowd in case of ructions. Stayne slipped into a vacant chair at Raymond's table. The young man glanced up, but Stayne was busily hunting through the piled heaps of papers and periodicals.

Without looking up Stayne handed over his card. "Colonel John Stayne," and underneath, in neat red capitals, the letters S.S.

Raymond looked up with a shock of sudden fear showing starkly on his face. But Stayne never moved. He continued to pore over the pages before him. Then slowly he passed over one of the damning ten-pound notes with Raymond's name across it, and a cold perspiration broke out over the younger man's face.

Raymond continued to stare furtively, almost wildly, like a wild animal caught in a new and sudden trap. Stayne was calmly writing, his steady fingers moving evenly over a sheet of paper on a tablet.

When Stayne had finished his writing he passed the sheet of paper across. With eyes that blinked incredulously the forger read the neatly written statement.

> *I, Arthur Raymond, formerly of the British Embassy staff in Paris, hereby declare that I have been guilty of forging plates for the reproduction of English banknotes of all denominations from Ten Pounds to One Thousand Pounds, and that these notes were printed on official bank paper supplied from London by the intervention and connivance of Lady Demorval, wife of Lord Demorval, also of the British Embassy staff here. I also declare that the first forgeries were committed unwittingly and that I*

had no idea that counterfeit notes were to be reproduced from my plates but that pressure was subsequently brought to bear on me, forcing me, under a threat of exposure, to complete the other plates. I furthermore declare that I have forged the scrip of all the stock certificates which the two men Perrigo and Canning have put up as collateral security for loans raised on European banks.

I herewith undertake to return to England immediately and to go straight to 8B, Curzon Square, remaining there until I am called upon to make a fuller detailed declaration of the activities of the company styling itself the South American Development Corporation, of which Perrigo and Canning are the sole instigators. I promise I will not move from that address until officially authorised.

Signed, in the Club Tabarin, Rue Pigalle, Paris,—

When he looked up from the document it was to encounter Stayne's eyes, no longer courteously formal, but cold and dominant, almost icy, in their bitter determination.

The forger was like a boxer on the verge of a knockout. The unexpectedness of the thing had stung his brain, stunned it. He seemed incapable of appreciating its full import. For a while he looked at Stayne as though he were some new and hitherto undiscovered specimen from the deep. His eyes blinked curiously and his lips moved. There was a frown across his forehead and he seemed to be trying to spell over in his mind a repetition of the words of that extraordinary document.

"You will sign that document—for your own good," said Stayne quietly.

Out in the central hall the voice of the black page drifted in in a nasal sing-song. "Mr. Canning, please—telegram for Mr. Canning, please!" The glaring uniform approached the *portière*, and the boy repeated his high-pitched drawl. He passed on the telegram on a silver tray in his hand.

Raymond licked his lips. His interlaced fingers were caught in a fierce grip between his knees.

"That," said Stayne distinctly, "is a wire from Perrigo. A panic wire. You'd better sign, my boy, before it's too late."

"You—you—I—" The words stuck and the young man's mouth shut tightly.

"I know you had no wilful hand in this," went on Stayne in a hard yet not unfriendly voice. "I know you were dragged into it unconsciously. That will be seen into later."

The Mystery-Maker handed over his pen and gently indicated the bottom corner of the tablet.

Raymond took the pen, but his fingers shook so badly he could scarcely hold it.

"Don't be frightened," said Stayne. "There will be no public scandal. That's what I'm here to prevent. But there will be if you don't put your signature to that statement. A very terrible scandal in which you will play a central part. Take my advice and rely implicitly on me. I know the facts. For the first time since you compromised yourself in this affair you've found a friend. Go back to London and stay there. The house is guarded by police and you will be quite safe. None of this scum here will be able to get at you. Trust me and I will see that the whole thing is satisfactorily squared-up—both for others and for you. Whitehall knows all about it. They are expecting you there."

As though in a dream Raymond gripped the pen, steadied his twitching nerves and wrote in his signature. He finished it with something like a gasp of relief breaking through his lips.

"That's fine," said Stayne. "The wisest thing you've done for months."

Outside they heard the soft scurry of hurrying feet on the carpet as Canning came hurrying down from an upstair room. He was white-faced and agitated. Clutched in his hand was a telegram, and they saw him hurry through the roulette-room, which Stayne and Tembridge had just left.

"Come on—quick," said Stayne. "Let's get out of this. That's Canning—he's after us. Make for the lift. Lady Demorval is in there, unconscious. He will find her and raise hell. Hurry!"

Stayne hurried out with Raymond, quaking and uncertain of his actions, close behind. Tembridge brought up the rear, sauntering out unostentatiously. His hand was still in his coat pocket, and he cocked a leery eye behind him to see if anyone was taking notice of their sudden exit. He strolled over to the bar, dropped a fifty-dollar bill on the counter, and told the delighted white-coat to keep the change.

The Colonel was hustling Raymond into the lift. As Tembridge was following they heard the rush of Canning's feet across the buffet. He whizzed round the corner and saw them just as Tembridge was trying to pull the gates shut.

"Duck your head," hissed Stayne savagely. Tembridge bobbed as though his head had been jerked down on a cord. A white paper parcel whizzed over his head and impacted on Canning's face with a hard thud. The tissue-paper burst and a yellow powder broke over his face. The man flung his hands up, clawed at the air, then fell over with a crash, prone on his face. Tembridge jammed the gates shut and Stayne sent the lift spinning down.

They hurried through the little shop below and hailed a passing taxi. "The Grand Hôtel du Pavilion," said Stayne, and climbed in. Few transport vehicles move faster than the Paris taxi. They were off with a rush, and in ten minutes were in the long, quiet lounge of the hotel in the Rue l'Echiquier, with its stained-glass roof and softly splashing fountain.

"Stay here a moment; have a coffee cognac—I've a little phoning to do," said Stayne.

He was gone nearly half an hour. When he came back it was with the air of a man with a tremendous load off his mind.

He beckoned to Raymond and took him out through the foyer. At the kerb stood the big car in which they had travelled down from Calais, and at the wheel sat Burdy, calm, serene, quite ready for another long pull back to the coast.

"In you get," said Stayne. "I like to clear things up as we go, and you will be one end of it well out of the way. Take this card"—he wrote a hurried line on it—"Belham will let you in and see to you in every way. You can catch the morning boat. A green and white car will be waiting for you at Victoria. Show this card to the driver and you will be taken straight to Whitehall. Number One wants to see you urgently. When you get back to my place, ring up the Strand Hotel. There's a little lady there desperately anxious to see you. Goodbye and good luck." He assumed a cheerful laugh. "You'll be passing Perrigo on the road—good joke."

The young man tried to speak, but a painful constriction had come over his jaws. He could only hang on to Stayne's hand with a grip that positively hurt. Stayne pulled himself away, slammed the door and signalled the driver off. As the car skimmed round the corner for the Gate du Nord he turned away abruptly.

"Oh, well," said a colourless voice behind him. "I guess there's plenty girls left. Somehow I'm rather glad things turned out that way. Hi, taxi!"

The commissionaire held the door for them.

"45 Rue Paysanne," said Stayne, "and when you get there—wait!"

They bowled along merrily towards the old fortifications. That end of the city was as dead as the district east of St. Paul's after nightfall. The streets were deserted and the great masses of the business premises reared up darkly into the night, gaunt and unlit, lost in the shadows above.

"Feeling good?" asked Tembridge softly. He was aware of a huge job nearing its completion. He sensed the climax working up. So far the luck had been with them. Coupled to fine management on Stayne's part was the indubitable fact that every one of their surmises had turned out right, every subterfuge had come off, and all they had hoped for had happened. Would it hold? Tembridge knew of the law of averages, knew that a break was due and overdue.

"We've a couple of hours yet. Raymond is out of the way. Lady Demorval won't be able to squawk for hours yet, and it will be nearly as long before Canning comes to. That's this end of it cleared up. There remains only Perrigo."

"What are we going to do about those two brutes?"

"They get theirs."

Stayne said the last remark very softly, but there was a world of deadly meaning in it. "If we find all we hope to at Rue Paysanne we must take the *Sûreté* into our full confidence. Corrective measures will have been taken by then—and the police can do their piece. I'll tell the Chief de Police as much as is wise and get him to hold them on the gambling and cocaine charges. That is all I ask of him—to spread the net. Perrigo and Canning will know the moment the word goes out. To have carried on the Club Tabarin so long and to have got away with murder there means that they must have friends in their pay at headquarters. They'll know all right. And they'll know that every gate out of Paris will be closed against them."

"That sure is so," commented Tembridge. "Paris isn't so easy to get out of as London."

"That's where we get them," said Stayne grimly. "The railway stations are all barriered and every road out of the city has its octrol gate."

A deep glitter came into his eyes, a look of relentless, implacable determination that boded ill for the two counterfeiters who had all but smashed their country's credit abroad.

"Yes," he muttered." They get theirs. There's no other way out. We can't prosecute and we can't let them go free. What they've done once they can do again. They've tasted blood—and their type don't stop at one taste. No. So long as I can get them on the run I think I've got them. There's only one way out of Paris once the net goes out. Even the airports are closed. There's one way. And I think the brutes know it. Simple and ingenious. And it's not open to pursuit. And it will take them beyond the French frontiers, let alone the gates of the city."

"Hm! That darn balloon?"

"That's the fellow. I hope they do, that's all. I wouldn't lift a hand stop them! Gosh—I'd help 'em in!"

Going to have a smack at 'em in the air from a plane?" queried Tembridge dubiously. The idea didn't sound any too promising to him.

Stayne laughed shortly. "Nothing so spectacular. They'll get in all right, and they'll get away with it—for a while. They'll be as lively as crickets. But there will be two dead bodies in that balloon when the basket touches earth again."

Stayne was gazing intently out of the windows as he spoke. They were already in the Rue Paysanne. "Here we are," he muttered as the cab drew up at a tall block of offices.

Tembridge was aware of a curious feeling of chill in the pit of his stomach. Stayne seemed to regard the eliminating of two men from life as of no more consequence in his daily round than the stepping on a couple of beetles or the posting of a couple of letters.

They left the cab and climbed up a wide flight of stairs. Glass-panelled doors confronted them, three, each opening from the landing in front of the stairs. Gilt lettering on the glass announced the occupants. Martin et Bruyère. Stayne did some rapid work with a set of thin skeleton keys, and in a couple of minutes had the private door open. They took not the slightest pains to conceal their movements, switching the lights on boldly. An inquisitive caretaker could be referred to the Chief of the Police, and anyone else could be introduced to the business end of a gun.

XLI

Stayne and Tembridge worked quickly, but in silence. Tembridge, without further instructions, sat down at one of the desks, and, pulling a sheaf of their official notepaper before him, began writing a round letter in his own handwriting. It was a plain-spoken, formal, business letter cancelling any such business matters as were under negotiation with the South American Development Corporation.

It was addressed: "To the Bank Manager" and read:

> *Dear Sir,—It is with regret that I have to announce the dissolution of the above Company. Revolutions in South America and persistent difficulties raised by various South American political bodies preclude any possibility of our doing further business with the States in question. We feel, therefore, that the sooner this Company is disbanded and its capital put to use elsewhere the better.*
>
> *You have in your vaults British securities covering the extent of your loan to us. Herewith we enclose cash currency to its value, cancelling the loan. Will you please dispatch the securities forthwith to the Bank of England, Threadneedle Street, London, to await the order of Mr. T. S. Hawker, of Scotland Yard, who will thenceforward be responsible for their safe custody to us.*

Note numbers, enclosed Series—to—, Total value —.
We beg to remain, dear sir,
For the South American Development Corporation,
J. Stayne and V. Tembridge,
Liquidators.

He duplicated the letter time after time until a heap of three dozen were completed, identical in every way, even to the blanks where the series number and totals were to go.

An inner office led out from the private secretary's room, and Stayne, knowing that that was the centre of the spider's web, had immediately set about getting in. The lock was intricate and difficult to force, but he opened it at last and went in, switching on another blaze of lights as he entered.

The room seemed comparatively bare. Stayne had half expected it. It is the French custom when erecting big business premises to build safes and strongrooms into the walls, or at least to camouflage them very successfully. And from what he knew of Perrigo and Canning they had only taken that office, from among the hundreds on offer, because of its strongroom. Millions of pounds' worth of cash currency are not generally trusted in ordinary safes.

He prospected around with an ebony ruler, and presently, in the far wall, his tapping sent back a deep, hollow ring.

The whole of that side of the wall was bare. So far as he could see there was not a knob or a button or a crack anywhere.

Tembridge poked his head in at the door. "Found it?" he asked.

"Yes. And no," answered Stayne. "It's a trick safe. Somewhere behind this wall is a wad of some millions of pounds. And I've as much chance of finding the key as a frog's got feathers."

Tembridge came over and took a look.

"That's a Yankee idea," he said speculatively. "Works on the telephone from police headquarters. Ring up the exchange and ask for the *Sûreté*. Try a bluff. Tell 'em who you are and ask 'em to complete the circuit. The 'Yard' there keeps a record of every call going through—and knows every time the safe's opened. It'll mean that they will send a man round to investigate: looks suspicious at this time of night. But we may just do it with a bit of a rush. I'm nearly through at my end. Risk it—you speak French like a Gaul."

Stayne picked up the instrument and asked for the *Sûreté Générale*. When he got them he asked to be plugged through to the "Safes."

"Martin et Bruyére speaking," he said. "Sorry to trouble you so late at night, but we're auditing. Will you open us up, please—you know the number."

Placidly the reply came back, "Oui, monsieur." A second or two later there came a harsh double click from inside the wall and then a buzzer rang softly. The reason for the unusual bareness of that inner room suddenly became apparent. The whole of the wall began moving out, swung on perfect balances from the inside comers. It stopped when the aperture was about a foot wide. Stayne and Tembridge crowded themselves into the corner and heaved the massive thing sideways.

The huge mass opened smoothly and easily, without a sound, blocking the view of the door when it came to a standstill. Behind it lay two deep shelves, on which reposed a pile of flat leather portmanteaux. They hauled them out, seven of them, surprisingly heavy, considering their compact bulk.

Stayne burst one open, and inside were neat heaps of French currency notes. Twelve heaps of them, six to a row. Each note was for ten thousand francs, and the full value of them all, in English sterling, was nearly a million pounds. Each bag held the same, except that the currency was that of a different country. Two bags contained American thousand-dollar bills, and two again were English banknotes, genuine ones. But no matter what the currency, each bag contained approximately a million pounds in cold cash.

Stayne wiped the perspiration from his forehead when they finished their scrutiny. In that office the whole plot was laid bare. The bills were drawn for six months' credit. In six months from the date of issue the whole carefully built scheme would have collapsed like a burst balloon. First interests would have been called for—and nothing would have been forthcoming. Meanwhile, inquiries would have revealed the fact that the offices of Messrs. Martin Bruyère were closed and that the birds had flown. There would have been nothing left but the ghastly realisation that the great banks had been milked of seven million pounds—with British credit abroad tottering to the crash, and the thieves safely tucked away in some delightful retreat below the Equator, as safe from arrest as eagles in the skies.

In the safe they found registration labels in blank all ready for filling in. Those cases would have been registered right through to their final destination, immune from inspection at the French frontiers. And by the time they got through to South America a good, hefty bribe would have got them through anywhere.

There were thousands of papers and documents which confirmed their guilt to the hilt. Stayne skimmed swiftly through them, but they were all so disjointed and disconnected that little could be gleaned from them. A staff of trained auditors would take a fortnight atleast to arrange and sort the various papers, bringing the whole reckless story to light step by step. But it could be done; all the evidence was there, clearly written down, even though scores of vital documents must have been destroyed as the scheme matured.

There in the safe, too, were steamer tickets, *two* only—Perrigo and Canning were aiming to leave their dupes flat, to let them face the music, right from the very start. And the tickets were for the round trip—Venezuela, Brazil, Paraguay, Uruguay, Chile, Peru, Ecuador, and right round the coast.

In special passport wallets were *visas* for every country named on the tickets, and the forgers had put them through in their own names. It was all very clean cut and perfectly arranged—and all the swag was there. Stayne took a look at the tickets. They were dated two days ahead, with Marseilles as the sailing point. The forgers had left it just a day too long.

In a strong box they found French notes for high denominations totalling nearly a hundred thousand pounds. Tembridge suggested that they were the proceeds of the nightly rookings at the Club Tabarin. The assumption was that Perrigo and Canning were going to use that money on the way out and on bribes through various customs.

Stayne took the lot. That odd money would help to reimburse the Bank of England in the false banknotes which it had accepted and honoured rather than precipitate a banknote panic on the Continent.

Methodically but with feverish rapidity they crammed the incriminating papers into the cases, distributing a sheaf in each, as many as each case would hold in addition to its currency contents. Then they relocked the bags. Stayne stowed the steamer tickets and *visas* in his hip pocket.

"Come on," he said. "Let's get this lot down into the taxi. This looks too good to last. I've got a shallow depression coming on—nasty sort of a feeling that all this is too good to be true."

"I should worry," retorted Tembridge. "We've done all we set out to do, haven't we? We've cleared up the mess—nearly; and we've kept the French police out of it—almost! And the authorities at home haven't been embroiled—hardly. All told I reckon we've ironed out a pretty hefty business, and we've done it without raising a ripple—or all but I should worry."

With a heave of his muscular young shoulders he flung his weight on the wall and rammed it ponderously back into position. And as the wall closed again they found themselves face to face with Gabriel Perrigo—Perrigo with his face convulsed with fury and the red light of murder blazing in his eyes. For a second he stood there, speechless, his face congested with a demoniac surge of passion. A great glittering gun was in his hand, and he suddenly flung it into the horizontal, full at Stayne.

At that same moment two things happened with the rapidity of a lightning flash. Stayne threw himself sideways against the vault wall, falling with a crash, and at the same instant there was a savage jerk forward of Tembridge's right arm. The American's own automatic whizzed across the room in a metallic blue-steel streak, and its full weight impacted with a smash on Perrigo's bunched fingers. The crash of a shot burst out from the nickelled gun as the two weapons collided, and the force of it sent both guns hurtling across the room.

Then Tembridge was at him, in almost the same movement, flying low at him and collaring him round the knees. The pair of them went down in a fighting, cursing tangle. A hard bony knee heaved up into the pit of the younger man's stomach. Tembridge grunted and rolled over, his face going yellow with agony. Perrigo was up with the agility of an acrobat, bloodstreaming in thin crimson lines from his burst knuckles. He leapt at Stayne like a wild tiger, his hands out and clawing for the throat.

Stayne stepped back and met him halfway. Quiet, unhurried and unflustered, exactly as befitted the appearance of the rather fragile, middle-aged gentleman he looked, he gave ground two paces as the maddened man came at him. Then he hit, a clean cut, beautifully timed blow to the point of the jaw, that came over with incredible power from such a frail-looking arm. Perrigo catapulted back against the door as though he had collided with a runaway fire-engine. His head struck the woodwork with a resounding thud. Stayne saw his eyeballs

"Close the gates against Perrigo and Canning," said Stayne grimly. "I ask nothing more than that: and I am as averse to involving the French police in this matter as you are yourself. I think it best that we keep our own dirty linen in our own wash. Send out the net. Bar the exits. And leave the rest to me. I'll promise you no further trouble from those two crooks. Paris has seen the last of Perrigo and Canning."

The Chief picked up his private telephone. "It shall be done, immediately, m'sieurs," he said.

Stayne heard the orders go through, and knew that he had the two arch-swindlers at his mercy.

A telephone message came through from the Rue Paysanne to say that Perrigo, released by an inquisitive office-cleaner, had left his suite and had been shadowed to the Club Tabarin.

"That is the best news today. Couldn't be better," said Stayne. "Good day to you, Chief—and—a thousand thanks." They shook hands warmly and both of them hurried out.

* * **

Stayne made but one call before posting himself for his last grim wait, and that was a short visit to a pharmacy. There he made three prefectly innocuous purchases—a two-pound roll of compressed lint, a saturated solution of tartaric acid crystals, and a bottle of salts of selenium. On the way to the Exhibition Grounds he took the blue paper from the lint and cut the great roll in half, stowing one in each pocket of his greatcoat.

In a few minutes they were at the entrance to the giant fair, that huge assembly of wonderful commercial exhibits that sprawls down both banks of the Seine and even includes one of the great bridges in its decorative scheme.

Stayne waited by the great balloon winch, sure beyond all doubt that the arch-swindlers would come. The fare for a five-minute trip was four hundred francs, split up between five—the load capacity of the balloon. But a single passenger could go up solo if he cared to pay the full five hundred francs. During the last day or two it had become quite fashionable among the gayer of the young engaged couples of the capital to take a little jaunt up alone, taking snapshots of each other in the swaying basket.

When the two men arrived there was a queue of about twenty all waiting to take their turns for a flight. As the balloon came down each time they rushed forward to hang on to the drag-ropes, steadying the straining thing as it came to earth. There was much laughing and high-spirited banter among them as they hauled on the tugging lines. Stayne and Tembridge joined in with the crush after registering for a run up.

Slowly the hours dragged by. Stayne still waited on, took his flip, and then waited again. Deep in his soul he hadn't the faintest doubt that sooner or later Perrigo and Canning would come. He allowed them a certain time to tap the other avenues of the city. In a little while they would realise that the exits were barred against them. Inevitably, through the long process of elimination, they would arrive at the last bold chance of a getaway in the lone balloon.

And so it proved. On towards dusk they came, furtively, their eyes roving interminably along the lines of people drawn round to watch the ascents. The queue had thinned considerably, most people preferring to take their aerial view of the city in full daylight.

They approached the kiosk and registered, paying their five hundred francs for a flight alone. The girl behind the grill informed them that they would take the third ascent from then. Stayne took out one of the fat rolls of lint and soaked it with the liquid from one of the bottles—the tartaric acid. When next the balloon was hauled down he put his weight on the drag-ropes and helped to hold the creaking basket steady on the ground while the passengers disembarked. Also with a deft movement he thrust the soaked lint down among the neatly piled sandbags that lined the bottom of the basket.

Up went the balloon again—twice more. On the third descent the second wad of lint, drenched with the selenium salts, was thrust far down amongst the ballast. Perrigo and Canning climbed in. Stayne and Tembridge faded into the crowd, and up went the swaying monster. At the height of its rise the crowd began to gasp. One of the passengers was seen, leaning far over, sawing away at the singing anchor wire with a steel saw. He was working like lightning. Someone in the crowd yelled to the winchman. He looked up, gesticulated wildly, and then thrust over the lever that worked the winch drum.

Slowly the monster bag came down, straining against its own tremendous lift.

Perrigo worked like a maniac till the saw went fiercely hot in his hands. Then the wire broke. With a loud "ping!" it parted and came snaking and constricting down to earth. The balloon shot up, going up in the light wind at a tremendous pace. Bags of ballast began to fall from it and the shrieking crowd scattered to give them falling room.

Down in the crowd Stayne stared up without even a hint of pity or remorse in his eyes.

"They've got it," he said quietly. "They've got it all."

Tembridge rubbed his chin. "I hope so," he muttered fervently, "but I'm everlastingly boiled if I can see how!"

"You'll know—when you find them, my boy," smiled Stayne, as he gazed up at the speck gliding along smoothly against the darkening sky. "And you'll find them by travelling east in the super-sports. Get into it now—I'm for home. The job's done, and when those two little babies in the wicker cradle come to earth I shall expect a wire from you at Curzon Square. You'll find 'em asleep—and they'll be sleeping quite peacefully!"

XLIII

Stayne was stretched out restfully in his big armchair before the fire in the main room of 8B, Curzon Square the following evening, enjoying one of his favourite cigars and idly turning the pages of a magazine.

Definite news of the end of the Perrigo-Canning case was yet to come, but he was certain as to the result—so certain that the affair was already listed in his records as an accomplished coup.

Tembridge was still on the Continent, where, Stayne did not know. But the westerly breeze having held, he must be many miles east of Paris in his pursuit of the truant balloon which had carried their prey high into the clouds above the city Stayne, following mentally the course of that guideless basket containing the two doomed criminals, anticipated a message from anywhere beyond the Alps.

The great jade clock on the mantelpiece chimed softly and struck eight. Stayne slumped back deeper in his chair, revelling in the relaxation that was his after the hectic action of the last few days. The respite, he knew, would be only temporary; within a few hours a call might come from Number One, and the Mystery-Maker would embark on a new case with all the vigorous energy, craft and pertinacity that always resulted in the success of his exploits.

Just as the clock ceased striking the golden idol on its bracket behind him tinkled out a summons.

Stayne laid aside his magazine, turned the knob under the arm of his chair, and spoke into space.

"Yes—what is it?"

The answer came immediately. "A visitor to see you, sir."

"What name, please?" inquired Stayne.

"Mr. Harris to see you, sir," was Belham's answer to Stayne.

"Oh, yes, show Mr. Harris up, please," said Stayne.

He pushed back the knob under the arm of his chair, and rose slowly to his feet, his lips crinkled in a quiet smile. "Mr. Harris," no doubt, had experienced some hours of worried speculation as to recent events in Paris, and particularly in regard to his own position as a pawn in the game.

Stayne walked to the window, opened it and stepped on to the balcony. There was no evidence of police vigilance before the house now; no loitering gossipers, no mendicants, no waiting taxi-drivers. A few pedestrians occassionally passed up and down, but intent obviously only on their own business.

The smile was still on Stayne's face as he stepped back into the room and greeted Templer Varris.

"I thought you'd be getting anxious," he said. "If it hadn't been that I've had every second of every minute more than fully occupied every hour since you dropped us near Dover Pier I should have wired you the good news, Varris. You got us down there with the speed and comfort that might have been expected from a trained chauffeur."

"And you got across all right, too?"

"Not in quite such comfort, but considering the circumstances the passage was very satisfactory."

Stayne's eyes scrutinised his visitor closely. Varris's attire was quite in keeping with that of a taxi-driver in mufti; a heavy, faded overcoat hung open, revealing a suit of navy blue serge which shone in those places most affected by wear; his feet were shod in thick-soled, ill-fitting boots, and the cap which he held in his hand was badly in need of replacement. Hands and face were far from clean, and a growth of beard spread from ear to ear.

"You can dispense with that outfit, Varris," said Stayne, offering him a cigar from a box which he picked up from his smoker's table. "In fact, you've finished with disguises now altogether."

"How on earth—" began Varris.

"Don't ask too many questions," smiled the Mystery-Maker. "But perhaps you noticed when you came here tonight that this house hasn't the same interest to the police that it apparently possessed some hours ago."

"Yes; but I broke prison—they must be after me still—"

"I shouldn't worry," drawled Stayne. "When an affair involves very intricate international problems, ordinary police procedure is sometimes—well—slightly affected."

"I see."

Varris, lighting his cigar, spent the few moments ensuing silence in very concentrated thought.

"You mean, then, that I can even resume my own identity without risk?"

Stayne nodded. "Without risk of any police interference, unless, ofcourse, you invite it by some act apart altogether from the present case. I suggest that your sister Marienne will welcome the news as much as you do—even though she has another very important matter to occupy her mind—and that you convey it to her without delay. She is at the Strand Hotel."

Varris seemed as though he was attempting to say something: he failed, gulped, and shot out his hand.

Stayne gripped it. Just a nod and a straight look, eye to eye, passed between the two men; then Varris turned and went from the room.

* * *

Half an hour later a wire reached Stayne from Tembridge. It informed him that the balloon containing Perrigo and

Canning had been found wedged in some trees in the Plain of Lombardy. Tembridge was returning immediately.

When Val Tembridge arrived he was in much the same state of bewilderment as when Stayne had left him with orders to follow the balloon from Paris.

"I've thought my brain sore," he said. "I told you over there that I'd be boiled if I could see how you could do it—and I'm still boiling."

"Just simmer for a moment," Stayne advised, "and tell me a few facts about the actual end of the story."

"The gas-bag has been taken out of the trees when I arrived. Hundreds of peasants were gathered around, registering curiosity to a perfection which no film producer will ever be able to obtain from his cast. I was in time to see two dead men lifted from the basket of that balloon. Suicide of course—they all said the same thing—officials, doctors, peasants; and I almost agreed."

"The case of Perrigo and Canning will, no doubt, become the most remarkable case of suicide on the records," observed Stayne quietly.

"*Suicide!* Tell me more!"

There was something of a twinkle in Stayne's eyes as he fixed them on his assistant.

"Never been up in a balloon, eh?" he asked. "Don't know that a balloon travels *with* the wind; therefore there is no wind in a balloon and no sensation of wind pressure, even in half a storm?"

"That's easy, but—"

"I stuffed two packets in the bottom of the basket, one tartaric acid, the other salts of selenium. They're harmless enough apart; they're used every day in foodstuffs, but once let 'em get together—"

"Oh, boy!" breathed Tembridge.

"That's how they got it," added Stayne. "By a process of double decomposition a lethal gas is given off. Those two wads of lint were touching, rammed down together. Perrigo and Canning were breathing in lungsful of that deadly gas, and they didn't know it—until it was too late. They collapsed on the bottom long before they reached Lombardy, and a jury of doctors won't be able to decide how they died."

And they never did. The Italians could make nothing of the extraordinary event that the two men who severed the anchor wire of the balloon at the Exposition de Paris were found dead in the basket.

And that was all that ever came to light of one of the most delicate cases that John Stayne, in his character of discredited Secret Service emissary, cashiered soldier and general social outcast, ever engineered to a successful conclusion.

When odd rumours of unorthodox happenings over in Paris began to circulate through the London clubs, Stayne was once more out on the fringe of things, a definite, integral part of the whole, but, just as he had always been before, a vague, nebulous somebody, moving at the back of the main story, unconnectable in any criminal way with the actual outcome.

The rest of it was contained in three telegrams.

1. From Number Three to Number One. "Sorry to hear news of suicide of Lady D. Rather saw it coming. Numbers Three and Twenty-two have the honour to submit we both remain on Risky List."
2. From Number One to Number Three. "Nice work: nice news: nice sentiments. Report immediately. Case awaits you—on Risky List."
3. From Colonel John Stayne to Miss Varris: "Sincerest wishes to you, Templer and Raymond for your perfect happiness. Regret I cannot be best man. Tembridge offers to deputise."

He had added, "Tembridge has no soul," but he rubbed that out.